Praise for David Gemmell and *Ravenheart*

"This poignant heroic fantasy explores familiar Gemmell themes: heroism and sacrifice. . . . As the plot of *Ravenheart* unfolds and a tragic ending looms, the tension rises to almost unbearable levels."
—The British Fantasy Society

"I love David Gemmell's work. He's one of the best out there today, and one of the reasons that fantasy is alive and well."
—R. A. SALVATORE

"David Gemmell infuses his narrative with gritty realism. His characters are earthy, vibrant, heroic, and engaging, the conflict heart-wrenching in its echoes of historical fact."
—*Romantic Times*

"Gemmell not only knows how to tell a story, he knows how to tell a story you want to hear. He does high adventure as it ought to be done."
—J. GREGORY KEYES
Author of *Newton's Cannon*

"Gemmell's great reading; the action never lets up; he's several rungs above the good—right into the fabulous!"
—ANNE MCCAFFREY

By David Gemmell
Published by Ballantine Books:

LION OF MACEDON
DARK PRINCE
KNIGHTS OF DARK RENOWN
MORNINGSTAR

Ravenheart

David Gemmell

BALLANTINE BOOKS • NEW YORK

A Del Rey® Book
Published by The Ballantine Publishing Group
Copyright © 2001 by David Gemmell
Excerpt from *Stormrider* copyright © 2002 by David Gemmell

All rights reserved under International and Pan-American Copyright Conventions. Published in the United States by The Ballantine Publishing Group, a division of Random House, Inc., New York. Originally published in Great Britain by Bantam Press, a division of Transworld Publishers, in 2001.

Del Rey is a registered trademark and the Del Rey colophon is a trademark of Random House, Inc.

This book contains an excerpt from the forthcoming book *Stormrider* by David Gemmell. This excerpt has been set for this edition only and may not reflect the final content of the forthcoming edition.

www.delreydigital.com

ISBN 0-345-43228-2

Manufactured in the United States of America

First American Hardcover Edition: July 2001
First American Paperback Edition: March 2002

OPM 10   9   8   7   6   5   4   3   2   1

Ravenheart is dedicated with love to the memory of Bill Woodford, a big, flawed, tough, and kindly man. During World War II he fought with distinction at El Alamein, Anzio, Salerno, and Monte Cassino, and was mentioned in Despatches twice for gallant conduct. In 1954 he married a woman he adored and raised her son as his own. As I said in the dedication to *Legend* back in 1984, without him Druss the Legend would never have walked the walls of Dros Delnoch. He was the heart of many of the heroes I have created over the years—none more so than Jaim Grymauch, whose story is told within these pages.

ACKNOWLEDGMENTS

Many people helped to make Ravenheart *the joy it was to create. To my test readers Jan Dunlop, Tony Evans, Alan Fisher, Stella Graham, and Steve Hutt, many thanks. I am also grateful to editors Steve Saffel of Del Rey and Selina Walker of Transworld for their valuable input, to Erik Lowenkron and Nancy Webbe for copyediting the United States and British manuscripts, and to Colette Russen, Kathleen O'Shea, and David Stevenson.*

Prologue

THE SUN WAS setting, and Lanovar sat slumped against the stone, the last of the sunlight bathing him in gold. There was a little heat in the dying winter sun, and the brightness felt good against his closed lids. Lanovar sighed and opened his eyes. The huge figure of Jaim Grymauch stood close by, gazing down at him.

"Let me carry you to the Wyrd, Lan," he said. "She'll cast an ancient spell and heal you."

"In a while, my friend. I'll just rest here and gather my strength."

Grymauch swore and turned away. Loosening the strap at his shoulder, he swung the massive broadsword clear of his back. The black hilt was almost a foot long, crowned with an iron globe pommel. The curved quillons were beautifully crafted to represent the flared wings of a hunting falcon. Drawing the fifty-two-inch blade from the scabbard, Grymauch examined the sword in the fading light. There were still bloodstains on the blade, and he wiped them away with the hem of his black cloak. Beside him Lanovar lifted clear the wedge of blood-soaked cloth he had been holding to the wound in his side. The bleeding had slowed, and the pain was almost gone. He glanced up at Grymauch.

"That monstrosity should be in the Druagh museum," said Lanovar. "It is an anachronism."

"I don't know what that means," muttered Grymauch.

"It means out of its time, my friend. That blade was created to rip through plate armor. No one wears plate anymore."

Grymauch sighed. Returning the blade to its scabbard, he sat down beside his friend. "Out of its time, eh?" he said. "It is like us, then, Lan. We should have been born in the days of the *real* highland kings."

Blood was leaking slowly from the cloth plugging the exit wound in Lanovar's lower back, a dark stain spreading across the outlawed blue and green cloak of the Rigante. "I need to plug the wound again," said Grymauch.

Lanovar made no complaint as the clansman pulled him forward, and he felt nothing as Grymauch pressed a fresh wad of cloth into the wound. Lanovar's mind wandered briefly.

He saw again the standing stone and the tall black-clad man waiting there. Regrets were pointless now, but he should have trusted his instincts. He had known deep in his heart that the Moidart could not be trusted. As their gaze had met, he had seen the hatred in the man's dark eyes. But the prize had been too great, and Lanovar had allowed the dazzle of its promise to blind him to the truth.

The Moidart had promised that the turbulent years would end: no more pointless bloodshed, no more senseless feuds, no more murdered soldiers and clansmen. This night, at the ancient stone, he and the Moidart would clasp hands and put an end to the savagery. For his part the Moidart had also agreed to petition the king and have Clan Rigante reinstated to the roll of honor.

Lanovar's black warhound, Raven, had growled deeply as they walked into the clearing. "Be silent, boy," whispered Lanovar. "This is an end to battle—not the beginning of it." He approached the Moidart, extending his hand. "It is good that we can meet in this way," said Lanovar. "This feud has bled the highlands for too long."

"Aye, it ends tonight," agreed the Moidart, stepping back into the shadow of the stone.

For a fraction of a heartbeat Lanovar stood still, his hand still extended. Then he heard movement from the undergrowth to the left and right and saw armed men rise up from hiding. Six soldiers carrying muskets emerged and surrounded the Rigante leader. Several others moved into sight, sabers in their hands. Raven bunched his muscles to charge, but Lanovar stopped him with a word of command. The Rigante leader stood very still. As agreed, he had brought no weapon to the meeting.

He glanced back at the Moidart. The nobleman was smiling now, though no humor showed in his dark, hooded eyes. Instead there was hatred, deep and all-consuming.

"So your word counts for nothing," Lanovar said softly. "Safe conduct, you said."

"It will be safe conduct, you Rigante scum," said the Moidart. "Safe conduct to my castle. Safe conduct to the deepest dungeon within it. Then safe conduct up every step of the gallows."

At that moment a bellowing war cry pierced the air. A massive figure rushed into sight, a huge broadsword raised high. His lower face was masked by a black scarf, and his dark clothes bore no clan markings. Lanovar's spirits soared.

It was Grymauch!

The surprised soldiers swung toward the charging warrior. Several shots were fired, but not one ball struck him. The massive broadsword swung down, slicing a soldier from shoulder to belly before exiting in a bloody spray. In the panic that followed the clansman's charge Lanovar leapt to his left, grabbed a musket by the barrel, and dragged it from the hands of a startled soldier. As the man rushed in to retrieve the weapon, Lanovar crashed the butt into his face, knocking him from his feet. A second musketeer ran in. The warhound Raven gave a savage growl and then leapt, his great jaws closing on the man's throat. Lanovar raised the musket to his shoulder and sought out the Moidart. The nobleman had ducked back into the undergrowth. More shots rang out. Smoke from the guns drifted like mist in the clearing, and the air stank of sulfur. Grymauch, slashing the great blade left and right, hurled himself at the musketeers. A swordsman ran in behind the clansman. Raising the captured musket, Lanovar fired quickly. The shot struck the hilt of the swordsman's upraised weapon and ricocheted back through the hapless man's right eye. Across the clearing three more musketeers came into view. Raven, his jaws drenched with blood, tore into them. One went down screaming. The others shot into the snarling hound. Raven slumped to the ground.

Lanovar threw aside the musket and ran toward Grymauch. The musketeers, their weapons empty, were backing away from the ferocious clansman. The swordsmen were dead or had fled into the woods. Lanovar moved alongside the blood-spattered warrior.

"We leave! Now!" he shouted.

As they swung away, the Moidart stepped from behind a tree. Grymauch saw him—and the long-barreled pistol in his hand. Vainly he tried to move across Lanovar, shielding him. But the shot tore through Grymauch's black cloak, ripping into the outlaw leader's side and out through his back. "That is for Rayena!" shouted the Moidart.

Lanovar's legs gave way instantly. Grymauch reached down, hauled him upright, and draped the paralyzed man across his shoulder. Then he ran into the thicket beyond the trail. At first the pain had been incredible, but then Lanovar had passed out. When he awoke, he was here on the mountainside and the pain was all but gone.

"How are you feeling?" asked Grymauch.

"Not so braw," admitted Lanovar. Grymauch had plugged the wound again and had settled him back against a rock face. Lanovar began to slide sideways. He tried to move his right arm to stop himself. The limb twitched but did not respond. Grymauch caught him and held him close for a moment. "Just wedge me against the rock," whispered Lanovar. Grymauch did as he was bidden.

"Are you warm enough? You look cold, Lan. I'll light a fire."

"And bring them down upon us? I think not." Reaching

down, he pressed his left hand against the flesh of his left thigh. "I cannot feel my leg."

"I told you, man. Did I not tell you?" stormed Grymauch. "The man is a serpent. There is no honor in him."

"Aye, you told me." Lanovar began to tremble. Grymauch moved in close, pulling off his own black cloak and wrapping it around the shoulders of his friend. He looked into Lanovar's curiously colored eyes, one green and one gold.

"We'll rest a little," said Grymauch. "Then I'll find the Wyrd."

Jaim Grymauch moved out along the ledge and stared down over the mountainside. There was no sign of pursuit now, but there would be. He glanced back at his wounded friend. Again and again he replayed the scene in his mind. He should have been there sooner. Instead, to avoid being seen by Lanovar, he had cut across the high trail, adding long minutes to the journey. As he had crested the rise, he had seen the soldiers crouched in hiding and watched as his greatest friend walked into the ambush. Masking his face with his scarf, Jaim had drawn his sword and rushed down to hurl himself at the enemy. He would willingly have sacrificed his own life to save Lanovar from harm.

The sun was setting, the temperature dropping fast. Jaim shivered. There was precious little fuel to be found that high. Trees did not grow there. He moved back alongside Lanovar. The Rigante leader's face looked ghostly pale, his eyes and cheeks sunken. Jaim's black cloak sat on the man's shoulders like a dark shroud. Jaim stroked Lanovar's brow. The wounded man opened his eyes.

Jaim saw that he was watching the sky turn crimson as the sun set. It was a beautiful sunset, and Lanovar smiled. "I love this land," he said, his voice stronger. "I love it with all my heart, Jaim. This is a land of heroes. Did you know the great Connavar was born not two miles from here? And the battle king, Bane. There used to be a settlement by the three streams."

Jaim shrugged. "All I know about Connavar is that he was nine feet tall and had a magic sword crafted from lightning. Could have done with that sword two hours ago. I'd have left none of the bastards alive."

They lapsed into silence. Jaim felt a growing sense of disorientation. It was as if he were dreaming. Time had no meaning, and even the breeze had faded away. The new night was still and infinitely peaceful.

Lanovar is dying.

The thought came unbidden, and anger raged through him. "Rubbish!" he said aloud. "He is young and strong. He has always been strong. I'll get him to the Wyrd. By heaven, I will!"

Jaim rolled to his knees and, lifting Lanovar into his arms, pushed himself to his feet. Lanovar's head was resting on Jaim's shoulder. Moonlight bathed them both. "We're going now, Lan."

Lanovar groaned, his face contorting with pain. "Put . . . me . . . down."

"We must find the Wyrd. She'll have magic. The Wishing Tree woods have magic."

In his mind he saw the woods, picturing the path they must take. At least four miles from there, part of it across open ground. Two hours of hard toil.

Two hours.

Jaim could feel Lanovar's lifeblood running over his hands. In that moment Jaim knew they did not have two hours. He sank to his knees and placed his friend on the ground. Tears misted his eyes. His great body began to shake. Jaim fought to control his grief, but it crashed through his defenses. Throughout his twenty years of life there had been one constant: the knowledge of Lanovar's friendship and, with it, the belief that they would change the world.

"Look after Gian and the babe," whispered Lanovar.

Jaim took a deep breath and wiped away his tears. "I'll do my best," he said, his voice breaking. His mind, reeling from the horror of the present, floated back to the past: days of childhood and adolescence, pranks and adventures. Lanovar had always been reckless and yet canny. He had a nose for trouble and the wit to escape the consequences.

Not this time, thought Grymauch. He felt the tears beginning again, but this time he shed them in silence. Then he saw Gian's face in his mind. Sweet heaven, how would he tell her?

She was heavily pregnant, the babe due in a few days. It was the thought of the child to be that had led Lanovar to trust the Moidart. He had told Jaim only the night before that he did not want the child growing up in the world of violence he had known. As they sat at supper in Lanovar's small, sod-roofed hut, the Rigante leader had spoken with passion about the prospect of peace. "I want my son to be able to wear the Rigante colors with pride and not to be hunted down as an outlaw. Not too much to ask, is it?" Gian had said nothing, but Lanovar's younger sister, the red-haired Maev, had spoken up.

"You can ask what you like," she said. "But the Moidart cannot be trusted. I know this in my soul!"

"You should listen to Maev," the raven-haired Gian urged, moving into the main room and easing herself down into an old armchair. One of the armrests was missing, and some horsehair was protruding from a split in the leather. "The Moidart hates you," she said. "He has sworn a blood oath to have your head stuck upon a spike."

" 'Tis all politics, woman. Peace with the highland Rigante will mean more tax income for the Moidart and the king. It will mean more merchants able to bring their convoys through the mountain passes. This will bring down the prices. Gold is what the king cares about. Not heads upon spikes. And as one of his barons, the Moidart will have to do what is good for the king."

"You'll take Grymauch with you," insisted Gian.

"I will not. We are to meet alone, with no weapons. I'll take Raven."

Later Maev had come to the hulking fighter as he sat in the doorway of his own hut. Normally his heart would beat faster as she approached him, his breath catching in his throat. Maev was the most beautiful woman Grymauch had ever seen. He had hoped to find the courage to tell her of this but instead had stood by as she and the handsome young warrior Calofair had begun their courtship. Calofair was now in the north, trading with the Black Rigante. When he came back, he and Maev would walk the tree.

Jaim glanced up as Maev approached. "You'll go anyway," she said.

"Aye, of course I will."

"You'll not let him see you."

Jaim laughed. "He's a bonny swordsman and a fine fighter, but he's a hopeless woodsman. He'll not see me, Maev."

Gian came walking across to them. Maev put her arms around the pregnant woman and kissed her cheek. Jaim Grymauch wondered briefly how it would feel if Maev did the same to him. He reddened at the thought. Gian stretched and pressed her palms into the small of her back. This movement caused her pregnant belly to look enormous. Jaim laughed. "Pregnancy suits some women," he said. "Their skin glows; their hair shines. They make a man think of the wonders of nature. Not you, though."

"Aye, she's ugly now, right enough," said Maev. "But when she's birthed the rascal, she'll become slim and beautiful again. Whereas you, you great lump, will always be ugly." Maev's smile faded. "Why does the Moidart hate Lanovar so?"

Jaim shrugged. The truth clung to him, burning in his heart, but he could not voice it. Lanovar was a fine man, braw and brave. He had many virtues and few vices. Sadly, one of his vices was that he found women irresistible. Before wedding Gian the previous spring, Lanovar had been seen several times in Eldacre town. Few knew the woman he had met there, but Jaim Grymauch was one who did. He suspected that the Moidart was another. Rayena Tremain was beautiful, no doubt about it. She was tall and slender, and she moved with an animal grace that set men's hearts beating wildly. The first affair with Lanovar had been brief, the parting apparently acrimonious.

Rayena wed the Moidart four months later in a great ceremony in Eldacre Cathedral.

Within the year there were rumors that the marriage was foundering.

Lanovar began acting strangely, disappearing for days at a time. Jaim, concerned for his leader and his friend, had secretly followed him one morning. Lanovar traveled to the high hills, to a small, abandoned hunting lodge. After an hour a lone horsewoman rode up. Jaim was astonished to see it was Rayena.

Beside him now Lanovar groaned, the sound jerking Jaim back to the painful present. Lanovar's face was bathed in sweat now, and his breathing was shallow and labored. "I was never . . . frightened . . . of dying, Grymauch," he said.

"I know that."

"I am now. My son is about to be . . . born, and I've . . . given him no soul-name."

In the distance a wolf howled.

◇ 1 ◇

THE THIN CANE slashed through the air. The fourteen-year-old youth winced but uttered no cry. Blood seeped from a split in the skin of his right palm. The tall, bony schoolmaster loomed over the black-haired boy. He was about to speak but saw the blood on the tip of his bamboo cane. Alterith Shaddler gazed at it with distaste, then laid the bamboo on the shoulder of the lad's gray shirt. Drawing the cane back and forth, he cleaned it, leaving thin crimson streaks on the threadbare garment.

"There are those," said Alterith Shaddler, his voice as cold as the air in the stone schoolroom, "who doubt the wisdom of trying to teach the rudiments of civilized behavior to highland brats. Since knowing you, boy, I am more inclined to count myself among their number."

Alterith placed the cane upon the desktop, straightened his threadbare white horsehair wig, and clasped his hands behind his back. The youth remained where he was, his hands now at his sides. It was a shame that he had been forced to draw blood, but these clan youngsters were not like Varlish boys. They were savages who did not feel pain in the same way. Not once did any of them make a sound while being thrashed. Alterith was of the opinion that the ability to feel pain was linked to intelligence. "No sense, no feeling," as his old tutor, Mr. Brandryth, was apt to say regarding clan folk.

The schoolmaster looked into the youth's dark eyes. "You understand why I punished you?"

"No, I do not."

Alterith's hand lashed out, slapping the boy hard upon the cheek. The sound hung in the air. "You will call me 'sir' when you respond to me. Do you understand *that*?"

"I do . . . sir," answered the youth, his voice steady but his eyes blazing with anger.

Alterith was tempted to slap him again for the look alone—and would have if the distant ringing of the dusk bell had not sounded from the Saint Persis Albitane School. Alterith glanced to his right, gazing through the open window and across the old parade square to the main school building. Already Varlish youngsters were emerging from the great doors, carrying their books. One of the masters came in sight, his midnight-blue academic cape shimmering in the afternoon sunshine. Alterith looked with longing at the old building. Within it were libraries filled with historical tomes, fine works of philosophy, and diaries of famous Varlish soldiers and statesmen. There were three halls and even a small theater set aside for great plays. The teacher sighed and returned his gaze to the cold stone walls of his own classroom. It was a former stable, the stalls having been ripped out and replaced with twenty ancient desks and chairs. Twenty chairs and fifty students, the unlucky ones sitting in ranks around the walls. There were no books there, the children using slate boards and chalk for their work. The walls were bare except for a single map of the Moidart's domain and beside it the daily prayer for the Moidart's continued health.

What a waste of my talents, he thought.

"We will recite the prayer," he said, offering the customary short bow. The fifty pupils in the class rose and, as they had been taught, returned the bow. Then the chant began.

"May the Source bless the Moidart and keep him in good health. May his lands be fertile, his people fed, his honor magnified, his laws be known, his word be obeyed, for the good of the faithful."

"Good day to you all," said Alterith.

"Good day, sir," they chanted.

Alterith looked down into the eyes of the black-haired

youth. "Begone, Master Ring. And bring a better attitude with you tomorrow."

The lad said nothing. He took one backward step, then spun on his heel and walked away.

One day, thought Alterith Shaddler, Kaelin Ring will hang. He has no respect for his betters.

The master sighed again, then moved swiftly across the room, lifting his greatcoat from its hook on the wall and swinging it across his thin shoulders. Despite the promise of spring, the highland air was still icy cold. Wrapping a long woolen scarf around his neck, Alterith left the old stable and walked across the parade ground into the school proper, striding down the now-silent corridor leading to the outer grounds. Several of the other teachers were sitting in the academic chamber as he passed. A fire was blazing in the hearth, and Alterith could smell the spices used in the mulled wine. It would have been pleasant to sit in one of those deep armchairs, his feet extended toward the fire. But then, unlike the members of staff at Persis Albitane, teaching was Alterith's only source of income, and he could not afford the chamber membership fee. Pushing thoughts of mulled wine and warm fires from his mind, he strode out into the cold air. The sun was shining brightly in a clear, bright sky. Immediately his eyes began to water. Alterith squinted toward the road and the lake beyond.

He could see the pony and open carriage already making their way slowly along the water's edge. Alterith's heart sank at the prospect of the four-mile journey to the Moidart's estate. He would be frozen and blue by the time they arrived, his teeth chattering, his mind unable to function properly. Alterith hoped the Moidart himself would not be present for his arrival. The last time they had met, Alterith, limbs trembling with the cold, had tried to bow only to see his horsehair wig slide off and land on the marbled floor at the Moidart's feet. Alterith blushed at the memory.

The sound of the pony's hooves could be heard now, and Alterith walked down to meet the carriage, anxious for the journey to begin as soon as possible. The driver nodded to him but said nothing. He was, as usual, wearing a thick overcoat and had a plaid blanket wrapped around his shoulders. Alterith climbed into the open-topped carriage and settled back, pushing his thin hands into the sleeves of his overcoat and trying not to think about the cold.

Kaelin Ring had no coat. He had lent it to his sick friend, Banny, though at this moment he was regretting the kindness. Banny had not come to school that day, which meant the coat was hanging on a hook in his hut and not keeping the wind's icy fingers from tugging at Kaelin's thin shirt.

Kaelin ran from the school yard out onto the cattle trail leading up into the hills. At least the cold made the pain in his hands less worrisome, he thought. Anger touched him then, warming him as he ran. He pictured old White Wig, tall and skinny, his thin lips constantly twisted in a contemptuous smirk, his pale eyes seeping tears whenever sunlight shone upon them. His clothes smelled of mothballs. That bony Varlish bastard will pay for every stroke he has ever laid upon me, Kaelin decided as he ran. He tried to think of punishments befitting such an ogre.

When I am a man next year, I'll nail him by his hands to the schoolhouse gates, then I'll take a whip to his hide. Five strokes for every one he's laid upon me.

Suddenly Kaelin's good humor came flooding back. He would need to be a great deal better at his arithmetic to tally such a sum. Perhaps he should ask old White Wig for extra lessons. The thought was so ridiculous that Kaelin slowed to a stop and burst out laughing. How would the conversation go? "I'm planning my vengeance on you. So would you kindly explain the multiplication so that I may lash your back to the exact number required?"

His laughter pealed out once more, then faded as he heard hoofbeats. Moving to the side of the trail, he waited. Five riders emerged from the trees. All of them were soldiers of the Moidart, or Beetlebacks, as the highlanders called them, referring to the black breastplates of baked leather they wore. The lead rider was a portly officer named Galliott. He was known widely as Galliott the Borderer, since his main role was to track and capture criminals and outlaws before they could cross the borders and leave the Moidart's jurisdiction. Just behind him was the thin, sallow-faced Sergeant Bindoe and three other soldiers Kaelin did not know.

Galliott drew rein and smiled at Kaelin: "Cold to be going without a coat, Master Ring." His voice, as ever, was friendly and warm, and Kaelin found it difficult to hold a dislike for the man. But it was not impossible if he worked at it.

"Aye, it is, sir."

"Perhaps your uncle Jaim will buy you one."

"I'll ask him next time he visits, sir."

"You've not seen him, then?"

"Has he broken the law, Mr. Galliott?"

The officer chuckled. "Always, boy. He was born to break the law. Two nights ago he was in a fight at Cock Crow tavern. Broke a man's arm and stabbed another in the face. Man was lucky not to lose an eye. If you see your uncle, tell him the owner of the tavern applied to the magistrate for damages to three tables, several chairs, and a window frame. Damages have been set at one chailling and nine daens, plus a two-chailling and six-daen fine. If it is paid by the end of the month, there will be no charges against Jaim. If not I am to arrest him and take him to the assizes for judgment by the Moidart."

"If I see him, I'll tell him, Mr. Galliott." Kaelin shivered.

"And get yourself a coat," said the officer. Heeling his mount, he rode away.

Kaelin watched as the riders cantered toward the town. Sergeant Bindoe glanced back, and Kaelin could feel the malice in the man. Beetlebacks were hated and feared in the highlands. Most—though not all—were Varlish and over the years had been responsible for many outrages. Only a month previously a woman living in an isolated cabin had walked into town and reported to the magistrate that she had been raped by three Beetlebacks. One of them had been Bindoe. Her story had not been believed, and she had been birched and jailed for two weeks for fabrication while under oath. After all, it was said, what self-respecting Varlish soldier would touch a lice-infested highland slut?

Kaelin waited until the Beetlebacks were out of sight and then ran on. The wind was less fierce within the woods, and he was soon sweating as he ran. The trail wound up, ever higher. He stopped at a break in the trees and gazed down over the hills below. Hundreds of small dwellings dotted the countryside, and many more, he knew, were hidden from his gaze, their sod roofs blending them into the land. Cattle and sheep and goats were grazing on the new spring grass, and some way to the west Kaelin saw more Beetlebacks riding along the Eldacre Road where it met the shores of the lake.

Cutting away from the main trail, he darted up a side slope, hurdling a fallen tree and sprinting along the final stretch to the crack in the cliff face. It had rained in the night, and glancing down, Kaelin saw that he was leaving footprints in the earth. He continued to run along the line of the cliffs until he reached higher ground, then climbed to the rock face. The face was sheer for some fifty feet, but Jaim Grymauch had taught him to overcome his fear of heights and glory in the joy of the climb. Wedge holds, hand hams, pressure holds—all were second nature to Kaelin Ring now, and he smoothly climbed the wall of rock, traversing back until he was once more alongside the crack in the face. Swinging himself inside, he edged along the narrow gap and then climbed again, emerging into a deep cave. A fire was burning in a roughly made hearth, and a man was sitting beside it, gently burnishing the blade of an enormous broadsword. Kaelin leapt to the floor of the cave and ran to the fire. The man glanced up. He had but one eye, the other covered by a strip of black cloth wound around his bald head, and his face was scarred and pitted. There was a large purple bruise on his cheek, and a cut on his lip was almost healed. Splashes of dried blood had stained the black cloak and kilt he wore.

"I hope you learned a goodly amount today," said Jaim Grymauch.

Kaelin settled down opposite the big man. "I learned that Connavar was a Varlish prince and not a clansman at all," he said.

"Aye, I've heard that. Did they also tell you that he shit pearls and pissed fine wine?" Putting aside the broadsword, Jaim reached out and took Kaelin's hand, turning the palm toward the firelight. "I see that you've been insolent again. What was it this time?"

"I told old White Wig that Connavar was Rigante and that the man who wrote about him being Varlish was a stinking liar."

"I'm a great believer in diplomacy, Kaelin, and it pleases me to see you mastering it at such a tender age."

"Oh, and I saw Mr. Galliott. He says you've to pay one chailling and nine daens for damages and you've been fined another two chaillings and six daens. He says it must be paid by the end of the month or you'll be taken before the Moidart."

"So how much do I owe in all?"

"A lot," answered Kaelin.

"I'm not good with numbers, boy. Calculate it for me."

Kaelin closed his eyes. Best to calculate the daens first, he thought. Nine plus six made . . . he counted it on his fingers. Fifteen. Suddenly he thought of Banny again, wondering if his cough had improved. Jerking himself back to the problem, he calculated that fifteen daens made one chailling and three daens. To which he had to add the fine: two chaillings. Making three chaillings and three daens. He told Jaim the figure.

"You've lost a chailling," said Jaim.

"I have not!"

"Forget the daens for a moment. How many chaillings was the fine?"

"Two."

"And how many for the damages?"

"One."

"Well that makes three already. Now you have fifteen daens. That makes one chailling and three daens. So I owe them four chaillings and three daens."

Kaelin scowled. "You told me you were bad at figures."

"I *am* bad at figures. I'm just not as bad as you." The warrior sighed. "I'm getting old, Kaelin. Was a time when the damages and fine always came to more than five chaillings. But now I'm weary before I've bent the second chair over some poor fool's head."

"You're not old," said Kaelin, moving to sit beside the grizzled warrior and enjoying the warmth of the fire. "You'll never be old."

"That's probably true." He glanced at Kaelin. "You staying long, boy?"

"Only an hour or so. Aunt Maev has chores for me. Why don't you come back and have supper with us."

Jaim shook his head. "I'm feeling solitary."

"You want me to go?"

Jaim grinned, then winced as the scab on his lip parted. He dabbed at it with a finger. "No, I don't want you to go. Sitting like this reminds me of times I sat with your father. You look just like him save for the eyes. His were strange, one green and one gold. You have your mother's eyes. She was a good woman, Gian. Deserved better."

Kaelin looked away and added some sticks to the fire. His mother had been killed two nights after he was born. Beetlebacks had raided the settlement. Few had escaped. Aunt Maev had been one of them, carrying the infant Kaelin in her arms.

"What was the fight in the tavern about?" asked Kaelin, changing the subject.

"I don't remember."

"You stabbed a man in the face, Grymauch. You ought to remember."

"Aye, that's true, I guess." The big man stretched himself

out beside the fire. "It was probably over a woman. Most fights are."

"Have you ever lost a fight?"

Jaim was silent for a moment. "I think that in a way I have lost every fight I've ever had." He sat up. "I'm like the Rigante, Kaelin. I have fought men in the highlands, in the south, and across the great ocean. No man has ever bested me in battle, and yet I sit in a hidden cave nursing my bruises. I own no cattle. I have no land."

"You should wed Aunt Maev."

Jaim's laughter pealed out. "She's too good a woman for the likes of me, lad. As she'd tell you herself."

"You like her, though?"

"Of course I like her. She's a woman to walk the mountains with."

"She's mean with her money, though," said Kaelin.

"Aye, she's careful. She needs to be. The Varlish don't like to see any highlander gathering wealth. It makes them uncomfortable."

"Why? She pays her tax to the Moidart and the king."

"They mock us and tell us we are stupid, but secretly they fear us, Kaelin. Wealth is power. The Varlish have no desire to see powerful highlanders. Now, enough talk. You tell Maev I'll be needing you at the week's end. The pass is open, and I've a hankering to see the ocean."

Kaelin laughed. "Will it just be the two of us?"

"Of course. Together we're an army, boy."

"And whose cattle will it be? Old Kocha?"

"I've not made up my mind. I like to spread my favors." Jaim chuckled. "They say the Moidart has brought in a new bull from the isles. Ten pounds, he paid for it."

"How much is that in chaillings?" asked Kaelin.

"Two hundred chaillings."

"For a bull?" Kaelin was amazed that such a sum could have been paid. "Are you joking with me, Grymauch?"

"I never joke about the price of cattle. I'm wondering how much Pinance would pay for it."

"How much do you think?" asked Kaelin.

"At least enough for my fine," Jaim Grymauch answered with a wide grin.

The ride had not proved quite as uncomfortable as Alterith Shaddler had feared. The wind had died down, the temperature hovering a few degrees above freezing. There was still snow on the high ground and the wheels of the carriage crunched over icy puddles, but Alterith believed he could finally feel spring in the air.

The carriage slowed as it neared the top of a rise. The driver cracked his whip above the pony's ears. The little beast lunged forward. Alterith felt a moment of motion sickness and took a deep breath. Then the carriage topped the rise, and the schoolteacher found himself gazing down over the magnificence of the Eldacre valley. The first sight to catch the eye was the mighty castle rearing like a giant tombstone on a hill above the town.

The ancestral home of the Moidart, Eldacre Castle was a monument to the power and ingenuity of the Varlish race. Alterith's heart swelled each time he saw it. It had walls forty feet high, boasting twenty jutting turrets and four massive gates of seasoned oak reinforced with iron. Fifteen thousand workers had labored for seven years to build it. The finest stonemasons and carpenters had been brought in from the south at vast expense. Many of them had stayed on in the valley after the castle was built, including Alterith's own ancestors, one of whom had been responsible for fashioning the curved rafters of the chapel within the great keep.

For three hundred years Eldacre Castle had been an impregnable fortress in times of war and a mighty symbol of Varlish superiority in times of peace. Just the sight of her massive walls and turrets, fashioned with murder holes and oil vents, was enough to quell any thoughts of rebellion within renegade highland hearts.

The carriage picked up speed as it moved down the hill.

Alterith's motion sickness returned. "Slow down, for pity's sake!" he yelled.

"Mustn't be late, sir," answered the driver.

Alterith sat miserably, praying that he would not be sick. It was bad enough that his wig had fallen off at the Moidart's feet. The prospect of arriving before the Moidart in a vomit-stained coat was more than he could bear. The Moidart would in all probability dismiss him, and Alterith could ill afford to lose the extra two chaillings a month. Steeling himself, he clung to the strap on the inside of the carriage door and tried to focus his mind on something other than his heaving stomach. He chose history.

Eldacre. Originally Old Oaks, the center of government in the ancient kingdom of the Rigante, once ruled by Connavar, Bane, Laguish, Borander, and Sepdannet the Leaper. Now a town of some twenty-five thousand souls with three mines, two of coal and one of gold, and five blast furnaces feeding a thriving industry making muskets for the king's armies, iron rims for wagon wheels, ornate buckles and accoutrements for officers and gentlemen, and swords for the military and for export. It was a prosperous community, a healthy mix of the industrial and the agricultural, with seventeen churches, a massive cathedral, and the Academy for the Instruction of the Righteous. Alterith himself was a graduate of the academy, having majored in the terms of the Sacrifice and the evangelical journeys of the Saint Persis Albitane.

At last the carriage began to slow, cutting away from the main highway and onto a narrow stone road leading between a line of fir trees. Leaning to his left and looking past the hunched figure of the driver, Alterith could see the wrought-iron gates that barred the way to the Moidart's huge country manor. It was here that the Lord of the Highlands spent the winter. Two musketeers stood sentry, the sunlight gleaming on the gold braid and bright brass buttons of their yellow jerkins. The first of them called out for the carriage to stop and, laying aside his long-barreled musket, stepped forward to inspect the vehicle. He looked closely at Alterith.

"Are you carrying any weapons, sir?" he asked.

"I am not."

"Be so kind as to step down."

Alterith pushed open the small door and climbed from the carriage. His black frock coat was tight-fitting but, he supposed, could still have hidden a small knife. The soldier expertly ran his hands over Alterith's garments.

"My apologies to you, sir, for the impertinence," said the sentry.

Alterith resumed his seat, and the second sentry opened the gates.

The sound of blades clashing was music to the ears of Mulgrave. Such was the skill of the fencing master that he did not even have to see a duel to judge the skill of the fighters. He had only to hear the sweet sword song of kissing steel. Mulgrave loved to fence and could have made his fortune as a duelist in any one of fifty major cities across the empire. The problem—though Mulgrave did not see it as such—was that he did not like to kill. There were those who thought him squeamish and others who whispered that the swordsman was a coward. None, however, were sure enough of either view to dare speak them to his face.

Mulgrave not only was a master swordsman, he *looked* like a master swordsman, tall, lean, and with reflexes that could make a man believe in magic. His eyes were a pale metallic blue, close-set and piercing, his features sharp, his mouth unsmiling. His hair, closely cropped to his skull, was the silver of polished iron despite the fact that he was not yet thirty years of age.

Selecting a slender rapier, the point capped by a small wooden ball, he bowed to the golden-haired young noble standing before him. His opponent pulled his face mask into place and took up his position.

"Are you ready?" asked the fifteen-year-old Gaise Macon.

"Always," answered Mulgrave, donning his own mask of fine mesh.

The young man darted forward, his rapier lancing toward the chest guard of the older man. Mulgrave sidestepped, avoiding the thrust. Gaise stumbled. Mulgrave's rapier struck the young man's leg in a stinging blow. "A nice idea but poorly executed, my lord," said Mulgrave. Gaise did not reply. Nor did he react to the blow except to assume once more the fighting stance. This pleased the master. Their blades touched and slid away, and the practice continued. The lad had fine balance and great speed of hand. Already he was more than a match for most men with rapier or épée. His saber work was not of a great standard, but then, he was of slight build. Maturity would add muscle to his frame and strength to his arm, Mulgrave knew.

Toward the end of the session Mulgrave allowed the young noble to score a partial hit. He did not want the lad to become discouraged.

"Enough!" said the master, offering a bow to his opponent. Gaise returned it, then swept the mask from his face, tossing it to the grass. His golden hair was sweat-streaked, his face red from his exertions—except for the star-shaped scar upon his cheekbone, which remained bone-white. Mulgrave removed his face guard and placed it on the ground.

"By the Sacrifice, you are not even warm, sir," Gaise said with a sudden smile.

Mulgrave gave the young noble a warning look, and the smile faded. Gaise unbuckled his quilted chest guard and glanced up at the house. A silver-haired figure dressed all in black was standing at the balcony rail, looking down on them. Then he was gone.

The fencing master saw the look of sadness that came to the young man's face. There was nothing Mulgrave could say or do. "You are moving well, my lord," he told the young man. "You almost had me in trouble twice."

"I think that he hates me," said Gaise.

Mulgrave took a deep, slow breath. "Your history teacher is due soon, sir. You should get out of those sweat-drenched clothes and towel yourself down. This is the weather for chills to take hold."

"Aye, 'tis a chilly house," Gaise Macon said sadly.

Mulgrave wanted to throw his arm around the young man's shoulder and say something to cheer him, but he guessed that the Moidart would be watching them from behind a curtain at one of the upper windows. It saddened Mulgrave to think that Gaise had every reason to believe his father disliked him. They rarely spoke unless it was for the Moidart to criticize some aspect of the youth's behavior, and often Gaise carried bruises on his face or arms that Mulgrave guessed came from beatings.

Mulgrave had been bodyguard to the Moidart as well as martial instructor to Gaise Macon for three years now and in that time had seen much of the Moidart's cruelty.

"This afternoon we will try out the new pistols," said Mulgrave. "They are beautifully balanced."

"I will look forward to it," answered Gaise.

How can the Moidart dislike the lad so? wondered Mulgrave. He is considerate and kind, deferential in all his dealings with his father, and has shown great dedication in learning the martial skills of riding, fencing, and shooting.

Mulgrave looked into the youth's odd-colored eyes, one green and one tawny gold. "You did well, sir," he said. "I'm proud of you."

"That means a great deal to me," answered Gaise. "I shall go and change my clothes. Would you make my apologies to Mr. Shaddler and tell him I will be with him presently?"

"Of course, sir."

Mulgrave watched the youth run lightly up the steps to the side doors. Just then the tall, spidery figure of Alterith Shaddler came into view. Mulgrave removed his chest guard and offered the teacher a short bow. "Good day to you, sir teacher," said the swordsman.

"And to you, Master Mulgrave. I trust that you are well."

"I am, sir. Lord Gaise has asked me to convey his apologies

for lateness. Our practice was delayed, and he is changing his clothing."

"The martial skills are always considered ahead of the cerebral," Alterith said without bitterness.

"Sadly, sir, I must agree with you. A true student of history would learn of the endless stupidity war brings out in men."

"And the nobility, Master Mulgrave," admonished the teacher. "That, too."

"Indeed. Nobility is found in great quantities among warriors. It is notably lacking, I find, in those who send them to war."

Alterith Shaddler blinked and licked his lips. "I must have misunderstood you, sir, for your words could be seen as a criticism of the king."

Mulgrave smiled. "We were talking of matters historical, sir. Not political. For example, one could read the essays on war of the emperor Jasaray. There is little nobility there—merely a vaunting ambition to conquer as much of the known world as possible."

"But there was great nobility in Conn of the Vars, who defeated him," observed Alterith.

Mulgrave chuckled. "Conn of the Vars? He was one of us, then? Fascinating. I'd always been led to believe he was a clansman."

"A common misconception among nonscholars, sir. The power of the Source brought him to this realm as a child in order that he could one day defeat Jasaray."

"Ah, yes, the Source," Mulgrave said with a grin. "I understand he is also of the Varlish."

"I believe that you are making sport of me, sir," Alterith said sternly.

"My apologies, sir teacher," Mulgrave replied, with a bow, "for indeed I am. When I was a child, my mother taught me of the Sacrifice. As I understand it, the early saints were people who preached peace and love. How strange it is that in their names we have conquered many lands, burned cities, slaughtered thousands. I'll wager the legendary Veiled Lady would turn her face from us in shame. We are no better than the savages she sought to convert."

All color drained from Alterith's face. "By the Sacrifice, man! You could burn for such remarks! The Varlish are the chosen race of the Source."

Mulgrave's pale eyes held to the schoolmaster's gaze. "Aye, I guess I could burn for the truth. Other men have."

Alterith sighed. "I shall not repeat this conversation, Master Mulgrave, but I would appreciate it if you did not repeat such heresy within my hearing."

"Agreed, we will not talk of matters religious. In the same spirit please do not insult my intelligence with nonsense about Conn of the Vars. It is enough that we destroy the culture of the Keltoi without polluting their proud history."

"Connovar's origins are a known fact," insisted Alterith. "The historian—"

"I'll tell you a known fact, sir teacher. Four years ago a small church some thirty miles from here, in the province of the Pinance, was undergoing renovation. They removed a cracked flagstone close to the altar. Beneath it was an old chest, and within it a number of old scrolls, yellow and crusty with age. Upon one scroll was written the table of Keltoi kings and their lineage. An elderly monk spent months deciphering the Keltoi script. Many of the stories contained in the scrolls were unknown to us, dealing with myths of the Seidh. The old monk became very excited. We always knew that Connovar carried the soul-name Sword in the Storm. We did not know why. One of the scrolls explained it. His name was actually Conn-a-Var, or in pure translation, Conn son of Var. His father's name was Var-a-Conn, Var son of Conn. He was not of the Var race at all. The scrolls also gave insights into known historical events, the battles, the philosophy of the Keltoi kings."

"I would have heard of such a find," argued Alterith. "It would have been priceless and much talked of."

"It would have been had word leaked out," said Mulgrave. "I knew of it only because I was studying some of the works held in the church library, and I got to speak with the monk. He sent a letter to the Pinance, telling him of the find. Soon after that a squad of soldiers arrived and forcibly removed the scrolls. They also took all the copies the old monk had made. He wrote to the Pinance, pleading to be allowed to continue his work. There was no reply. He wrote to his bishop, requesting that the king be petitioned, detailing in the letter all that he remembered from the scrolls.

"On my last day at the church a carriage came for him. I saw him climb into it. He was happy, for he believed he was going to be taken to the castle of the Pinance, there to continue his work. His body was found two days later in a stream some three miles from the church."

"You are saying the Pinance had him killed?"

"I am saying nothing of the kind. The Pinance disavowed all knowledge of the carriage or the men riding with it."

"Then what are you saying?"

"I am saying that history is always written by the victors. It is not about truth but about justification. The Keltoi were a proud warrior race. It does not suit us that they should remain so. So we denigrate their culture, and what we cannot denigrate we suppress. I do not know if the scrolls were true. How could I? The old monk could have been wrong in his translations. But I do know they have never surfaced again for other discussion. That tells me much."

Alterith sighed. "Why do you persist in telling me things that could put your life at risk, Master Mulgrave?"

"Because I am a good judge of men, Master Shaddler. Your head may be filled with nonsense, but deep down you have a good heart."

The teacher blushed. "I thank you for the . . . the half compliment, sir, but from now on, let us hold to conversational topics that do not bring visions of the noose or the flame."

Kaelin had never seen a more magnificent bull. As tall as a horse, black as a raven's wing, the enormous beast stood in the moonlit paddock like an enormous statue cast from coal.

Hidden behind a screen of gorse on the hillside above, Kaelin sat quietly beside Jaim Grymauch.

"I have never seen horns so wide," said Kaelin. "They must be seven feet from tip to tip. Is it a freak?"

"No," whispered Jaim. "It is an isles bull. One and a half tons of short-tempered unpredictability. One flick of that head and the horn would pass right through a man."

"Then how are we going to steal it?"

Jaim Grymauch grinned suddenly. "We'll use the old magic, lad. I'll summon a Seidh spirit."

"You shouldn't joke about such things," the youth said sternly.

"There's nothing in this world that I cannot joke about," the man told him, his smile fading. "Sometimes, deep in the night, I believe I can hear the gods laugh at us. If they did create us, Kaelin, they created us for a joke. Nothing else. And a bad joke, to boot! I'll mock the Seidh and I'll mock the Sacrifice. I'll mock any damn thing I please!"

Kaelin Ring loved and trusted the scarred warrior, but he knew when to fall silent. Jaim was just like one of the bulls he lived to steal: brooding, short-tempered, and wholly unpredictable. Dawn was still a little way off, and Kaelin hunkered down into his borrowed coat. It was thick and warm and smelled of woodsmoke, coal dust, and sweat. He closed his eyes and dozed for a while. Pain woke him, and he cried out.

"Quiet, boy! What's wrong?" hissed Jaim.

"I've a cramp in my calf," muttered Kaelin, reaching down and trying to ease the pain. Jaim knelt beside him, his huge fingers closing firmly over the knotted muscles. It was excruciating. Jaim dug deep into the tortured tissue. Kaelin tried to make no sound. Gritting his teeth, he held his breath for as long as he could. Just as it seemed he could take the agony no longer, the muscles eased, the pain sliding away.

Jaim patted the youth's thigh. "Good lad," he said. Reaching up, Jaim pulled clear the black cloth headband that protected his ruined eye. The empty socket had been stitched some years before and was now sealed tight. Jaim rubbed at the scars. "It baffles me," he said, "how an eye that is long gone can still itch." Settling the cloth back into place, he glanced back down the hillside. There was still no sign of herdsmen even though the sun had been up for some minutes. "They breed 'em lazy in these parts," he said with a grin.

Kaelin did not reply. He was gently massaging his calf. They had crossed the mountains the previous day, and though Kaelin was strong and as fleet as any youngster of his age, he had struggled to keep up with Jaim Grymauch, especially when they had reached the pass. Jaim had said it was now open, yet still they had had to dig their way through one snow-blocked section and make a precarious climb across a high icy ledge. Kaelin had been relieved to see the glittering water of Moon Lake, the paddocks and outbuildings of the Moidart's western estate nestling by its banks.

He and Jaim had slept in a derelict shack close to a long-deserted coal quarry. Jaim lit a small fire, while Kaelin roamed the area in the twilight, gathering fragments of coal that still dotted the hillside. Kaelin loved to watch coal burn. It was a mystery to him how the black rock could catch fire and how the flames could suddenly hiss and turn blue.

They slept on the floor of the shack, and Kaelin was awakened by Jaim three hours before the dawn. "Time to find the watching spot," said Jaim. Sleepily the youth followed the big man out into the darkness and down into the lower gorse-covered hills. Using a broad-bladed knife, Jaim cut several thick branches of gorse, handing them to Kaelin for carrying. The youngster handled them with care, for the needle-sharp thorns could lance through skin as easy as winking. Jaim cut more gorse, then moved farther down the hillside, seeking a hiding place. Deciding on an old gorse bush skirted with heather, Jaim cut an entrance into the eastern side of the bush; then, from within it, he and Kaelin built up a layered outer wall of the branches they had cut. When the hiding place was completed, Jaim squirmed across to the western-facing branches and gently parted them with his hands. Satisfied that he had a good view of the outbuildings and paddocks, he squatted down, delved deep into his leather undershirt, and produced two hard-baked oatcakes. He passed one to Kaelin.

"Are you bored, young Ravenheart?" he asked.

Kaelin shook his head. The truth was that he loved to roam the mountains with Jaim Grymauch. It made him forget for a while that as a highlander he had no real future in a world ruled by the Varlish. He could not even publicly claim to be a Rigante. The clan had been outlawed twenty years before. The wearing of the pale blue and green Rigante plaid was an act punishable by death. All Rigante males in the area had been forced to change clans, most becoming Pannone. Those who refused and took to the hills were ruthlessly hunted down and murdered by the Beetlebacks. A few hundred had fled into the bleak northern mountains, where they survived by raiding and stealing. They were known now as Black Rigante, and every few years strong forces of Beetlebacks and musketeers would enter the mountains seeking them out. Ten years earlier a small settlement of Black Rigante clansmen had been surrounded and slaughtered, though almost eighty Beetlebacks had been killed in the raid and two hundred had been injured. They lived now in an uneasy truce with the Beetlebacks.

No, Kaelin Ring was never bored while with Jaim. "Do you have a poem for the bull yet?" he asked.

"I thought I had," replied Jaim, "but now that I've seen him, I realize it is inadequate. I shall work on another."

Kaelin grinned. There were some who thought Grymauch's bull-stealing verses were merely indications of the man's vanity. The one-eyed warrior was as well known for his rhymes as for his raiding. Many of his songs were sung at festival feasts, and Kaelin knew at least twenty bull songs by heart. He also knew that vanity had little to do with Grymauch's poems. Aunt Maev reckoned it was merely Grymauch's deep, hypnotic voice and confident movement that mesmerized the animals, but Kaelin believed the verses were the links in a magical chain between Grymauch and the bull. He had twice seen the big man walk into starlit fields, take the chosen bull by the nose ring, and gently lead him away from all he knew.

"Tell me the soul-name story again, Grymauch," he urged.

"By the Sacrifice, boy, do you never tire of it?"

"No. It brings me closer to my father somehow."

Jaim reached out and ruffled Kaelin's black hair. "Where would you like me to start it? The fight with the Moidart, the flight to the mountain, the coming of the stag?"

"The stag. Tell it from the stag."

The sky was lightening as Jaim began his tale. "We were sitting on a ledge of glistening gray rock. Your father was mortally wounded and knew it. He had few regrets, he said, for he was a man who—in terms of the clan he led—always did what he thought was right. He had lived true. Yet he was filled with sorrow that he would not see you grow and that he had found no soul-name for you." Kaelin closed his eyes, picturing the scene. "We sat quietly, him and me, and then we heard the howling of the wolves. They were hunting. Canny creatures, wolves. They know they cannot outrun a stag. It has far more stamina than any wolf. So they hunt as a team. Four or five of them will harry the stag, chasing it for a mile or two. The forest lord is not concerned at first. He knows the wolves cannot outlast him. What he does not know is that the wolves have formed a circle of death and that others of the pack are waiting farther down the trail. As the first wolves begin to tire, the second group takes up the chase, driving the stag toward a third in a great circle. The killing run goes on and on, the wolves tightening the circle, until at last the exhausted forest lord turns at bay. By now all the wolves have come together for the kill. This, Kaelin, is what your father and I saw. A proud and massive stag, a right royal beast if ever there was one, was upon the hill opposite to where we sat. He had a wonderful spread of horn, and he stood weary yet defiant as a dozen wolves closed in on him. Ah, but it was a sight to see. The bravest of the wolves darted forward and was tossed high into the air, his body dashed against a tree, his back broken. Then the other wolves charged. There was no way for the stag to win. No way. It was finished."

"And then came Raven," prompted Kaelin, excitement in his voice.

"Hush, boy! 'Tis I who am telling this tale."

"I am sorry, Grymauch. Go on, please."

"No more interruptions, if you please. As I said, the stag could not win. Yet he fought magnificently, giving no ground. As the wolves closed in, something dark came rushing from the undergrowth. At first I could not see what it was, but it charged into the wolves, scattering them. Your father had better eyesight than mine—and I had both my eyes then! He said: 'By heaven, it is Raven.' We had both thought the hound slain in the fight with the treacherous Moidart, but there he was, ripping into the startled wolves. There was blood on his muzzle and two more wolves dead when the others panicked and ran." Grymauch paused, lost in the memory. Kaelin did not prompt him. The warrior sighed. "And—for the merest heartbeat—I saw Raven and the stag standing together, looking at one another. Both were bloodied. The forest lord dipped its head toward Raven as if in thanks, though I doubt it was. Then it bounded away into the trees, and the hound continued across the hills toward us. He had followed the scent, you see, and wanted to be reunited with Lanovar. I saw him stumble twice, but he carried on, more slowly than before. Aye, he was a brave hound, right enough. I swung around to see that your father was in his last moments. My heart was pierced as I watched him then. It has never mended. I held him close. We said nothing. Then the hound reached us, and I saw that it, too, would not survive the night. Musket balls had pierced him deep, and he was bleeding badly. He settled down alongside Lanovar, his head on his master's lap. I think they died together. If not, there were only a few heartbeats between." Jaim fell silent.

"What about my soul-name?" asked Kaelin.

"Oh, yes. Forgive me, boy. I was lost in moments past. As we watched the hound attack the wolves, Lanovar whispered something. I didn't hear it quite, so I moved alongside him. 'Ravenheart,' he said. I didn't understand at first. Then he drew in a breath and said: 'My son . . . Ravenheart.' I knew then, and I promised him I would see that your mother was told that this was to be your soul-name."

"Most of my friends don't have soul-names," said Kaelin.

"The Varlish fear them. The names hold us to the land and give us pride. The Varlish need to see that pride eaten away, so they claim soul-names are a sign of heresy and paganism. Few parents want to risk a visit by the knights of the Sacrifice and then be staked above the fire."

"Why do you think Raven rescued the stag?" asked the youngster.

"I don't believe that he did intend to rescue the creature. Raven was a wolfhound. He was born to fight wolves and protect cattle. I think he was just trying to reach Lanovar and the wolves were in his way. Once he came upon them, instinct took over. The stag was irrelevant."

"I think it was a magical stag," said Kaelin.

"Magical? Why would you think that?"

"Because it brought me my soul-name and because the Wyrd told me."

"Be careful, Kaelin. The Wyrd knows some ancient spells, and she's dangerous to know."

Kaelin smiled. "We are sitting on a hillside waiting to steal the Moidart's prize bull, and you tell me the Wyrd is dangerous to know. *You* are dangerous to know, Uncle."

"Aye, well, I guess that's true, right enough."

Jaim fell silent as a group of men emerged from a thatched building to the north of the paddock. They walked to the fence and stopped to gaze at the bull. The animal swung its shaggy head and stared at them, then pawed at the ground. Jaim chuckled. "Settle back, Kaelin. Now we'll see how skilled they are." Three of the men clambered up to sit on the fence. A fourth ducked through between the posts and approached the bull, hand extended. Wind noise, whistling through the heather, prevented the youth from hearing what the man was saying, but Kaelin knew he would be speaking softly, making soothing, friendly noises to calm the beast. Jaim was watching the scene intently. "That's good. That's good," he said softly as the unknown man below moved alongside the animal. The bull was a little calmer now. "Ah, he has a talent, the man," said Jaim. "But don't get cocky now. He's still not sure of you. Just stay away from his head."

Kaelin smiled. Jaim was probably not even aware that he was speaking aloud. The man below was stroking and patting the bull's flanks. The animal ceased to paw at the ground and was standing quietly. The man eased himself around the huge horns and reached for the bull's heavy nose ring. "Too soon!" whispered Jaim. The bull lunged forward. The man was hit hard by the bull's forehead. Instinctively he grabbed the horns. The head dropped, then flicked upward. The cattleman was hurled up. One hand lost its grip on the horns, and the other clung tight. The man came down across the bull's back, the impact causing him to let go of the horn. Half-stunned, the cattleman fell to the earth. His comrades on the fence shouted at the bull, seeking to divert its attention. They succeeded better than they hoped. The bull charged, its massive head thundering against the fence post, which split down the middle. Two of the men managed to jump clear just as the bull charged. The third fell headfirst into the paddock. The bull swung on him. Kaelin saw a streak of crimson smear the air. The man was flung some ten feet across the paddock. He landed heavily and did not move.

The first cattleman, still dazed, staggered across the paddock toward the fence. The bull ignored him as it ignored the fallen man. Kaelin saw blood dripping from one of the horns. He transferred his gaze to the fallen herdsman. "Is the man dead?" he asked Jaim.

"He most certainly is."

"Are we still going to steal the bull?"

Jaim nodded. "Aye, but I'll need a stronger bull song, by heaven!"

◇ 2 ◇

FOR SEVERAL HOURS Jaim sat unmoving, watching the bull. For part of the time Kaelin dozed. He felt safe there, hidden at the center of a gorse bush, the giant Jaim Grymauch alongside him. Jaim was a ferocious fighter, and even though he had not brought his mighty glave—clansmen were forbidden, under pain of death, to own swords—he was carrying two broad-bladed hunting knives held in horizontal sheaths stitched at the back of his wide belt. Kaelin doubted if even a black bear would have the nerve to face Jaim Grymauch in battle.

The youngster yawned and stretched. He moved alongside Jaim and, looking through the parted gorse branches, saw that the body in the paddock had been removed. Several men were repairing the fence, and Kaelin could just hear the distant sound of hammering.

"They'll not try to move the bull today," Jaim said suddenly. "Time to stretch our legs and see the country."

"Will we go back to the shack?"

"No. We'll grace the town with a visit. I've a hankering to taste smoked fish soup and fire-black bread. Aye, and a pint or two of brandy barrel ale."

"You'll get into a fight, Grymauch! Then we'll be in trouble," warned Kaelin.

Jaim Grymauch chuckled. "You listen too much to your aunt Maev. Women exaggerate matters. It is in their nature. Anyway, it will be an education for you, Ravenheart. Moon

Lake boasts one of the last of the timber castles. You'll not see their like again."

Grymauch eased himself back across the hide and pushed aside the interlaced branches. Staying low, he moved back through the gorse and the heavy undergrowth until he could no longer be seen from the outbuildings. Kaelin followed him, and they were soon walking across the low hills toward the woods above and behind the Moidart's western estate.

"Why do we steal cattle?" Kaelin asked him as they entered the trees.

"It is an honorable tradition, my boy. A man should always treat with respect the traditions of his elders."

"If it is that honorable, why do you not steal from clan herds?"

Jaim laughed. "Balance, Kaelin. The Varlish have stolen our lands, our cattle, our homes, even our traditions. My stealing of their cattle—and on occasion horses—brings me a sense of harmony, of balance."

"Do you hate them, then?"

"Hate them? A man might as well hate the sea for the friends who have drowned in it. No, boy, I don't hate them. I don't *know* them all, and it is a principle of mine never to hate a man I do not know. It just so happens that I *have* come to dislike all the Varlish I *do* know. Their arrogance works into my skin like a thorn."

"I hate Mr. Shaddler," said Kaelin. "One day I'll show him!"

"I fear you won't," said Jaim. "Teachers are never *shown*, for they are never wrong. If you rise up to be a great man, respected and admired by all who know you, Mr. Shaddler will swell out his bony chest and say: 'I taught him all he knows.' If you become a brigand and a terrible killer, he will say: 'I always knew he was bad. I told him so to his face every day.' "

"Perhaps I'll just kill him," snapped Kaelin.

"Whoa now!" said Jaim, pausing in his walk and turning to face the black-haired youth. "No, Kaelin, *that* you must never do. The man may be Varlish and misguided in much that he teaches—though I doubt he is in *all* that he teaches—but he has still chosen a profession of *service*. He is a poor man, this Shaddler. There are rats where he lodges. He owns no house and has no private income. His topcoat is threadbare, and his shoes have soles like paper. He could earn far more chaillings in Eldacre, in commerce or in the law. He teaches because he wants to serve, to pass on knowledge to the young. And he suffers poverty for his dedication. Hate him, by all means, for the stick across your hands or the corrupting of our history but never, ever consider killing him. You understand, boy?"

"Yes, Grymauch," Kaelin lied, unable to comprehend how killing a worm like Shaddler could be considered wrong.

They walked on, pushing up a long rise until they crested a hill and gazed down on the town of Moon Lake. Along the shores were fat-bellied fishing boats and tall net huts, while the town itself was draped like a necklace around a steep hill upon which stood a circular keep. The hill was deeply terraced, and Kaelin could see a broken line of crumbling ramparts.

"It doesn't look like timber," said Kaelin, staring hard at the white-walled keep.

"Looks can be deceiving. The keep was crafted from timber, then covered in plaster and faced with pebble stone. When it was first built, the rampart walls would have extended around the town as protection. Back then the Varlish who constructed it were on hostile soil. Clansmen would attack them at regular intervals. Back around five hundred years ago a Pannone uprising saw every Varlish male within the castle and its baileys put to the sword."

"Did they build a new castle then?" asked Kaelin.

"What do you mean a *new* castle?" responded Jaim.

"After the Pannone destroyed it."

"Ah, I see. No, Kaelin, they didn't. They didn't have to. The Pannone killed all the men, then went away. They left the castle standing. The Varlish just reoccupied it and then, using it as a base, brought up an army. It was led by the knights of the Sacrifice, and they all but annihilated the clan."

"They were powerful, then, these knights?"

"Aye, they were. Still are. They become squires when they are your age, almost fifteen. Then they spend five years training with sword and mace, pistol and musket. At least half of them fail the stringent tests conducted every year. I was told that of a hundred men seeking to become knights, only fifteen receive the white cloak. Tough men. A long time ago a hundred knights bested a thousand rebels. There is no give in them. Aye, and no mercy, either."

"The Pannone should have burned the castle," said Kaelin.

"Aye, they should. That, however, is the downfall of the Keltoi peoples. We win great battles and lose all wars."

"Why should that be?" asked the youth.

Jaim shrugged. "We were never besotted with the idea of conquering lands. If an enemy comes, we fight and defeat him. Then we go home. If the enemy keeps coming, then eventually he is going to win. The only way to thoroughly destroy your enemy is to follow the example of the knights. Go to his home and burn it. Kill him, kill his wife, kill his bairns. Those you allow to survive you enslave, and you hold them in thrall with harsh laws. When they transgress, you flog, burn, or hang them. We just never developed a taste for that kind of butchery."

"But Bane fought against Stone and captured it," argued Kaelin. "He took his army across the sea and all the way to the heart of the empire."

"Yes, he did. Then he brought the army home again. He sacked Stone, but he did not destroy it. He was a great warrior king. No doubt about it. Yet within twenty years of his death the armies of Stone had conquered all the southlands. Within fifty they had hill forts at the Rigante borders."

The two travelers moved on down the hill toward Moon Lake. As they came closer, Kaelin caught the smell of fish in the air. It was thick and acrid. "It stinks," he said.

"You'll adjust to it faster when you have some fish inside you," said Jaim. "There's a market close to the shoreline, and within it a food hall. I've eaten there a few times. They know me."

"If they know you, will they still serve you?" Kaelin asked with a grin.

"They'll serve anyone with a copper coin in his pocket, you cheeky rascal."

Their good humor faded as they entered the town and saw the four-rope gibbet in the square. A ten-man squad of Beetlebacks was guarding the structure. Four bodies dangled from the gibbet. Kaelin saw that there were two men, a woman, and a youth of around his own age hanging there. The oldest of the men had suffered the agony of having his eyes burned out and his hands cut off.

The crowd moving through the square did not pause by the gibbet but moved on, eyes downcast. Kaelin could not take his eyes from the scene and slowed. A man behind walked into him and cursed loudly. Jaim grabbed Kaelin's arm and drew him on.

The market beyond the square was thronging with people as Jaim and Kaelin eased their way through. At the far side was an eating area with a series of bench tables set around three fire pits and several long stone-built grills. It was crowded, but Jaim found a couple of seats and he and Kaelin sat, awaiting one of the many serving maids rushing hither and yon, bearing trays laden with food.

A stout, round-shouldered woman with buckteeth approached the table and stood before Jaim. "So, it is you, is it?" she said, her voice cold.

"Good to see you, Meg. You look lovely," said Jaim.

"You cause any trouble today and I'll see you dungeoned. I swear I will!"

"I'm just here with my nephew for a little breakfast," said Jaim, nervous now, for several of the other diners were staring at him. "Kaelin, this is Meg, the finest fish cook this side of Caer Druagh." Kaelin rose and bowed. "Meg, this is Kaelin, the son of Lanovar."

The woman's hard face softened momentarily. "Aye, you

are a handsome lad," she said. "You have your father's looks and your mother's eyes. You are also, it seems, blessed with good manners. You should know, though, that a man is judged by the company he keeps."

"Only until his deeds are known," said Kaelin.

"*His* deeds are known," snapped Meg, returning her attention to the one-eyed clansman. "He is a drunkard and a troublemaker. He should have stayed in the north with the Black Rigante. However, since you, at least, are the son of a hero, I'll give him the benefit of the doubt and feed you both. You can have the soup and the bread," Meg told Jaim. "No ale, though. And it'll be payment now, if you please."

"You're an unforgiving woman," muttered Jaim, delving into his money pouch and producing two copper coins. Meg took the coins without a word and moved off toward the main building.

"She really dislikes you, Grymauch," observed Kaelin.

Jaim forced a smile. "How little you understand women. She adores me, boy. I sang her a song once, and her heart is mine. Oh, I'll admit she struggles against it. 'Tis only show, however."

Kaelin said no more on the subject. He had seen—and recognized, despite Jaim's attempt to hide it behind a display of good humor—the embarrassment and shame the big man had felt. The woman had treated Jaim scornfully, and Jaim had accepted it. This surprised Kaelin, for had it been a man who had spoken so slightingly, Jaim would have reacted with sudden and extreme violence. Not that the youngster would expect Jaim to strike a woman—no clansman worthy of the name would ever commit such a heinous act—but for the warrior to meekly accept such treatment without at the very least rebuking the woman was beyond Kaelin's understanding. It left the youngster feeling vaguely uncomfortable. He felt that one of life's lessons had been laid out before him, yet he could not quite grasp the significance of it. He shivered as the wind shifted, then pulled up the collar of his coat.

Jaim seemed lost in thought, and Kaelin did not disturb

him. Instead he thought back to the four-rope gibbet and the people hanging there. He wondered what their crimes had been and what the oldest of them had done to deserve having his eyes put out and his hands cut off. He shivered again.

" 'Tis getting colder," said Jaim. "Could snow today, I reckon."

"What was the crime, do you think, Grymauch? You know . . . for the man on the gibbet. The one who was maimed first."

Jaim shrugged. "I'm not a great student of the law. I know the punishment for cattle stealing, but I don't know what a man would need to do to suffer having his hands cut away."

The buck-toothed woman laid a wooden tray on the bench table. Upon it were two deep bowls of fish soup and a loaf of crusty bread. "Best not to ask about the hanging," she told them. Dropping her voice, she leaned in close to Jaim, though Kaelin could just make out what she told him. "The trial was in secret, but it is said that a Varlish noblewoman claimed the man climbed into her bedroom and assaulted her."

"What did the others do?" asked Kaelin.

"The woman was the man's wife, the other two his sons. Apparently they lied to the Beetlebacks about his whereabouts."

"They hanged his whole family for that?" said Kaelin, shock making him forget to keep his voice down.

"Hush, stupid boy!" hissed Meg: "You want to hang with them?"

Red-faced and angry, Meg walked away. Kaelin leaned in toward Jaim. "You think she was telling the truth?" he asked.

"Probably, boy. Eat your soup."

"I have lost my appetite, Grymauch."

"Eat, anyway, you'll need your strength later."

"I think I can hate the Varlish without knowing them all," Kaelin said suddenly.

"I hope not," Jaim said sadly.

The moon was bright in a clear sky above Moon Lake, the dark water glistening and still. Jaim Grymauch crept down the hillside, his young apprentice moving silently behind him. With great care they approached the outbuildings of the Moidart's estate. Jaim led Kaelin to a log stack, and the two of them crouched down behind it and waited. After a short while two guards came wandering along the shoreline, talking in low voices. They passed the paddock on the western side, skirted the fence, then swung toward where Jaim and Kaelin were hidden.

The black bull stirred, its great head swinging toward the walking men and fixing them with a baleful stare. "Should have killed it," Kaelin heard one of the guards say. "It near ripped Ganna apart."

"He's a fine beast, though," said the other. "No denying it."

"I'll remind you of those words when you're lying on the ground with your guts in your hand."

The men were closer now, and Kaelin, peering through a gap in the logs, could see their faces in the moonlight. Both looked powerful. They wore no swords, but one carried a staff while the other had a long knife scabbarded at his hip.

Jaim drew the youngster back as the guards strolled past the log stack. As they moved out of sight, the huge warrior came smoothly to his feet and followed them. Kaelin heard a grunt, then a stifled cry, followed by the sounds of a scuffle. Grabbing a length of wood from the stack, he ran around the corner of the building. Two guards were stretched out on the ground, but two others, who had arrived unseen, were grappling with Jaim. One of them drew a knife. Moonlight glinted on the blade. He lunged. Jaim parried the knife with his left forearm and hammered a swift counterpunch, a straight right that sent the guard hurtling back unconscious. The fourth man also drew a knife just as Kaelin moved in behind him, swinging his makeshift club. The wood thudded against the back of the guard's head. There was a tremendous crack. The guard's legs buckled, and he toppled to the ground. Jaim moved to the fallen man. Kaelin saw blood seeping through Jaim's left shirtsleeve.

"You are hurt," whispered the youngster.

Jaim did not answer. He knelt by the guard, his fingers pressed against the man's throat. "Is he dead?" asked Kaelin, worried now. Jaim relaxed.

"No, thank goodness. I'd not want a man to die for the sake of a bull." Reaching out, he took the club from Kaelin's hand. "The wood has split through. When I heard the crack, I thought you had broken his neck. But his pulse is strong, and I think he'll be fine. Damn, boy, there was a time I could have taken four men without help."

They dragged the unconscious men back behind the log stack. Jaim took a ball of tough twine from a pocket sewn into his cloak. Rolling the first man to his belly, he looped twine around the man's ankles and up to the hands, which he tied behind the guard's back. As Jaim was working with the twine, Kaelin gagged the man. Only when all four guards were securely bound and gagged did Jaim set about bandaging his own wound, a shallow cut to the forearm.

"You can't go into that paddock smelling of blood," said Kaelin. "Let us just leave!"

"No, Kaelin. I've set my mind on a stroll with the beast," Jaim said with a smile.

Then he walked out toward the paddock. The gate was held closed by a hinged iron hoop. Jaim lifted it clear and stepped into the enclosure. Kaelin watched him from the log stack, fear causing his heart to pound.

Kaelin saw the bull's tail twitch. He pawed at the ground. Then Jaim spoke, his voice soft, his tone mesmeric.

> "There was a time,
> The old man said,
> Before the dream,
> Beneath the sky,
> When bulls were born
> With iron horns
> And golden eyes."

Jaim continued to move across the paddock. Kaelin was scarcely breathing now as the big man approached the deadly horns.

> "That was the time,
> The old man said,
> Between the stars,
> Before the ring,
> When bulls could fly
> And graze the sky
> On silver wings."

The black bull was no longer pawing at the ground, and he did not turn his mighty head as the man walked by his horns. Kaelin watched as Jaim stroked the bull's dark flanks. It seemed as if even the wind died as Jaim spoke, and Kaelin believed he could hear a soft, distant music echoing from the stars. He blinked and watched the bull. Moonlight was gleaming on its horns, and Kaelin's mouth was dry as the one-eyed warrior stood beside the beast.

> "Then came the time,
> The old man said,
> Beyond the song,
> Beside the lie,
> When bulls wore rings
> Instead of wings
> And learned to die."

Still stroking the bull, Jaim moved completely around it and then strolled back toward the gate. He stopped at the entrance and held out his hand.

> "Come walk with me tonight, my friend.
> On moonlit trails we'll talk awhile,
> Of olden days when bulls were gods
> With iron horns and golden eyes.

We'll walk together to the end
Of weary trails and dusty miles."

For a moment the bull remained statue-still, then it seemed to shiver as if waking from a trance. It walked forward slowly, toward the outstretched hand. Jaim's fingers curled around the ring in the bull's nose, and together man and beast walked from the enclosure and away into the night.

Gaise Macon awoke with a start, his heart pounding. He sat up and looked around. Moonlight was shining through the open window, illuminating the leather-topped desk and the assortment of quills, ink pots, and papers scattered there. The breeze had lifted some of the papers, causing them to flutter to the floor. Gaise pushed back the covers and swung his legs from the bed. As always when he awoke, the star-shaped scar on his right cheekbone was itching, the white, puckered burn feeling tight and uncomfortable. He rubbed the spot gently, then gathered up his papers.

Mr. Shaddler had set him to write an essay on the warrior king Connovar, and Gaise had scoured the library for information. Much of it was either contradictory or cloaked in ridiculous fable. Mr. Shaddler had urged him to prepare his piece "only on what is truly known. Try to avoid conjecture, Lord Gaise." It was an odd assignment. Mr. Shaddler would normally direct him to specific historical tomes.

In the end Gaise had employed a different method of analysis. He had removed all references to gods, demons, and sprites, treating them as exaggerated representations of more human virtues and frailties. Connovar was, for example, said to have been enchanted by Arian, a Seidh goddess of mischief and torment. By her he had a son, Bane, half man, half god. It seemed to Gaise that Arian was more likely to have been a Rigante woman who bore Connovar a bastard son.

He had worked for some hours, his thoughts focused entirely on this man from the far past.

Perhaps it was this that had caused the dream.

It had been so intense, so real. He had become aware of walking in a wood, the smell of decaying leaves and moss filling his nostrils. He had felt the breeze cool upon his skin, the earth wet and cold beneath his bare feet. There was no fear. In fact, quite the opposite. He felt at one with the forest, in harmony with the beating hearts of the unseen animals all around him: the fox by the riverbank, the white owl perched on the high branch, the tiny mouse in the mound of leaves; the badgers wakening below the ground.

The smell of woodsmoke drifted to him, and he walked toward a small campfire set within a group of stones. A white-haired woman was sitting there. There were tools at her feet: a small ax, a long knife with a curved serrated blade, a shorter knife with a hilt of bone. In her hands was a length of curved wood. She was carefully stripping away the bark.

"What are you making?" he asked her.

She glanced up at him, and he saw that her eyes were green, her face unlined. It was a face of great beauty, ageless and serene.

"I am crafting a boughstave longbow."

"Is that elm?"

"No, it is yew."

Gaise sat down and watched her. "It does not look like a bow," he said, seeing the knots and dimples on the rough wood.

"The bow is hidden within the stave. It is beautiful and complete. It merely needs to be found. One must seek it with love and care, gently and with great patience."

Gaise shivered at the memory.

The room was cold. His father allowed him only one bucket of coal per week, and with only four lumps left and three more days to go, Gaise had decided not to light the fire that night. Instead he had put on warm woolen leggings and a nightshirt before climbing into bed. The sheet and the two thin blankets did little to keep him warm, and he had draped an old cloak over the blankets to add a little weight and warmth.

The young noble swung the old cloak around his shoulders

and padded across to the fireplace. There was kindling there and several chunks of wood beside the coal bucket. Anger flared in the young man. The Moidart desired him to be tough, so he said. That was why he kept his son cold in the winter, why he mocked his every effort, why he had killed Soldier. This last thought leapt unbidden from an unhealed wound in the young man's mind. He had loved that dog, and even though three years had passed, the hurt he had felt at its slaying still clung to him with talons of grief. It had been an accident, the Moidart had said. The hunting musket had had a faulty hammer spring. It had struck flint before the Moidart had placed his finger on the trigger. The red-haired retriever had been sitting alongside the Moidart, and the lead ball had smashed his skull. Not for a moment had Gaise believed the tale. As a child he had loved a white pony, which the Moidart then had sold. After that it had been Soldier, which the Moidart slew. When Gaise had first attended school and made friends, he had arrived home full of joy. The Moidart had removed him from the school, hiring Alterith Shaddler and others to tutor him privately. Then there were the beatings, administered when Gaise failed to achieve the high grades the Moidart demanded for his schoolwork. The beatings had stopped since Gaise had reached fifteen, though it was not, he believed, his coming of age that had ended them. It had more to do with the rheumatics that had afflicted the Moidart's shoulders and back. He could no longer lay on the lash as once he had.

Gaise wondered if life would have been different if his mother had survived the assassination attempt. Perhaps then his father would not have hated him so. He shivered again as a cold wind blew through the curtainless window behind him.

Gathering the cloak more tightly about his shoulders, Gaise leaned forward and, upon an impulse, picked up the pewter tinderbox, struck a flame, and applied it to the crumpled paper and wood shavings beneath the kindling in the fireplace. The paper caught first, orange flames licking out over the kindling. Gaise felt the first of the warmth touch him, and he shivered again, this time with pleasure. As the larger kindling accepted the fire, Gaise added several chunks of wood and two of his precious coals.

Fire shadows danced on the walls around him, and a golden glow filled the room. Gaise felt the muscles of his shoulders losing their tension, and he relaxed before the flames. It must have been thus for the caveman, he thought, safe and warm, free for a time from the many perils of the day. He thought again of Connovar and pictured him sitting before an open fire, planning battles against the armies of Stone.

The dream came back to him then, the walk in the woods and the damp musty earth, the woman crafting the bow. She was quite small, with long white hair pulled back from her face and tied in a single braid hanging between her shoulders.

"How do you know that a beautiful bow is within the stave?"

"The yew whispered it to me. That is why I picked it up."

"Wood cannot speak," he said.

"It cannot speak to those without a name, young man," she told him, her voice low and musical.

"I have a name," he had told her. "I am Gaise Macon."

"Not a name recognized by the trees that surround you. Not a name whispered in the valleys or borne on the wind toward Caer Druagh. Not a *soul*-name."

"You are speaking nonsense. Who are you?"

"I am the Flame in the Crystal, Gaise Macon. My mother was the Shadow on the Oak. Her mother was the Sheltering Cloud. You wish to hear the names of all my line?"

"I note you do not mention the men involved in your ancestry," said Gaise. "Did they have no soul-names?"

"Sadly they did not," she said. "My grandfather was a Varlish captain, my father a merchant from Goriasa, across the water, where they have robed the magic in stone and thus imprisoned it. When this happens, men forget the magic of soul-names."

"Why did you bring me here?"

"I brought you nowhere, Gaise Macon. You walked to my fire. You will walk away from my fire. Or run or fly. Whatever pleases you."

"I am dreaming," said the young man. "You are not real."

"Aye, you are dreaming. But it is a *real* dream, Gaise. A dream of *meaning*. A moment of magic, if you will. Would you like to see a story?"

"You mean hear a story?"

"I know what I mean, Gaise Macon."

"Then, yes, I would like to see a story."

The woman raised her hand and pointed toward a small stream a little way to her right. Water rose up from it in a shimmering sphere as large as a man's head. It floated some three feet above the grass and hovered before the astonished young noble. Then it swelled and flattened, becoming a circular mirror in which Gaise could see his own reflection. He saw that he was wearing a patchwork cloak of many colors fastened with a silver brooch. The brooch was the crest of his house, a fawn trapped in brambles. He was about to ask the woman about the cloak, but the mirror shimmered, and he found himself gazing on a distant moonlit mountainside. Two men were there. The images came closer, and he saw that one of the men was wounded. The scene changed. Now a stag was at bay, a great and majestic beast surrounded by wolves. His heart went out to the stag. A black hound, blood upon its flanks, charged at the wolves. They scattered, though not before three were dead.

The images faded away. Water began dripping from the circle, first as a few drops and then as a rush, falling to the earth and soaking through the soil.

Gaise sat very still, trying to make sense of what he had seen. A dying man and a wounded hound. A brief battle with a wolf pack.

"Do you know what a *geasa* is?" asked the woman.

"No."

"It is a prophecy of a kind. King Connavar's *geasa* was that he would be killed on the day he slew the dog that bit him.

And he was. What you have seen today is part of your *geasa*.
You are the stag, Gaise Macon. You will stand against the
wolves."

"And who is the hound who will rescue me?"

"He will be a kinsman."

"I have no kinsmen. Only my father. I doubt he would risk
himself for me."

"All will be revealed in its own time. Would you like a
name that the mountains can hear, that the leaves can whisper
and the rivers sing?"

"I am Varlish. Why would I want a Keltoi soul-name?"

"Come to me again when you do," she told him.

That was when he had felt the cold sweep over him and had
awoken in his bed. Now he was troubled and did not know
why. Gaise sat by the fire until it began to die down. He
reached for the coal bucket only to see that he had used all
four lumps. Anger swelled again, and with it the first seeds of
rebellion stirred in his heart. He was the heir to the earldom.
One day he would be the Moidart. Yet he sat here in this cold
room with no fuel for his fire despite the huge store of coal
stacked alongside the rear kitchen wall.

Gaise rose smoothly to his feet, pulled on his boots, took
up the brass coal bucket, and opened his bedroom door. Beyond it was the gallery overlooking the entrance hall. No
lanterns were burning, and Gaise stood for a moment, allowing his eyes to grow accustomed to the darkness. The
faintest sign of light could be seen at the foot of the stairs,
where a heavy velvet curtain had not been fully closed. Gaise
moved across the gallery landing until he reached the safety
rail. Keeping his hand to the rail, he edged to his left and onto
the stairs. His heart was beating fast now. If the Moidart discovered him stealing coal, he would no doubt punish him
severely. In that moment Gaise did not care. Slowly he descended into the hallway, then through to the kitchen. There it
was lighter, for there were no curtains on the paneled glass of
the window. The rear door leading to the yard beyond was not
locked. This surprised Gaise, for the Moidart was strict about

security within the Winter House. Gaise smiled. When he returned with his coal, he would lock the door, thus saving some poor servant from a flogging.

He stood silently, waiting for one of the sentries to pass by the kitchen window. It would not be wise for the Moidart's son to be seen collecting coal. All the guards were obliged to note down every unusual activity while on watch. The Moidart would scan their records every week. Gaise waited. The grounds of the Winter House, though large, were easily patrolled at night. It would not take a man more than a few minutes to walk the perimeter of the house. Time dragged on. No guard passed the window. Gaise felt a flicker of annoyance. It was getting very cold standing there in nothing but his nightclothes.

Moving to the door, he lifted the latch. The guards were obviously huddled somewhere out of the cold. Gaise stepped out and made his way to the coal store. With great care he half filled the bucket and then returned to the kitchen.

A dark figure flitted past the window. Gaise jerked. The man was moving fast, and Gaise barely glimpsed him. Yet he saw enough to know that it was no soldier. Retracing his steps, Gaise walked back to the hallway and saw that the main doors were ajar.

Fear touched him. Stories of night creatures, demons, and blood drinkers swept up from the depths of his imagination. Angrily he forced them away. He had seen a man. No more than that. Probably one of the servants returning from an assignation with a serving girl. Gaise reached the staircase and began to climb. The coal bucket was heavy, and his arms were still weary from the sword work earlier in the day.

He was halfway up the stairs when he heard a cry that echoed from the gallery. There was a crash, and a pale figure appeared at the top of the stairs. The light was not good, but Gaise could make out the Moidart's sharp features. He was wearing a white nightshirt stained at the shoulder by something dark. A black-garbed figure rushed at the Moidart, and the two men grappled and fell to the floor. Another man came

into view. Gaise saw the gleam of a blade. With a great heave
Gaise hurled the coal bucket at the knifeman. It struck him on
the shoulder, knocking him back. Gaise ran up the stairs two
at a time. He could hear the Moidart shouting: "Assassins!
Assassins!" But no guards came.

Gaise rushed at the knifeman. The blade slashed out. Gaise
swerved and threw himself to his right. The assassin was fast.
Gaise managed to block a thrust with his forearm. The knife
blade slid along his sleeve, ripping the cloth and creating a
shallow cut in his skin. Gaise leapt at the man, ramming his
elbow into the assassin's face and following it with a head
butt to the nose. The assassin cried out and fell back, half-
stunned. In that split second Gaise sensed someone behind
him and threw himself to his left. Something heavy cracked
against his right shoulder, sending searing pain into his neck.
Gaise fell to the floor. The new attacker, wielding an iron
club, ran in. His foot twisted on a lump of coal, and he, too,
fell. Gaise rolled to his feet and launched a kick into the
newcomer's face. The man made a grab for Gaise's foot and
missed. Gaise ran back to the gallery wall. It was decorated with shields and ancient weapons: lances and spears,
broadswords and bows. Gaise tried to lift clear a sword, but it
was held too firmly in place. Instead he grabbed a hunting
lance, wrenching it from its bracket. The man ran at him.
With no time to turn the spear point toward his attacker, Gaise
spun on his heels, the haft of the lance cracking against the
man's temple. With a grunt he toppled to the floor. Bringing the lance to bear, Gaise hurdled the fallen man and
plunged the lance into the side of the attacker struggling with
the Moidart. The man gave out a terrible scream and dropped
his knife. The Moidart took up the weapon, ramming it into
the assassin's throat. Pushing aside the corpse, the Moidart
wrenched the blade clear and rose to his feet.

The last of the assassins hefted his dagger. "I'll kill you
yet, you black-hearted bastard!" he yelled. He rushed at the
Moidart. A gunshot boomed. The assassin staggered, blood
pumping from a great tear in his throat. He grabbed the

gallery rail and tried to pull himself toward the Moidart. A second shot echoed in the gallery. The assassin's head snapped back. Gaise saw that he had been shot this time through the right eye. The young noble swung to see the tall figure of Mulgrave walking along the gallery, two long-barreled dueling pistols in his hands. Gaise ran to a curtain, wrenching it open. Moonlight bathed the gallery.

Mulgrave placed the pistols on a nearby table and moved alongside the Moidart. "You are cut, my lord," he said.

"It is nothing," said the Moidart, his voice cold. "I see one of these wretches still lives," he said, pointing to the unconscious man Gaise had struck with the lance butt. "Take him to the cells. I will attend his questioning myself."

"Yes, lord." Mulgrave glanced at Gaise. "You fought well, sir," he said. Gaise bowed and returned his attention to his father.

The Moidart did not look at him but walked back toward his room. "Send the surgeon to me," he told Mulgrave. Then he paused and stared down at the carpet. He swung toward Gaise. "I see that you were stealing my coal. We will speak of this another time."

At thirty-one Maev Ring was a handsome woman, tall and green-eyed. Her hair, still a lustrous red, now shone with faint streaks of silver. She was regarded by many clansmen as cold and remote, largely owing to the fact that following the death of her husband ten years before, she had refused all advances from the many widowers among the clan. Maev had been just sixteen when she had wed the young warrior Calofair. It was widely accepted that they were the best-looking couple in the highlands. Many of the young men envied Calofair's luck. Maev not only was beautiful but also was the sister of Lanovar, the chieftain, and all men knew that this brilliant and gifted warrior would bring prosperity to the clan. Through his efforts, the Rigante name would be restored to the Scroll of Clans and lands stolen from the clan would be returned to their rightful owners. Those were days of golden promise.

But Lanovar had been murdered by the Moidart, and the Beetlebacks had descended on clan villages, killing and burning. For years those with Rigante blood were forced to stay away from towns and settlements, building homes in the bleak highlands. They survived by raiding Varlish settlements and convoys and stealing cattle and coin or any merchandise that could be useful. Life was harsh back then.

Maev Ring remembered it without sentiment: the squalid sod-roofed dwellings, the sickness and death among the old and the weak. As she sat now by the kitchen window of her six-room house, she thought again of Calofair, his flesh eaten away by the fever, the wound in his chest festering and angry. He had been beyond speech at the end, only his eyes showing any sign of life. Maev had sat with him, holding his hand. And then, as the light of life had faded, she had kissed his brow. She had been tempted to take a dagger and slash open the veins at her wrists, to fly away from the woes of the world and travel with the spirit of Calofair. She shivered at the memory. Four-year-old Kaelin had approached her, tears in his eyes. "Will Uncle get better, Aunt Maev?"

It was a summer night, and the last of the sun's rays was shining through the roughly wrought door of the hut. By its light the twenty-year-old Maev could see the flea bites on the child's ankles and wrists. His face was pinched and sallow. Maev put her arms around him, drawing him into an embrace. "Uncle *is* better now," she told him. "He is walking across green hills with comrades he has not seen in years. He is tall and proud and wearing the colors of the Rigante."

"He is still in the bed, Aunt."

"No, Kaelin," she said softly. "All that lies in this bed is the coat of flesh that Calofair wore. And we must bury that coat, you and I."

Ten years on, and even now the memory brought a tear to Maev's eye. Angrily she brushed it away and rose from her seat. She gazed around the kitchen at the furniture crafted from pine and the iron stove set upon a bed of slate in the hearth, at the windows with leaded panes of clear glass, at the floor with its neatly fitted flagstones. Pots and pans hung from brass hooks above the worktops, and the larder had food aplenty.

Kaelin walked into the kitchen and sat down at the bench table. "Shula is sleeping," he said. "I left Banny with her."

"She should have come to me sooner," Maev said sternly.

"Aye, she should," he agreed. "Banny said she went into Eldacre to the poorhouse to ask for food. She was turned away."

"Where did she get the cuts and bruises?"

"Banny says it was Morain, Galliott's wife. She and several other women beat her as she was making her way home."

"There is a deep well of bile in that woman," said Maev. "It shames us all that Morain has Rigante blood."

"Will Banny's mam be well again, Aunt Maev?"

"We will do our best for her, Kaelin. We will feed her and keep her warm. Do you still have that chailling Jaim gave you?"

"I do."

"Then go to the store man and buy a dozen eggs and three jars of honey. Then go to the butcher and tell him I want double the amount of beef for Holy Day. Then . . . " She paused. "Can you remember all this, Kaelin?"

"Aye, a dozen eggs, three jars of honey, double the beef. What else?"

"Go to the apothecary Ramus and tell him I need some powders for fever and a potion for the cleansing of the blood. If he has any fat hen weed, I will take that, too. The woman has a festering wound on her lower back. Tell him that."

"Is that all?" asked Kaelin.

"Aye. Is Jaim still in the front room?"

"Yes, Aunt."

"Send him in to me and then be on your way."

Kaelin smiled at her, then swung away. Maev walked to the

larder and lifted down the stone milk jug. She filled a cup, then sipped the creamy liquid.

"You wanted me, Maev?" said Jaim Grymauch. She finished her milk, leaving the huge, one-eyed warrior standing in the doorway. Then she turned and looked at him. Jaim normally radiated a physical power that was almost elemental, but he was nervous now under her gaze.

When she finally spoke, her voice was hard and cold. " 'Tis said that one of the Moidart's men was killed when two raiders made off with his prize bull."

"Whisht, woman! No one died. 'Tis a terrible lie."

"It is also said that the Moidart has offered a five-pound reward for the naming of the criminals."

"Five pounds. That is a lot," Jaim said with a grin. "By heaven, I'm tempted to hand myself in for such a reward."

"Wipe that smirk from your face!" snapped Maev. "Will you be smiling when they take Kaelin and put the rope around his neck?"

Instinctively Jaim touched two fingers to his lips, then tapped them upon his chest in the sign of the Sacrifice. "Do not say such things. Not even in jest. Kaelin wasn't seen. When I took the bull to the Pinance, I made the boy stay back in the woods." He stepped in closer. "Now tell me the truth. Are you angry with me for stealing the bull or for carrying the sick woman here?"

Maev was shocked. "Do you think so little of me, Grymauch? Bringing her here was to your credit. No, I am angry because of your stupidity." Maev sighed. "It is more than the bull, Grymauch. I think you want to die. I don't pretend to understand it, but there is a need in you to spit in the eye of the Devil. Had I known you were planning to rob the Moidart, I would have refused Kaelin permission to go with you. All cattle owners know that some of their stock will be lost. Largely they accept it. Not the Moidart. He will not rest until the thieves are found and hanged. You will take Kaelin on no more raids. You understand?"

"He'll be a man within the year, Maev. He'll make his own choices then."

"Aye, he will. But until then no more raids. I'll require your oath on that."

Lifting the black headband clear of his face, he rubbed at the stitch marks above the empty socket. "It troubles me still. Can you believe that?"

Maev was unmoved. "Your oath, Grymauch."

"Aye, all right, woman," he snapped. "You have it. No more raids until he is a man. Then perhaps you can find him employment licking the boots of the Varlish."

She stepped in close, her green eyes blazing with anger. Even so her voice was calm and controlled. "And what will you teach him, Jaim Grymauch? How to puke after too much ale? How to break the bones of men you do not know? How to hide in the heather while other men gather crops or tend cattle? Where is your home, Jaim? Where is your wife? Where are your bairns? You have none. So what are you?" Maev moved in even closer to the big man. "You're a seed blowing in the wind. You cannot settle, you cannot change, you cannot grow. When you die, Jaim Grymauch, it will be as if you never were. You will leave nothing behind save a few memories, and even they will fade in time. Lick the boots of the Varlish, you say? How long would it take them to defeat us if all men were like you? One generation, Jaim. Then we'd all be gone." She swung away from him and moved to the larder, returning the milk jug to its place on the shelf.

"It might be better if we were," he said softly. "Once we were wolves; now we are puppy dogs to be kicked and thrashed by the Varlish. And look at you, Maev. You are bright and intelligent. Aye, and you are rich. But you wear old clothes, and Kaelin has threadbare shirts. And why? So that you will not appear to *shine* before the Varlish. They will accept a wealthy clanswoman only so long as she does not stand out. Do not lecture me, woman, especially not on the subject of a wife and bairns. I had a wife and two sons. Varlish soldiers ripped out her throat and drowned my boys in the weir.

But tell me, Maev, where are *your* sons? Where is your gift to the future of the Rigante?"

"The man I loved died," she said. "You know that."

"Aye, he died. But it was you who chose to shrivel up inside and turn into a harridan."

Maev Ring swung away from the shelf and moved swiftly across the room. Her hand lashed out. Jaim made no attempt to block the blow, and her hand slapped against his face.

"Well, at least there's still *some* fire in you, lass," he said.

Then he turned and walked from the room.

◇ 3 ◇

ARLEBAN ACHBAIN SAT by his mother's bedside. What he saw frightened him. Shula's eyes were sunken, her cheeks hollow. She was scarcely breathing. A large bruise had formed on the right side of her jaw, and her lips were split. Banny could not understand why Morain and the women in Eldacre had set upon his mother, but then, he had never understood why both clan and Varlish youngsters used to torment and beat him. It was not that he did not *know* why. He had been told often enough. It was understanding he lacked. His mother had fallen in love with a highlander. A union between Varlish and Pannone, though not illegal, was highly unusual, and both had suffered as a result. The clan had turned its back on his father, while the townsfolk, most of them Varlish, had shunned his mother. Even so their love had endured for some years. But it had been worn down and eroded season by season by the relentless hatred washing against it. Banny was seven when his father left home, never to return. He had gone north to find employment in an area where no one would know of his wife's tainted blood. He would send for her and the boy, he promised, when he had found a place to settle. They never heard from him again.

From then on Banny and his mother barely scraped together a living. In the growing seasons they gathered mountain herbs for the Old Hills apothecary, Ramus. Every week she would collect the few coppers she earned, buy food at the store, and carry it home to their dugout. She always saved a farthing from every payment. This would help feed both her and Banny through the harsh winter months. Last year's summer had been poor, and the herbs were not so plentiful. Their money had run out weeks earlier.

Shula's mouth was open, and Banny saw that she had lost two teeth on the upper right side. Banny's own teeth were loose. He could move them with his tongue.

Outside the sun was shining, and for the first time in months there was genuine warmth in its rays. Banny wanted to walk out in the sunshine and feel the heat upon his skin. But he was too weary, and there was no strength in his legs.

He heard a movement and looked around. Kaelin's aunt was coming into the room. She was an imposing woman, tall and fierce-eyed. Banny was a little frightened of her. Back in the summer, when he and Kaelin had come running into the house, she had grabbed him by the shoulder and marched him outside. "You will play out here," she had told him. "I'll have no fleas on my furnishings, if you please!" It had been a shaming experience.

As Maev leaned over the bed and laid her hand on Shula's brow, Banny turned his gaze back to his mother. She would not die, he decided. It would be too unfair. A trembling began in his stomach, and he felt his throat tighten. Tears spilled from his eyes. Fighting for control, Banny sat very still, making no sound. He squeezed his eyes shut to prevent more tears from shaming him. Then he felt Maev's hand upon his shoulder.

"Sleep is good. Sleep is healing," she told him. "Now you come with me. You need to eat again and then to bathe. You have both lice and fleas, and there is no room for either in my house. Come now."

Banny rose on trembling legs and followed her into the kitchen. It seemed like a palace to the twelve-year-old. He sat down at the pine table and stared at the golden sheen on the wood. Aunt Maev placed a deep bowl of beef gravy soup and a hunk of bread before him.

"Do not chew on the bread," she said. "Your teeth are already loose, and we don't want them falling out. Just dip it into the soup."

"She won't die, will she?" whispered Banny.

"Not if I have a say in it," said Aunt Maev. "Now eat your soup, Banny. Take it slow."

It was almost a week since Banny had eaten solid food, and that had been a gnarled root his mother had dug from the edge of the forest. It had been bitter and had made him nauseous. His stomach was still queasy, and when he gazed down at the soup, he felt suddenly sick and dizzy.

"Be strong now," said Aunt Maev, moving swiftly alongside him. She tore off a small hunk of bread and dipped it in the warm soup. "Here. Just hold it in your mouth and let the juices run." Banny opened his mouth, allowing her to feed him like a babe. The juices of the meat flowed on his tongue, awakening his hunger. His stomach cramped, and he almost choked on the bread. Carefully he chewed the morsel, then swallowed it. It tasted divine.

"That's good, Banny," whispered Aunt Maev. "Take a little more now."

Banny sat very still, staring down at the soup bowl. It was white-glazed, but only on the inside; the outside was the golden brown of lowland clay. It was a pretty bowl. His mind swam, and he felt himself falling. He did not care. Maev's arms held him close, and when he opened his eyes, he found to his surprise that he was still sitting at the table. It seemed to Banny that he had fallen from the world, spinning down and down into a blessed darkness where there was no hunger, no pain, no fear. "I'm sorry," he whispered. "I have fleas."

Maev said nothing, but she dipped more bread into the now-cold soup and lifted it to his lips. Banny ate until both the soup and the bread were gone. "I think we'll forget about the bath for now," said Maev. "Let's get you to bed."

Banny's legs were unsteady, but Maev helped him up the stairs to a small room. The window shutters were closed, but thin lines of golden light could be seen between the slats. They shone on a patchwork blanket that covered the single bed of pine that nestled against the far wall. Maev drew back the coverlet and the two thick blankets beneath. "Let's get you out of these clothes," she said. She took hold of the torn and filthy shirt he was wearing. Banny raised his arms, and she lifted it clear. His ragged trews were held up by a length of string. He fumbled with the knot. Maev gently moved his hands aside and swiftly undid it. Banny stepped out of the garment, too weary to feel shame at being naked before a woman.

He sat down on the white undersheet and became aware of the ingrained dirt on his arms and hands and the red flea bites on his belly and thighs. "I should bathe," he said.

"Later, Banny. Lay your head upon the pillow, there's a good boy."

He had no strength to refuse. The pillow yielded beneath him, soft and inviting, and he felt the blankets and a soft over-sheet being drawn up around his thin shoulders.

Once more the world spun away, and Banny's mind cried out in the joy of it.

The apothecary Ramus was a small man. Round-shouldered and stooping, he rarely looked into the eyes of his customers. He would nod continuously as he listened to their requests and, when they had finished, mutter, "Good, yes, very good," as if complimenting them. His movements were quick and sure, his judgment of weight uncanny. He would tip powder or shredded leaf into small bags of muslin and rarely weigh them. Occasionally a new customer would ask to see the item weighed on his small brass scales. He would nod and smile and say, "Good, yes, very good." The scales would then show the exact weight in ounces the customer had asked for.

But then, the silver-haired Ramus had been an apothecary for twenty-nine years. Judgment to the quarter ounce, he considered, was a small enough skill to acquire in almost three decades and certainly not one to cause undue pride. Ramus was not wealthy, nor was he poor. He lived in a small house with a slate roof and a half acre of ground on which he grew many herbs. Other plants and fungi were gathered for him by women who lived in the barren empty areas of the high hills.

The apothecary Ramus had no friends and no wife, for he was not a man comfortable with intimacy of any kind. Neither did he have enemies. He was not even disliked, which was unusual for a Varlish living among clan folk. Ramus was punctiliously polite to all, Varlish or Keltoi, and never offered an opinion except on matters herbal and never entered into debate with anyone. It was, he had long ago decided, safer that way.

Ramus cast a quick, nervous glance at the black-haired youth standing at his counter. He felt uneasy around Kaelin Ring, though in truth he could not think why. "Fever, you say? What is the nature of the fever, Master Ring?" He listened intently as the young man told him of finding Shula Achbain and her son on the verge of death from starvation and cold.

"Aunt Maev said to ask you to select herbs to heal them. She told me to ask also for fat hen and something for a festering wound."

"Good, yes, very good," said Ramus. "Please take a seat, Master Ring, while I prepare the necessary ingredients." Ramus was anxious to please Maev Ring. She had become a powerful personality in Old Hills and, truth be told, in Eldacre itself. More than sixty women were now employed by her in the making of dresses, shirts, blouses, and other articles of clothing. It was said that she was a shareholder in three other ventures, though Ramus knew of only two. Maev Ring now had minority interests in the businesses of Gillam Pearce the bootmaker and Parsis Feld, owner of the forge and armory in Eldacre town. Both men had been in danger of bankruptcy and debtor's prison, but Maev Ring had settled their debts. As soon as she acquired her stake in the businesses, their fortunes changed. Orders came in, and prosperity followed. Other merchants talked of Maev Ring being lucky. It was easy to see how they would think that, but Ramus was not fooled. Once might be luck, not twice. No. Maev Ring was a clever woman with a sharp eye for opportunity.

The apothecary stood for a moment surveying the scores of earthenware jars on his shelves. Each jar was marked with a symbol or a series of letters. The first he chose bore the legend "DHS" in black. Uncorking the jar, he scooped out a portion of the contents and then, with his left hand, opened a small bag of muslin into which he tipped the powder.

"What is that?" asked Kaelin Ring. Ramus jerked. He had not heard the young man leave his seat and move once more to the counter. It unnerved him a little. Had it been anyone else, he would have asked him politely to return to his seat. But this boy was the nephew of Maev Ring and therefore needed to be treated with a little more respect.

"It is the leaf of the dwarf honeysuckle," said Ramus. "I shall give you four half-ounce bags. The powders must be boiled with sugar to make a jelly. It will help dispel the fever.

"For the festering wound I shall also make up a potion with honey wort and saffron. Your aunt will know what to do with it. You may expect some immoderate movements of the bowels in the early stages of their recovery. To alleviate this I recommend myrtle berry extract. This is, however, expensive. It is six daens a bottle, and you will need two bottles."

"A whole chailling?" said Kaelin Ring, astonished.

"Aye, Master Ring. The myrtle tree does not grow in the highlands. Indeed, no one has successfully grown it on this side of the sea. The extract needs to be shipped from Goriasa and then brought overland. It is, however, as effective as it is costly."

"I'll take the one bottle," said Kaelin. "But I'll have to owe you."

"Not a problem, Master Ring. I trust you implicitly." Ramus carefully gathered all the herbs and powders, then took up a swan feather quill and dipped it into a small pot of ink. In immaculate copperplate script he wrote out the details of the purchase and the sums required, sanded the finished receipt, and, when he was sure the ink had dried, folded the paper and handed it to Kaelin. The young man pocketed it, then heaved a large canvas shoulder bag to the worktop. It was already half-full. Ramus opened the flap at the top and packed his powders and potions among the contents. The bottle of myrtle extract he placed within a wooden box half-filled with straw. "Be careful with this, Master Ring."

"I will, sir."

A commotion began outside, and Ramus could hear voices being raised.

The outside door was thrust open, and a young man pushed inside. He was red-faced, his eyes wide with excitement. "There was an attempt on the Moidart's life," he said. "Assassins broke into his home last night. There are soldiers all over Eldacre, and there have been many arrests."

"Was the Moidart injured?" inquired Ramus.

"No one is saying, sir."

"Thank you, Master Lane. Most kind of you to let me know."

The young man nodded excitedly, moved back to the street, and entered the bakery next door. His voice could just be heard through the thick walls, but only the occasional word sounded clearly. "Moidart . . . assassins . . . arrests . . ."

"We live in perilous times, Master Ring," Ramus said with a sigh.

Kaelin Ring lifted the canvas bag to his shoulder, offered a short bow to the apothecary, and walked out to the cobbled street beyond.

Ramus could see people gathering in the street and wandered back into his storeroom, sitting himself down in an old wicker chair. Leaning back against the embroidered cushions, he closed his eyes. So much violence in the world, he thought sadly.

On the table beside his chair was a package of herbs and ointments he had prepared for the Moidart only that morning, soothing balms for the old burns on the skin of the lord's arms and neck. Those wounds had come from yet another act of violence, when assassins had set fire to the old Winter House. Eleven people had died in the blaze—all of them servants. Before that, some fourteen years ago, there had been the murder attempt that had seen the Moidart's wife strangled and the Moidart himself stabbed in the groin while trying to save her. He had almost died from that wound. It had been the Moidart's good fortune that Ramus had been summoned. There was much internal bleeding, but the apothecary had managed to stem the flow and halt the onset of infection. Even so, it was a full four months before the wounded man recovered sufficient strength to walk unaided. Years later the angry scar was still occasionally leaking pus and causing the Moidart bouts of fever.

Ramus sighed. Acts of violence were beyond his imagination. Never in his life had he desired to hurt anyone.

This latest attempt on the Moidart's life would cause great anger among the Varlish. It was likely there would be riots and bloodshed in Eldacre, followed by more arrests and hangings.

Ramus felt the weight of sadness heavy upon him.

Thirty-two years earlier his own father had been hanged for stealing a sheep. He had not stolen the sheep, and the true culprit was discovered later. The lord of Goriasa had sent five pounds in gold coin as recompense for the mistake. The family had used part of the money to pay for Ramus' tuition at the apothecary college. His mother had spent her remaining years hating the lord, her soul corroded by bitterness and resentment. Ramus' brother, Aborain, had taken to the hills for a life of outlawry and murder, culminating in his execution on the same scaffold that had claimed his father.

On the night of Aborain's hanging armed soldiers had come for Ramus, taking him before the lord.

"Do you wish revenge?" the lord of Goriasa had asked.

"No, sir."

"Yet you hate me?"

"I hate no one, sir. My brother deserved to die for the sins of his life. My father did not deserve to die. But his killing was an error and not born of malice."

"You know why you are here?"

"You are considering whether it would be prudent to kill me."

"You seem very calm, young man."

"I cannot prevent you from killing me, sir, if that be your will."

The lord had sat silently for a while, watching the young apothecary. Then he had drawn in a deep breath. "I will not kill you. Equally, I cannot have you living within my realm. It would concern me that you might one day discover hatred in your heart. I shall give you coin, and you will travel far from here. There is always a need for apothecaries. So where will you journey?"

"I have always liked mountains, sir."

"Then cross the sea, Master Ramus. Travel to the north and find a home in the Druagh mountains. I am told it is very beautiful there."

"I will, sir. Thank you."

"A man should not be thanked for resisting evil. I wish you well, Master Ramus."

"And I you, lord."

The sound of shouting cut through the old man's memories. Angry voices could be heard.

Ramus rose from his chair, pushing shut the heavy storeroom door.

Now there was silence.

Mulgrave reined in the chestnut and sat gazing out over Old Hills Lake. The water was shimmering in the afternoon sunshine, the jagged lines of the western mountains reflected on the still surface. The sight of the lake calmed him. "We are such fleeting creatures," he told Gaise Macon. "Here for a heartbeat and then gone forever."

"Why do you say that with a smile?" asked the young noble, drawing his palomino gelding alongside Mulgrave's mount.

"It makes the evil of men more bearable to know that it is largely of no account," replied Mulgrave.

"If that be the truth," said Gaise, "then the good that men do is also of no account."

Mulgrave chuckled. "Now, *there* is something worth

debating, sir." The smile faded. A cold wind blew off the lake, a gust billowing Mulgrave's gray cloak. The sudden movement caused the palomino to rear. Gaise fought for control, calming the horse. A lesser rider would have been thrown. "You handle him well, sir," said Mulgrave.

"He is a skittish beast," said Gaise, leaning forward to stroke the palomino's golden neck. For a moment the two riders sat silently as Mulgrave once more returned his attention to the glittering water.

"Why did you want me to ride with you to the apothecary?" asked Gaise.

Mulgrave sighed. He was entering unknown territory here. "I wanted to tell you that your actions last night filled me with pride, sir. You tackled armed men. You did not run. You saved your father's life. Of that there is no doubt."

Gaise Macon reddened. "I was stealing coal," he said.

Mulgrave swore suddenly and swung in the saddle to face the younger man. "You are a fine man, Gaise. You have it in you to be a great one. Do not let the man's malice change you."

"It would be a help to know why he hates me," replied Gaise. "But we should not speak like this, Mulgrave. The Moidart is the law. Your words could see you hanged if reported to him."

"Aye, sir, that is true." He chuckled. "You are not the first to offer such a warning. The truth will be the death of me yet. Come, let us find the apothecary." Mulgrave gently heeled the chestnut forward.

"Time to ride!" shouted Gaise Macon. The palomino surged into a run, thundering along the shores of the lake. Mulgrave's chestnut followed, and for the remainder of the short gallop the swordsman's burdens fell away.

Gaise cut to the left, racing toward a fallen tree. Fear touched Mulgrave. It was not that the palomino could not jump the obstacle but that Gaise could not possibly know what lay beyond it. There could be jagged rocks, or rabbit holes, or twisted roots. The palomino could snap a leg. Mulgrave had seen riders crippled or killed by such falls, their backs snapped, their limbs flopping. The palomino rose majestically. Mulgrave's breath caught in his throat. It seemed as if the golden horse hung in the air for an eternity. Then it sailed over the fallen tree, landed smoothly, and ran on. Mulgrave's chestnut followed. As Mulgrave leaned in to the jump, he saw that the falling tree had broken several saplings, which now jutted from the earth like spears. The chestnut, as had the palomino, just missed them. Furious now, Mulgrave rode to where Gaise waited.

"Did you see the broken trees?" raged the swordsman.

"Yes," said Gaise.

"That was monumentally stupid! You could have been killed."

"Aye, I could." The young man shrugged. "Did you not say that our lives were fleeting and of little account? So what would it have mattered?"

"Your life is of great account to *me*, sir. I do not like to see you risk it for so small a matter as a moment of recklessness."

Gaise shrugged. "It was not a small matter, Mulgrave," he said. "I needed that jump."

"Why?"

Gaise did not reply instantly. Instead he leaned forward and ran his fingers through the palomino's white mane. Mulgrave sensed the sadness in the young man. Gaise looked up. "Last night, as I returned to my bed, I could not sleep. I began to tremble. I felt fear like I have never felt it before. You complimented me for saving my father. Yes, I did that. I did it through instinct, not through any considered courage. You understand? The fear came later, and with it a terrible doubt. I came close to death. If I was faced with the same situation again, would I react differently? Would the fear unman me? Would I run? Would I cower and cry like a babe?" He fell silent.

"So, with the tree you were facing your fears?" prompted Mulgrave.

"Aye, even so." Gaise smiled.

"He either fears his fate too much,
or his desires are small, that dares not
put it to the touch, to gain or lose it all."

"Fine words, sir, but I'd sooner have seen the poet make that jump than yourself. In my experience poets are like politicians. They talk like lions and live like weasels."

"Let us hope they are not all like that," said Gaise, "for I wrote the words myself last night."

Mulgrave saw the young man laughing at him. "Ah, give me a moment, sir, while I prize my boot from my mouth."

"Do you still think me foolish for making the jump?"

"I have to say that I do, sir, though I better understand the reasons for it. You doubted yourself, but you did not have the confidence—or the patience—to wait for a better moment to test yourself. It was reckless and unnecessary. Had you asked me, I would have told you that you have all the courage a young man could desire. And I would have set you tasks to prove it to you. You have a fine future ahead of you, sir. Yet, but for a stroke of fortune, I could have been kneeling beside your crippled body, your legs and arms useless, your life ruined. Within a day the Moidart would have had me hanged for failing in my duty. You think the risk was worth it?"

Gaise laughed. "One can only measure deeds by results. I made the jump, and I feel free of fear, and strong, and young and happy. Therefore, the risk was worth it. Now let us debate it no more. You will not lecture me, and I will jump no more fallen trees. Agreed?"

"Agreed, sir," answered Mulgrave. But he remained troubled. He knew then that Gaise Macon was cursed with a reckless spirit, and such a vice could prove deadly. Given time, he thought, I can cure him of it.

The two riders moved on. "I wish I had killed the poor wretch," Gaise said suddenly.

Mulgrave remained silent. The screams from the captured assassin had been terrible and had lasted for hours. There was no escaping them. At last there had been silence, and the

Moidart had walked back from the cells, his clothing drenched in blood. Then he had written out a list, and soldiers had ridden into Eldacre to arrest those named on it.

The assassins had killed three of the four guards. The fourth was missing, but a warrant for his arrest had been issued.

"He should not have been tortured," said Gaise. "Hanged, yes, tortured, no."

"The Moidart needed to know if others were involved in the plot," said Mulgrave.

"You heard him, Mulgrave. By the end he would have named Saint Persis Albitaine as a coconspirator."

"The saint was arrested once, I understand," said Mulgrave, "and taken to Stone for execution. I think it was the time that Bane fought for the Veiled Lady."

"Not Bane," said Gaise. "It was a gladiator named Rage. And you are changing the subject."

"It is probably best we do not discuss the Moidart's methods, though I will say that I agree with you. I wish the man had died before he did."

The gray stone schoolhouse could be seen now and the cobbled streets leading into the village of Old Hills. As they approached the town, Mulgrave saw a crowd gathering. A fight was just starting.

A black-haired youth was being set upon by two—no, three—larger men.

Taybard Jaekel had always disliked Kaelin Ring. If asked why, he could have come up with a number of reasons, though none of them were entirely convincing, even to himself. The powerful young Varlish would have said that Ring was "too cocky for his own good" or that the clansman looked "down on him." Taybard knew that those statements did not convey anything like the real reason, yet even he could not say exactly why the mere sight of Kaelin Ring would set his blood boiling. The easy, graceful way he moved infuriated Taybard. The fact that the local girls—even Varlish girls—smiled at him and hung on his every word was like salt on an open wound to Taybard Jaekel. Now Chara Ward, the girl of Taybard's dreams—who had never even given Taybard a second glance—had set her cap for Kaelin Ring. Everyone knew it. Taybard Jaekel would have walked through fire to see Chara look at him the way she stared at the clan youth. And so his dislike had distilled into a cold hatred.

Taybard and his friends had been earning coppers in the market, fetching and carrying for the shoppers, when news had come in of the assassination attempt on the Moidart. All business had stopped momentarily as people paused to discuss the dreadful incident. Most of the residents of Old Hills were Varlish, and many could remember the last clan uprising fourteen years before. Those had been bloody times, days of rape, pillage, and murder, ending only when the Beetlebacks had crushed the last of the Rigante. An attack on the Moidart might be the herald of a new uprising.

Kaelin Ring had come walking along Market Lane, a canvas bag hanging from his shoulder. He had not seen Taybard and his friends, nor did he seem to notice the gathering crowd. It looked to Taybard as if Ring felt that the worries of the townsfolk were somehow beneath him.

Kammel Bard, one of Taybard's companions, an overweight redheaded youth, saw him staring at Kaelin Ring. "He can't be bothered with the likes of us, Tay," he said.

"He will today," snapped Taybard. He ran across the lane, catching up to Kaelin Ring just as he reached the gates of the school. "Heard the news, Ring?" shouted Taybard.

Kaelin Ring stopped and turned. "I've heard. What do you want, Jaekel?"

"Stinking clansmen attacked our Moidart."

Ring said nothing and swung away to continue his walk. "Don't you turn your back on me, you bastard!" shouted Taybard, rushing forward. Kaelin Ring sidestepped as Taybard grabbed at him. Taybard felt himself falling and landed hard on the cobbles, bruising his knees. Kammel Bard and Luss

Campion came running over. "He's attacked Tay!" shouted Kammel.

Taybard pushed himself to his feet. The crowd moved out, forming a half circle around the two young men. Kaelin Ring still had his canvas bag on his shoulder. Taybard advanced more warily. At least a head taller than Kaelin Ring and twenty pounds heavier, he was known for his street-fighting skills. His heart pounded, and a savage exultation filled him. He would make Ring beg for mercy. Taybard darted forward. Kaelin Ring ducked, moved to his left, and hooked his foot over Taybard's instep. Taybard stumbled and fell once more. A sharp stone slashed his leggings and cut a shallow wound into his leg. Taybard cried out more in anger than in pain. He looked up. Kaelin Ring was still holding his bag. Twice now Taybard had hit the ground. He scrambled to his feet, aware of laughter in the crowd. It stung him worse than a whiplash. He advanced on Kaelin Ring. The black-haired clansman laid his sack on the floor. Taybard moved in and let fly with a straight left. Kaelin swayed aside from it and delivered a right uppercut to Taybard's belly. Air whooshed from his lungs, and he sagged forward into a powerful head butt that smashed his nose. Taybard fell back, blood streaming. Fat Kammel ran at Ring and grabbed him. Kaelin Ring slammed an elbow into Kammel's face. As he did so, Luss Campion ran in and thundered a punch to Ring's cheek. The skin split, and blood sprayed out. Kaelin Ring lashed out with his foot, kicking Luss Campion's feet from under him, then hit Kammel twice more with his elbow. Kammel let go and threw a clumsy punch. Ring blocked it and hit the fat youth in the jaw with a straight left followed by a right cross. Luss Campion had regained his feet and ran in behind Ring, grabbing him in a bear hug and pinning his arms. The clansman leaned forward, then threw his head back. His skull struck Campion full in the face.

Taybard watched Luss fall back. Blind rage and pain from his smashed nose overcame his reason, and he drew a small knife from a sheath at his belt. Kammel had grabbed Ring again, and Luss ran in, hurling blow after blow at the clansman. Taybard moved in, ready to grab Ring's hair, pull back his head, and rip open his throat.

Just as he reached the struggling trio, a shadow moved across him. He glanced to his left. A golden horse surged forward, its shoulder slamming into Taybard, knocking him once more to the cobbles. Two officers of the watch, one of them the famed Sergeant Bindoe, moved through the crowd and pinned the arms of Kaelin Ring. Luss Campion smashed two blows to the clansman's face while he was being held. The officers holding him did nothing to prevent the attack.

"That is enough!" shouted Gaise Macon. "Release that man."

The watch officers let go of Kaelin Ring, who half stumbled and then righted himself.

"Sir, this man attacked a Varlish citizen," said Bindoe. "It was witnessed by most of the people here."

"I also witnessed it," Gaise Macon said coldly. "Three men against one. And he almost had the beating of them." He turned his palomino toward Taybard Jaekel. "And you, sir. Let me inform you that had you used that knife, I would have seen you hang for murder. Now begone from here."

In that moment all anger drained away from Taybard Jaekel. It was not the threat that caused it but the realization that he had come close to killing an unarmed man. Shame swept over him, and he swung away.

He did not go back to the market but instead ran down to the lake, where he sat on a fallen tree and offered up a prayer of thanks to the blessed Saint Persis Albitaine for preserving him from murder. Kammel Bard and Luss Campion found him there.

Taybard's broken nose was deeply painful, and a headache was pounding at his temples. Luss had a lump on his cheekbone, and Kammel was sporting a swollen, blackened eye.

"We'll get him another time," said Luss Campion.

Taybard did not respond.

"We'd better be getting back to the market," put in Kammel. "You coming, Tay?"

"No. I'll sit here awhile." His friends strolled away. Taybard moved to the water's edge and gently washed the blood from his face. His head felt like it could burst at any moment. He sat down heavily, dizziness swamping him.

A white-haired woman came alongside him. "Drink this," she said, offering him a small copper cup brimming with a murky liquid. "It will take away the pain."

"What is it?" he asked.

"Drink," she ordered him.

Taybard did so. The taste was bitter upon the tongue, but within moments the sharp, jagged pain receded, replaced by a dull throbbing ache.

"Thank you," he said.

"How did you hurt your nose?"

"It was . . . a fight."

"Did you win?"

"No."

"And that saddens you?"

"No. I didn't . . ." He paused and took a deep breath. "I didn't deserve to win. I almost killed a man. I would never have forgiven myself."

"Then be glad, for you learned a lesson that some men never learn. It will change you and change you for the better. This has been a good day for you, Taybard Jaekel."

He turned toward her, his gaze taking in her ragged clothing. "Who are you, and how do you know my name?" he asked, looking into her green eyes.

"I am the Wyrd of the Wishing Tree woods," she told him, "and I know all the children of the Rigante."

A heavy weariness flowed over him, and he lay down on the soft earth. "I am Varlish," he said sleepily.

"You are Taybard Jaekel, and your line goes back to the days of greatness and beyond. In you flows the blood of Fiallach, Connavar's iron general. He, too, was a man of uncertain rages. Yet he was loyal unto death."

He wanted to reply, but his eyes closed, and he slipped into a velvet sleep.

Kaelin Ring could feel the blood on his face, and his head was pounding. Taybard and the others had left the scene, but the hatchet-faced Sergeant Bindoe was standing close by, staring at him malevolently. Kaelin ignored him and reached for his shoulder bag.

The golden-haired young nobleman dismounted. "You are bleeding," he said. "Let us check the wound."

"It is nothing," answered Kaelin, pressing his fingers to the cut on his cheekbone. "It will seal itself." He wanted to be away from there, away, indeed, from all things Varlish.

"I expect that it will," said Gaise Macon. "I am sorry that I did not arrive more swiftly."

"You were swift enough," said Kaelin. He paused, aware of how ungrateful he sounded. "I thank you," he managed to say, having to force the words out.

A second man approached them, tall and lean with prematurely white hair. "You fought well, lad. Fine balance. Who taught you those moves?"

"My uncle Jaim. No one can fight like him."

"He is a good teacher." The soldier put out his hand, and Kaelin put down his sack and shook it. The grip was firm, and despite himself, Kaelin warmed to the man. Then he spoke again: "My name is Mulgrave. The gentleman who saved you is Gaise Macon."

"The Moidart's son," said Kaelin, stiffening.

"That is so," said Gaise, his friendliness fading as he saw the cold look in Kaelin's eyes. "You know my father?"

"No. He knew mine," said Kaelin. With that he stepped back, swept up his sack, and walked away, his heart beating fast. He was angry now. Just for a moment he had found himself relaxing in the company of the Varlish, one moment that now felt like a betrayal of his blood. This man's father had treacherously killed Lanovar and hundreds of other Rigante men, women, and children. Now the son had saved his life. It was galling.

Kaelin trudged on past the school and up into the hills. The blood dried on his face, the bruises on his flesh throbbing in the cool wind. He had known fear—real fear—for the first time in his life when he had seen Taybard Jaekel advancing on him, the knife glittering in his hand. He saw the scene again and shivered. It was not the knife that frightened him or even the prospect of death. It was that he had been helpless, his arms pinned. He would have been slaughtered like a feast bull.

The strange thing was that he had never hated Taybard. He did not much like Luss Campion or Kammel Bard, but Taybard, he had always felt, was essentially good-hearted. He had once, so Banny had told Kaelin one day, stepped in to save Banny from taking a beating. He had also been heavily involved in the rescue of little Jassie Wirrall when she had fallen into the weir and almost drowned. Taybard had hurled himself into the rushing torrent, grabbing the child and holding her head above the water until Galliott had thrown a rope and dragged them both to the bank.

He found it hard to understand the youth's hatred of him. Yes, Taybard was Varlish, but only nominally. Everyone knew there was clan blood in his line.

Kaelin walked on, keeping a wary eye out for Taybard and his companions in case they had decided to waylay him farther from town.

Up ahead was a cluster of dwellings used by the families of timber yard workers. Several women were hanging clothes out to dry on rope lines strung across the open ground. The houses had been built more than a hundred years before, the outer shells constructed of gray granite slabs, the sloping roofs of black slate. Freezing in winter, cold in summer, they stood colorless and drab against the bright green wooded hills. One of the younger women saw Kaelin and called out. He glanced up to see Chara Ward moving toward him.

Kaelin paused, his mood lifting. Chara was tall for a girl,

and she walked in a way that caused Kaelin's pulse to race
and his mind to focus on thoughts that were entirely inappropriate. She was dressed in a pale blue blouse and a flowing
gray skirt that hugged her body as she walked. As she neared
him, she smiled, her hand moving up to sweep back the long
blond wisps of hair that had fallen clear of her bright blue
headband. The lifting of the hand caused the blouse to press
against her body. Kaelin could not keep his eyes from the
plump, perfect outline of her breasts. Guiltily he looked away.
As she came closer, Chara saw the blood on Kaelin's face.

"What happened to you?" she asked, suddenly concerned.

"A scrap. Nothing serious," he answered.

"Who did that to you?"

"It is not important." He shuffled from foot to foot as she
came closer, her hand reaching out to touch his face.

"It is very swollen. You should come inside and let me
bathe the cut."

"It is nothing, Chara. You look beautiful today," he said,
catching hold of her hand and kissing the fingers.

She smiled, and a faint blush touched her cheeks. "You
shouldn't do that," she whispered. "Mother is watching."

Kaelin recalled that Chara's mother had recently been sick
with yellow blight, a fever that caused the skin to pale. Yellow
blight was rarely fatal, but sufferers lost great amounts of
weight and were liable to bouts of weakness that might last
for months. "Is she better now?" he asked.

"She is still a little weak, but she is improving. Thank you
for asking. Will you come in and sit with us for a while?"

"I would like to," he told her, "but I must be getting home. I
have medicine for Banny and his mother."

"I heard about the attack," said Chara. "It was shameful. I
sometimes think Morain has a streak of wickedness in her.
Will Shula be all right?"

"I don't know. She is very ill."

For a few moments they stood together in comfortable silence. Then Chara spoke again.

"Will you be attending the feast come Sacrifice Day?"

"I thought that I might," he said.

"Would you like to walk there together?" she asked.

"You know that I would. But it might be best if we did not."

"I don't care what people say, Kaelin."

"It is not about what they *say*."

"I'm not frightened of them, either. You are my friend, Kaelin. I value that friendship, and I'll not hide it to please bigots."

An older woman called out: "There is work still to be done, child."

Chara laughed. "I must be going. Will I see you at midday, then, or will you want to be walking there sooner?"

"Midday is good," he said. She smiled and swung away.

Kaelin watched her and found himself imagining her without the skirt and blue blouse. Then he caught the older woman staring at him. It was as if she could read his thoughts. He blushed and continued his way along the lane.

Cutting across the fields, he was within sight of his home when he saw the Wyrd sitting at the edge of the trees. He had not seen her in some months and waved at her. She gestured for him to join her. Kaelin strolled over, laid down his bag, and sat beside her on a fallen tree.

"My, but you have been busy today, Ravenheart," she said. "So much of import in so little time."

"I have merely been to town and had a scrap," he told her.

"You have seen the stag and set in motion events that will shape the future of the Rigante."

He shook his head and looked into her green eyes. "I have seen no stag."

"What did you think of Gaise Macon?"

"What was there to think? He is a Varlish nobleman."

"Did you like him?"

"I don't know him."

"Come, come, Ravenheart, I have no time for word games—unless of course they are mine. Did you like him?"

"Aye, sadly I did."

"Nothing sad about it," she told him. "Gaise Macon is a

fine young man—doomed but fine. I'm glad you took to him, and I am delighted he took up for you."

"Why do you say he is doomed?"

"He lives to ride the storm horse. No man can ride it for long. Those who do are bonny and brave—aye, and doomed."

Kaelin chuckled. "Every time we meet, you add a little riddle to the conversation. Stags and storm horses."

"You enjoy it, though?"

"Aye, I do. Will you come home with me and share a meal?"

"No, though it is kind of you to ask. I have a long journey ahead. I am going back to the Wishing Tree woods. I need to rest awhile and seek the wisdom of the Seidh."

"I thought they had gone from the world."

"Not from the world, Kaelin. Only from Caer Druagh. There are still places where they walk the wild woods and leave their magic in every footstep."

"Why did you say I had seen a stag?"

"Not a stag, Kaelin. *The* stag."

"You have lost me."

"Of course I have." She smiled at him, and he wondered anew just how old she was. When she smiled, her face seemed suddenly youthful. "I am as old as I choose to be," she said.

Kaelin jerked as if stung. "You can read my thoughts?"

The Wyrd's laughter pealed out. "That is no great talent. You are still young, and your expressions are honest. You have not yet learned to disguise what you are thinking. Though you should—at least when you are around Chara's mother."

Kaelin chuckled. "She's a fine-looking girl. I think she knows magic, for my heart beats like a drum whenever she is close."

"All women know *that* magic," said the Wyrd.

"Even you?" The words were out before he could stop them. "I am sorry," he said swiftly. "That was rude."

"Yes, but it was honest. Yes, even the Wyrd. I have chosen

to hold that magic within me. It strengthens my powers to be celibate. Why that should be, I don't know." Her green eyes locked to his dark gaze. "However, my time in Old Hills is short, and I've little of it to waste on matters philosophical."

"Nor I," said Kaelin. "Aunt Maev will be angry about the fight, and I need to be getting home. I don't doubt she'll scold me over it. Scolding is one of her talents."

"Aye, she's a hard woman. Difficult to live with."

Kaelin laughed. "I'll vouch for that."

"You know how you came to live with her?"

Kaelin looked away. "I know my mother was killed two nights after I was born. The Beetlebacks came into the village. They slew all who could not escape to the woods. After that Aunt Maev raised me."

"It was a night of sickening slaughter," said the Wyrd, her voice low. "Some women managed to run to the woods. However, Maev, instead of fleeing, ran back to your mother's hut. The soldier who killed Gian was standing over her body when Maev slammed a dagger into his throat. She killed him, Kaelin. She avenged Gian and took you from your crib and carried you to safety."

"She has never spoken of it," said Kaelin. "I did not know."

"She is Rigante, Ravenheart, and in her flows the blood of Ruathain and Meria, two of the great heroes of our past. Aye, and Lanach and Bedril, who held the pass. Maev is old blood. As are you. As is Gaise Macon."

"Varlish blood. Murderer's blood."

"Chara Ward is of Varlish blood, Kaelin," said the Wyrd. "Do you hate her?"

"No, of course not."

"Then think before you speak, Ravenheart. Chara Ward is good and kind." The Wyrd suddenly seemed sad. Kaelin expected her to speak, but instead she reached down to a canvas sack at her feet and opened it. From it she took a muslin pouch. "Now, listen to me. Ramus has given you good herbs, and they will help Shula a little. They will not, however, save her life. When you get home, put this in a pint—no more—of boiling water, then leave it until the water is merely warm to the touch. Make her drink at least half of it. When she does so, she will fall into a deep sleep. It will be like death. You may not be able to detect a pulse. Do not fret. She will recover, but she will sleep for at least three days. You understand?"

"Aye. Thank you, Wyrd. And now will you tell me about this stag?"

The Wyrd smiled. "I'll tell you this for now: When Raven the hound came to the rescue of a stag, it brought you your soul-name. It linked you to the land. Yet it was also a prophecy, Ravenheart. One day you, too, will need to rescue the stag. Now get off with you and take my herbs to Maev."

◇ 4 ◇

BANNY HAD NOT yet regained anything like his full strength, and the walk up to the hidden meadow had all but exhausted him. He lay on the grass watching Jaim Grymauch and Kaelin Ring practicing with wooden swords. The sun was shining, and the grass felt soft as a feather bed beneath him. Jaim and Kaelin were laughing and joking as they circled each other. Banny felt privileged to have been invited to join them. Even wooden swords were outlawed among the clans, and Banny felt a glow within that these two full-blooded clansmen should trust him so.

Everything seemed to be going well now. His mother had slept for three solid days but had awoken feeling stronger. She had eaten a good breakfast, and it seemed to Banny that there was color in her cheeks.

"Don't think, boy!" roared Jaim Grymauch. "Just do!"

Kaelin leapt at him, cutting and thrusting. Jaim swayed aside. He moved very fast for a big man, parrying Kaelin's blade and whacking his own against Kaelin's shoulder. "I'd have had your arm off!" he shouted gleefully. "Concentrate now."

"How can I concentrate while I'm not supposed to be thinking?" answered Kaelin.

"Concentrate on not thinking," answered Jaim.

"That doesn't make any sense."

"I know, but that's what old Lanash taught me."

"Was he drunk at the time?"

"He was always drunk."

"Is that someone coming up the hill?" Kaelin asked suddenly.

Jaim turned. Kaelin leapt in and struck him a blow on the buttocks. "You cheeky rascal!" yelled Jaim, and the two began to hack at each other yet again. Banny rolled to his back and stared up at the sky, wondering what it would be like to have wings like an eagle and soar through the clouds, to look down on the green earth far below, safe from any danger. Would it be cold up there, or warm because you were closer to the sun?

Banny yawned. He had spent the last few days resting, eating, and sleeping. It was a strange feeling to be without the call of hunger or the pressure of the cold, to sleep under warm and heavy blankets, his head resting on a soft pillow. Banny pressed his tongue against his teeth. They were firm now.

Life was good.

The spring feast was tomorrow. Banny, who rarely had an opportunity to eat fine foods—honey-roasted pig, wine-marinated steak, stuffed goose—was looking forward to it. Unfortunately, there was a touch of dread within the anticipation. In a crowd someone was bound to pick on him: Luss Campion or Kammel Bard—any one of a dozen Varlish youngsters. He had hoped to spend most of his time with Kaelin, but now his friend was going to the feast with Chara Ward.

Banny sat up and watched Kaelin fight. He moved swiftly and with confidence, unafraid of the pain that would come if Jaim's wooden sword pierced his defenses. Banny wished he, too, could learn to be unafraid. The two fighters closed in on each other. Jaim tossed his sword away and grabbed Kaelin in a bear hug, and the two fell to the ground, struggling and laughing.

"Enough! Enough!" shouted Jaim, releasing the youngster. The one-eyed warrior sat up and glanced across at Banny. "Would you like a try with the swords, lad?"

"No, thank you, sir," answered Banny.

Jaim rose to his feet and wandered across to sit beside him. For a moment Banny remembered the first time he had seen

Jaim Grymauch and the terrible fear that had swept through him. Banny had been very young then. Five or six? He could not remember. What he did recall was seeing this gigantic creature striding toward their little hut. Grymauch was so ugly that the child thought he must be a demon. His one eye seemed to glare balefully. He had a bulging sack on his shoulder, and Banny was convinced that the bodies of other little boys were held within it. As Grymauch approached, Banny screamed in fear and ran for his mother. Hearing his cries, Shula came from the hut. Seeing Grymauch, she curtseyed. Grymauch smiled, and in that moment Banny's fear drained away. The smile was broad and infectious. Even so, Banny hid behind his mother's skirt, peeking out at the giant.

"I know your man is away seeking work," said Grymauch, "so I thought you might like a little extra meat."

"Thank you, Master Grymauch, but we are doing well."

"I didn't doubt that," he said swiftly, "but I owe your husband a small debt, and having no coin, this was the only way I could think of repaying him." Dropping the sack, he opened it and drew out a large hank of ham and several small sacks. "There is sugar here, and salt, and a pot of that mustard the Varlish are so fond of. No offense," he added.

"None taken, Master Grymauch. I shall tell my husband when he returns that you have repaid your debt."

"Oh, this is only part of the debt," he told her. "When I have the time and the coin, I'll come back."

With that he had wandered away. Jaim Grymauch had often visited after that time, dropping off food and sometimes a few daens. Banny had come to realize that there was no debt to his father. Jaim never came into the hut. Always he would stop outside, chat briefly, then leave.

The previous week, when his mother had been too weak to move and Banny had been semidelirious, Grymauch had entered. Kaelin had been with him. Banny had struggled to sit up. Grymauch had leaned over his mother's bed and lifted her to his arms. Her dress was filthy and vomit-stained, her face covered in a sheen of sweat. "You hang on, lass, and we'll take you home," he remembered Grymauch saying.

Kaelin had helped Banny to his feet and half carried him after the departing Grymauch.

Now, days later, Banny was feeling strong and the giant Grymauch was sitting beside him. "How is your mother?"

"Better, sir. Almost strong, I think."

Jaim placed his huge hand on Banny's shoulder. "Do not call me 'sir.' My name is Grymauch. It is a good name, and my friends use it."

Banny nodded, unsure of how to respond. Kaelin joined them. He sat quietly, rubbing his forearm. "Those swords are heavy," he said.

"The wood is hollow," Jaim told him. "There is a center rod of lead to give them the same balance as a steel blade." He grinned at Kaelin. "I hear you are soon to walk the tree with a young Varlish girl."

"There's no talk of marriage," said Kaelin. "She is my friend, is all."

"Then you'll be walking your Varlish friend to the Beltine Feast?"

"You mustn't call it Beltine. It is the Feast of the Veiled Lady. Beltine is a pagan festival, born of devil worship."

"Pah! What nonsense." Jaim leaned in close to Kaelin, sniffing loudly.

"What are you doing?"

"I'm picking up traces of Varlish bullshit on you, boy."

Kaelin burst out laughing. "That coming from the man who last had a bath when the world was young. By heavens, Grymauch, your armpits could fell an ox."

Banny lay back on the grass and listened to their argument with great pleasure, feeling himself a part of their easy camaraderie. After a while Jaim fetched a canvas sack and from it drew a bottle of golden Uisge. He took several deep swallows and offered it to Kaelin, who shook his head.

"Good for you, lad. Cleans the blood."

"I've no wish to get maudlin," Kaelin told him. "In a

few minutes you'll be talking about the old days when men were men."

"Ah, true enough," admitted Grymauch. "So tell us about this walk to the feast with the beautiful Varlish maiden."

"Why do you keep saying Varlish?" snapped Kaelin.

"Because that's what she is, Kaelin. Are you in love with her?"

"I don't know. I like her company, and . . . she is very beautiful."

Grymauch took another drink. "Have you kissed her? Be honest now."

"A man shouldn't talk about such things," said Kaelin, embarrassed.

"Aye, maybe he shouldn't. So let me say this: If you *have* kissed her and you still don't know whether you're in love, then maybe you aren't. Beautiful women are a wondrous temptation, Ravenheart. But by all accounts Chara is a good lass. So you listen to your uncle Jaim. Don't bed her until you are sure that you want to walk the tree with her."

"I don't want to talk about this," said Kaelin. "It is not seemly."

"If you must sow your seed," continued Grymauch, ignoring his protestations, "and I fear a man must, then there are plenty available who will not have their hearts broken by it. I myself visit the Earth Maiden at the old mill house."

"Parsha Willets?" said Kaelin, pulling a face. "She must be close to forty."

"She's a good girl and bighearted," said Jaim.

Kaelin laughed aloud. "By bighearted you mean she extends credit?"

"I do," said Jaim.

"You are a disgraceful man, Grymauch," Kaelin put in, chuckling. "It is no surprise that decent people avoid your company."

"Will you be attending the feast, Grymauch?" asked Banny, more to practice the use of Jaim's name than anything else.

"Perhaps, lad. I'm still considering it."

"You won the fistfighting two years ago. There's another tournament this year, they say."

"Not for me, Banny. The Varlish will gather around the circle and bay and cheer as clansmen whack and thud at each other. I've no mind to add to their entertainment."

"The tournament is open this year," said Kaelin. "There's thirty chaillings to be won. I've heard that there will be Varlish looking to win it."

"Is that so?" replied Jaim, taking another deep swallow.

"According to Captain Galliott, two fighters are coming up from the south. Big men. Varlish champions. I expect they'll be looking to show that clansmen are easy meat."

Jaim chuckled. "You are trying to goad me, boy. I'm not so drunk that I cannot see it."

"I am not trying to goad you," Kaelin told him with a wink to Banny. "You are getting too old to fight, Grymauch. You've said it yourself. I think you should let the tournament pass."

"Too old, am I? You rascal! It may be that I will show these southern Varlish the error of their thinking."

"Thirty chaillings is a great sum," put in Banny.

"There'll be more to be made on the side betting," said Jaim. "I'd say the winner of the tourney would clear maybe four . . . five pounds."

"How much is that in chaillings?" asked Banny, who had never seen a pound.

"Tell him, Kaelin."

"Twenty chaillings to a pound . . . one hundred chaillings."

"That is a fortune," whispered Banny. He closed his eyes. There were twelve daens to a chailling. He knew that much. The sum was the equivalent of twelve hundred daens. Enough to feed Banny and his mother for . . . for . . . He tried to calculate the sum, but it was too large. Shula had managed to scrape together enough food for them on three daens a week. Ten weeks, then, would be thirty daens.

Concentrating hard, Banny carefully built the sums in his

mind. A year would cost 150 daens; ten years, 1,500. The difference was three hundred, or two years.

According to Banny's calculation, the winner of the tourney would have enough money to feed himself and his mother for eight years!

"Could you teach me to fight, Grymauch?" he asked, sitting up.

"I could teach any clansman to fight. It's in the blood."

"I'm not a clansman," Banny told him. "My mother is Varlish."

Jaim put down his bottle. Removing his black headband, he scratched at the empty socket. He turned his one-eyed gaze on Banny. "This Rigante eye is magical," he said. "It sees into the hearts of men. And when I look at you, young Banny, I see a clansman. And that's an end to it."

Banny felt as if his heart would burst. His throat tightened, and he could not speak. He glanced away so that the others would not see the tears in his eyes.

"Let's be getting back," said Kaelin. "Shula has made a fruit pie."

"It's a good one," said Jaim. "I had a little taste before coming to meet you boys."

The apothecary Ramus drew rein on his small, fat-bellied pony and carefully dismounted at the gates of the Moidart's Winter House. A soldier expertly searched him, then opened the gate. Ramus did not remount. A small man with an arthritic hip, Ramus needed a mounting step or a box in order to climb to the saddle. Slowly he walked toward the house, leading the pony.

A servant came out to meet him. Ramus recognized the old retainer Maldrak and greeted him with a smile. The pony picked up its paces as Maldrak approached. He knew the old man would feed him carrots or sweet apples.

"Good morning, Apothecary," said Maldrak. "Are you well?"

"I am, sir. Is the nettle tisane still keeping the rheumatik at bay?"

"Mostly. Except when the weather is bad."

Ramus nodded. "No herb can completely repair the ravages of time." Maldrak took the reins, and the two men walked side by side toward the rear of the house. Some two hundred paces to the north, almost hidden by the trees, Ramus could see the blackened remains of the old house. Weeds had grown over the ruined walls, and a tree was growing through the collapsed roof. "You were here, were you not, when fire consumed the old house?" said Ramus.

"Aye. A terrible night that was. The screams of the trapped were terrible to hear. Even some of those who got out, their clothes on fire, died later." Maldrak shivered at the memory. "We all thought the Moidart would die. But he's tough, the man."

Another male servant, a round-shouldered young man, met them at the side door. Ramus patted the pony's neck, removed his small pack from the saddle, and followed the servant into the house, through the kitchen, and onto the stairs. His right hip ached as he mounted the stairs and continued his walk along the corridor toward the Moidart's private rooms. The servant tapped on a paneled door, then, on hearing a command from inside, entered. He reappeared moments later. "The lord will see you in a few moments, Apothecary. Please be seated."

Ramus gratefully sank onto a couch by the balcony rail and gazed up at the paintings adorning the wall. Mostly they were of the Moidart's ancestors, dressed in martial fashion, shining plate armor, swords in their hands. There were occasional hunting scenes and, closest to where he sat, a stunning portrait of a young woman with golden hair. She was standing beside a tall horse and was dressed in riding garments of velvet and silk, a long split skirt that had been high fashion half a century earlier. Ramus always found himself captivated by her. He had first seen her as a real woman just before her death some ten years before. She had been old then, her skin wrinkled and leathery, her eyes sunken. Here, in this portrait, she was young, and the artist had captured the fire of her spirit and the quintessential lure of her femininity. The face had strength and yet compassion, sensitivity allied with a steely determination. She was the Moidart's grandmother, and people still spoke of her with reverence and love.

The door to the apartments opened, and a young officer stepped to the balcony. His face was flushed. "You may enter now," he said, then walked stiffly to the stairs.

Ramus pushed himself to his feet and moved to the doorway. The room within was double-aspected, tall windows looking out to the north and east. Glowing coals burned within a red brick fireplace. A single armchair was set before it. Beneath the eastern window was a broad desk with yet another single chair behind it. No one else could sit in the Moidart's presence.

The Lord of the North was standing by the northern window, hands clasped behind his back. Dressed all in black, his silver hair shining in the sunlight, he stood motionless. A distant gunshot sounded, followed instantly by another. Ramus remained in the doorway.

"Come in, Apothecary," said the Moidart, his voice, as ever, without emotion. "And close the door. It is creating a draft."

Ramus did as he was ordered and stood before the desk. The Moidart remained where he was for several seconds, then returned to his desk, seating himself. Then he looked up into Ramus' eyes. Ramus thought he had prepared himself for this meeting of eyes, but it was always a shock. It was not that the man had a malevolent gaze or even that Ramus could see the cruelty and power of the lord. No, it was that the Moidart's eyes were empty, devoid of emotion. The look seemed to say: "You are nothing, a speck, insignificant and disposable."

"My scars have been causing me discomfort," said the Moidart. "In cold weather the skin still cracks and weeps even after fifteen years."

"Most men would have died, lord," said Ramus. "The burns were severe."

"I am not most men. Did you bring me salves?"

"I did, lord. They should be used sparingly, for they are most potent."

Ramus waited, still unsure why the Moidart had summoned him. Usually a retainer—Mulgrave or one of the other officers—would collect the balms, salves, and powders required.

"You are an artist, I see," said the Moidart.

"An artist, lord?"

The Moidart opened a drawer at the front of his desk and removed a glazed jar. It was from the apothecary, and upon it was a hand-painted label showing the leaf and flower of a honeysuckle. Beneath it in delicate script were written the instructions for preparing the tisane. "You drew this?"

"Yes, lord. I am a sketcher. No more than that."

"One of my retainers is also a . . . sketcher." The Moidart rose and moved around the desk, gesturing for Ramus to follow him. He walked to the rear of the room. A framed painting had been hung on the western wall. Light from the window shone upon it. Ramus gazed at it, awestruck. He had never seen the like. It was a winter scene of mountains and pines laden with snow. There was no delicacy in the brushwork, which was vibrant and swift, creating an elemental power that was both immediate and stunning. Ramus stood before the canvas. The trees were breathtaking for their depth. Ramus felt he could step into the canvas and walk in that winter forest.

"What do you think?" asked the Moidart. "Does the man have talent?"

"It is majestic," whispered Ramus. "One can almost feel the cold emanate from the mountains and hear the birdsong within the trees. And the light shining on the pines. Oh, sir, this is exquisite. How did the man create such depth?"

"Lighter layers upon darker backgrounds," said the Moidart, "then further highlighted with just the corners of a two-inch brush."

Ramus glanced at the Moidart, knowing in that moment that he was the artist. The Moidart saw the realization in his face. "You did not guess?" he asked.

"No, sir. Not until you spoke of method. It is an amazing piece. How long have you been painting?"

"Many years. You are the first to see my . . . efforts."

"I am honored, sir. More than I can say." The words were spoken with genuine feeling, for Ramus was not skilled in the art of flattery.

"The hardest part was the water upon the lake and obtaining the reflection of the mountains and trees. I discovered it by error. One merely pulls the bristles of a dry brush down in sharp motions. Would you like this painting?"

"I could not afford such a . . . a masterpiece, lord," Ramus said, astonished.

"I am not some peasant who needs to sell his wares. It is finished. I have no more use for it."

"Thank you, lord. I don't know what to say." He paused. "Are there others? I would love to see them."

"No."

"But what of the paintings you have completed over the years?"

"Time for you to go, Master Apothecary. I have much to do. I will send the painting to you."

Ramus bowed deeply. The Moidart ignored him and returned to the window.

The little apothecary walked to the door, then realized he had not unpacked the salves from his sack. With a sigh he left it behind and stepped from the room.

His mind was reeling as he descended the stairs.

In the town center of Eldacre twelve corpses were hanging from the Moidart's gibbets. Three of the men had been tortured, their eyes burned out before their execution.

And the man who had ordered such brutality was an artist

of exquisite talent who could capture the beauty of a moment
and the raw majesty of nature in a few brushstrokes.

As Ramus emerged into the light, he saw the young Gaise
Macon and the soldier Mulgrave approaching the house. He
stopped and bowed.

"Good morning, Apothecary," said Gaise Macon. The
young man seemed suddenly concerned. "Are you all right,
sir? You seem very pale."

"I am well, lord. I heard you practicing," he said, pointing
to the two silver-embossed flintlock pistols in the young
man's hands.

"Yes, they are fine pieces."

The old servant Maldrak came into sight, leading the pony.
Ramus bowed once more to Gaise Macon. The young man
stepped in. "Allow me to assist you, sir," he said, cupping his
hands and helping Ramus into the saddle.

"Thank you, lord. Most courteous," said Ramus. The sun
broke through the clouds, its light shining on the young man's
face. His strange green and gold eyes glinted in the sunlight.

Just like the portrait in the gallery. "You have your great-
grandmother's eyes," said Ramus.

"So I have been told, sir," answered Gaise Macon. "I wish I
had known her, but I was a small child when she died and remember only a stern woman who dressed in black."

"She was greatly loved," said Ramus. "During an outbreak
of the lung sickness she and her ladies-in-waiting worked in a
hospital, tending the sick. She was a woman of great courage
and compassion."

"Compassion is not a word one hears often in talk of my
family," Gaise said with a bitter smile. "It was good to see
you, Apothecary."

Maev Ring closed her book of accounts and replaced it in the
bottom drawer of the pine cabinet. There was ink on her fingers, and she walked out into the sunlight, drawing up a
bucket of water from the well. Dipping her hands, she washed
her fingers but could not quite remove the stains.

Glancing up at the sky, she saw that rain clouds were bunching over the mountains. Shula Achbain emerged from the main building and curtseyed as she saw Maev. She was painfully thin, but Maev was pleased to see some color in her sallow cheeks.

"I have cleaned the rooms upstairs, ma'am," she said.

"I told you to rest, Shula. And do not call me 'ma'am.' I am Maev Ring, a clanswoman by birth."

Shula gave a shy smile, curtseyed again, and went back into the house. Maev sighed. Shula was Varlish, albeit "kilted Varlish," as the poorer people were known even among their own kind. Even so, it would normally be unthinkable among her people to call a clanswoman "ma'am." No wonder Morain and the other Varlish women hated Shula. She had no sense of place. Bad enough, they would think, to marry a highlander without treating them as your betters. But then Maev knew that Shula's sense of self-worth was almost nonexistent. She had no confidence.

However, questions of Shula's broken personality were not uppermost in Maev's mind as she stood by the well. Following the assassination attempt on the Moidart's life, twelve men had been executed—all of them clansmen. That was not in itself surprising, but three of them had been successful businessmen in Eldacre. Maev had known two of them well and doubted they would have taken part in any such murderous enterprise. No, their crime had been to be too successful in the Varlish world. One, Latimus Esher, had run a pottery enterprise, his wares shipped as far south as the capital. That burgeoning enterprise was now owned by the Moidart.

Best be careful, Maev, she warned herself. Her own businesses were booming, and she had now invested in three cattle farms in the far north. It seemed that anything she turned her mind to became profitable. Already she had more than five hundred pounds in gold hidden in the house.

There was movement on the hillside, and shielding her eyes, she saw Jaim, Kaelin, and young Banny returning from

the high meadows. Her mood softened as she thought of
Jaim. Born out of his time, he was a true clansman no matter
what she said to his face. He was strong, proud, and angry,
and his heart chafed constantly against the Varlish yoke. One
day his temper would get the better of him, and he would do
something even more rash than usual and be walked to the
gallows.

The thought made her shiver. There had been a time when
she had believed Jaim Grymauch desired her, when they had
both been young. She had waited for him to approach her, but
he never had. Then Calofair had wooed her. He had been a
good and kind man, brave and strong. Though she had loved
him, she had never felt as easy in his company as she did with
Grymauch. Whenever Jaim was absent—which was often—
Maev would find herself gazing out over the hills, longing for
his return. Yet whenever he did come back, she would find
herself becoming angry with him, often for no reason that
she could fathom later.

Kaelin idolized him. For Maev this was double-edged.
There was much to admire about the big man, yet she did not
want Kaelin to imitate him. The thought of her child with a
rope around his neck was more than she could bear.

He is not your child. The thought was a surprising one. No,
Kaelin was born of Gian, but Maev had raised him from a
babe. I could not love any child of mine more, she thought.

They reached the house. Kaelin waved at her and took
Banny inside. Jaim strolled across to the well and dipped
a gourd into the bucket. "I have washed my hands in that,"
said Maev.

"Then it will taste all the sweeter," Jaim answered with a
grin. He took a long drink. "He will be quite a swordsman,"
he said. "He moves well, and he is fearless."

"A useless talent for a clansman these days," she observed.

"Times change," said Jaim. "There's talk of unrest in the
south. The king is not popular in all quarters. Only last month
I heard merchants talking of the risk of civil war. A nice
thought, eh, all those Varlish killing one another?"

"It is never nice to think of killing. I only ever killed one man, and I can still see his face."

"He deserved killing," said Jaim, his face darkening. "He murdered Gian."

"Aye, he did. Let's talk no more of killing. So will you be coming with us to the feast?"

"You want me to?"

"I don't care, Grymauch. But I'll not have you shaming me again by getting drunk. If you come, you must promise to avoid the brandy tents."

"I shall give you that promise, Maev. There'll be little time for drinking. I plan to enter the bouts."

Maev took a deep breath, seeking to calm the angry words she felt clawing their way toward her throat. "Do you never learn, Grymauch? There'll be Varlish in the tourney this year. Champions, I'm told. Men who make their living by stalking the circle."

"I can handle them."

Her left hand whipped into his cheek, the slap sounding like a distant gunshot. Jaim stepped back, his face angry. "By heaven, you go too far!" he shouted.

"Do you still not understand, Grymauch?" she said softly. "You did not see the blow coming. You are blind in one eye. I can understand how a clumsy clansman might not take advantage of it in a friendly feast bout, but a Varlish fighting man? He'll whip in hooks and crosses and turn your face to pulp."

Jaim stood silently for a moment. "Aye, there's truth in that. But the bastard will have to be on his feet to do it." He bunched his fist. "You know what this is? It's the Rigante hammer. I'd like to see the Varlish who can stand against it. It strikes like thunder and brings only darkness." Suddenly he winked at her. "And if you ever strike me again, woman, I swear I'll put you over my knee and let the hammer fall on your buttocks."

Her hand flashed out. Jaim caught her wrist. "Fool me once, shame on you; fool me twice, shame on me."

"Let go of me, you lummox."

"Only if you promise not to hit me."

Maev did not struggle, but she glared at him. Jaim grinned and released her arm. "Will you place a bet on me, Maev?"

"I do not gamble, Grymauch. But I'll place a cold compress on your bleeding face at the close. I promise you that."

He held to her arm for a moment more, and she felt the power in his grip. His expression changed, and just for a heartbeat he seemed wistful. Then he let her go, and they stood together in awkward silence. It seemed to Maev that Grymauch was struggling for the right words.

Then Kaelin called out from the kitchen. "You greedy hog, Grymauch. You ate the whole pie!"

Jaim turned toward the lad and grinned. "And mighty fine it was, too. Though I am a little peckish now." Grymauch strolled toward the house.

Maev rubbed at her wrist. She could still feel where his fingers had held her.

On the outskirts of Eldacre was the common land known as Five Fields. It was only nominally common land these days, for much of it was permanently fenced, ready for the four major feast days of the Sacrifice calendar. The fencing had been installed more than thirty years earlier, effectively segregating Varlish townsfolk from the clans. Stewards patrolled the entrances to each section, preventing any Pannone from entering the wrong enclosure.

Mulgrave had arrived early to ensure that the Moidart would be as secure as possible against assassination. He interviewed the officers of the lord's guard, making them aware of all the necessary precautions. "Watch the crowd always," he told the assembled soldiers. "Ensure that no one comes within twenty feet of the lord. Watch especially for those with very pale faces. When a man is about to commit an act of premeditated murder, his blood runs cold and his features whiten. Watch also the hands of those closest to the lord. If they slip inside their cloaks or coats, move to block their view of the lord."

Dismissing the soldiers, he then gathered the red-cloaked stewards who would be patrolling the entrances. "Be good-natured if you find someone in the wrong enclosure," he told them. "Do not insult them; merely escort them to the correct area. Be always in pairs. If you suspect there is danger, one man should fetch help while the other merely watches the likely offender. The most obvious reason for a clan man or woman to be in the wrong enclosure is that a child has wandered and they are seeking it. Assure them that the child will be sought and brought to them and then escort them from the enclosure. You understand this?"

"Why be polite to clan vermin?" asked a tall, thin man standing at the back.

"Your name?"

"Jannie Clippets."

"You are no longer a steward, Jannie Clippets. Hand back your cloak to the feast marshal."

"I only asked a question," shouted the astonished man.

"If I see you in a steward's cloak this evening, I shall have you flogged for impersonating an officer of the Moidart," Mulgrave told him. "Do the rest of you understand my instructions?"

Some of them muttered "Aye," while others merely nodded.

Mulgrave strolled away. Guarding the Moidart was never easy, for the man was hated. At feast times it became nightmarish. Some eight thousand people would fill the Five Fields, moving between tents and stalls, shows and exhibitions. A killer probably would come dressed as a Varlish in a white wig and black cloth. Obtaining an entry disk was not difficult, and the Moidart would be in full view of the crowd for much of the afternoon. One pistol ball, well aimed, and no amount of guards could prevent a murder. And there was likely to be other trouble.

Largely the clan folk did not trespass on the Varlish areas.

The punishment was too severe: twenty lashes at a public flogging. The same was not true in reverse. Many Varlish townsfolk liked to wander the clan sections, watching the boulder hurl, the rope war, and the fistfighting tourney. Food and drink were cheaper, and this year there was the added complication of the fist tourney being an open event. It was foolishness, the thinking behind it obvious and crude. Bring up Varlish champions to hammer the clumsy clan farmers and cattle workers, thus displaying Varlish superiority in matters martial. No one seemed to have considered the possibility that a clansman might prove just the opposite. The Moidart had said nothing about the plan, but Mulgrave sensed he was irritated by it. Cruel he might be, stupid he was not. He had made it clear to Mulgrave that he would not be present for the final bouts.

The feast was organized by the Eldacre Elders, a committee of wealthy town merchants of which the chairman was the bishop of Eldacre. Their plan of events had been, as usual, posted and advertised without reference to the lord. The Moidart's power was based on the twin pillars of tax and defense. He had no say over Sacrifice feasts, which came under the jurisdiction of the church.

Mulgrave walked across the first of the fields to where the best of the fighting circles had been constructed on a raised wooden dais. Two channels led away from the circle, one to the clan area and one to the Varlish. At the circle itself the crowd would again be segregated, the Varlish area containing tiered bench seating and the clan folk being obliged to stand in the mud. Mulgrave sighed.

He saw two men approach the circle and climb to the fighting area. Both were large, but his eyes were drawn to a powerful black-haired figure with a large, flat face and huge hands. Mulgrave recognized him. He was Chain Shada, a former soldier who had become wealthy through his fistfighting skills. It surprised Mulgrave that a professional such as Shada should have been interested in such a small event. He had once earned two hundred pounds fighting in Capital

Park before a crowd of forty thousand. It was said he owned several properties in the capital and two racing stables near Baracum. What would such a man be doing traveling hundreds of miles for a thirty-chailling purse?

Intrigued, Mulgrave waited until the two fighters had examined the circle and climbed down to the ground. "Good day to you, Master Shada," said Mulgrave. "It is an honor to have you visit our town."

"I'm sure it is," said Chain Shada without a hint of humor. He was several inches over six feet tall, wide-shouldered and bull-necked. His face, though showing the marks of more than a hundred fights—scarred eyebrows, a broad flattened nose—was still savagely handsome. His eyes were dark and wide-set, his voice deep. "Who are you?"

"Captain Mulgrave. I will be in charge of security."

"Will the Moidart be watching me in the final?"

"Sadly, no."

"Pity. He'll miss a fine exhibition. I expect it will be against Gorain here," he added, slapping the shoulder of the powerful man standing alongside him. "He's good. In a few years he'll be even better. Luckily I will have retired by then."

"I saw you fight the champion from Goriasa," said Mulgrave. "It was at Werwick Castle four or five years ago. You broke his jaw in the first period, but he fought on for nigh on an hour."

"Aye, he was tough, that one," said Shada. "Had a good left-right combination and knew how to use his head. Split my nose with a good butt in the eleventh period. Thought I'd gone blind. Are you a fight follower?"

"No. I was on duty that day also. But I recall your footwork was exquisite. Always in balance, even when in trouble."

"It's all in the legs, Mulgrave. Every punch comes from the toes, and every blow received is absorbed and lessened by correct footwork. Tell me, are there any highland men who should merit concern?"

"Fistfighting is not a sport here, Master Shada. It is not even considered a craft. In the highlands a fight involves two men throwing punches until one falls down. But there will be some big lads facing you, and you'll take a few whacks before the final."

"Not so," replied Chain Shada. "I am here only to fight the final. The bishop offered me fifty pounds. He is a fight follower and my greatest supporter—or so he tells me."

Mulgrave fell silent for a moment. "That is hardly sporting, sir. The man you face will have fought maybe five . . . six opponents before he steps into the circle with you."

"I shall go easy on him. As I said, it is more of an exhibition and will give Gorain an opportunity to test himself. I'm hardly likely to want to batter my own apprentice."

"Indeed, I can see that. However, there is always the possibility that you will not be facing Gorain."

"You think some highland lout can beat me?" sneered the other man. "Nonsense!"

Mulgrave looked at him. Like Chain Shada, his face was broad, the cheekbones and brows rounded and therefore less likely to suffer cuts. There was a brooding power in the man, but Mulgrave took an instant dislike to him. There was something in the man's eyes that spoke of cruelty and malice.

"A lucky blow, sir," said Mulgrave, "a slip, a rush of blood to the head. It could happen."

"In a pig's eye!" snapped Gorain. "I am unbeaten in seventeen fights. No stinking sheep shagger will beat me. You can wager your fortune on that, Captain."

"I don't gamble, sir."

"It wouldn't be a gamble," said Chain Shada. "Gorain has the talent to be the best I have ever seen. I intend to make twice the fortune from his career that I have made from my own. Next month he will be fighting in Baracum, in the King's Tourney. There he will make a name for himself. And now we must be going. The bishop has promised us steak and Uisge. It is said there is no finer steak than that found in the highlands."

"The same can be said of the Uisge," Mulgrave told him.

"I may try it, but only after the tourney," said Chain Shada. "A fighter needs a clear head."

"An *old* fighter, maybe," said Gorain.

Mulgrave saw a momentary flash of irritation cross Chain Shada's features. "It was good to meet you, Captain," he said. "Perhaps we can meet for a dram of Uisge later tonight."

"I shall look forward to it, sir."

The Wyrd was close to exhaustion. She had traveled far, and her work had barely begun. It was cold now, deep within the Wishing Tree woods, and she shivered and drew her tattered cloak more firmly around her shoulders. Resting her back against the bole of a twisted oak, she tried to rest her mind.

There was so little magic left now in Wishing Tree that all her efforts amounted to little more than adding a drop of perfume to a stagnant pond. The analogy annoyed her, for it made her life's work seem futile. I will not become defeatist, she told herself. I will persevere.

The Seidh were long gone, the land having become increasingly barren without them. Yet the Seidh alone did not create the magic that once flowered across the land. They merely harnessed it. It lived within the hearts of all living things, but it radiated most from man. Acts of love and unselfishness, heroism and duty, all added to the magic, feeding the earth and the trees, flowing across the mighty mountains, carried in the rivers and streams. A mother singing to her child, a farmer giving thanks for his crops, two lovers arm in arm by a riverbank, a hero standing alone on a wooden bridge defying the enemy. Thus was the land enhanced.

Sadly, the opposite was also true. Acts of selfishness and vengeance, thoughts of greed and avarice, and dark deeds of savagery and murder robbed the land, draining it of harmony. The Varlish were not inherently evil, but their arrogance and lust for power blinded them to the majesty of their surroundings. The mountains were merely lumps of rock, yielding coal and gold and silver, the forests sources of timber for their ships and buildings. Their furnaces polluted the sky with black smoke, their cities of stone became breeding grounds for disease, and their endless rapacious need for war and conquest brought with it oceans of despair, sorrow, and hatred. Like a plague of locusts descending on a cornfield, the Varlish ate into the magic of the world, corrupting its soul.

The Wyrd felt anger touch her and quelled it swiftly. She could not allow their malice to find a place within her soul. "They do not know what they do," she whispered. Much like a child running around and stamping on the ants beneath his feet. They have no sense of what they are destroying.

A water rat emerged from a stream close by and scampered across the clearing, pausing to look at the Wyrd before vanishing beneath a bush. The Wyrd closed her eyes, seeking calm. She rested there for an hour, dozing and dreaming of her youth and remembering the first day she had met the spirit of Riamfada. She was a seven-year-old gathering herbs for her mother on the edge of the Wishing Tree woods. He stepped from the trees and spoke to her. He seemed to be just a young clansman, fair-haired and sweet of face. "Walk with me," he said.

"We should not enter the woods," she told him. "It is forbidden."

"Not for you and me, Caretha."

"Doom will fall upon any mortal who ventures into the wood. Everyone knows that."

"Not every mortal. Connavar walked here. Bane walked here. Trust me. Come."

Looping her herb sack over her shoulder, Caretha took his hand and walked into the woods. It still surprised her that she had done so. Her mother had warned her of strangers and their dark ways.

Riamfada brought her to a little clearing. A fire was burning, and upon it was a copper pot hanging from a tripod. Steam was rising from the pot. It filled the clearing with a sweet smell, a perfume she had never forgotten. Riamfada sat by the fire and plucked a small blue flower from the ground close by. He held it up for her to see. The flower was almost dead, its petals fading and brown at the edges. He closed his hand around it and reached out. The child leaned forward. His hand opened. What he held was no longer dying but vibrant with color, the blue of a summer sky at sunset, its center white as new snow. His fingers curled over the bloom once more. This time, when they opened, the flower had gone, replaced by a small silver brooch in the shape of the bloom.

"That is a clever trick," she said. "Can I touch it?"

"You may touch it and you may keep it, Caretha."

The child pinned it to her dress. "It is very beautiful," she said.

"Only you will be able to see it."

"Why?"

"Because it is magic, and it is yours alone."

"Does it work spells?"

"Not yet. But it will."

"When?"

"When I have taught you all you need to know."

She touched the brooch. It was warm and made her fingers tingle. "Do you live near here?" she asked him.

"No. I died near here," he replied.

Back in the present the Wyrd smiled, recalling that the child had not been at all surprised at such a statement. Her memories of Riamfada were fond ones, and she felt refreshed. Glancing down, she touched the tiny brooch on her faded green dress. It tingled still.

Rising, she returned to her work.

Unwrapping the crystal from its covering of black velvet, she held it in her hands and began again the chant Riamfada had taught her so many years before. Freeing her mind of all stresses and burdens, she focused on all that was clean and clear: the freshness of the air, the birdsong in the trees, the rustling of the leaves above and around her. She pictured the energy flowing from the sun, golden and invigorating; from the waters of the stream, white as a saint's conscience; from the trees, healing and green.

"I am a vessel, empty and pure," she chanted, feeling the

power begin to fill her. The crystal in her hands became warmer and warmer. Slowly the color changed from white to gray and then to black. Threads of gold grew within it like blades of yellow grass. They thickened and swelled until the crystal itself had ceased to be, replaced by a block of what appeared to be solid gold.

The Wyrd let out a weary sigh. Rising to her feet, she carried the golden block to the center of the clearing and laid it on the sun-dried yellowing grass. Kneeling beside it, she spoke the seven words of power.

The crystal began to glow. Around it the grass thickened, becoming emerald green. The Wyrd closed her eyes. Blue flowers sprang to life as the magic rippled out from the crystal, flowing across the clearing until it touched the ancient oaks.

When she opened her eyes, the clearing was verdant, the grass rich and velvet, the trees swelling with new life. The air tasted as sweet as honey, and the sunlight sparkled on the waters of the stream.

She lay down on the grass and fell into a deep sleep.

In it she saw Riamfada. He was walking in the shadow of mountains she had never seen. It was a land of exquisite beauty, filled to overflowing with magic: vast lakes swarming with birds, huge plains rich with grass and wildlife.

"Where is this place?" she asked him.

"Home," he told her.

It had taken Chain Shada no more than a few minutes to realize that he disliked the bishop of Eldacre. Within the hour he had come to loathe him. The Source alone knew what he would have felt if he had had to spend a day in the man's company.

He and Gorain had dined with the bishop at his fabulously appointed mansion behind Albitane Cathedral. Built of limestone faced with marble, the mansion boasted eastern rugs of silk, curtains of lace, furniture covered with the softest leather. Red-liveried servants were everywhere, polishing and cleaning, fetching and carrying. The bishop was at the center of it all like a vast, bloated red spider. To be honest, Chain realized, he had begun to loathe the man on sight. As a fighting man and an athlete he despised gluttons, and the bishop was so fat that it seemed his skin would burst. Chain could not take his eyes from the golden rings the man wore on every finger.

The meal he had promised them turned out to be a feast: three roasted geese, a suckling pig, several roast chickens, and platters of steamed vegetables coated in butter. There were cakes and pastries, wines, ales, and spirits, and the twenty guests tore into the meal as if they had not eaten in a month. Chain ordered a steak with gravy and some fried bread. He drank no wine or ale and was irritated that Gorain did not abstain from the golden Uisge.

"You are fighting in less than two hours," he warned him.

Gorain grinned at him. "I fight better on a full stomach."

No one fights better on a full stomach, thought Chain, but he did not argue. This was, after all, more a pleasure excursion than a real tourney.

The bishop sat Chain beside him on his right and began by telling him how privileged he was to have the legendary Chain Shada at his table. "I have seen almost all of your bouts. Remarkable. I was a fighter in my youth, you know." He made a pudgy fist. "I had quite a mighty punch."

And now you have a mighty paunch, thought Chain. A serving maid refilled the bishop's golden goblet with rich red wine. The fat man grinned at her, then reached out, patting her behind. Chain looked away. He had noted that no words of thanks had been offered to the Source for the food, and now he had seen that the bishop was a lecher as well as a glutton. It was dispiriting, to say the least.

He listened politely to the bishop's conversation, the story of his vastly successful life, the seemingly endless anecdotes illustrating his wisdom, his intellect, and the huge respect he enjoyed throughout the empire. ". . . The king complimented me on it. He said he had rarely met a man with so much . . ."

Wind, thought Chain.

"Why did you invite me to take part in your tourney?" he asked, more to change the subject than to hear the answer.

"These highlanders need keeping in their place," the bishop told him. "They are a troublesome, rebellious people. Only recently they tried to kill our Moidart. It will be good for them to see the superiority of the Varlish fighting man."

"And they shall," said Gorain, leaning in to the bishop. "I shall break their bones, their hopes, and their hearts." He drained his goblet and raised it toward the serving girl.

"You have drunk enough Uisge," said Chain.

"What are you, my mother?" Gorain asked with a laugh.

Something inside Chain Shada snapped. He looked at Gorain and for the first time allowed himself to see beyond the man's talent. Yes, he had the potential to be great, but not the discipline.

Chain took a deep breath. "No, I am not your mother," he said. "I am the man who thought you were the heir to my crown. I was wrong. Do as you please, Gorain. You are my protégé no longer." Chain rose from his seat and bowed to the bishop. "My thanks for the meal, sir. And now I must prepare."

"Wait, Chain," Gorain called out. "There's no need for this. I'm sorry. All right?"

Chain ignored him and walked away.

Gorain's face darkened. "I don't need you," he called out. "I'll fight my way to the top without you."

Chain was angry with himself as he left the mansion. He turned away the offer of a carriage to return him to his lodgings and strolled out through the gates and down the wide avenue that led to the cathedral. It was an imposing building, twin-spired and shaped like a vast white crown. The doors were open, and he walked inside, enjoying the cool, calm atmosphere. Statues of the saints lined the walkways, and the rows of pews were scattered with red velvet cushions. A young priest was placing sheets of paper on the seats.

"Good day, Brother," he said. "May the Source bless you."

"Mostly he has," said Chain. Many of the statues were decked with golden laurels, and there were paintings on the wall in gilded frames. "This is a rich church, I see."

"Indeed, Brother. Our congregation numbers the finest citizens of Eldacre, rich and powerful men who see to our every need."

"In my experience the rich are seldom the finest," Chain told him. "But I am just a poor fighting man, born in a hovel. What would I know?"

The priest gave him an uncertain smile, then carried on laying prayer sheets on the pews.

Chain walked around the cathedral for a while, then returned to the sunlight.

Be honest with yourself, he thought. You always knew Gorain was undisciplined and uncouth. So why end it now? He still has more talent than any fighter you've seen in ten years. He could still make you a fortune.

You are thirty-six years old, he reminded himself. Soon you'll have to retire or endure the indignity of some young, strong challenger beating you to your knees.

Why now? The question came back at him. It was seeing Gorain in the company of the fat lecher and realizing that Gorain himself was little better. He was a braggart and, like most braggarts, filled with fear. Some men fought because they loved winning, others because they feared losing. Gorain was in the latter group. He would never be a champion.

"I'll fight on for a while," Chain told himself aloud. "And when some young bastard sinks me, he'll at least know he beat the best."

◇ 5 ◇

TAYBARD JAEKEL DID not enjoy feast days, though he pretended to. Sometimes he could almost convince himself. Today was not one of those days. Dressed in his best shirt and breeches and an old coat of his father's, he joined others from Old Hills on the two-hour walk to Eldacre. The threadbare white wig had belonged to his grandfather, and he could feel the sweat prickling his scalp as he walked.

The day was fine, but there were rain clouds in the distance, and the air was still chilly with the memory of winter. Some way ahead he could see Kaelin Ring walking with Chara Ward. She looked beautiful in a simple dress of corn yellow and a pale blue shawl. Taybard watched her closely. Every now and again she would reach out and touch Kaelin's arm as she chatted to him or lean in to whisper something, allowing her shoulder to brush against his. Taybard tried not to stare. He transferred his gaze to Kaelin's aunt Maev. She was strolling beside the huge one-eyed clansman Jaim Grymauch. Everyone said he was little more than an outlaw destined for the rope, but Taybard had a sneaking admiration for the man. The previous summer he had fought three tough men in a tavern brawl, emerging victorious. Behind them came Banny and his mother, Shula. Taybard liked Banny. There was no malice in the boy, and Taybard had stopped Luss Campion and Kammel Bard from tormenting him. For some reason Luss hated Banny, though when pressed, he could not explain why.

There were maybe fifty people on the road now, with more joining as they passed the outer houses of the village.

Slowly they trooped up the hill, cresting it to see the distant castle and the sprawling town below. The wind was picking up. Taybard was relieved to see the rain clouds being pushed back over the mountains.

Luss Campion and Kammel Bard emerged from the last house, saw him, and strolled to join him.

Both young men were wearing black coats and sporting ill-fitting wigs. "Looks like the rain will keep off," said Luss.

"Aye."

Luss and Kammel were also wearing their best clothes, though, as in Taybard's case, "best" meant least mended. There was a patch on Luss' coat, and Kammel's breeches were thin, the original black now showing as powder gray. Taybard's polished shoes had holes in the soles and had been packed with paper.

True, they were smarter than most of the clan folk, but once they were segregated at the feast, all three of them would look exactly what they were: "kilted Varlish." All around them would be the citizens of Eldacre in their finery, spending silver money at the many stalls. Taybard had three copper daens in his pocket: enough for a jug of ale and a piece of pie in the Varlish area.

"Have you heard about Grymauch?" asked fat Kammel Bard.

"What?" inquired Taybard.

"He's entered the bouts."

Luss laughed. "He obviously hasn't heard about Gorain Wollam and Chain Shada. Either one will rip his bald head from his ugly shoulders."

"Chain Shada is going to fight?" asked Taybard, astonished. The man was a legend.

"So my father says," Kammel replied.

"Varlish against clansmen? Is it allowed?"

"Maybe our boys will fight with one hand tied behind their backs," said Luss. "Make it more even."

Taybard said nothing. Chara Ward had linked arms with Kaelin Ring. The sun was glinting on her golden hair, and Taybard felt as if someone were slowly twisting a knife in his gut.

"That shouldn't be allowed," said Kammel Bard. "It should be an offense for clan filth to match with Varlish girls. My father says it pollutes our bloodlines. Weaker races should be forbidden to wed outside their own kind."

"Your grandmother was Pannone, for heaven's sake!" snapped Taybard. "Everybody knows it. Does that make you polluted, Kammel?"

"That's a stinking lie! You take that back."

"That's not a good thing to say to a friend," put in Luss Campion.

The moment was broken by the sound of hoofbeats on the road. The column moved aside as four Beetlebacks cantered by. Taybard recognized Sergeant Bindoe in the lead. He slowed his horse as they neared Kaelin Ring and Jaim Grymauch, but he was not looking at them. He was staring at Chara Ward.

"There's someone else who doesn't like to see our Varlish blood tainted," said Luss Campion. "Uncle Jek knows how to treat the bastards."

"I do not like the man," said Taybard.

"Maybe you'd like to tell him *he* has clan blood," snapped Kammel Bard.

Taybard turned to his friend, seeing the hurt on his face. "I am sorry, Kammel. Friends should not cause each other pain." He held out his hand.

Kammel ignored it. "Do you take it back?"

Taybard felt his anger rising. "I tell you what. Tomorrow you and I will go the church and look at the records of births. They go back two hundred years. We will find the entry for your grandmother and see what it says. If it says Varlish, I will drop to my knees and beg forgiveness."

"A pox on you!" shouted Kammel Bard. "You are my friend no longer." With that he stalked away.

"Why did you do that?" asked Luss Campion.

"By the Sacrifice, Luss, you *know* he has Pannone blood. So how stupid is it to talk of taint and pollution? Most of the Old Hills Varlish have some highland links. Everyone knows it. It's why when we get to the feast, the town Varlish will look down their noses at us. It's why they call us 'the kilts.' Do you feel you are a lesser man for it?"

"There's no clan blood in my line," said Luss Campion. "And I'll kill anyone who says different. My blood is strong. My blood is Varlish."

"Strong blood? These clansmen crossed the sea and sacked Stone hundreds of years ago. They crushed every army that came against them. We defeated them by burning their villages, destroying their crops, butchering their women and children. They are not weak, Luss. They are just conquered."

"Which is what makes them weak. The Varlish are unconquered and invincible. However, it is obvious where your loyalties lie. But then, just like poor Kammel, you are also part clan. At least he has the strength to resist the call of his tainted blood and desires to be Varlish. What is it you desire, Tay? A clan wife and a little home carved from dirt?"

Taybard could think of nothing to say. Thoughts whirled in his mind, but he could find no voice for them. Yes, he was proud of being Varlish, but why did that fact need to be allied with contempt for others? And if the clans are so weak and spineless and lacking in ambition, why do we fear them? he thought.

Luss Campion walked away from him to join Kammel Bard.

Taybard was irritated with himself for alienating them. He had experienced no difficulty with traditional Varlish values before he had met the Wyrd. He had believed in his people with iron simplicity.

His trouble had begun when she had told him he was Rigante.

Her words had washed across his soul, and his heart had soared, though he knew not why.

* * *

The various entrance channels to the Five Fields were growing busy as the first of the arrivals from Old Hills approached them. Red-cloaked stewards stood at the entrances. The Varlish spectators produced small red disks stamped with their family tax numbers and were ushered to the right, while the clan folk waited patiently to be allowed through to the left.

Kaelin Ring was feeling uncomfortable. Once again Chara Ward had linked arms with him and showed no desire to separate and follow her Varlish neighbors through. Luss Campion and Kammel Bard had already passed the entrance, and Taybard Jaekel was presenting his disk to a steward. A Beetleback moved through the throng. Kaelin glanced at him. It was Sergeant Bindoe, his thin hatchet face wearing a scowl. He approached Chara Ward.

"This way, miss," he said, beckoning her to follow him. Chara seemed uncertain. "The Varlish area is to the right," he told her. "You are standing in the wrong line."

"I know where I am standing, Sergeant," she replied. "It is not unlawful to enter the clan area."

"That's right, miss. Once the festivities are under way, there is freedom of movement for all Varlish. But the festivities are not under way, and you have not yet presented your disk to the steward. Once you have done so and entered the correct area, you can do as you please." People were staring now, and Chara reddened.

"Best go, lass," said Jaim Grymauch. "We'll see you later."

Chara stood for a moment, then disengaged her arm from Kaelin's and crossed to stand behind Taybard Jaekel. Sergeant Bindoe followed her, then leaned in and whispered something that Kaelin did not hear. Taybard Jaekel did, however, and Kaelin saw the young man's face go white with anger. He swung around, but Bindoe had walked on.

Chara seemed close to tears. Kaelin heard Taybard say: "Ignore him, Chara. I'd be proud for you to walk with me, and I'll escort you back to the clan area once we're through."

The clan line began to move. Kaelin glanced back, but

Chara and Taybard had vanished into the throng. Jaim laid his hand on the young man's shoulder. "I have to register my presence for the tourney. I'll see you by the pieman's stall in a while." Kaelin nodded, still distracted by the events at the entrance.

Aunt Maev hooked her arm in his. "Don't let Bindoe get to you, Kaelin. The man is scum. Put it from your mind. Look!" she said, pointing across the field. "There are jugglers. I have always loved to watch their skills."

Banny tapped his friend on the arm. "Shall we explore?" he asked.

"Why not?" answered Kaelin.

For some while the two young men wandered the area. Already there were thousands of spectators, and fresh columns of new arrivals could be seen on the hill roads leading from Eldacre. The Five Fields were filling fast. To the north was the equestrian area, largely a Varlish entertainment, since most highlanders owned no horses. Special collapsible fences had been erected to reduce the risk to the horses and riders, while at the far end straw dummies had been fastened to several rails for the martial events. Kaelin enjoyed those events, watching the horsemen thunder across the field, their sabers shining in the sunlight as they slashed at the heads of the dummies. The skill of the horsemen was high; as the straw men were attached to ropes and hidden, men would tug and sway them as the riders approached. The object was to lop the heads from as many straw men as possible in four passes.

Most of the stalls in the large clan area had already been set up; crafts such as pottery, jewelry, clothing, and cutlery had been placed around the eastern perimeter. Cattle dealers and merchants selling agricultural merchandise were in the south. Here there was much activity. Clansmen loved to engage in barter. A man could sit happily for several hours arguing the merits—if he owned it—of a particular plow or work ox or the demerits of a pony or a wolfhound if he did not.

Kaelin and Banny moved through the throng, heading for

the cluster of food stalls and the rough benches set close by.
Kaelin kept glancing across to the Varlish area, seeking sign
of Chara Ward.

The smell of roasting meats from cooking pits made him
realize how hungry he was, and the slab of dark bread and
fresh butter at breakfast seemed insubstantial after the two-
hour walk. He fingered the few coins in his pocket and decided to wait until dusk.

At the center of the field three circles had been marked out
with ropes, and already two men were fighting within one of
them. As the blows rained in, the crowd moved closer. Kaelin
recognized one of the fighters, a herdsman from the High
Pines settlement, half a day south of Old Hills. The fight was
brutal and short, the herdsman catching his opponent with a
high right cross that hurled him from his feet.

"I didn't think the fights were due to start yet," said Banny.

A tall clansman standing close by turned and said: "This is
not the tournament proper. There were thirty-three entrants,
so two had to scrap to decide which of them would be allowed
to take part." The man suddenly swore. Kaelin saw he was
staring at a big dark-haired man who was strolling away from
the bout. Despite the heavily muscled upper frame, he moved
with easy grace.

"Who is he?" asked Kaelin.

"Chain Shada. He is the Varlish champion. One hundred
bouts, they say, and never defeated. He gets to crush the
winner of the tourney." The anger and contempt in the man's
voice surprised Kaelin.

"Why do you say 'crush'?"

"Think on it, lad. Thirty-two fighters. The man who faces
Chain Shada will have fought five times in a single day, while
Shada himself will be untouched by pain and exhaustion. In-
deed, look at it the other way. If Chain Shada had to suffer five
tough fights, *I'd* probably be able to take him in the sixth.
Still, it won't be so bad," the man added with a rueful smile.
"The other Varlish fighter is said to be almost as good as

Shada, so I guess they'll fight each other in the final. It will be good to see one Varlish pound upon another."

"My uncle Jaim will beat them all," Kaelin said loyally.

"Grymauch is fighting?"

"Aye."

"I'm not sure I'll stay to see that," the man said sadly.

"He is a great fighter."

"I know that, lad. He is also one-eyed." He held up his hand. "How far is my hand from your face?"

"Just over two feet."

"Do you know how you estimated that?"

"Of course. I can see it."

"Yes. Both your eyes focused on the hand. It is why we have two eyes, so that we can estimate depth and distance. A one-eyed man has no true perception of depth. Added to which his field of vision is restricted. Grymauch is tough, and by heaven, he's a highlander to walk the mountains with, but I don't want to see him step into the circle with either of those bastards. He'll be lucky if he isn't blinded."

Aunt Maev had raised a similar objection, and Kaelin felt suddenly fearful. He had goaded Grymauch into fighting, and if anything happened to the big man, it would be his fault. He moved away from the circle, scanning the crowd. Banny came alongside.

"You think he was right?"

"Can you see Grymauch?"

"No."

Together they made their way back across to the food area. Eventually they found Jaim sitting beneath a dead tree. He was drinking from a clay cup. "I hope that is not Uisge or ale," said Kaelin, dropping down to sit beside him. "Aunt Maev will cut off your ears and give them back to you as a necklace."

Jaim grinned. "It is water, Ravenheart."

"I don't want you to fight, Grymauch," said Kaelin.

Jaim looked surprised. "You don't want to see me pound on those Varlish? Why?"

"You could be hurt by them."

"I *will* be hurt by them. No one steps into the circle without knowing there will be pain. Now, what is really troubling you?"

Kaelin sat silently for a moment. "They are circle warriors. They do this all the time. It is their craft. Chain Shada has fought a hundred times and never lost."

"I know. I saw him fight once. He moves like a dancer. Every time his opponent hit him, he rolled and swayed. It must have been like trying to punch a leaf in the wind. It was beautiful to see."

"And you think you can beat him?"

"It is not about beating him, Kaelin," said Grymauch. "It is about being willing to face him. We are a conquered race. I cannot argue with that; it is a sad fact of history. But I am not conquered. I am Rigante. There is no man on earth I am frightened to face."

"You have only one eye. You could lose it."

"Aye, and a tree could fall on me. Now, you two lads go off and enjoy yourselves. I have a bout in a short while, and I need to focus my mind. Off with you." Grymauch leaned back against the tree and closed his eye. Kaelin wanted to say more, but Banny tapped his shoulder, and the two youths walked away.

"I wish I had never mentioned the tourney," said Banny.

Chain Shada watched Gorain's first two bouts and felt a sense of embarrassment. All the Varlish fighter's bouts had been scheduled to take place on the raised wooden circle so that he would not have to suffer the indignity of crossing into the clan area and fighting on mud surrounded by rope.

Gorain's first fight had lasted no more than three or four heartbeats: a heavy straight left followed by a crushing right cross. The big highlander had hit the wooden floor face first, where he lay unmoving. The Varlish crowd had roared its approval. The second bout had been longer but only because

Gorain had toyed with the man, a bearded cattle herder with ten times more guts than skill. He had kept coming, walking into Gorain's lefts, which had snapped back his head. Gorain was pulling his punches, picking the man apart with ease. When he finally went to work in the fourth period, he all but tore him apart, keeping him on his feet with wicked uppercuts before sending him sprawling to the canvas with a clubbing left. The man's face was cut to pieces, and attendants had to carry him away before wiping the blood from the boards.

Chain had had enough. Rising from his seat, he wandered across to one of the select dining areas. The red-cloaked steward bowed as he entered. "I think the kilts will remember your visit, sir," he said.

Chain nodded and moved inside. A young woman brought him a goblet of crushed apple juice, and Chain walked through to the rear, where several benches had been set close to an iron brazier filled with glowing coals. He saw the young white-haired officer—Mulgrave, was it?—talking to several stewards and beyond him a black-garbed, hawk-eyed nobleman in conversation with the fat red-caped bishop. Chain cursed inwardly and was about to swing away when the bishop saw him.

"My dear man," he boomed. "Do join us. Let me introduce you to our Moidart."

The fighter approached them, towering over both men. He bowed to the Moidart, and their eyes met. Chain felt something cold touch his blood. This, he knew instinctively, was a dangerous man.

"I am honored to meet you, my lord."

"I trust you will ensure that this nonsense ends well," said the Moidart. The bishop's face was flushed with embarrassment.

"How should it end, sir?" countered Chain.

"It should never have begun, sir," the Moidart told him. "It is foolishness in the extreme. But at close of day the arm raised in victory must be Varlish. You understand this? Anything else would be . . . perilous. For all concerned."

"It is merely an entertainment for our people," put in the bishop. "There is no peril, my lord."

"You are an idiot. You explain it to him, fighter. Tell him the danger."

Chain looked into the bishop's eyes. The man was frightened. "Even the strongest fighters, the finest champions, can be caught by a lucky punch which scrambles their brains. Or they can meet a man who just won't quit. Or they could slip on a blood-covered board just as their opponent throws a wild blow. Nothing is certain."

"But . . . but . . . Gorain said he could defeat any clansman."

"In theory he should do just that," said Chain.

"If he does lose," said the Moidart, "you will destroy the man who beats him."

"I am here to fight an exhibition bout, my lord. If Gorain should lose—which is extremely unlikely—the man who beats him will have fought five or six times today. He will be in no condition to face me."

"Then you will have little difficulty in crushing him," said the Moidart. "The consequences of any alternative outcome will be severe." The Moidart walked away without another word, the bishop trailing after him.

Chain was angry now, though he did not allow it to show. Leaving his drink untouched, he left the area and walked out into the crowd. Everywhere he went people smiled and waved; some even bowed as he passed.

He did not return to the raised dais but wandered instead into the clan area. There no one bowed, but he felt eyes upon him. Coming north had been a huge mistake. He had lost his protégé and was now caught in the middle of a potential crisis.

"You don't look so tough," said a voice. Chain glanced to his right and saw a burly highlander wearing a ragged kilt and a long cloak. The man was holding a jug and was swaying slightly.

"Looks can be deceiving," Chain said mildly.

Two stewards moved in swiftly, grabbing the man. Chain realized they had been following him. "Let him go. Now!" said Chain. "We were having a conversation."

"Sir, we are instructed—"

"Leave him and go about your business. I do not need an escort."

The men stood for a moment, then released the highlander. "Now, I thank you for your concern, boys, but leave me be."

The two stewards seemed uncertain, but they left and returned to the Varlish field.

The drunken highlander swore at Chain. "Always need backup, don't you?"

"Certainly seems that way," Chain told him. The fighter moved on. Another bout was under way in one of the mud circles. He paused to watch. A huge one-eyed man was fighting. His opponent was younger, with good shoulders and a long reach. The two circled for a few moments, then the young man moved in swiftly, feinting with a left and then throwing a right. It was a good move. The one-eyed man swayed away and delivered a chopping left that exploded against the younger man's jaw. His legs gave way, and he pitched to the ground.

"Grymauch! Grymauch!" chanted the crowd. The one-eyed man raised his arms and bowed to them. Then he saw Chain.

"Would you like a little lesson, Varlish!" he called.

"Perhaps later. That was a good blow."

"The . . . Pannone . . . hammer," said the man. Chain noted the hesitation. So did the crowd, and they laughed.

"You need to look to your comrade," said Chain. "I fear he is drowning in the mud."

The fighter glanced down, then dropped to his knees, rolling the unconscious man to his back. It was true. His mouth and nostrils were caked with mud. The one-eyed man wiped it away, and the stricken fighter suddenly gasped for breath.

Chain walked on, stopping by a stall selling trinkets. They were cheap, mostly of copper or bronze, but one or two shone with silver. As he was looking at the jewelry, a man came alongside him. He saw that it was Mulgrave.

"Are you enjoying yourself, sir?" asked the white-haired young officer.

"I like to see the sun shine. Are you now escorting me?"

"It would be . . . unfortunate to suffer an incident on a feast day. There is a good deal of strong drink available everywhere, and a riot could ensue if a drunken highlander were to attack the Varlish champion."

"Let us walk awhile," said Chain.

"It will be my pleasure, especially if we walk back to the Varlish fields."

"As you say, Captain." The two men crossed the field and went through the entry channel. "What is going on here?" asked Chain as they paused by a small wood at the northern tip of the Varlish field.

"In what way?"

"This absurd need to crush the highlanders' spirit."

Mulgrave sighed. "You are asking the wrong man to justify it. However, I will try to explain it. It is, you will hear, a historical problem. You are from the far south. You have no idea of the festering hatreds in these mountains. Old men still remember the rebellions, the clans sweeping down upon townsfolk and farmers, the savagery and the bloodshed. The clans do not forget the days—not so distant—when soldiers raided their settlements, killing their wives and children. The fear among our own people is that if pride is allowed to seep back into clan mentality, they will rise again. This is why the Moidart is angry about the tournament. Is Gorain going to win it?"

"He should," said Chain.

"He'd better," said Mulgrave. "The Moidart does not suffer disappointment lightly."

"I would guess that."

The sun shone brightly for much of the afternoon. Gaise Macon, riding the palomino, won the first of the equestrian events, the twelve jumps. His victory was received with great acclaim from the citizens, though Gaise himself seemed less than ecstatic. Captain Mulgrave won the saber event, lopping eleven "heads." Gaise finished fourth in that event and seemed far more pleased than he had with his own victory.

As they groomed their mounts, Mulgrave asked him about it. The young man put aside his brush. "I won because the last rider's horse balked at the water jump."

"I saw."

"Did you also see that the rider intentionally balked?"

"I did," agreed Mulgrave.

"So it was not a win at all. The rider allowed the Moidart's son to claim the crown."

"I am glad you spotted it," said Mulgrave. "Many men would not have. It was done skillfully, and I doubt many in the crowd noticed it. However, there were some fine riders today, and second place—which you won fairly—is a matter for pride."

"Why did he do it, Mulgrave?"

"You do not really need to ask that, sir. Your father is not a forgiving man, and the rider was one of his officers. I expect that he feared retribution."

"A sad state of affairs," muttered Gaise. "But understandable, I suppose. Have you seen Gorain yet?"

"I have. Most accomplished. A fine example of Varlish manhood."

"Who is he fighting next?" asked Gaise.

"I understand it is a blacksmith from the Pinance's region. Last year's champion. I believe his name is Badraig."

"Yes, I saw him last year. Big man, very powerful. What about the other semifinal?"

"I do not know the result, sir. They were fighting while we were competing in the sabers. A one-eyed man was taking part."

* * *

By late afternoon Kaelin had still not found Chara Ward, and he was growing irritated. There were thousands of people in the fields now, and trying to hunt down one girl was like seeking a single leaf in an autumn forest. At one stage he had even lost touch with Banny, finding him by accident as he sought the latrine area.

Kaelin watched Jaim Grymauch win his semifinal in a fight that lasted only a few minutes, congratulated his uncle, then once more sought out Chara. Had he had any sense, he would have shouted out a meeting place to her as she vanished into the Varlish area. He and Banny wandered through the various stalls close to the fighting circles, then angled out toward the cattle markets. "Why would she be there?" asked Banny. "Her relatives are not herders."

"She won't be, but it is higher ground," Kaelin told him. "We'll be able to see better."

As they walked, they heard a sudden roar from the Varlish field. Kaelin glanced back. From there he could see the small figures in the wooden circle. One man was down. Attendants were gathering around him. Banny, whose eyes were not strong, asked: "Is it the Varlish?" Kaelin shook his head. Gorain was standing, hands on hips. Then he pulled a towel from his belt and wiped his face. Moments later another roar went up. "What are they cheering for now?" asked Banny. "The fight is over."

"I don't know, Banny. I'm not there, am I?"

"Sorry, Kaelin. Hey, there's Tay. Maybe he knows where Chara went."

Kaelin saw the stocky figure of Taybard Jaekel making his way up the hill. Crowds were swirling around below, groups of people gathering and speaking in an animated fashion. They saw Taybard stop and listen, then the young Varlish began to climb once more. Kaelin did not want to have to talk to him. He was still nonplussed over the fight and had no wish to find himself in another disagreement. And yet he needed to know. With a soft curse he moved to intercept the youth. Taybard glanced up as he saw him. He neither scowled nor smiled but stood still, his eyes wary.

"Have you seen Chara?" asked Kaelin.

"No. Bindoe said he wanted to talk to her and told me to go away. I lost them in the crowd then."

"Why is everyone gathering below?" asked Banny.

"Gorain killed Badraig. Broke his neck."

"That's what the Varlish swine were cheering," hissed Kaelin.

"Aye," Taybard Jaekel said sadly. "That's what the swine were cheering. Makes you sick, doesn't it?" With that he walked away.

"Your uncle fights him next," said Banny.

Kaelin was staring after Taybard Jaekel. The youth was heading out through the gates toward Old Hills and home.

"What did you say?"

"Grymauch fights him next."

"Aye." Kaelin was less worried than he had been. Grymauch had fought four times, and not one bout had lasted long. He had a swelling on the cheekbone under his empty left socket and a few bruises on his upper body, but he had emerged triumphant. Kaelin could no longer imagine any man thrashing him. He glanced again at the forlorn figure of Taybard Jaekel. On impulse Kaelin ran after him, calling out as he ran. Taybard stopped and waited.

"If you want a fight, I'm not in the mood," Taybard said as Kaelin paused before him.

"I don't want a fight, Tay. But the feast is only an hour away. It would be a shame to miss it. Why don't you come with Banny and me?"

"You want a Varlish at your feast?"

"Whisht, man, you're an Old Hills neighbor. We'll watch Grymauch whip the southerner and then eat till our bellies swell."

Taybard stood silently, his mind racing. He wanted to apologize to Kaelin for the fight. He wanted to say how sorry he was that men cheered when a highlander died in the circle.

He wanted to tell him about the Wyrd and about his jealousy concerning Chara. He looked into Kaelin's dark eyes.

"Aye, I could eat," he said.

And the three youths walked back to the clan fields.

◇ 6 ◇

THE VARLISH SEATING tiers around the fighting circle were
full, and hundreds more townsfolk crowded around the
base as the two fighters made their way to the boards. On the
other side of the circle clan men and women were packed so
closely together that there was little room for movement.

The sun had gone down, and tall lanterns had been set
around the circle, casting flickering shadows over the two
large men who were about to fight. Gorain, bare-chested and
wearing tight-fitting gray leggings and knee-length riding
boots, waved to the Varlish crowd, cocking his fist and laughing. He was unmarked, only the last of his bouts having
stretched beyond a few periods. He was perhaps an inch
shorter than his opponent, but his breadth of shoulder was
enormous, and the lantern light glinted on his finely sculpted
muscles. On the other side of the circle Jaim Grymauch
seemed ponderous and massively ugly. He, too, sported huge
shoulders and arms, but there was nothing of the beauty of
Gorain. Stripped to the waist, he looked more like a bear than
a man, clumsy and slow.

Sitting on the highest tier, Gaise Macon could feel the fear
emanating from the clan crowd. It was as if they were wit-
nessing an execution rather than a contest. Gorain began to
move through a series of stretches, cartwheeling his arms and
swaying from side to side. The one-eyed clansman watched
him. The keeper of the sands took his place beside the circle,
and the two white-cloaked adjudicators held a short confer-
ence before one climbed into the circle. The crowd fell silent.

The adjudicator, facing the Varlish tiers, bowed. "This contest," he called out, "will be of unlimited duration, ending only when one of the contestants can no longer climb to his feet before the sands run out. Each period will end when either contestant drops his knee to the board and will resume when the sand keeper orders the horn to be blown. No blow shall be struck after a contestant has indicated the end of a period. Under the rules of valorous combat any contestant who grapples, gouges, bites, or kicks will have the prize forfeited."

Gaise listened as the adjudicator named the contestants. The roar for Gorain shook the tiers, and the fighter responded by raising both arms and bowing. The clans cheered for the one-eyed fighter, but the sound was muted.

Gorain walked to the side of the circle and called out to one of the attendants. The man brought him a strip of black cloth, which he tied around his head, obscuring the sight in his left eye.

"A noble act," said Gaise to Mulgrave.

"Indeed, sir, unless it is meant as mockery."

The bright moon emerged from behind a cloud, and a chilly wind blew across the circle, making one of the lanterns gutter. An attendant relit it with a taper.

Gaise looked around and saw Chain Shada sitting some twenty feet to his right. He was leaning forward, his chin resting on his fist. He, too, wore the fighting leggings. A blanket was draped over his bare shoulders.

The adjudicator climbed down from the circle, and the keeper of the sands raised his arm. A single horn blast sounded.

Gorain moved swiftly across the circle. Grymauch advanced to meet him. Gorain feinted with a left, then sent a right hand whipping toward Grymauch's blind side. The clansman stepped inside the blow, hammering a right uppercut to Gorain's belly that almost lifted the Varlish from his feet. Air whooshed from Gorain's lungs. Grymauch followed it with a left cross that cracked against Gorain's cheek. The

Varlish managed to roll with the blow. Regaining balance, he blocked a right and sent a straight left slamming into Grymauch's mouth, snapping back his head. The clansman was forced back. Gorain bore in, punches thudding into Grymauch's belly. Grymauch suddenly sidestepped to the right while snapping out a left hand that took Gorain high on the right cheek. The Varlish, off balance, stumbled and almost fell. Grymauch followed in. Gorain ducked his head and counterattacked: three punches to the belly and a left uppercut to the face. Grymauch stumbled. Gorain threw a big left, but the covering of his left eye made him misjudge the depth, and the blow sailed harmlessly past Grymauch's jaw. The clansman attacked again. Gorain hit him four times without reply, big meaty blows that rocked the highlander. The Varlish were cheering themselves hoarse. Gorain hammered a punch to Grymauch's bearded chin that half spun him. Gorain rushed in, hitting him twice more but missing with a flurry of punches as Grymauch swayed and rolled. An overhand right cannoned into the blind left side of Grymauch's face. Blood splayed from a gash to his cheek. A huge roar greeted the blow, and for a moment Gaise thought the clansman was about to fall. Instead he leapt forward, slamming a bone-jarring left into Gorain's face. As Gorain fell back, Grymauch dropped to one knee, ending the period. The Varlish crowd booed and shouted.

"Canny," said Mulgrave. "He needs time to clear his head from that big right."

"They seem evenly matched," put in Gaise.

"In raw talent, perhaps," said Mulgrave. "But Gorain has more learned skill. He is also younger."

"You think he will win?"

"He should, sir. He has the skill and the strength. The question is, Does he have the heart?"

That was a question occupying the mind of Chain Shada as he watched the first period. Gorain had been foolish to don the eye patch. The clansman was well used to being single-sighted, whereas many of Gorain's punches were missing their mark and others were landing off target. Gorain had taken the man too lightly. That first uppercut had winded him badly, sapping his strength. Gorain had also made another mistake that could prove costly. Unused to being at the center of attention, he had gloried in it and not taken rests between bouts. Instead he had moved among the crowd, bathing in the adulation. He had also, as Chain had witnessed, been drinking.

Under normal circumstances, having already severed his connections with Gorain, Chain would have been unconcerned by his stupidity. Not so now. They were linked in a political game that left a filthy taste in Chain's mouth. Both fighters were tired, and if the fight were to end now, Chain knew he could beat them both—probably at the same time. Which was exactly the point that caused the foul taste. Chain Shada was a fighting champion. He fought the best—at their best. Here—if events turned bad—he would merely be an executioner.

The second period followed the pattern of the first, with Gorain landing more blows but the highlander absorbing them and putting in two or three powerful strength-sapping counters. Gorain came back strongly at the end with combination rights and lefts that rocked the clansman, pitching him to the boards on his back. Gorain walked to the edge of the circle and raised his arms once more to the Varlish, who yelled and bayed in their joy.

Chain Shada watched the clansman. The man rolled to his knees and sat back quietly, gathering his strength. There was blood on his face streaming from a cut to his cheek and another to his mouth. He did not rise but sat watching the keeper of the sands. As the keeper raised his hand, so, too, did the highlander rise.

The crowd expected the fight to be finished now. Chain Shada did not.

Gorain rushed in, believing his opponent to be weakened

and groggy. He was met by a hard left and a right cross that pitched him from his feet, slamming him headfirst into the boards. There was silence from the Varlish crowd, but it was more than made up for by the thunderous sound erupting from the clan area. Chain noted that the fighter did not acknowledge the crowd. He was standing quietly, taking deep, even breaths, allowing his body to recuperate. Not so Gorain, who angrily pushed himself to his feet. There was blood on his mouth, and he stalked to the side of the circle, calling for water. An attendant handed him a cup. He swished the liquid around in his mouth, then spit it out.

Chain knew what Gorain was feeling. Twelve years earlier Chain had met a man who just would not submit. He absorbed every blow and kept coming back. Such a man became a living question that wormed its way into the soul of a fighter, shrinking his courage, eating away at his self-belief. The fight had been a watershed experience for the young Chain Shada. It had lasted for forty-four periods before, weary almost to the point of surrender, he had unleashed one last murderous combination. His opponent had gone down hard and had not been able to rise. Only Chain ever knew how close he had come to quitting.

Now Gorain was facing the same maggot in the soul.

Chain watched his former protégé intently. Gorain reached up and pulled clear the eye patch, hurling it out of the circle. The horn sounded, and he once more moved in. For the next three periods he pounded the clansman, blows raining in from every side, seeking to overpower his opponent with sheer strength. But Gorain was tired now, and many of the punches lacked penetration. He, too, was taking punishment. Grymauch had begun to work the body, slamming big punches to Gorain's midsection. All three periods ended with the highlander dropping to one knee. On the last Gorain threw a low blow after the clansman touched the boards. The surprise punch slammed into Grymauch's good eye, hurling him to his back.

Chain could not believe it. In full view of the adjudicators

Gorain had broken the rules of valorous combat: no punch to be thrown after a period was ended. Even the Varlish crowd was silent, awaiting the disqualification. It did not come. Shame gripped Chain Shada then, deep and lingering. Everywhere there was silence. Grymauch rolled to his knees, shaking his head to clear it. Even by the lantern light Chain could see that the man's eye was swelling badly. Pretty soon he would be totally blind. Chain rose from his seat and walked down to where the adjudicators were standing.

He spun toward the first. "You are a disgrace," he said. The keeper of the sands was about to raise his arm. Chain grabbed it. "Not yet," he said, lifting the sand glass and turning it once more. "You will at least give him another minute after such a cowardly attack."

One of the adjudicators spoke: "The blow was struck before the clansman touched the boards."

"Be silent!" hissed Chain Shada. "There is not a man or woman here who did not see the truth. You make me disgusted to be Varlish."

Inside the circle Jaim Grymauch had rolled to his knees. His eye was almost closed, his body a sea of pain. It surprised him that he had not heard the horn, but truth to tell, he was glad he had not. Wearily he pushed himself to his feet and looked out past the crowd at the distant, moonlit mountains of Caer Druagh. All his life he had been cursed by the yoke of the Varlish. Now, here in his own mountains, he had a chance to defeat his enemy and stand triumphant before the spirits of his ancestors.

Rigante ancestors.

"I am Rigante," he whispered. He looked across at Gorain. "Come feel my hammer, little man," he said.

The horn sounded. Gorain advanced. Jaim Grymauch, his eye closing, leapt to meet him. Gorain's first blow smashed into Grymauch's face. Blood sprayed from a new cut under his right eye. A cold fury began in Grymauch then, feeding his exhausted muscles. He slammed a hard left into Gorain's jaw, following it with a right uppercut to the belly and a left cross that half spun the Varlish. Hardly able to see, he followed in with lefts and rights. The Varlish tried to cover up, dropping his head and shielding his face with his fists. Jaim stepped back and sent another right uppercut between the fists. It pulped Gorain's nose, snapping him upright—and into a murderous left hook that hurled him across the boards and out into the clan crowd. Attendants ducked under the rope sections separating Varlish from clan. They tried to lift Gorain, but the man was unconscious.

Chain Shada leaned across the keeper of the sands. The man had not turned the glass. Chain Shada did it for him. A terrible silence had fallen upon the Varlish crowd, while clansmen were dancing and shouting.

Grymauch stood in the center of the circle, trying to see through the narrow slit in his swollen eye. Time was draining away, and still Gorain had not moved.

A chant began in the Varlish crowd: "Chain Shada! Chain Shada!" Louder and louder it grew. The clans fell silent. A horn blew. The fight was over. Grymauch had won.

But entering the circle from the far side came a tall figure wearing dark gray leggings. A towel was tucked into his belt.

Grymauch stared sullenly at him. "Come for your lesson now?" he asked.

"Perhaps later," answered the man, moving closer. Grymauch's fists came up, but Chain Shada ignored them. Pulling his towel from his belt, he said: "Let me look at that eye."

Carefully Chain Shada wiped away the blood. "You need a cold compress on it, but you should be fine."

The crowd began to boo and shout. Items began to rain down on the circle. Cushions and debris, food scraps, and even a pewter tankard bounced over the wood.

An angry murmur went up from the clan ranks, and a waiting squad of Beetlebacks armed with muskets moved into position, their guns trained on the clans.

"Coward! Fight him!" screamed someone in the crowd.

"Can you walk?" Chain asked Jaim Grymauch.

"Aye, but not far."

A young dark-haired youth and a redheaded woman had climbed into the circle. "Let me take you from here, Grymauch," she said.

"Ah, you're not going to scold me, are you, Maev?"

"Not tonight. Come on, let's be going home." She looked at Chain Shada. "I thank you for your kindness, sir," she said.

Chain smiled. It seemed to him the words had been as difficult as crawling naked over broken glass. "It was a great pleasure, lady. I will see that his prize is delivered." A cushion struck Chain Shada in the back. "But it is probably best you leave now. Matters here seem to be getting out of hand."

Then, just as suddenly as it had begun, the shouting began to fade away. People in the Varlish crowd began to look toward the woods to the north. The silence when it fell was almost eerie.

"What is happening?" asked the black-haired youth.

Chain Shada walked across the debris-strewn circle. He spoke to an attendant, then walked back to where the woman was supporting the clan fighter.

"A young Varlish woman has been found dead in the woods," he said.

Galliott the Borderer would describe himself a pragmatic man. He had no ideology, though he voiced with apparent passion the prevailing political view of Varlish superiority, and no religious beliefs, though he attended church every week, sang in the choir, and held the position of honorary deacon. Galliott's belief system, if such it could be called, was based on the maintenance of the status quo: everything—and everyone—in its place. When people obeyed the Moidart's laws, society ran smoothly. When society ran smoothly, Galliott's job was easy, his life content. Principles of right and wrong played little part in Galliott's thinking, except that what was right maintained the balance, allowing society to function in the time-honored fashion, and what was wrong caused dissent, confusion, and anarchy.

In short, Galliott was a political animal. When faced with small evils, he would consider "the larger picture." This view he was now struggling to maintain.

As he stood in the lantern light looking down on the corpse of Chara Ward, he was not content. Not only because a girl was dead but because her death would—unless he acted with great care and skill—cause grave complications both to society and to his own well-being.

The apothecary Ramus was kneeling on one side of the corpse, Captain Mulgrave on the other. The rope was still about Chara Ward's neck, and her face was mottled and dark, her mouth and eyes open. When she had been discovered hanging from a high limb, Galliott had been irritated. Questions would have to be asked, forms filled in. Why was the wood not patrolled? Why had his men not seen her entering the area? At least, however, the case had been complete in itself. A young girl, obviously deranged, had come into the woods with a rope and hanged herself. The case would have been put to rest within a day or so.

Not so now, thanks to the interfering little apothecary. The officer Mulgrave glanced back to where crowds had gathered beyond the roped-off area. "Move those people back, if you would, Captain," he asked Galliott. The Borderer summoned several soldiers and relayed the orders to them. The crowds were pushed back, many of them grumbling.

Ramus was examining the dead girl's hands now, while Mulgrave held a lantern close. Chara Ward had been a pretty girl, bright and vivacious. Now she was a problem. Galliott moved in closer to the two men. "There is no evidence that she did not climb the tree and throw herself off," said Galliott. "Can you be sure, Apothecary?"

The little apothecary turned the dead girl's hand, showing the palm to Galliott. "The bole of the tree is covered in moss and fungi. The outer bark is rotten. There are no marks upon her palms, and if you examine the trunk of the tree, you will see no scuffing."

Ramus noticed that the girl's eyes were still open, and he closed them gently. "Your eyes are better than mine, Captain," he said to Mulgrave. "Take a look at her fingernails. What do you see?"

Mulgrave took the girl's hand and leaned in close. "I think it is blood," he said.

"I concur. I believe she scratched her assailant—or assailants."

Ramus transferred his attention to the lower part of the body, lifting the heavy skirt.

"What on earth do you think you are doing?" asked Galliott. Ramus ignored him and drew back the garment. Galliott turned his back on the scene, ordering his soldiers to do likewise. Had he been alone with Ramus, he would have stopped him forcibly.

Unfortunately, as the officer in charge of security, Mulgrave was the ranking soldier, and he seemed content to acquiesce in this disgusting examination.

"You may turn back now, Captain," said Ramus. "The investigation is complete."

"And what did you discover, pray?" asked Galliott, struggling to keep the anger from his voice.

"Either the girl was a virgin before the attack or a sharp implement has been used on her. I would guess the former, since there is very little blood. She was raped before being murdered."

"I agree," said Mulgrave, rising from beside the body. "There are deep foot marks beneath the limb. After the rape she was strangled before being hanged from the bough."

"How do you arrive at such a conclusion?" asked Galliott. "Why would she have been strangled first?"

Mulgrave moved away from the body. "I think it unlikely that rapists would have come ready with a rope. My guess would be that she fought for her honor and was then killed. The killer—or killers—realizing what they had done, set out to disguise their deed. They fetched a rope and strung her body up, making it appear to be suicide."

"You keep saying 'they,' Captain Mulgrave."

"She was tall and not unduly slender. I think a single man would have experienced difficulty hauling up her body and then tying the rope to the trunk."

"No witnesses have come forward," said Galliott, "and the ground around the body has now been churned. It will be difficult to identify the culprits."

"Witnesses *will* be found," said Mulgrave. "Someone carried a rope from the Five Fields and entered the wood. Others will have seen that. Added to which there is blood under four of her fingernails. At least one of the men is carrying her mark, probably on his face or neck."

Galliott felt his belly tighten. "I shall order my men to begin inquiries tomorrow," he said.

"Tonight, Captain Galliott, while the crowds are still gathered. The main questions to be asked are: Did anyone see Chara Ward enter the woods, and did anyone see men carrying ropes toward the trees?"

"It will be as you order, Captain Mulgrave. My thanks for your assistance in this matter. You too, Apothecary."

Galliott walked away, his mind racing. Mulgrave was right. Someone would have seen men with a rope. He took a deep breath. Only an hour earlier he himself had seen Sergeant Bindoe with deep scratches on his face. Bindoe maintained that they had come from a highland woman who had entered the Varlish area and refused to be escorted quietly back. Even without that damning evidence everything about the crime pointed to Bindoe. Twice before he had been accused of rapes against highland women, and twice Galliott had found ways of saving him. Not for his sake but for the honor of the Beetleback regiment.

If Bindoe was found guilty of this crime, it would throw a harsh light on previous accusations. That light could prove embarrassing to Galliott himself, perhaps resulting in his dismissal. Or worse.

Galliott weighed these thoughts in his mind as he left the woods. The girl was dead, which was a tragedy, but nothing would bring her back. Equally, nothing would be achieved if a fine officer like himself was made a scapegoat for a piece of filth like Bindoe.

I should have rid myself of him long ago, he thought. Galliott would have, except for the fact that Bindoe was an expert tracker and a fine fighting man. He was also, within his dark limitations, loyal to Galliott and the regiment.

As the Borderer walked down the short slope to where the crowds were still gathering, he spotted Sergeant Packard, an eight-year veteran and a friend of Bindoe's. Galliott called him over.

Swiftly he relayed the orders given by Mulgrave to question the crowd. "We will need all the men we have here, and any others not on watch should be sent for," he said. "After the debacle of the fight tourney there may be unrest later."

"Yes, sir."

Galliott paused, aware that he needed to choose his words with care. "Sergeant Bindoe did ask me for compassionate leave earlier. One of his relatives has taken sick in Scardyke. Find him and tell him he can leave immediately."

"I believe he has already gone back to the barracks, sir," said Packard. "He was injured by a highland woman earlier."

"I see," said Galliott. "Well, give out the orders first, then relay my message to Sergeant Bindoe."

"Yes, sir. What happened up there, sir?"

"That has still to be ascertained. We'll know more by morning."

Satisfied that he had done all he could to rectify and restore the situation, Galliott proceeded across the field to the main feasting pits. His wife, Morain, was in charge of the roasting, and she was a fine cook, probably the best in Eldacre.

As he walked through the throng, many people spoke to him, prominent citizens and merchants and even two members of the Sacrifice clergy. All wanted to know the circumstances of the girl's death. Galliott assumed the expected expression of grave concern and answered them with reassuring banalities: The situation was under control, the investigation was proceeding, his men were even now questioning possible witnesses.

"Could it have been highlanders?" asked the bishop.

Would that it could, thought Galliott. It would muddy the proceedings wonderfully. Unfortunately, the area leading into the woods was entirely within the Varlish field. He pondered the possibility of several highlanders climbing over the patrolled fence on the far side of Five Fields and making their way through to the Varlish area unnoticed. At another time it might have been expedient to let this theory fly for a while, but not today. The Gorain-Grymauch fight had left a bad feeling in the air, and it would not take much for a riot to ensue. Such a disturbance would reflect badly on Galliott's ability to control the crowd.

Aware that others were waiting for his answer, Galliott raised his voice. "No highlanders were involved," he said. "It is possible that the young woman took her own life. If not, then her assailants were certainly Varlish."

"Incredible," muttered the bishop.

"Indeed so, my lord. I am heartsick at the possibility. But be assured I shall not rest until this matter is resolved. If the girl was killed, we will hunt down her killers and make them pay."

Galliott bowed and moved on.

Despite being an animal, Bindoe was no fool. The message to take compassionate leave would be understood. He would flee the country. Then this whole sorry mess could be allowed to fade away.

The smell of prime beef wafted to his nostrils.

As he approached the roasting pit, he saw Morain coming toward him, holding a platter of meat, gravy, and freshly baked bread. He smiled at her.

"Was it that strumpet Chara Ward, as people are saying?" Morain's pinched face was set in a stern expression of disapproval.

Reaching out, Galliott stroked his wife's dark, graying hair. "Aye, it was."

"Serves her right for taking up with highland scum. Women with no sense of morality always come to a bad end."

"Indeed they do, my dove," he said, leaning in to kiss her cheek.

She was a good wife, he thought. The best.

Kaelin Ring was numb with shock and grief. The moment Chain Shada had spoken of a dead girl, he had known with terrible certainty her identity. Even so he had allowed himself to hope that it was not Chara Ward. That hope had been short-lived.

Aunt Maev had urged him to return home with her and Jaim and Banny, but he had refused. Taybard Jaekel was sitting on the ground close by, his head in his hands. Kaelin approached him and squatted down. "It's not your fault," he said.

Taybard's shoulders sagged, and when he looked up, Kaelin saw that his eyes were wet with tears. "It *is* my fault. She walked through with me. I let Bindoe lead her away. I loved her, Kaelin. And I let her down."

"We both let her down, Tay," Kaelin said softly.

"How did she die?"

"I don't know."

"I can't believe this. It's like the worst of dreams." Taybard Jaekel pushed himself to his feet. "I can't stay here. I need to be alone. Look at me. I'm weeping like a child." He walked off toward Old Hills, and Kaelin was left alone to deal with his own roiling guilt-filled thoughts. He should have found her. He should have waited by the entrance after Bindoe had forced her to pass through the Varlish entrance.

Bindoe.

The man's hatchet face appeared in his mind. Twice now Bindoe had been cleared of attacks on women. And Taybard Jaekel had seen him walking away with Chara Ward. Anger touched the young Rigante, deep and burning, tearing at his heart with talons of fire.

He was leaning on the separation fence, watching the woods, when he saw the white-haired officer Mulgrave walking down the slope. The apothecary Ramus was with him. Behind them came a stretcher party. Kaelin watched as the stretcher came into view. A blanket had been hastily thrown over the body, but a section of Chara's heavy skirt was hanging free. Kaelin felt a terrible tightness in his stomach, but the shock was still heavy upon him, and he had not yet had time to register his grief. He called out: "Captain Mulgrave! Captain Mulgrave!" The officer turned, saw him, and walked across to where he stood.

"What can I do for you, young man?"

"We met at Old Hills. Your master saved me from a beating."

"Ah, yes, I remember. Kaelin, isn't it?"

"Yes. Chara is . . . was . . . my friend. How did she die?"

"Did you see her today?"

"Yes. We came to the feast together, but she was not allowed to walk through to the clan area. She had to register first as a Varlish. She was to meet us later."

"I am sorry, Kaelin. She was murdered. We are looking for her assailants."

"You think to find them?"

"One of them at least was badly scratched—probably on the face. I think we will locate him. He will then tell us the names of his associates."

Kaelin pondered this for a moment. "Do you know Sergeant Bindoe?" he asked.

"I have heard the name," answered Mulgrave, his voice suddenly noncommittal.

"He was seen taking Chara away from the crowd."

"I see. Where did you come by this information?"

"A Varlish named Taybard Jaekel told me. He was one of the boys I was fighting when you helped me. He was in love with Chara."

"I will look into what you say."

"Aye, but will there be justice?" said Kaelin, the words tumbling out before he could stop them.

"Why should there not be?" countered Mulgrave.

"She was 'kilted Varlish.' Her family is poor, and she was seen walking with a highlander. Justice doesn't visit such people. Bindoe has twice raped highland women. Both times he has been declared innocent. I have no great expectation that this time will be any different."

"I'll not be drawn into talking of a man's guilt before I have spoken with him, but let me tell you this, highlander: When I find the people responsible, they will hang. You have my word on it."

Kaelin thanked him and walked away. Mulgrave seemed a good man, but twice now Bindoe had escaped the noose. Who was to say it would not happen a third time?

The thought continued to occupy his mind as he left Five Fields and began the long walk back to Old Hills. The numbness of shock began to wear away, leaving grief to rise in its stead. Kaelin saw again the bright smile of Chara Ward and heard her voice whispering in his mind. She had set off for a day of sunshine and laughter and had had her life ripped away in a lonely wood. Kaelin paused by a hedge and wept for Chara Ward.

He heard a whispering voice and looked around. The road was empty. The voice came again, and he recognized it as the Wyrd. It was as if he were listening to an echo from far away.

"Kaelin, can you hear me?"

"Aye," he said, pushing aside the branches of the hedge, expecting to find her on the other side. The field was empty. "Where are you?"

"I am in the Wishing Tree woods. I cannot hold this spell much longer. So do not talk—just listen. I saw the killing. I have tried to touch the spirit of the white-haired officer, but he is not of this land and my words whisper past him. Go to him. Urge him to find Bindoe. He is at the barracks, but not for long. He plans to take the Scardyke Road. If he is not apprehended now, then by dawn he will have reached the old log bridge and then will go into the lands of the Pinance. You understand me, Kaelin. Find the officer."

The words faded away.

Kaelin Ring stood very still. Yes, he could run back to Eldacre and try to find Mulgrave. What then? Bindoe had been accused twice of rape and both times had walked free. The second time his accuser had been birched for "falsehood under oath." Would there be justice? Mulgrave seemed a fair man, but then, so did Galliott the Borderer. Yet he had spoken up for Bindoe, telling the court that the sergeant had been in his company when the second rape had taken place.

The choices seemed simple to the young clansman: trust in Varlish law or find Bindoe and show him Rigante justice. A terrible stillness settled on Kaelin Ring. The night air seemed charged as he gazed at the stark outline of the distant mountains.

Do you have the nerve? he asked himself.

The old log bridge was nine miles east and south of Old Hills. If he moved swiftly, he could make it home and be at the bridge an hour before dawn.

Kaelin began to run, long easy strides that ate the miles between Five Fields and Old Hills. Just under an hour later he slipped into the rear door of Aunt Maev's house. He could hear Grymauch snoring, but apart from that the house was silent. He made his way to the old teak cabinet in the sitting room. Opening the lower door, he carefully removed the bottles of elderflower wine Aunt Maev kept there. Behind them was a polished panel. Kaelin reached in and with great care eased it out. Hidden behind it was a dusty walnut box some eighteen inches long. Kaelin lifted it and carried it to the table by the window. As he opened the lid, moonlight fell on two ornate silver dueling pistols. Beside them, in cunningly crafted compartments, were a silver powder horn, a small phial of oil, a packet of gun cotton wadding, and a box of lead balls. Once, when Maev had been away on business in Eldacre, Grymauch had shown him the pistols. "They belonged to your father," he had said. "One day they will be yours."

They had spent an hour loading and firing the pieces before cleaning them and replacing them behind the hidden panel. For a highlander to be in possession of projectile weapons such as these was a hanging offense.

Kaelin loaded both pistols and tucked them into his belt. Then he replaced the panel and lifted the wine bottles back into the cabinet. Rising, he slowly climbed the stairs to his room. From the back of a drawer he pulled clear his bone-handled skinning knife. The four-inch curved blade was as sharp as any razor. Placing knife and sheath into his coat pocket, Kaelin descended the stairs to the kitchen and stepped out into the night.

A cold breeze whipped against his face. What are you doing? he asked himself. You are a boy, for heaven's sake.

No, I am a man, he corrected himself.

I am Ravenheart.

◇ 7 ◇

Luss Campion closed his eyes tightly, but he could still see the dead face of Chara Ward, the eyes staring sightlessly up at him. The horse stumbled beneath him, and he almost fell from the saddle.

"Hell's bells, boy," said Jek Bindoe, "get a grip."

"I can't stop thinking about her," he told his uncle. "We did a terrible thing."

"She asked for it. Look at my face!"

Luss did not want to look at Bindoe, but he did, seeing the four angry gashes starting under his right eye and slicing down across his lip. Luss had gashes of his own, but they were on his soul, and he feared they would never heal.

"I don't see why I have to come with you, Uncle Jek," said Luss. "Nobody saw me with . . . her." He could not bear to say her name.

"No, but someone would have seen you when you fetched the rope. I told you to put it under your coat. Didn't I say that? Should have listened to your uncle Jek, boy. We'll get some coin in Scardyke, then head south. Maybe the capital. I've friends there. They'll find us a berth. Truth to tell, I was getting tired of the highlands, anyway."

He seemed untouched by the horror of the night, and Luss Campion felt as if he had wandered into a crazed nightmare.

"You shouldn't have done it," he said before he could stop the words.

Jek Bindoe drew rein. "*We* shouldn't have done it. You stuck your meat in her, too, boy."

"I didn't kill her."

"Oh, really?" Bindoe answered with a cruel smile. "You think she was dead *before* we hoisted her up?"

Luss remembered his hands on the rope. His eyes had been closed, but he had felt the weight as they had hauled her body up. Tears fell from his eyes. "We are going to burn in hell," he said.

Jek Bindoe's hand slashed across the youth's cheek. "You can shut up with that," he said harshly. "There ain't no hell. She was just a tart. Now she's a dead tart. Not a great loss to the world. There's plenty of tarts. Always has been, always will be. One—or two—less don't make no difference to nothing."

They rode on in silence, Luss remembering the walk to the feast and the angry exchange with Taybard Jaekel. He remembered also Chara's carefree movements as she linked arms with Kaelin Ring. Closing his eyes once more, Luss began to pray to the Source, begging forgiveness. It felt as if his prayers were seeping out into a great emptiness, echoing unheard among the stars. He made promises in his mind never, ever to commit another evil act, to spend his life doing good works. Instinctively he knew that no amount of good deeds could wash away the stain on his soul. He was damned.

They rode slowly through the darkness. Occasionally Bindoe would move up to higher ground and scan the back trail. It was unlikely, he said, that anyone would be following yet. Best to be sure, though, he told the despairing youth.

Luss half hoped they would be followed. Aye, followed and caught. Then he could hang like poor Chara Ward, and maybe his death would cancel out his sin.

Toward dawn they angled down a steep slope leading to the river. An old log bridge spanned the narrow crossing. "Best dismount and lead your horse across," said Bindoe. "Them boards is pretty slippery this time of year." The soldier stepped down and advanced onto the bridge. Luss followed him.

A dark shape moved into sight on the far side. "Who's there?" called out Jek Bindoe.

"Kaelin Ring."

"What do you want?"

"I want your heart in my hand, you murdering piece of filth."

Luss saw that Kaelin was holding two pistols. His heart began to beat faster, and fear rose in him like a forest fire. A few moments earlier he had wanted to be caught and punished. Not now. Now he just wanted the chance to ride south with Uncle Jek.

Bindoe slowly drew his cavalry saber. "I hope you know how to use them beauties, boy," he told Kaelin Ring. "Because I'm going to rip out your bowels if you don't." As he spoke, he rushed forward.

Luss saw Kaelin raise one of the pistols and pull the trigger. The flash pan flared, but no shot followed. The second pistol came up and fired. The ball smashed into Bindoe's face, shattering the teeth on the right side of his mouth and exiting in a bloody spray over his cheekbone. He staggered and almost fell, then righted himself. With an angry roar he charged at Kaelin Ring.

Instead of running, Kaelin dropped both pistols and reached into his pocket, coming up with a small knife. Flinging the sheath aside, he darted in to meet Bindoe. The saber slashed through the air. Kaelin Ring ducked under it. The knife slid into Bindoe's belly and ripped upward. A scream of mortal agony came from the dying soldier as his entrails spilled over the hands of his killer. Kaelin wrenched the knife up farther, then slammed it deep into Bindoe's chest. Pushing the soldier away, Kaelin kicked him in the chest, hurling him to the boards. His guts splayed around him, Bindoe began to shake and scream. Kaelin Ring knelt beside him. Grabbing his hair, he hefted the skinning knife and carved seven letters into his brow. As he reached the seventh, Bindoe gave out one last shuddering sigh and died.

Luss Campion saw Kaelin Ring rise up from beside the body and walk toward him. His hands and arms were covered in blood, and in his eyes there was a fury that Luss found almost inhuman.

"I'm so sorry," he said. "So sorry. I didn't want . . ."

Something cold swept across his throat. There was little pain. He tried to speak, but only a garbled noise came out. His vision swam, and he pitched to his knees. Blood was pumping from his neck. He tried to reach up and stem the flow, but Kaelin Ring pushed him to his back. The knife cut into his brow.

There was no pain.

Kaelin Ring knelt by the water's edge in the shadow of the old log bridge. The dawn sun shone down on him, and by its light he stared at his blood-covered hands and arms, at the gore-drenched white shirt, and at the red streaks and splashes on his leggings.

The frenzy had passed now, and he felt weak and disoriented, his mind numb. He found himself looking at the reflections in the water, the glints of light sparkling on a jutting white rock, and the newly opening yellow flowers on the riverbank. He wondered what made the flowers open in sunlight and close in darkness. On the far bank he saw two rabbits emerge from their burrow. Birdsong filled the trees, and the land seemed to sigh with awakening.

Kaelin's hands were sticky, and he plunged them into the water. The movement caused the rabbits to flee back to their burrow. Kaelin watched the blood swirl on the surface. Not so long ago the same blood was flowing in the veins of living men, now headless corpses sprawled on the bridge above. The water was cold, but Kaelin waded out into it, ducking down and scrubbing at his shirt, trying to remove the stains. He was shivering as he emerged some minutes later. The front of his shirt was still pale pink. He stripped it off and scrubbed it again, beating it against a rock until no sign of his excesses could be seen on the garment.

He had not known what to expect or what he would feel if he avenged Chara's murder. But there ought to have been at least a sense of satisfaction, of balance. There was none. A sweet girl was dead, and no amount of vengeance could alter that. "The blame is mine," he whispered, remembering her words in the lane outside her home.

"I don't care what people say, Kaelin."

"It is not about what they say."

"I'm not frightened of them, either. You are my friend, Kaelin. I value that friendship, and I'll not hide it to please bigots."

I should have refused, he thought.

And there was a deeper guilt. Grymauch had asked him if he was in love with Chara Ward. The truth was that Chara was a dear friend, no more than that. Her beauty touched his body but not his soul. He was not in love with her. It felt like betrayal of her memory even to acknowledge it. Would love have grown had she lived? Kaelin would never know now. What he did know was that a sweet and loving person had been murdered. She would never experience the joy of watching her children playing at her feet nor hold the hand of her husband as they watched a sunset. Chara Ward was gone, her life torn from her in a dark wood by evil men. Tears fell from Kaelin's eyes. A wracking sob burst from him, and he wept again for all that Chara Ward would never know.

Cold and trembling, Kaelin Ring at last wiped away his tears. As he did so, he smeared congealing blood to his face. He looked at his hands, picturing the deaths of Jek Bindoe and Luss Campion, recalling the awful sounds Bindoe had made as his guts spilled out and his lungs were ripped apart. Kaelin's hands began to shake, and he felt his stomach heave. For a moment he thought he would vomit, but he did not.

Rising from the river's edge, he draped his wet shirt over his shoulder and climbed to the bridge. He did not look at the mutilated corpses. Instead he gathered the silver pistols, Bindoe's saber, the skinning knife, and the discarded sheath. Pushing the pistols into his belt, he walked to Bindoe's horse and tried to mount. The horse backed away, and Kaelin half fell.

Leaving the horses where they were, he walked out across the hills, heading for home.

The morning brought fresh drama to the people of Eldacre as word spread of astonishing events that had happened during the night. People gathered on street corners to discuss the shocking news. The fighter Gorain had hanged himself, leaving behind a scrawled note expressing his shame and explaining that he had placed bets against himself and had thrown the fight against the highlander. Incredibly, it seemed that Chain Shada had been a party to the crime, and when officers of the watch had gone to question him, he had attacked them without reason. Three officers had been seriously injured and were now under the care of the surgeon. A fourth had been thrown through a window and rendered unconscious. Chain Shada had then fled, and a warrant had been issued for his arrest.

Eldacre was in an uproar. Some who had seen the fight with the one-eyed clansman remained silent, but most agreed that a fixed fight was the only possible explanation. It all made sense. How else could an untrained and clumsy highlander defeat the pride of the Varlish? The fact that Chain Shada might be involved was surprising, but his attack on the innocent officers surely proved his guilt beyond doubt. Some even began to voice doubts about Shada's right to be considered Varlish. "I heard his mother was a tribeswoman from south of the old city of Stone," said one. Others recalled hearing that Chain Shada's father was a mercenary soldier from Bersantum, a non-Varlish city-state far to the east.

Such talk was even heard among the ten soldiers who rode behind Mulgrave as he set out on the Scardyke Road. Galliott the Borderer was alongside him as they departed from the town. Mulgrave was still angry. He had not slept that night but had continued seeking witnesses who might have seen the killers of Chara Ward. It was painstaking work. Galliott's officers had been moving through the crowds, so Mulgrave had visited every stall with a view of the woods, talking to stall holders and servers. After four hours he had learned nothing of importance. Then a young woman had approached him as he sat on a fence rail eating a slice of pie. She had been helping her sister and brother-in-law earlier that evening on a stall selling riding accoutrements. Business had been good, and she had returned to the main premises to fetch more items. That was why she had missed Mulgrave's earlier visit to the stall. She told him that around dusk she had seen a young man carrying a rope into the wood, and soon afterward she had seen him in the company of a soldier. Both men had walked past the stall. The soldier had had blood on his face.

"Do you know the soldier?"

"Yes, sir. It was Sergeant Bindoe."

Mulgrave had gone immediately to Galliott, requesting men to arrest Bindoe. "I need to question her myself," said Galliott. "It could be that she is mistaken."

This further questioning had taken an inordinate amount of time as Galliott took her through her story half a dozen times. "Have you ever had dealings with Sergeant Bindoe?"

"No, sir."

"Has he ever arrested any members of your family?"

"No, sir," she said, indignantly.

"Friends, perhaps?"

"He once cautioned my husband's brother for being drunk."

"Ah, I see."

"What do you see?" demanded the woman. "I'm telling you the man came from the woods and had blood on his face. What is it you think you see? My husband is an Eldacre councillor, and if you are implying that I would lie, I'll seek redress from the Moidart himself."

"I am not implying anything of the kind," Galliott said smoothly. "But we must be sure that any evidence we receive is properly examined."

"Indeed we must," said Mulgrave. "We must also ensure that the suspects are not given time to escape the jurisdiction of the court. It is my belief that the balance between the two objectives is now seriously in jeopardy. Do you concur, Galliott?"

The Borderer looked into Mulgrave's gray eyes. "We will go to the barracks and question Sergeant Bindoe," he said. "I believe the man is about to take compassionate leave. I would imagine he is packing."

Bindoe had packed and gone by the time Mulgrave and Galliott arrived.

Now, with a squad of Beetlebacks in tow, Mulgrave rode from Eldacre and out onto the Scardyke Road. He had no wish to speak to Galliott, nor was he happy to have the man's company.

They pushed the horses hard for several miles, and it was during a pause to rest them with a slow walk that Mulgrave heard the soldiers talking about the "fixed" fight. Some were recalling how Chain Shada had stormed down to the circle, forcing the keeper of the sands to give the highlander extra time to recover from a blow. Mulgrave's anger grew. He was tempted to point out to them that the extra time was given because Gorain had thundered an illegal punch to Grymauch's head. Hardly the act of a man trying to throw a fight. He stayed silent. Men would believe what they wanted to believe. Mulgrave did not believe for a moment that Gorain had hanged himself. The Moidart had been coldly furious at the outcome of the fight. That alone told Mulgrave that someone would have to die.

The ride continued for another hour, and then Galliott finally spoke. "We are almost at the borders of the Pinance's territory," he said. "It would appear that we have lost them."

Mulgrave did not reply. Once they reached the log bridge, he would allow Galliott and his men to return to Eldacre. Mulgrave, however, planned to ride on. He would find Bindoe, arrest him, and bring him back, no matter what the distance.

Galliott seemed to read his mind. "We have no jurisdiction beyond the bridge," he pointed out.

"I have some friends in Scardyke," said Mulgrave. "And I am also owed leave time."

Galliott's handsome face darkened. "The rule of law should always be maintained, Captain. It is not helped by individuals who flout its principles."

"Indeed it is not, sir. Those who flout its principles should be brought to justice." His voice became cold as he struggled with his anger. He fixed Galliott with a hard look. "I am not a great believer in the value of the rack and the screw. However, when Bindoe is brought back, I shall question him myself. When I am finished, he will have told me every vile thing he has ever done. He will also tell me who has aided him in his iniquities. I shall then see that every person so named is hanged, for, like you, I have no tolerance for those who flout the law."

Without waiting for a response, he touched heels to his mount and cantered up the short rise. Some fifty feet ahead was the log bridge. Mulgrave reined in. The other horsemen rode up. They, too, pulled up their mounts and gazed in shock at the bloody scene below. Two heads had been wedged on the bridge posts. Beyond the heads lay the mutilated bodies. Blood had spread across the timbers and was still dripping through to the river below.

"Sacred heaven!" whispered Galliott. No one moved for several heartbeats. Then Mulgrave urged his horse on. The gelding was uneasy with the smell of blood, and Mulgrave dismounted, tethering the beast to a bush.

He approached the first of the heads. It was that of a man close to middle age. Scratch marks could be seen on the graying skin of his left cheek. His right cheek was torn away, several teeth smashed. One eye was open. Something had been carved into his brow. Mulgrave looked at it, but flowing blood had obscured it. He could make out a J and an S. Moving to the second head, he saw that this was a younger man. He, too, had the marks of savage cuts on his forehead. Galliott came alongside the officer.

Taking a cloth from his pocket, he wiped away the blood

on the youth's brow. Now the word could be seen clearly: JUSTICE.

Galliott threw aside the cloth and stepped out onto the bridge. "Bindoe was gutted like a fish," he said, "and castrated. The youth has no marks on his body that I can see. I would imagine his throat was cut."

Two horses were grazing on the far side of the river. Stepping carefully to avoid the slippery blood, Galliott crossed the bridge and led the horses back across. Once there, he searched the saddlebags, removing a heavy pouch, which he opened. "Bindoe was carrying a deal of silver," he told Mulgrave. "He was not robbed."

Mulgrave was lost in thought. He was staring at Bindoe's head. It looked as if he had been shot in the face before being knifed. The killer or killers had been waiting there to exact revenge for the murder of Chara Ward. But why? How could they have known that Bindoe would take this road at that time? He glanced at Galliott. The man seemed infinitely more relaxed now than he had been some moments before.

Had Galliott sent men to have Bindoe murdered?

Mulgrave dismissed the idea. Had the Borderer done so, the bodies would have been merely buried somewhere, never to be found. Hacking and mutilating the corpses had been the work of someone filled with fury and a burning desire for revenge.

The officer moved out across the bridge. There was a bloody footprint on the earth, leading down to the river. Mulgrave climbed down to the water's edge. There were more footprints there and marks of blood on the earth. Curiously, there was also a footprint below the water that had not yet been washed away by the flowing river. The killer had waded into the river in his shoes.

Shoes. Low-heeled shoes. Not a rider, then.

Mulgrave sat back and thought the evidence through. The killer had been covered in blood and had splashed into the river to clean himself. He had not removed his shoes first, which indicated he was acting instinctively, without conscious thought. He was therefore probably in a state of shock at his actions.

Mulgrave saw where the killer had walked back up to the bridge. He followed the prints and saw that the man had walked away to the northeast.

Toward Old Hills.

"This is the work of a clansman," Galliott said as Mulgrave returned to his horse.

"What brings you to that conclusion?" asked Mulgrave.

"Look around you, man. Would any civilized man commit such a barbarous act?"

"Let us not get into debates about civilized behavior," said Mulgrave. "How civilized was it to rape a young virgin and then hang her from a tree?"

"That, too, was appalling," said Galliott, "but since Sergeant Bindoe was offered no opportunity to explain his scratches, there is no evidence to convict his memory. He died innocent according to the law."

"Aye, he did," admitted Mulgrave. "More's the pity."

Excitement mounted in the week that followed. Eldacre had not known such a turbulent period for a great many years: an assassination attempt on the Moidart, the drama of the fixed fight between Gorain and the highlander, then the murder of a young girl and the savage slaying of two Varlish travelers. Those events were discussed endlessly in the bars, taverns, and meeting places. Added to which there was the continuing hunt for Chain Shada. Stories and theories abounded. Did Chain kill the girl? Was the murder of the—now—well-loved Sergeant Bindoe the first hint of a new highland uprising?

Beetlebacks rode through the highland settlements, questioning men about their whereabouts on the day Bindoe was killed. The questioning was often harsh, and if a man could not adequately answer their questions, he was taken in chains to Eldacre Castle. One man died there, apparently of heart failure.

Jaim Grymauch recovered swiftly, though the bruises on

his face lingered for some time. He had gone into Eldacre to retrieve his prize money only to be told that since the fight had been fixed, no monies would be forthcoming. On the surface Jaim shrugged off the loss, but Kaelin knew he was seething inside.

Maev Ring was subdued. She had seen her nephew come home just after dawn on the day after Chara's murder. She had been making her bed and had watched him emerge from the old barn that now served as a workshop for Maev's spinners. They had not yet arrived for work, and Kaelin had had no reason to be in the empty building. Maev had waited until the end of the day, when the twelve workers had gone back to their homes. Then she had searched the workshop's upper loft, where she had found the two pistols and a cavalry saber hidden beneath an old rug. Returning the pistols to their original hiding place in the cabinet, she had carried the saber into the woods and buried it.

Under normal circumstances Maev liked to bring problems out into the open. Not this time. Less said, soonest mended, she decided.

When the ten Beetlebacks came to the house the following day, she greeted them courteously, offering them water for their horses and some bread and cheese. Galliott led them, and the men behaved with cold civility in his presence. Kaelin, Jaim, and Banny stood by while the soldiers moved through the house, searching for weapons.

When they crossed to the old barn, Maev glanced at Kaelin. If he was tense or frightened, he did not show it. When the soldiers returned empty-handed, Maev saw the surprise register briefly.

"I am sorry to have inconvenienced you, Maev," said Galliott. "But we are obliged to search everywhere."

"Of course, Captain."

He approached Jaim. "I see your bruises are healing, Grymauch. I want you to know that no one holds you to account for the vile behavior of Gorain. You fought well and honestly."

"Aye, that's true," said Grymauch. "He was a talented man, that Gorain."

"In what way?"

"When I registered to fight, I made my mark and I saw his. Just like mine, a large **X**. Though his did have a little flourish above it. Like Gorain, I never did learn to read and write, Captain. But one must surely admire a man who learns to do so in a single night just so he can write a farewell note before he hangs himself."

Galliott sighed. "You will talk yourself into a noose one of these days, Grymauch. I will be sad to see it."

"Aye, Captain. Without rogues there'd be no need of Beetlebacks, I guess."

Galliott laughed. "Quite so. Well, I must be leaving. We have another thirty homes to visit today."

"Have you found Chain Shada yet, sir?" asked Maev.

"No, Maev, but we will. He will be cold and hungry by now. The Moidart has sent for Huntsekker and his trackers. They will find him."

"I do not like the man," said Maev. "He is a killer. What has Chain Shada been convicted of that he should be hunted by the Harvester?"

"It is not for me to question the orders of the Moidart, Maev," said Galliott. "I share your dislike of Huntsekker. It must be said, however, that he rarely fails to find those he tracks."

"And then he scythes off their heads," snapped Maev. "It is vile."

"Why should you be concerned for Shada?"

"He helped Jaim. He could have destroyed him. That is what the mob was baying for. That he did not does him credit."

"Helped me!" muttered Grymauch. "The man cost me thirty-eight chaillings. Did you know they refused me the prize money?"

"Aye, that was unfair," Galliott agreed, with a smile. "I'll speak with the bishop. Maybe with a little money in your pocket you'll be less likely to go roguing." Galliott walked to his horse and mounted. The Beetlebacks rode from the house and turned toward the south.

Kaelin strolled toward the old barn. Maev called out to him. "There's nothing there for you. Let the girls get on with their work." Then she walked up to Jaim and linked arms. "Come walk with me a ways," she said.

"You want something from me, lass?"

"Why do you say that? Why should I not want to walk with an old friend?"

He laughed. "Now you are scaring me. Scolding I understand. Hell, I even enjoy it. But I'm not comfortable with this strange softness." Maev forced a smile, and the two of them walked out into the calf meadow. Once there she released his arm and sat down on a split log. "Where do you think Chain Shada might have gone?"

"How would I know?"

"We owe him, Grymauch."

"For what?"

"You didn't see him grab the keeper of the sand. He forced the man to give you extra time after the foul blow. More important, as you just heard me say to Galliott, he did not rip your stupid head from your shoulders as the crowd urged him to."

"Stupid head? Now that's the Maev I know and love."

"Be serious, will you. He knew that by not crushing you he would be in trouble. I doubt he realized his life depended on it, but even so. It was—though I hate to admit it—a noble and selfless act. He risked himself for you, Grymauch. Now he is alone and hunted. Find him."

"Just like that? An army is seeking him, but old one-eyed Grymauch can just walk into the mountains and the big Varlish will emerge from behind a bush? I don't think so, Maev."

"You'll not do this thing?" she asked, surprise in her voice.

"No."

"This is not like you, Grymauch," she said, staring at him intently.

He was suddenly uneasy under her green-eyed gaze. "Maybe it isn't like me," he admitted. "But then, maybe it's time old Grymauch started looking out for himself. You heard what he said. Huntsekker is on his trail. I don't want that scythe on *my* neck."

Maev rose from the log, still holding to his gaze. "I know you, Grymauch. I know you better than you know yourself."

"Obviously not," he retorted, taking a step back.

"You are not frightened of Huntsekker."

"All men are frightened of something. Shada will either escape or he won't. No sense in us getting involved."

Maev was about to speak, then Grymauch saw her relax. She smiled and stepped in close. "Damn, but you already have him, don't you? Where is he? In that cave of yours?"

"Whisht, woman. Have you taken leave of your senses?"

"You went out three nights ago and only came back this morning. I thought you were whoring with Parsha Willets. But you weren't, were you, Grymauch? You went into the mountains and found Chain Shada. Look me in the eye and tell me you don't have him."

"I don't . . . ," he faltered. "Damnit, woman, but I think you're a witch." He glanced around to see if anyone was in earshot. "Yes, I have him, but I didn't want to put you in peril by sharing the secret. I'll get him across the river tomorrow night."

"That's my Grymauch," she said fondly. "He'll need coin once you bring him to the Pinance's territory. I'll give you two pounds for him."

"Two pounds, is it? You've never given me two pounds."

"You're not worth two pounds," she snapped. "Now, there is something else we must discuss. How does Kaelin seem to you?"

Grymauch shrugged. "He's a mite withdrawn since they killed the lass. He'll get over it."

"He has not spoken to you, then?"

"About what?"

"The murders of Bindoe and the boy."

"No. Why would he?"

"The killer is said to have shot Bindoe in the face and then stolen his saber."

"So I heard."

"Kaelin came back that morning and hid Lanovar's pistols and a saber in the old barn."

Jaim Grymauch stood silently for a moment. "I'm sorry to hear this," he said at last. "Not that they didn't deserve to die, you understand."

Maev nodded. She knew he was thinking about the manner of their deaths and trying to come to terms with the fact that such crazed behavior had come from his beloved Kaelin. "He liked the girl, you know," he said. "His mind must have been . . . unhinged."

"Yes," agreed Maev. "A killing frenzy." Jaim turned away from her for a moment, staring out over the mountains. Maev could see the sadness in him. He stood silently for a while.

"Why did the soldiers not find the weapons?" he asked finally.

"I put the pistols back, Grymauch, and I buried the saber. My guess is that you showed Kaelin the pistols when I was away at some time. It doesn't matter now. What does is that he has killed two Varlish. He is just like Lanovar, and I fear for his life. As he grows older, he will resent more and more the Varlish domination. He will not exist within it like you or I. He will resist it. He will oppose it. And they will kill him as they killed his father."

Jaim sighed. "Is there anything that I can do, Maev? You have but to name it."

"I have purchased property far away in the northwest, a farm that borders the Black Rigante country. You have friends among them. Come summer I want you to take Kaelin north. I want him far from the Moidart and his Beetlebacks. I want him to find a life away from the Varlish."

"Come summer he will be a man, Maev. He may choose not to go."

"That's why I need you, Jaim. He admires you, and I think he would travel with you if you asked him."

"Why wait until the summer?"

"Life in Eldacre will be calmer then. There is too much excitement and suspicion now. Let Kaelin finish his schooling and then you can go."

"Will you want me to come back?" he asked her.

"What kind of question is that?" she countered. He stood silently, watching her, his expression grave. Maev felt uncomfortable. "Of course I will, you lummox," she told him. "I'd have no one to scold. Now, you be careful tomorrow. Huntsekker will be close. Vile the man may be, but he's no fool."

"I'll avoid him, and don't you worry, I'll not take Kaelin with me."

"Yes, you will, Jaim," she said sadly. "He has killed now, and he is a man, with all the sorrow that brings. I want him close to you from now on. There is much he needs to learn from you. You were a killer once, and you changed. Help Kaelin change."

"I'll do my best, Maev."

"Aye, I know. You're a good man, Grymauch."

◇ 8 ◇

THE FEELING OF sadness did not fade as the Wyrd moved across the countryside toward the old log bridge. Rather, it deepened. There was no pulsating magic in the ground below her feet, no silent music in the trees. Here and there she could sense tiny fragments of what once had radiated from the land: a glint of golden light on the surface of a stream, a shard of harmony in the shadow of a great oak, a whisper of past glory on the gentle breeze.

Even that faded as, leaning heavily on her sycamore staff, she reached the bridge. Death hung in the air. Recent rains had washed away most of the blood, and the bodies had been removed. Yet the horror remained, swirling unseen over the river, tainting the trees and the grass.

To restore harmony to the scene would take days of mind-numbing toil, endless prayers, and fasting. It was ever thus, she thought. The sculptor labored for years to carve the perfect statue from marble, every muscle shaped with perfect beauty. One talentless man with a hammer then destroyed it in a moment. Creation took time and love, destruction merely a heartbeat of madness.

The Wyrd had spent half her life becoming one with the land, sacrificing all that most humans held dear: love, children, family. At times like this she could almost regret it.

"Oh, Ravenheart," she whispered. "What have you done to yourself?"

Dusk was approaching, and the Wyrd settled down to rest, drawing her tattered cloak around her. The first of her labors would take place when the moon was high, and she needed to be strong. From a small canvas pouch she took a pinch of shredded leaves, placing them under her tongue. The taste was bitter, and she felt her heartbeat quicken. The scents of the forest sharpened: the musty earth, the damp fur of the nearby rabbits, the harsh and pungent fox urine, the soft, heady perfume of the spring flowers by the river.

The Wyrd relaxed, allowing the weight of forest memories to flow over her. From somewhere deep within she heard the sounds of men laboring. Distant sounds, echoes from the past. Closing her eyes, she focused on the sounds. Laughter came, and with it a sense of camaraderie. The Wyrd saw the soldiers of Stone putting aside their breastplates as they cut down the trees to make this bridge, creating a passage through to the heart of Rigante territory. It would allow their army to march on Bane's stronghold. The Wyrd could hear their voices now. The old tongue of Stone, which she did not know. Yet she could feel their soaring confidence, their belief in their invincibility. Bane would destroy that less than three weeks after this bridge was completed. The Rigante would fall upon the Stone army and annihilate it utterly.

Slowly the Wyrd opened her eyes. She could see the men now, splitting the logs and hauling them into place. They were not true spirits, merely reflections in the mirror of time. There could be no interaction with them. Their labors had merely become part of the memory of the forest.

For an hour the Wyrd rested, then she moved to the riverbank, cupping her hands and drinking deeply. As she did so, the narcotic herb she had taken linked her to another image. She *saw* Kaelin Ring sitting beside the water, weeping. The Wyrd sighed. Her spirit was in tune with the people of the Rigante, and she often experienced glimpses of their futures. Chara Ward had been full Varlish, and the Wyrd had not seen the perils she faced.

The moon was above the mountains now, though scurrying clouds obscured it for long periods. Running wet fingers through her hair, she stood and stretched. Once there had been bears in these mountains, great ambling creatures that would hunt the salmon in the clean, sparkling waters. Once there had been wolves, running wild and free. Man had killed the bears and all but destroyed the wolves, driving them far to the north.

The Wyrd climbed to the bridge, took another pinch of shredded herbs, and sat down on the logs.

The murder of Chara Ward had been savage, born of lust and hatred. The slaying of her killers had been more than that. It had been premeditated and vicious in its execution. That it should have been Ravenheart who had committed the crime was almost more than the Wyrd could bear. In him she had hoped to find the best of the Rigante. But like his ancestor Connavar he carried the best and the worst.

The night grew chilly.

"Come to me, Jek Bindoe," whispered the Wyrd.

Mist swirled over the logs, and the Wyrd shivered. Her skin prickled as something cold touched the back of her neck. She did not turn. Instead she emptied her mind. Within the whispering wind she heard a voice, the sound growing stronger. "Kill you, bitch! Kill you!" Icy, insubstantial fingers raked at her neck.

"You are dead, Jek Bindoe," she said softly. "You can harm no one now."

A shrill scream sounded. Mist flowed over her, re-forming before her eyes, taking the shape of a thin hatchet-faced man. "I'll show you dead!" he shouted, slashing at her face. His fingers clawed at her, but all she felt were tiny whispers of cold against her skin.

"It is time for you to go, to leave this place. The world has no more use for you, Jek Bindoe."

"I need to rest," the ghost of Bindoe said suddenly. "This is a dream. In the morning I'll ride south to Scardyke. Just a dream."

The Wyrd began to chant in the old highland tongue. The wind picked up, tugging at Bindoe's shimmering form.

"What are you doing? You stop that, bitch! It is hurting me."

"Then do not resist it."

He began to swear and shout and scream. The chanting began again. Bindoe's voice faded, and the mist vanished.

"Where has he gone?" asked the ghost of Luss Campion.

"To the place he has earned with his deeds," said the Wyrd, "but I do not think you will be joining him there."

"Am I dead, too?"

"Yes," she said sadly.

A low moan came from the spirit. There was silence for a while. "I didn't want Chara to die," he said. "Truly I didn't."

"I know that, Luss Campion. You were bred to hate, and that is a dangerous and terrible thing to do to a child. You do not need me to send you to your destination. You can hear it calling you. Let go, boy. Just let go."

"I don't have any way to make amends now, do I?"

"No. That chance was taken from you. But it is good that you desire to."

"I feel so lost. So sad." The Wyrd felt the soul of Luss Campion vanish. And she wept.

Kaelin Ring sat quietly, watching and listening to the two men. Jaim he knew and loved, but the big Varlish was another matter entirely. Kaelin was still unsure why they should be risking themselves for this enemy. Yes, he had not punched Jaim when the highlander had been virtually helpless. But that had been *his* choice. It seemed unreasonable that for that one act he and Jaim should put their lives in peril.

They were sitting in Jaim's cave, a fire burning, a lantern set high on a natural rock shelf. Jaim was in his traveling clothes: black trews and walking shoes, a dark shirt, and a black cloak. Chain Shada wore riding boots with thick heels and a heavy, double-shouldered coat of shimmering brown leather. Kaelin felt out of place alongside these massive men and had moved to sit a little distance from them. He was almost at the mouth of the cave and could feel the cool night air against his face.

In the days since Chara's death he had not slept well. He

had dreamed of her, and in his dreams she was alive and happy. Upon waking, the full realization of her passing would strike him like a hammer blow, wrenching at his guts. Everything seemed different now, and Kaelin took no pleasure from the sun on the mountains or the breeze whispering through the trees. He moved listlessly through the days, then slept fitfully, his nights disturbed and full of sorrow.

"So who is this Huntsekker?" he heard Chain Shada ask.

"He is a southerner and has served the Moidart for twenty years," Jaim told him. "He is a skilled tracker. And canny."

"You know him?"

Jaim grinned. "Oh, we've crossed each other's trails now and again." Removing his headband, he rubbed at the empty socket. "So tell me, why did the mighty Chain Shada come this far north for such a small contest?"

Chain Shada shrugged. "I needed the money, and I thought Gorain could have become champion in my place. Needless to say, I wish I hadn't."

"How could you need the money?" Kaelin asked suddenly. "It is said you've won every fight you ever had. It is also said you are rich."

"I made the mistake of marrying a woman for her beauty," said Chain. "The face of an angel and a body like a goddess. I was totally besotted with her. She had a brother who was a merchant. She convinced me to invest heavily in his ventures. When she left me, I discovered I had no wealth left." Chain Shada shrugged. "Nothing more foolish than a man in love."

"Or more grand," countered Jaim. "Did you go after them?"

"No," answered Chain. "They fled across the narrow sea to Goriasa. The ship was caught in a storm and sank. She—and my gold—now sit at the bottom of the ocean." Chain Shada lapsed into silence and stared at the fire for a few moments. Then he took a deep breath. "So I had to go on fighting. I had already beaten most of the good challengers, so the purses shrank as I fought lesser men. Then one day I realized I no longer had quite the power or speed I once had had." He smiled. "I never met a man I couldn't conquer. Yet no man conquers time."

"Uncle Jaim would have beaten you," said Kaelin, "had he been fresh and strong."

"No, he wouldn't, lad. I'd have blinded him within three periods. He can't protect his left. Gorain was too stupid to see that."

"I think you are wrong," said Kaelin, irritation in his voice.

"No, he's not, Kaelin," put in Grymauch. "Fighting with fists is what he does. He couldn't steal a bull or swing a glave like me. He couldn't run as fast as you or ride as well as Mulgrave. Every man has his talent. There is no shame in being beaten by a man who has mastered his craft. It doesn't make him a better man."

Kaelin fell silent and reached for a clay goblet and a water jug. As he did so, one of the silver pistols in his belt dug into his ribs. Straightening, he pulled the pistol clear, laying it on a rock beside him. "May I see it?" asked Chain Shada. Kaelin hefted the piece and walked across to the fighter. The gun seemed small in Chain's massive hand.

"It was made by Emburley of Knights Walk," said Chain. "His mark is the silver lion rampant, which you can see on the pommel at the base of the grip."

"They are good pistols," said Jaim. "They belonged to Kaelin's father."

"They are fine," said Chain. "Emburley's engraved pistols sell for more than one hundred pounds apiece. A matched set would probably auction for two hundred and fifty."

Kaelin was aghast at the sum. "That is madness," he said. "A pistol in Eldacre costs eight chaillings."

"I expect so," agreed Chain. "However, you can buy an old workhorse for five chaillings. A proven racer will set you back a hundred times that. Maybe more. Emburley's pieces are bought by kings and dukes and lords. They are prized for their accuracy and the perfection of their construction."

"That one misfired the last time I tried it," he said.

Chain hefted the piece and cocked it. Then he flicked open

the cover of the flash bowl and examined it. "It will misfire the next time also," he said. "Come and see." Kaelin moved alongside him. Chain lifted the pistol close to his eyes. "You see this little hole here?"

"Yes."

"When the flash pan ignites, a flame needs to pass through this hole to fire the main charge. As you can see, it is blocked. You have a pin?"

"No."

Jaim removed his cloak brooch and passed it to Chain, who gently inserted the brooch pin into the hole. "This tiny hole is vital," said Chain. "Like so much in life, it is the small which dictates the success or failure of the large. There. Now it will work." Chain pressed shut the cover and carefully uncocked the weapon. Kaelin took out the second pistol and examined it. The fire hole seemed clear, but he inserted the brooch pin to be sure.

"Always thoroughly clean the pistols after they have been discharged," said Chain. "Never leave them loaded for more than a day or two. The black powder is corrosive."

"I'll remember that," said Kaelin.

"So when do we leave?" Chain asked Jaim.

"Another hour. It will be safer when the night is at its darkest."

"Does this Huntsekker work alone?"

"No. He has four men with him."

"What kind of weapons do they carry?"

"Swords and knives. They are highlanders and are not allowed guns. Huntsekker will have a gun, though. I saw it once. Half as long as a musket, with a trumpet-shaped barrel. Makes a noise like whistling thunder."

"Blunderbuss," said Chain. "The whistling is the sound of perhaps fifty tiny pieces of shot, tacks, or small nails. At close range it will blow a man apart. At twenty feet it will pierce him from face to groin. You have a plan if we meet them?"

"No," Jaim said cheerfully. "But I think fast when I need to."

"We kill them," said Kaelin. The words hung in the air, and

the cave seemed suddenly quiet. Kaelin felt uncomfortable in the silence. Neither of the two men was looking in his direction. Jaim transferred his gaze to the far wall, apparently watching the fire shadows dancing there, while Chain Shada lifted a goblet of water and drank.

After a while Jaim spoke, but not to Kaelin. "Maev has given me some coin for your journey," he told Chain. "I think it will be enough to see you to Varingas."

"That will not be necessary, my friend," said Chain, "though thank her for me. The Pinance is an old friend. Gorain and I stayed with him on the way up from the capital. I will lodge with him for a while, until I decide on a destination."

"Take it, anyway," said Jaim. "You've no idea of the tongue on that woman if I don't give you the coin."

Chain smiled. "I will find a way to return it to her."

Kaelin felt as if he had been snubbed, as if these men regarded his words as unworthy of attention. Anger flared in him. Had he not slain the murderers of Chara Ward? He was a boy no longer, only they could not see it. Well, they *would* see it if Huntsekker was unlucky enough to cross their path.

Kaelin's hand dropped to the pistol, curling around the engraved grip.

They would see it as a lead shot ripped through Huntsekker's black Varlish heart.

Screened by a stand of gorse, Huntsekker squatted on the ground, surveying the open land to the north. A large round-shouldered man wearing a full-length coat of black bearskin, he scanned the hillsides for signs of movement. The moon emerged from behind a cloud. Instinctively Huntsekker ducked lower behind the gorse, fearing that the moonlight would glow from his face and the twin spikes of white beard that grew from either side of his shaved chin.

The distant grass shone like silver in the new light, and Huntsekker saw three badgers moving across the open ground. Turning to his left, he could see the old log bridge. At this time of the year, with the river swollen, it was one of only three crossings to the territory of the Pinance. The other two involved climbing the steep passes over the mountains. Huntsekker, unlike Galliott, did not believe Chain Shada was friendless. Someone was hiding him, and Huntsekker believed that someone to be Jaim Grymauch. Jaim knew the mountains and might well have guided Chain Shada over that route. Huntsekker doubted it. It was three times as long and therefore offered three times the risk of capture. The bridge was only a few miles from Old Hills, and most of the way would be through dense woods within which two men could pass unobserved.

Only the bridge itself offered danger to the runaways.

That would appeal to Jaim Grymauch. The man loved calculated risks.

Huntsekker thought this stupid, yet he had to admit to a grudging admiration for the one-eyed clansman. News of his exploits always made Huntsekker smile.

Even the time Grymauch had made off with his own prize-winning bull.

For most men such a reversal would have been a humiliation. For Huntsekker it was a golden moment. Even now he did not quite know why. When he had acquired the animal, he had made it clear that anyone who attempted to steal it would be hunted down mercilessly. His reputation was such that he believed that no one—except Grymauch—would have the nerve to attempt the task. He had kept the bull tethered close to his house and guarded day and night. A long cord was cunningly concealed at the base of the paddock gate, attached to a series of bells. Anyone opening the gate would set them ringing. Farther up the trail he had had a ditch dug that would prevent anyone from leading the bull toward the south.

He had known Grymauch would still make the attempt, and night after night Huntsekker had sat up, his blunderbuss loaded, waiting for the moment when he would catch the man.

Truth to tell, he had no intention of killing him. The highlands would be an immeasurably poorer place without Jaim

Grymauch. No, he would catch him, then have a drink with him before releasing him.

But Grymauch had not come. For fifteen nights Huntsekker had kept watch. On the sixteenth he had dozed. Not for more than a few moments. When he had opened his eyes, the paddock had been empty. Huntsekker had roared with anger and rushed out into the night, waking his herdsmen. The two guards had been trussed behind a water trough. Neither had seen the attacker. The hidden bell cord had been neatly sliced. Huntsekker and his men saw tracks leading south and raced in pursuit. When they came to the ditch, they found that two heavy planks had been laid across it. For most of the night they searched, finding nothing.

At dawn they trudged wearily back to the farm—to see the bull back in its paddock, a sprig of heather tied to its horn.

Huntsekker chuckled at the memory. Not that he would ever admit to enjoying the affair.

His good humor faded away as his mind returned to the task at hand. If Jaim Grymauch was with Chain Shada, then Huntsekker would be forced to take his head. There would be no choice. He had not wanted this mission, but no one refused the Moidart. It was not healthy, as Chain Shada and his comrade had discovered. Huntsekker had taken no joy in hanging the fighter Gorain. The man had been blubbing and begging as he had been taken to the tree. Huntsekker had struck him a blow to the back of the head, then had looped the rope over his neck. Dal and Vinton had tried to haul him to the bough, but the unconscious Gorain had been too heavy and Huntsekker had been forced to help them. Then he had left the note the Moidart had supplied and had returned home. He had had no idea what the note said, being unable to read, but he had heard the stories the following day. They irritated him. He had seen Grymauch fight the man. How could people believe such nonsense? Yet they had. They had lapped it up like dogs at the gravy.

Huntsekker caught signs of movement on the far hill. Two

men were moving into sight. They cut away to the right, entering the trees.

Easing himself back, the big man ran down the hillside to where his men were waiting. Dal Naydham was sitting with his back to a tree, eyes closed. Vinton Gabious was hunched in his cloak. The brothers Bass and Boillard Seeton were asleep. Huntsekker nudged them awake with his boot. Bass surged upright, a double-edged knife in his hand. Huntsekker stepped back as the knife flashed out. "They are coming," said Huntsekker.

Turning away, he strolled to where Dal Naydham was rubbing his eyes. Dal was a small man, round-shouldered and balding. He had been with Huntsekker for more than twenty years. "Is it Grymauch?" he asked.

"Too far away to tell."

"I do hope not."

"I share that hope," Huntsekker admitted.

Boillard Seeton joined them. He was tall and thin, long black hair framing his sallow face. He looked like a priest, thought Huntsekker, his large deep-set brown eyes radiating compassion. "Can I take the heads, Harvester?" he asked. "I've never taken heads."

Huntsekker disliked being called Harvester, and he was already regretting hiring the brothers. "I take the heads, Seeton. It is what I do. Now take your positions."

"Just one head, then?"

Huntsekker reached down and grasped the black handle of the scythe at his belt. It leapt clear, moonlight gleaming on the crescent blade. The point pricked Boillard's skinny throat. "Anger me further, scum bucket, and I'll take yours," he said.

"No need to get tetchy," said Boillard Seeton, stepping back. "No harm in asking."

His men hidden in the undergrowth, Huntsekker moved back to a large gnarled oak and primed his blunderbuss. He was on edge. The breeze whispered through the leaves above him, flowing up from the old log bridge. The air smelled fine, and

Huntsekker felt a moment of peace settle on him. He glanced back to where moonlight was glinting on the river. He had seen the old bridge a thousand times since he had moved to the highlands twenty-four years earlier, yet somehow he had never really noticed it. It seemed to him curiously beautiful now; ageless and solid in an ever-changing world. Huntsekker wondered who had built it.

Damn, but I should have found a way to avoid this mission, he thought. When Chain Shada had refused to pound on the crippled highlander, Huntsekker had felt a surge of pride. It had largely erased the shame at the foul blow Gorain had hammered to Grymauch as the highlander was kneeling on the boards. Now here he was, ready to take the man's head.

It was not always this way, he realized. When he had first used his tracking skills, it had been to catch murderers and thieves, men who were seeking to escape justice. His success had brought him to the attention of the Moidart. Huntsekker laid his blunderbuss against the trunk of the tree and scanned the crest of the hill. Still no sign of them. Idly he tugged at the twin spikes of his silver beard. Don't come, Grymauch, he thought.

"The two fighters disobeyed me and betrayed the honor of the Varlish," the Moidart had said. "Unless they are dealt with, we face civil disobedience and perhaps a revolt. It is up to you, Huntsekker, to see that this does not happen. You will find the man Gorain, take him into the woods, and hang him. You will leave this paper under a rock close to the body."

"Yes, lord. What of the other fighter?"

"Galliott will arrest him and bring him to me. Once here, he shall answer for his impertinence."

Huntsekker had little doubt about the nature of Chain Shada's punishment. He would be tortured and killed in the dungeons below the Winter House.

Still, it was not his problem.

Except that Galliott had failed. Chain Shada was no one's fool and had broken free of the soldiers, escaping into the town and from there into the countryside. Now it was

Huntsekker's task to kill him and anyone with him. The breeze touched him again, and once more he found himself staring back at the bridge. This was a magical land. Huntsekker had felt drawn to it from the first moment he had marched there with the Second all those years ago. Having completed his nine years, Huntsekker had taken his pension and found work on the high farm, buying it from the aging owner six years later.

Dal Naydham and Vinton Gabious had been with him since that time. Both men had married since and now had houses on Huntsekker's land. Dal's wife had died the previous year in childbirth, and his three children now lived in Vinton's house, alongside his own six boys.

Huntsekker shook his head, trying to free himself from such thoughts. Any moment now the two victims would appear, and he needed to be ready. Taking up the blunderbuss, he stared again at the crest. They should have reached it by now.

He pictured the route they must take, across the open field and into the woods, down the short slope, and through to this trail. There was no other way they could have gone without being seen.

A pistol shot sounded. Huntsekker jerked. Boillard Seeton came running from the undergrowth to the north. The sleeve of his gray shirt was stained and dark. A powerful figure came running after him, followed by a youth carrying two pistols. There was no sign of Dal, Vinton, or Bass. With a curse Huntsekker stepped out from behind the tree. "Down, Boillard," he shouted, bringing up the blunderbuss. Boillard Seeton hurled himself flat, screaming as his injured arm struck the earth.

Something cold touched Huntsekker's throat. "Best be putting that dreadful thing down, Harvester," came the voice of Jaim Grymauch. "I'd hate to be cutting your throat on such a fine night as this."

"Aye," agreed Huntsekker. " 'Twould spoil the moment." Carefully he uncocked the piece and laid it against the tree.

"Now step forward, if you would, and join your friend."

Huntsekker walked across the clearing. Chain Shada was kneeling beside Boillard. "The shot bounced off the bone," he said. "It didn't break it. A few stitches and you'll recover, though you'll hurt for a while."

"What of the rest of my men?" asked Huntsekker.

"Bruised and sleeping," said Chain Shada.

"That's a relief to me. They are family men."

Jaim Grymauch moved from behind Huntsekker. His clothes were wet through. Huntsekker smiled. The old rogue had slipped down to the river and swum to the bridge, coming up behind him. "You'll catch a chill, Grymauch," he said. "You're not as young as once you were."

"Maybe I'll take that bearskin coat," replied Jaim. "That'll keep me warm."

"It's too big for you, son. Takes a man to wear a coat like this."

Grymauch chuckled and moved to Chain Shada. "The way is clear," he said. "Time for you to be going."

"What about these two?"

Jaim Grymauch swung to face Huntsekker. "It is a good question, Harvester. What are your plans?"

"I'll go back to my farm and tend to my cattle. As far as I am concerned, I got here too late and the fighter had already crossed the bridge. I saw no one else."

"And you?" Grymauch asked Boillard Seeton.

"The same," answered the injured man.

"Well, that's it, then," said Grymauch.

"The hell it is!" stormed the youth, his voice shaking with anger. "I say we kill them." Huntsekker saw the pistol come up. It was pointed at his face. He stood very still.

"We'll kill no one!" said Jaim Grymauch.

"We can't trust them. They'll betray us as soon as they get to Eldacre."

"Aye, maybe they will. That's for them to decide," Jaim said softly, moving to stand between Huntsekker and the youth. "Killing shouldn't be easy, boy. Life should be precious."

"How precious would it have been had *he* caught *us*?"

"I am not responsible for the way other men live their lives," Grymauch told Kaelin. "Only how I live mine. If a man comes against me and I have no choice, I'll kill him. But I'll not murder unarmed men. Put away that pistol."

"You are making a mistake, Grymauch."

"Maybe I am. If so, I'll live with it."

"I never thought you a fool till now," said the youth. Huntsekker watched him uncock the pistol and walk away. Grymauch turned to Chain Shada, offering his hand.

"The boy might be right," said the Varlish fighter, taking the hand and shaking it.

"Aye," agreed Grymauch. "Time will tell."

"Be lucky," said Chain Shada. Without another word he swung away and walked down to the old bridge.

"How's that bull of yours?" asked Grymauch.

Huntsekker shrugged. "Broke his leg last year. We ate him, and he was mighty fine."

"Damn shame," said Grymauch. "That was one good bull."

"I have another now. Even better."

"I might just drop by and see him."

"If you do, you'll be picking shot out of your arse for a month."

Grymauch laughed. "Take care, Harvester," he said, then he, too, strolled away.

Huntsekker watched him go, then walked into the undergrowth to check on his men. They were all still unconscious, though their heartbeats were strong. He returned to Boillard Seeton.

"I've never seen the like," said Boillard. "One moment it was all silence, the next that big bastard was right there. Three blows and the others was down. I pulled my knife, then that bastard kid appeared and shot me. By the Sacrifice, I'll see him swing and I'll piss on his grave."

"No, you won't, Boillard. You gave your word."

"Under duress," argued Boillard. "Don't count."

"Mine does."

"Well, I'm not you, Harvester. You do as you wish. Nobody shoots Boillard Seeton and gets away with it." The man pushed himself to his feet. "Damn, but I'll enjoy seeing them hang."

"I don't think so." Huntsekker's scythe whispered from its sheath, then plunged through Boillard's thin back, spearing his heart. With a sickening wrench Huntsekker pulled the blade clear. Boillard toppled forward. The cool breeze blew again across Huntsekker's face.

This time there was no magic in it.

◇ 9 ◇

MAEV RING PATROLLED the old barn, watching the work of the twelve spinners, stopping here and there to offer advice to the newest of the women, who was having trouble coordinating the foot pedal of the bulky machine while feeding the yarn to the wheel with her left hand. "Keep it steady and not too slow," said Maev. "It will come."

The woman smiled nervously. The twelve machines had cost Maev three pounds each. They had been carted in pieces all the way from the capital, Varingas, and reassembled in the old barn. It had taken months for Maev to learn the process and acquire enough skill to train others. The enterprise had been fraught with irritating delays and mistakes, but after two years Maev's spinners were creating enough good thread to supply the majority of Eldacre's shirt and clothing makers. The five weavers were creating rugs that were now highly prized, and the small dyeing plant Maev had acquired by the river in northern Eldacre meant that she could hire even more women to knit brightly colored and heavy woolen overshirts. They were immensely popular among the Varlish in winter.

Maev Ring could have grown mildly wealthy with those enterprises alone.

But she had a problem. It was one that most Varlish would have given anything to share. Maev's other business ventures were so successful that she was becoming seriously rich. The seeds of her dilemma had been planted when she had acquired a forty percent share in the business of Gillam Pearce the bootmaker. His work was of exceptional quality, but his business acumen was nonexistent. He had been facing debtor's jail before Maev had entered his workshop five years earlier. Gillam, a small man, round-shouldered and red-faced, was sitting at his bench, applying a third coat of polish to a pair of riding boots.

"What can I do for you, madam?" he asked Maev, affecting not to notice the highland shawl and heavy gray work skirt, which in a world ruled by the Varlish negated the need for any courtesy.

Maev Ring approached his bench and placed a heavy pouch upon it. "It is my understanding, sir," she said, "that despite your skill you are in need of funds."

His thin lips tightened. "My affairs should not be the subject of gossip. Please leave."

"I am not here to gossip, Master Pearce. Be so kind as to open the pouch."

He did so. The glint of gold caught his eye, and he tipped the contents to the bench. "By the bones of Persis," he whispered. "There is thirty pounds here."

"And more to be had if you are willing to listen."

"Gold has a way of making me attentive, lady," Gillam said, rising from his bench and moving around to fetch a chair for Maev. She sat down, and he returned to his seat. "Please speak what is on your mind."

"Your boots and shoes are beautifully made, though you do not use the finest of leathers."

"They are too costly," he said, interrupting her.

"Indeed. But this is why the rich do not buy your boots. In serving the poor you have been forced to underprice your wares. In short, you need a change in direction."

"The highest-quality hides must be shipped from—"

"Masacar, three hundred miles from the old city of Stone," she said. "I know. A small shipment will be arriving in the next week. I have acquired it."

"You are a bootmaker?"

"No. I am a highland woman with coin to spare. If we become partners, I believe we would both benefit."

"Partners? Apart from money, madam, what will you bring to this partnership?"

"Profits," said Maev Ring.

For some time they talked. Maev agreed to finance the buying of leather and the settling of debts in return for a forty percent holding. She then produced an old pair of riding boots from a heavy canvas shoulder bag. She passed them to Gillam Pearce. He looked at them closely. "Fine leather," he said, "but poor stitching. The wear on the heels is uneven, and the left boot is too small by a fraction. See here where the wearer's toes have stretched the leather."

"Could you make a pair of boots for this man that would better these?"

"Assuredly, madam."

"Then do so. Create a work of art, Master Pearce."

"Will he be coming to me for a fitting?"

"No. When finished, they will be a gift from you."

"Who is to be the lucky recipient? Your husband?"

"The Moidart. These boots were discarded some weeks ago. One of his servants brought them to a friend of mine, who brought them to me. If your gift finds favor, Master Pearce, others will hear that you craft footwear for the Moidart. Where the lord goes, others will follow. Then there will be no more two-chailling boots from Gillam Pearce. You can hire others to craft them."

"You are very confident, Madam Ring."

"That confidence is well founded, Master Pearce."

The Moidart had been delighted with the gift. The boots had been of black Masacar leather as soft as silk yet durable. He had not sent any message of thanks to Gillam Pearce, but three weeks after the delivery of the gift two of Eldacre's richest noblemen had visited his workshop, ordering similar footwear. By the end of the summer Gillam Pearce's order book was full despite the obscenely extravagant prices Maev Ring had insisted he charge.

As Maev left the old barn and walked across the open area

to the kitchen, she calculated once more the returns from Gillam Pearce alone. Sixty pounds to settle his debts, twenty-eight pounds and eighteen chaillings to ship in quality hides, and eleven pounds and nine chaillings to refit his workshop and acquire higher-quality tools. In total ninety-two pounds and seven chaillings. In the four years they had been partners Maev had earned 417 pounds and four chaillings in excess of that sum.

The forge and armory previously solely owned by Parsis Feld now supplied some three hundred pounds per year. Other businesses—the dye works, the cattle auction dealers, the three furniture makers, and the Eldacre abbattoir—supplied 140 pounds more.

The profits were becoming singularly dangerous. The law governing the clans was harsh. No highlander could purchase a Varlish business or acquire land of more than two acres. No highlander could own a horse above fourteen and a half hands, and then only if it was a gelding. No highlander could lodge coin with a bank or borrow monies above five chaillings. Any highlander found in possession of a sword, longbow, gun, or horse above fourteen and a half hands and virile would be judged a rebel and hanged.

Despite the fact that Maev had broken no laws, she knew that this would prove no defense. It was the spirit of the law that counted. Succesful highlanders were perceived as a threat to the governing order and were dealt with one way or another. Then why go on getting richer and richer? she asked herself. It was not the first time the thought had come to her. Maev had thought about the problem often. It was not the money. Heaven knew, there was little enough that a highland woman could spend it on. No, as she had explained to Jaim, it was the challenge.

He had not understood. "We were out walking last week," she said. "We passed a section of wall that had tumbled. You stopped and spent an hour restacking the stones."

"The cattle would have wandered," he said.

"Aye, they would, Grymauch, but they were not your cattle. It was not your wall. That's how it is for me. I see the potential in a business, and it irks me when it is not realized."

"Is it worth risking your life for?"

"No, it is not," she agreed. "I cannot explain it—even to myself. It is my talent, and I feel obliged to use it. I keep telling myself I will draw back and stop one day. Yet I don't."

Maev moved through to the long kitchen. Shula was kneading dough at the wooden worktop. The shy Varlish woman had proved a boon around the house, and Maev had made it clear to her that she was welcome to stay as a guest. Instead Shula worked like a servant, constantly at some labor or other, cleaning, dusting, washing blankets and sheets, repairing Kaelin's clothes.

Maev climbed the stairs and entered the west-facing bedroom used by Jaim Grymauch. He was still asleep. Maev sat down on the bed and nudged him. He groaned and rolled over but did not wake. Maev caught the smell of ale on his breath.

"Wake up, you ox," she said, shaking his shoulder.

Jaim's one good eye opened. It was bloodshot. "What is it?" he mumbled.

"I need to know what happened with Chain Shada. Kaelin came back and would say nothing. Now he and Banny are off in the hills. And you—you drunkard—did not stagger in until dawn. Well, the sun has been up for five hours now, and no self-respecting man would still be sleeping."

"Give me a few minutes to find my brain, woman."

"By heavens, Grymauch, you'd need ten expert trackers and a wizard to find such a mythical beast. I'll be downstairs. Get yourself dressed and join me there."

"A cooked breakfast would be nice. Bacon, eggs, a steak, and some mushrooms."

"Such a breakfast is for working folk who rise early. I'll slice you some bread and cheese."

Maev rose and glanced at the clothes so carelessly slung on the floor. She hefted Jaim's cloak, which was still damp, and sniffed it. "Did you fall in the river?"

"I didn't *fall*. I swam." Grymauch threw back the covers and swung his legs from the bed.

"You vile man!" she said. "How dare you show your nakedness to me?"

"You told me to get dressed!"

"When I'm gone, man." Maev flung the cloak aside and stalked from the room. Only when she reached the stairs did she allow herself to smile. She wondered what the difference would be between having Jaim Grymauch and having a pet bear living with her.

Her good mood lasted only as long as it took Jaim to dress, eat his bread and cheese, and tell her of the events of the night before. "You didn't kill them?" she said, astonished.

"No, I didn't kill them."

"Oh, Jaim, you idiot. Now they'll be coming for you and Kaelin. What were you thinking?"

"I was thinking that I am a Rigante, not some murdering Varlish. The boy has already killed two men. And he was willing, Maev. He was even eager to add to that tally. Two prisoners. He would have shot them down without a thought. That's not right."

"Better them than us, Jaim."

"We'll have to agree to differ. I have killed men. You know that. I carried rage in my heart, and I slaughtered the enemy wherever I found him. I regret every one of those dead now. Even the bad ones. Had we killed Huntsekker and his man, we'd likely have had to go back into the undergrowth and kill the other three. Then we'd have been forced to bury them in un-marked graves, hoping no one would ever stumble upon them. Dal Naydham and Vinton Gabious have children who would never know what happened to their fathers. Bass and Boillard Seeton care for their elderly mother, who is blind now. Aye, maybe Huntsekker would be a small loss to the world. I can't say for sure. But the day will never dawn again when I cut down defenseless men. Not ever, Maev."

Maev walked to the window, staring out at the distant mountains. "We must bring the plan forward," she said. "You and Kaelin will leave today for the north. Find him and take him to the cave. Send Banny back here. Tomorrow at dawn be at the fork in the Great North Road. I will be there with a wagon."

"We don't need a wagon, Maev. It will slow us down."

"The wagon will be carrying much of my wealth, Jaim. I need to get it away from here. You will take it to my farm in the north. Once there, you will remove the gold and bury it in the woods behind the main house."

"Gold? How much gold?"

"Two thousand pounds."

"Is there that much money in the world?" he asked, astonished.

"Why in heaven's name did you get drunk last night when you knew I'd be worried sick?" she countered.

"I stopped off at the tavern for a quick one. My bones were cold through. While I was there, I heard that an old friend of mine was hanged south of the border. Public execution, Maev. Hundreds of clansmen and women gathered to watch him dance on the rope. I wish I had known."

"What difference would it have made?" she asked.

"I'd have taken my glave and marched down the main street and cut him free."

"There are usually two squads of soldiers at every execution. Twenty men, Grymauch."

"I know," he said sadly.

"So what you are saying is you'd have thrown away your life needlessly."

He suddenly grinned. "Not at all. I'd have hacked a path through the soldiers and freed him, anyway. After all, what are twenty Varlish to a man of the Rigante?"

"A pet bear would be less trouble," she said.

"What?" he asked, mystified.

"Never mind. Find Kaelin and be at the fork at dawn."

The black-lacquered coach bearing the fawn in brambles crest of the Moidart stood waiting, the matched black horses standing patiently. Behind the coach ten lancers also waited in lines of two. The driver, dressed in a heavy double-shouldered coat, sat hunched, the reins in his hands.

A white-wigged Gaise Macon, his long pale blue cloak flaring in the breeze, walked back and forth, occasionally staring toward the gates of the castle. It was nearing noon, and there was no sign of Mulgrave. At last Gaise removed his cloak, opened the door of the coach, and climbed inside. The seats were of polished hide, and embroidered cushions were scattered upon them. Gaise tapped twice on the front panel. The driver flicked the reins, and the coach rumbled over the cobbles and out onto the hill road above Eldacre.

Gaise was disappointed that he had not been able to say farewell to his mentor. Mulgrave had been a good friend these past few years. Lifting his booted heels to the seat opposite, Gaise leaned back. It would be a long journey to Varingas, the capital. Eight days of mind-numbing boredom. It would have been so much more satisfying to ride the palomino and camp beside streams. But this was inappropriate for the son of the Moidart. No, his journey to the capital had to be made in style, with a ten-man escort and not even a wave good-bye from his closest friend.

Mulgrave had been much occupied during the last few weeks trying to solve the riddle of the murders of Jek Bindoe and the kilted Varlish boy. Gaise guessed that the soldier had his suspicions about the identity of the killer but would not voice them. Then had come the killing of Boillard Seeton. Like Bindoe, he had been shot before being stabbed. Mulgrave was convinced that the man who had shot Boillard had also been responsible for the other murders.

"It is a highlander for sure," he said. "The killer did not ride from the old bridge. He walked. I followed the tracks for a while, but then they vanished in a stream. I rode that stream looking for an exit print. I found none. But there were many areas where either the ground was rocky alongside the water or overhanging branches reached down. The man was canny, as they say in these parts. He was also not heavily built. The prints were not deep. Judging by the ground he covered, I would also assume him to be young and strong."

"What does it matter, my friend?" asked Gaise Macon. "Bindoe was a rapist and a murderer. He deserved to die. Boillard Seeton was a hunter of men and a man of poor reputation. Added to which I am glad Chain Shada escaped."

"It matters, sir, because a highlander has killed three Varlish. It would not be a good precedent for him to escape justice."

"It has not sparked a rebellion, Mulgrave."

"No, sir, but it has planted a seed."

The coach rumbled on. Gaise looked out the window at the houses flowing by and the people walking the narrow streets of Eldacre. Most of the men were wearing white wigs and the high-collared black coats once so popular in the south. A dog ran alongside the coach, barking furiously. A lancer broke formation and clouted the animal with the haft of his lance. The dog yelped and ran away.

Gaise pulled off his wig and scratched his head. Already he was sweating, and the journey had scarcely begun. The coach rumbled on past Five Fields, which was empty now. Gaise thought back to the night of the fight. He had been impressed by Jaim Grymauch. Just for a moment, after he had downed Gorain for the last time, the man had seemed like a giant, his huge frame silhouetted against the mountains.

He recalled an old description of the clansmen: "men with mountains on their shoulders." It was certainly true of that clansman.

And yet we treat them in the same way the lancer treated the dog alongside the coach, he thought. At first sign of independent thought we come down on them with whips and guns and the hangman's noose. It was no way to govern a people.

But it was the way of the Moidart.

Gaise felt himself tensing as he thought of his father and the man's last words as servants had carried his trunks down to the coach.

"Do nothing to make me ashamed," he had said.

Gaise wished he had found the courage to say: "If only you could do the same."

The senseless murder of Gorain had saddened the young noble. The fighter had given his best and been beaten. For that he had been dragged away in the dark of the night and hanged from a tree. Then, for a noble gesture that epitomized the greatness of the Varlish, Chain Shada had been hunted like an animal. It was monstrous.

Gaise was glad to be leaving the area. Perhaps in Varingas he would learn to feel pride in his race again. The Academy of Martial Thought was run by some of the finest soldiers ever to lead Varlish armies, and the books in its libraries were written by or about the greatest military geniuses of the last thousand years. All twelve of Jasaray's campaign memoirs were there. Gaise had also been told that the six books on cavalry warfare by the legendary Luden Macks were presented to every new student upon arrival.

The road curved sharply to the west for a while, and, glancing through the window, Gaise saw the towers of Eldacre Castle sharp against the sky. He stared morosely at the gray fortress.

Many of the great stories he had read talked of the joys of home. Gaise had never known such joys. Assassins had killed his mother while he was still a babe, and his father had always been a cold and vengeful figure. Eldacre Castle contained no fond memories. He could not recall one incident where his father had ever praised him or hugged him. In fact he had rarely seen the man smile.

Maybe he will die in the four years I am at the academy, he thought. Perhaps when I return, I will be the Moidart.

The thought saddened him, though he did not know why.

The road swung south, the castle disappearing from sight.

Gaise stared out now over the snowcapped mountains and found himself recalling the words of the woman in his dream: *You have no soul-name.*

What difference could it possibly make?

For the next hour Gaise tried to read. It was a book about the capital and its sites of interest: the White Tower, the Burning Bridge, the restored stone amphitheater, where plays were performed before the king, the Royal Park where red deer roamed, the gardens of Gavaras—twenty-five acres of plants brought from all corners of the known world. Gaise flicked through the pages, trying to concentrate. Every now and again he would look out the window at the mountains.

I shall miss you, he thought. I will miss the land.

The coach entered the woods, keeping to the old Scardyke Road.

Bored now, Gaise considered climbing to the seat beside the driver and engaging the man in conversation. As he prepared to do so, he heard the driver call out, "Whoa!" The coach came to a stop. A rider moved past the window. Curious now, Gaise swung open the door and climbed out.

Mulgrave was tethering his chestnut gelding to the rear of the coach. Gaise smiled as he saw him.

"I thought you had forgotten I was leaving."

"Hardly," replied the officer. "May I travel with you a while, sir?"

"Of course." Gaise returned to the coach. Mulgrave, removing his sword belt, joined him.

"Why were you not at the castle?" asked Gaise.

"Your father dismissed me from his service late yesterday. Since my main role was as your tutor and you were leaving for Varingas, he said he had no further use for me. To be honest, I had anticipated this. So I wrote to an old friend who had once offered me a position to inquire as to whether the offer was still good. He wrote back to say that the post was mine whenever I required it. So here I am, sir, on my way to Varingas."

"That is marvelous news," Gaise said happily. "We will be able to see each other in the capital."

"Indeed, so, sir."

"Have you been there before?"

"I served there for two years."

"Then you can be my guide. You can show me the wall on the White Tower from which Kaverly dived to freedom."

"He dived from the west tower, sir, but yes, I will be glad to show you the sites."

"Ah, but this is most fine, Mulgrave. My day is complete. So tell me, did you identify the murderer?"

"Only to my own satisfaction, sir."

"Will you share the secret?"

Mulgrave shook his head. "Only this far, sir. On the night of the murders a young highlander spoke to me concerning Bindoe. He doubted that Varlish justice would prevail. When I saw that the word "justice" had been carved into the brows of the murdered men, I guessed that this highlander had played a part in the killings. Just before your father dismissed me I rode out to see Huntsekker."

Gaise grinned. "My father was angry with the old man for failing."

"Aye, he was. Huntsekker claimed he was struck from behind and did not see his attackers. This was not true. I rode to the scene and read the tracks. Huntsekker stood for a while talking to the men. The one who died—Seeton—had run to the spot where he died. Several other footprints were close by, three of them made by large men. The last of them was a smaller foot. Huntsekker wears moccasins with no heel. His track was easy to read. The second of the large men wore riding boots. This I took to be Chain Shada. There is no question in my mind that Huntsekker saw the men who killed Seeton."

"Why, then, would he refuse to name them?" asked Gaise.

"More important, sir, why did they not kill him? Seeton was stabbed through the back, possibly as he was running. Having murdered one man, why not two? Indeed, why not the others, who were merely stunned?"

"Did you put this to Huntsekker?"

"Yes."

"What did he say?"

"He said that life was always more interesting while mystery prevailed. He then asked me if I intended to report my suspicions to the Moidart. In turn I asked him what his thoughts were on the subject. He walked across the room and returned with a curious weapon, a hand scythe with a heavy crescent blade. He laid it on the table. Then he said: 'Do you believe in magic, Captain?' I told him that I didn't know whether supernatural powers existed but that it would not surprise me if they did. He sat down and hefted the weapon. The man is large; his hands are huge. He said: 'I believe in magic. This scythe has killed men. It has taken the heads of murderers and thieves. It has—only once—claimed the life of the innocent. And even then the man wasn't *so* innocent.' 'You believe the scythe is magical?' I asked him. 'No, not the scythe,' he told me. 'This is an old land with old magic. I have studied it. There are certain men who feed the land, men unaware of their own greatness. I will not kill such men regardless of who orders it. I thought I could. I thought my own strength was such that I could overpower the will of the land. I was wrong. Chain Shada deserved to walk free. There is no doubt of that. The men who helped him deserved to walk free. I know this, too.' I sat silently for a moment. Then I said: 'Despite the fact that they killed your man, Seeton?' 'They killed no one,' he said. 'Seeton died because he was an oath breaker. A man should stand by his promises.' It was then that I realized Seeton had been killed by the scythe. Huntsekker had slain him."

"By the Sacrifice!" said Gaise Macon. "Why? What else did he say?"

"He said nothing, sir. He replaced the scythe in a black sheath and asked me if I would join him for dinner. After that we spoke of many things but did not again touch upon the events by the river. After the meal he walked me to my horse and asked me what my report would say. I told him there would be no report, since it was likely I would be leaving Eldacre for the capital in the next few days. He wished me well on my journey."

"So why did Huntsekker kill the man?"

Mulgrave shrugged. "My guess would be that Huntsekker promised the highlanders he would not reveal their identities. Seeton must have made the same promise. Huntsekker did not believe he would keep it."

Gaise was mystified. "Why would the highlanders trust Huntsekker?"

"Why indeed? And yet they could."

"So how did all this lead you to the identity of the man who killed Bindoe?"

"Bear in mind, sir, that I already had my suspicions, based on that conversation the night the girl was killed. I followed the tracks from the river. The younger, smaller man headed back toward Old Hills. The larger man cut away north. His tracks led to a small settlement and an unsavory tavern. I spoke to the tavern keeper, asking him who had been drinking there the night before. I told him I was interested only in one person, a large man standing over six feet tall. He said he couldn't remember. I offered him two choices: a silver chailling or a visit from Captain Galliott. He accepted the chailling and gave me the name. Once I had the name, I knew the identity of the young man who had been with him."

"And you chose not to divulge it to the Moidart. Why?"

"I truly cannot say, sir. There is little doubt in my mind that Bindoe was warned to run, probably by Galliott. The young man was in all likelihood correct in his assumption that Varlish justice would not have prevailed. As to Chain Shada, I have to agree with Huntsekker. The man deserved to escape. All in all, nothing would be served by seeing two more highlanders swinging from the gibbet."

"My father would not agree with you, my friend."

"Indeed he would not. He is not an agreeable man. It pleases me that he will be irritated when he learns of my new post."

"Why should he be irritated?"

"I am to be the fencing instructor at the Academy of Martial Thought and therefore one of your new teachers. Are you aware that you will be obliged to call me 'sir'?"

◇ **10** ◇

As Kaelin Ring swiftly discovered, the world was very different two hundred miles northwest of Eldacre. In those high, forbidding snowcapped mountains highlanders massively outnumbered the Varlish and a mere two hundred Beetlebacks and musketeers patrolled an area of almost eighteen hundred square miles. The towns were small, and the Varlish businesses were almost totally reliant on the custom of clansmen. Kaelin found people less friendly than in Old Hills, viewing him with a degree of suspicion. In some ways it was amusing. For most of his life Kaelin had thought of southerners with contempt, for they were almost all Varlish. To the townspeople of Black Mountain Kaelin himself was a southerner and Varlish-tainted.

Maev's farm was two miles from the town of Black Mountain, nestling in the mighty shadows of a range of towering peaks. It was cooler there than in Old Hills, and Jaim explained that they were now many thousands of feet above sea level. The air was thinner, which was why Kaelin had at first felt breathless when joining Jaim and the other five workers in felling trees for winter fuel.

The farm boasted two herds, each numbering some six hundred short-horned shaggy animals. The first herd was kept in the high pastures to the west, the second in a series of fields between the farm and Black Mountain. There were also thirty milk cows pastured within a half mile of the main house.

The numerous farm buildings were old and much repaired

over the years. The main house was more than two hundred years old, two-storied, built of gray stone, and roofed with timber and black slate. It was a cold house, grim and unwelcoming. Fifty paces to the west was a long, low building housing the cook house and a living area for the workers, and beyond that was the churning hall, where women from Black Mountain made butter, clotted cream, and cheese. A little way from that was the high barn, a shambling structure containing an old wagon, two swaybacked ponies, ten abandoned stalls for riding horses, and a loft for storing hay. A little farther on was a roughly built stone abbatoir and a salt storehouse.

Kaelin missed Old Hills and his friend Banny. He felt out of place there among strangers.

Jaim had stayed only a month, and in that time they had reestablished—at least in part—their easygoing relationship. Kaelin loved the fighter, but it was hard to overcome his disappointment at the man's softness when dealing with Huntsekker and his crew. Had they killed the man, Kaelin would not now be laboring in a foreign land where men treated him with cold courtesy.

Just the other morning he and Finbarr Ustal and his brothers, Jabe and Killon, had been out in the high pasture repairing a drystone wall. The brothers, all redheaded and pale-skinned, had been chatting in a language Kaelin did not know. He had asked Finbarr about it. Conversation ceased immediately. Finbarr scratched at his thin red beard. "It is Keltoi, Kaelin. The language of the clansman. Does no one speak it in the conquered lands?"

"No."

"A shame, that is, to be sure," said Finbarr, swinging back to his brothers and beginning the conversation again.

Kaelin could make no inroads with these men or with Bally Koin and Senlic Carpenter, the two senior herdsmen. Senlic was the friendliest, if "friendly" could be used to describe the fact that he would at least acknowledge Kaelin's presence with a nod or a wave.

Yet Jaim had no difficulty with them. With him they would chuckle and swap jokes, engaging in easy familiarity.

Kaelin continued to work patiently alongside them, believing that in time their suspicions of him would fade and that they would accept him as a clansman.

Then came the visit of Call Jace.

Kaelin was strolling back from the abattoir, where he had sold two steers to one of the Black Mountain butchers. He saw the gray-haired Senlic Carpenter and Finbarr Ustal standing with two tall kilted highlanders and what he took at first to be a boy. What was surprising was that all three highlanders wore swords and had pistols tucked into their belts. Kaelin walked toward the group. He saw Senlic speaking swiftly to the leader, a tall man nearly as big as Grymauch. The man wore a bonnet cap sporting an eagle feather and a cloak of pale green and blue intersected with red horizontal and vertical lines. As he came closer, he realized the third highlander was not a boy but a young red-haired girl dressed in buckskin leggings and a bright green woolen overshirt. She also sported a bonnet cap, but without a feather. Her face was pretty, her eyes deep green, her mouth divine. Kaelin could not take his eyes off her. She was without doubt the most beautiful girl he had ever seen. Suddenly aware of the growing silence, he dragged his gaze from the girl and spoke to the leader.

"Good morning," said Kaelin. "Are you here on business?"

"If I am, what is it to you, boy?" answered the man. His eyes were pale blue, his beard close-trimmed and black with touches of silver.

Kaelin could see he was angry, though he could think of no reason why. Kaelin's greeting had been courteous. "My aunt Maev owns this farm," said Kaelin, "and I speak for her."

"She should have known better than to leave a boy in charge," said the man. "I'll conduct my business with Senlic."

Now Kaelin felt his blood grow hot. "No, you will not," he said. "And if you call me 'boy' again, you can leave my property and seek business elsewhere."

"Is that so? How, then, does 'whelp' sound to you?"

The highlander was taller than Kaelin by around six inches and much heavier. Despite that, Kaelin dropped his shoulder and sent a straight left that crashed against the man's jaw. It was a good punch and knocked the surprised highlander back a pace. Kaelin followed in with a right to the belly and a left cross that almost spun the man from his feet.

Something struck him hard across the back of the head. Kaelin stumbled and fell to his knees. Dizziness swamped him, but he fought it and struggled up. He saw that the second highlander, a young man with a thick red beard, had struck him with a pistol butt. Kaelin could feel blood flowing down his neck, and his head was pounding.

With a great effort he pushed himself to his feet. He stood and swayed. Finbarr and Senlic were standing by quietly. The leader was rubbing his jaw. No one spoke. Kaelin backed away, turned on his heel, and walked to the house. He was unsteady, but the power of anger surging through his veins gave him strength. In his own room he pulled the walnut box from beneath his bed, opened it, and lifted clear the two pistols. Swiftly he loaded them. Then he walked back into the sunshine.

The men were still there, only now Finbarr's brothers, Jabe and Killon, had joined them. The tall man Kaelin had struck was the first to see him. He said something, and the men spread out. The highlander who had hit Kaelin with the pistol butt saw the guns in Kaelin's hands and dragged his own weapon clear, cocking it and bringing it to bear. Before he could shoot, Kaelin's pistol roared. He had aimed for the chest, but the shot struck the highlander on the side of the head. The man dropped his pistol and slumped to his knees before toppling to the ground. Senlic Carpenter ran to him, rolling him to his back. "It did not penetrate," he told the other highlander. "It creased his scalp. He'll be all right."

Kaelin heard the words but did not care. The remaining silver pistol came up, pointing directly at the face of the leader. He walked forward until the barrel was inches from the man's face.

"Feel free to use the word 'whelp' again, you scum-sucking goat turd. It will be the last word you utter. Come on! Say it!"

"You want me to kill him, Father?" said the young woman.

Kaelin flicked a glance to his right and saw that the girl had drawn her pistol. It was cocked and pointed at his belly.

"Yes, shoot," said Kaelin. "Do it now! It will not prevent me from exploding what passes for his brains all over the yard."

"Nice pistols," said the man, his voice calm, his eyes angry. "They look like Emburleys." He turned to the girl. "Put it down, lass. There'll be no more shooting today."

The man on the ground groaned and tried to sit. Then he fell back.

"Carry him inside," the tall man told Senlic and the others. They moved instantly to obey him.

"Stand fast!" ordered Kaelin. The men froze. "If he cannot walk," he told the leader, "you can carry him to his home, wherever that may be."

The highlander stood for a moment, holding to Kaelin's gaze. He said nothing and moved to the fallen man. Leaning down, he hoisted him to his feet. Before he could fall, the leader ducked down and hefted him to his shoulder. Then he walked away. The girl stood for a moment. "You were lucky today," she told Kaelin. "But when Bael recovers from your cowardly attack, he will seek you out."

"And I'll bury him," said Kaelin. "Now get off my land."

He watched her walk away, then swung to the waiting men. "You speak in Keltoi, you talk of conquered lands, and you regard southerners as little more than hounds of the Varlish. And yet beneath it all you are scum, all talk and no honor. Back in Old Hills, when a man takes a wage, he works—and fights—alongside the man who pays him. It is called loyalty where I come from."

"*You* do not pay the wages," said Finbarr Ustal. "They come from Maev Ring. The man you threatened is Call Jace,

the clan leader of the Rigante. I'd fight and die for him willingly, and I'd need no wage for it."

"Then go and do it, Finbarr. Pack your things."

"I have a wife and three bairns to support," said the
shocked man.

"I'm sure Call Jace will support them for you, you being
such a loyal follower."

Finbarr stood stunned. Senlic Carpenter stepped forward.
"This must not get out of hand, Kaelin," he said. "No one
knew you were about to strike Call Jace, and when Bael hit
you with the pistol, it took us all by surprise. None of us would
have allowed any further harm to come to you. You have my
word on that. Finbarr is right, though, in one respect. Call Jace
is admired throughout the mountains. He holds to the old
ways. Even the Beetlebacks will not ride into his territory."

"What did he want here?"

Senlic looked away, then took a deep breath. "He was here
for his tribute, sir. Two steers a month. Your aunt agreed to it.
Every farmer and merchant pays Call Jace. If they didn't, he
would steal the steers anyway."

Kaelin stood very still. He was angry enough to tell them
all to pack their belongings and leave and to add that if
Call Jace stole one cow, he would kill him. Yet he did not, for
he knew it would be foolish. With no one to run the farm he
would be reduced to hiring men he did not know. As to the
tribute, if Maev had agreed to it, then that was all there was to
it. He stood silently staring at them, his contempt obvious.

"Am I dismissed, then?" asked Finbarr Ustal.

Kaelin's head had begun to pound. He reached up and felt a
lump the size of a sparrow's egg. The skin was split, though
blood was no longer flowing.

"Pick out two steers for the tribute and deliver them yourself," said Kaelin.

" 'Tis a two-day walk to his settlement," said Finbarr.

"Then you'd best take supplies," answered Kaelin. "You
still have a place here, Ustal. But if you cross me again, I'll
kill you."

Senlic Carpenter spoke. "Call Jace may want more steers, sir. Because of the . . . embarrassment," he concluded lamely.

"I don't care what he wants." Kaelin swung back to face the silent Finbarr. "Tell Call Jace that Maev Ring set the tribute and I will abide by it. Tell him also that as leader of the clan, he is welcome at my house."

"That is all? No . . . apology or . . . gesture of friendship?" asked Finbarr.

"No."

Kaelin walked toward the house. His legs almost gave way, and he staggered but then righted himself. Once inside, he sat down in front of the fire.

Then he passed out.

He awoke some hours later. Moonlight was filtering through the window, and the fire had gone out. His head was thudding like a drum. Rising from the chair, he groaned and walked through to the kitchen. There was a pitcher of water on the table, and he poured himself a drink. The water made him feel sick. He made it out into the yard before vomiting. Feeling weak and disoriented, he struggled up the stairs to the west-facing bedroom and lay on the bed, too weary to remove his clothing.

He felt better by the time the dawn came up, though his head still hurt. Blood had matted his hair and stained the pillow. Moving downstairs, he cooked three eggs and ate them with the previous day's bread, which he fried in beef fat.

The sun was bright as he made his way to the well, drawing up a bucket of water and splashing it to his face. Senlic Carpenter was bringing in the dairy herd. He and Bally Koin would spend most of the morning milking. The cart, with the four girls who churned the butter, was just cresting the eastern hill. Kaelin found that the brightness of the sunlight hurt his eyes. Bally Koin strolled past him but made no sign of acknowledgment. Even Senlic looked away as he led the cows in.

So this is how it will be, thought Kaelin.

For the next three days Kaelin Ring lived in a world of

silence. No one spoke to him unless to respond to a question he asked. All eyes avoided him. By the second day even the churners looked away as he walked past, and the butchers who arrived to dicker for fresh meat seemed a little more distant.

On the morning of the fourth day Finbarr Ustal walked into the farmyard and approached Kaelin.

"Did he accept the tribute?"

"Aye, sir. He has invited you to dine with him at his home should you wish to travel there."

Kaelin looked into Finbarr's eyes. The man was at pains to disguise his expression, but Kaelin sensed he was enjoying the moment. "How do I get there?" asked Kaelin.

"You walk due west, following the mine road. You will be met."

"And when is this invitation for?"

"Whenever you choose to arrive, sir. Will you be going?"

"Why would I not?"

Finbarr shrugged. "You might feel that the Black Rigante were bringing you into a trap. You might think that you were meant to die in the wild country."

"Would you advise me to accept, Finbarr?" asked Kaelin.

"It's not for me to offer advice."

Kaelin stayed silent but held to the man's gaze. The silence grew. Finbarr seemed uncomfortable. "What? What do you want me to say?"

Senlic Carpenter moved into view. "He wants you to tell him whether they plan to murder him, Finn."

"How would I know what they plan? He doesn't have to go."

"Is Bael recovered?" asked Senlic.

"He has a sore head, but he's walking." Finbarr exchanged glances with the old herdsman. "All right. All right. Bael will probably challenge him to a duel." He looked back at Kaelin. "What did you expect? That it would all be forgotten?"

"Don't go, Kaelin," urged Senlic. "It will blow over."

"It's time I saw the mountains," said Kaelin Ring. "You stay in charge until I get back."

Once inside the old house, Kaelin went to his room and stood at the window, staring out at the western mountains. He wished Grymauch was there. When Finbarr Ustal had spoken of the invitation, Kaelin's stomach had tightened. Fear of this kind was alien to the young highlander and all the more powerful now as a result. Turning from the window, he caught sight of his reflection in the square mirror above the pine dresser.

He looked older than his fifteen years, his face angular, his dark eyes deep set. Kaelin was pleased that the raging fear inside did not appear to show on the stern young features. No one would guess that he was quaking inside.

The reality was that he had brought this situation on himself. The man Bael had been protecting his chief. He could have stabbed Kaelin or shot him. Instead he had struck him once with the butt of his pistol.

The events that had followed had been entirely of Kaelin's making, and he felt relieved that he had not killed Bael.

Even so he had managed to anger and humiliate the leader of the Black Rigante, a clan known for its murderous ways.

Now he was to pay, probably with his life.

You don't have to go, he told his reflection.

Yet deep in his heart he knew he had no choice. If he refused, it would be a second snub to Call Jace, and that would mean total enmity. Then they would come for him. At some point, as he mended a fence or traveled into Black Mountain for supplies, clansmen would appear and cut him down. And even if they ignored him, everyone would know that Kaelin Ring was too frightened to walk into the mountains and face Call Jace.

He recalled the words of Jaim Grymauch: "Always listen to fear, Kaelin. Never be ruled by it. Fear is like a cowardly friend. His advice is not always wrong, but given the chance, he will drag you down into the pit he dwells in."

Kaelin moved to the chest at the far wall and took out a thick double-shouldered hunting shirt of oiled doeskin and a pair of buckskin trews. Discarding his clothes, he dressed and pulled on a knee-length pair of moccasins and strapped on a belt containing a powder horn, a pouch of lead shot, and a nine-inch hunting knife. Retrieving the Emburleys, he loaded them and placed them in his belt.

If any Beetlebacks were patrolling the mountain roads, he would be arrested and hanged for sure.

From a drawer in the dresser he pulled clear a gray blanket, which he folded and rolled before draping it over his shoulder and walking downstairs.

Senlic Carpenter was waiting in the main room. Beside him was a canvas shoulder sack.

"There's some food in here," said the old man. "Muslin-wrapped cheese, oats, and some salt beef. You'll find streams aplenty for water. I've put a tinderbox and an old pot in there, too. Watch where you camp. There's few wolves left in the mountains now, but there's bears. Some of them can be right grumpy at this time of year."

"Thank you."

"You don't need to do this," said the old man, rising from his chair. The words were said without conviction.

"Always good to do something new on your birthday," said Kaelin.

"Birthday, is it? How old are you? Eighteen? Nineteen?"

"Fifteen," Kaelin told him.

Senlic was surprised. "I thought you older. Damnit, Kaelin, don't do this! If Call Jace knew you were not of majority, it would make a difference."

"I am of majority from today. If I don't return, tell Jaim Grymauch what happened. Will you do that?"

"I will. Were you there when he fought the Varlish champion?"

"Yes. It was a grand battle."

Senlic smiled. "We heard of it. Wished I'd seen it."

"It was a sight," agreed Kaelin, hoisting the shoulder sack and slipping his blanket underneath the strap.

"Take care, Kaelin. And stand tall. Call Jace admires a man who does that."

Kaelin Ring left the stone farmhouse and walked out. The other men were standing some distance away. No one spoke, and Kaelin did not look at them.

He journeyed west for several hours, the ground steadily rising. His headache cleared by noon, and truth to tell, he was starting to enjoy the walk. He had not realized quite how stultifying farm life had become with the endless writing in ledgers, the collecting and storing of coin, the checking of supplies. Out there in the open he felt free of such obligations. He thought of Alterith Shaddler. Without the man's teaching he would not have been able to keep Maev's books in order. The man might have known little about the Rigante, but he knew how to teach sums. And how to use a cane, thought Kaelin. He smiled at the memory of the man. It reminded him of Old Hills and a time without fear.

There was only one road west, and Kaelin held to it, always listening and watching for riders. Occasionally he saw men in the far distance, some herding cattle, others working, repairing sod roofs, or tilling the earth.

The land was growing more rugged now, outcroppings of rock piercing the shallow earth, stands of pine silhouetted against the clear blue sky. Kaelin paused, admiring the green against the blue. It seemed to him then that these were the colors of life. It was as if he were seeing pines against the sky for the first time. His heart soared. Surely it was this grand sight that had inspired the blue and green Rigante cloak.

The wind was strong and easterly, cold from flowing over the snow-topped peaks. It was bracing, and Kaelin enjoyed it. Every now and again he would remember why he was making this trek, but even the grim prospect of the Black Rigante could not dent his mood in this high, mighty country.

High overhead two golden eagles banked and flew off toward the west.

Kaelin walked on. Toward dusk he left the road, climbing to a rocky outcrop where a stream tipped over pale stones in a series of tiny waterfalls. Filling his small copper pot, he added a handful of oats and set a fire beneath a spreading pine. The camp could not be seen from the road, and the thin smoke would be dispersed by the branches.

When the fire had been going for a little while, enough for coals to form, he laid his pot upon it, stirring the contents with a wooden spoon. The air was filled with the scent of pines and woodsmoke, and Kaelin felt free for the first time in months.

With the porridge bubbling, he took two large sticks and lifted the pot from the fire, setting it on a rock to cool.

When I get back, he thought, I will write to Aunt Maev asking if Banny can join me. He would like it here. No one need know of his mixed blood. Not that it would matter, he realized, since Banny was a southerner like himself and would largely be ignored. Kaelin smiled. Banny had always wished to be treated like a clansman. Here he would be accepted as such and treated the same, anyway.

After a while he ate the oats, enjoying the deep warmth in his belly. Then he chewed on some salt beef, drank from the stream, and settled down beside his fire. Lying on his back, he looked up at the stars. And fell asleep.

The sleep was dreamless and good.

A noise awoke him just after dawn. It was the sound of snuffling and tearing. Lying very still, he opened his eyes. A large brown bear was ripping at his food sack.

Kaelin stayed motionless. The bear pushed his head into the bag, then shook it. The oats spilled out, followed by the salt beef and the cheese. Kaelin considered discharging one of his pistols to frighten the beast away, but there was little point now. The sack was ruined, the food spread over the ground. It did not take the bear long to devour Kaelin's supplies. It padded around the campsite, then ambled toward where he lay. Kaelin closed his eyes. He felt the bear's nose brush against his cheek and smelled the musty odor of its fur.

Then it swung away and padded off into the pines.

Kaelin waited until it was gone from sight, then rose. The sound of soft, contemptuous laughter came to him. Whipping his knife from its sheath, he spun toward the sound—to see the redheaded girl who had been with Call Jace sitting on a broad branch ten feet above the edge of his campsite. She no longer wore the bonnet cap, and her hair hung free, framing her face.

"What are you laughing at?" he asked, aware of the foolishness of the question even as he spoke it.

"Do you learn nothing in the south?" she countered. "What kind of a fool sets his camp alongside the tracks of a bear? Could you not see that this is where old Shabba comes to drink in the morning?"

"Obviously not," he replied, reddening.

Sheathing his knife, he moved to the canvas sack, which was ruined, and retrieved the tinderbox, the cooking pot, and the spoon.

"It will be a hungry day for you," she said, reaching into a pouch hanging from her belt and pulling clear an oatcake, which she began to eat.

"I'm surprised you didn't slit my throat while I slept," said Kaelin.

"Bael will do that," she said. "Would not be fair to rob him of his fun."

"I take it I'll get dinner first," he said.

"Of course. We are not barbarians." Rising, she walked lithely along the branch and began to climb down the trunk. Reaching the ground, she strolled over to him. Kaelin looked into her green eyes and felt lost for words. "Now you are gawping again," she said. "Did you not get into enough trouble for that last time?"

"Gawping?"

"You were staring at me. It made my father angry, which is why he spoke as he did. Do you learn no manners in the south?"

"Obviously there is much we do not learn in the south," he said, anger rising.

"I didn't think you would come," she said, moving away from him to the stream. Squatting down, she cupped her hands and drank. "You are not a wise man, Kaelin Ring."

The sound of his name from her lips was like music. Returning to the center of the camp, she also sat down. "My father likes those pistols. Perhaps if you gave them to him, he would forgive you."

"What is your name?"

"Chara."

His face registered his shock. She was surprised at his reaction. "You do not like the name?" she asked.

"It is a good name," he said sadly.

"Then what is wrong?"

"Nothing." He pushed himself to his feet. "Let us be on our way."

Chara Jace had not been truthful with the young southerner. She *had* expected him to agree to her father's invitation. In fact, she had pressed her father to offer it. Chara tried to convince herself it was so she could watch the arrogant boy being humiliated. That was not so.

As she walked alongside him, she could not stop herself from occasionally glancing at him. He was handsome, his face strong, his movements graceful. His handling of the situation with the bear had impressed her. Many men, upon waking, would have reacted with sudden shock. They might have shouted or leapt up. He had lain still and calm even as old Shabba had nuzzled his face. Yet this same calm young man had reacted with cold and terrifying violence when struck by Bael. He had not lashed back. He had walked back into his house and emerged with two silver pistols. It was a miracle that Bael was still alive.

Bael had recovered his senses after an hour and had been able to walk unaided. He had talked in camp that night of returning and killing the southerner. Call Jace would have none of it. "I allowed the matter to get out of hand," he said. "I should not have insulted him. He may be Varlish-tainted, but he is still Rigante. By heaven, he showed that!"

"The brat shot me!" said Bael. "I cannot allow it to pass. And you had every right to insult him. Hell's teeth, Father, he all but stripped Chara with his eyes."

"I know." Call had turned to Chara then. "What do you think we should do, lass?"

"I don't care, Father."

"I didn't ask if you cared. How would you deal with this situation?"

"He did not pay the tribute, so he has broken the agreement made by his aunt. We should take all his cattle from the high pasture, drive them south, and sell them."

"Aye, that's a good thought. But what of the man himself? You think he should die?"

Chara had thought about this, recalling the dark-eyed young man and how she had felt with those eyes upon her. "I'll need to think on it further," she said.

"Good. Decisions about life and death should never be made in a hurry," he said.

The following day Finbarr Ustal had arrived with the tribute and the message from Kaelin Ring. "I am welcome at his house?" said Call Jace.

"That's what he said, lord," replied Finbarr.

"And nothing else?"

"Not a word. I asked him if he wanted me to apologize on his behalf, and he said no."

Call swung to Chara. "Any further thoughts, lass?"

"Aye, Father. Invite him to visit. If you are welcome at his house, then he should be welcome at yours."

"I like that plan," said Bael. "My head will ache the less when I've cut him a little."

"You will stay the night, Finbarr, and enjoy our hospitality," said Call Jace. "Then tomorrow you will go home and pass on my invitation to the southerner."

"Yes, lord."

Toward noon Chara led Kaelin away from the road and down to the shores of a small lake. The sun was bright in a clear blue sky, the air fresh and cool. "Do you swim, southerner?" she asked him.

"Not well."

"This is Crystal Tears Lake. It is said to have been blessed by the Seidh a thousand years ago. If you dive deep, you can see into the past."

"How can anyone see into the past?"

"Swim with me and I'll show you."

"Why not?" said Kaelin Ring.

Chara pulled off her green woolen shirt and leggings and shoes and waded out naked into the cold water. Kaelin stood for a moment watching her. She looked around. "Are you going to stand there gawping again, or are you going to swim?"

Sitting down, Kaelin tugged off his moccasins, undressed, and followed her. She dived below the surface. Taking a deep breath, he followed. The water was clear, and Kaelin saw an old pike dart behind some rocks. Chara was just ahead. She paused in her swim and pointed at what at first seemed to be a pillar of rock. Kaelin swam closer. It was the head of a colossal statue half-buried in the earth. The head was fully twenty feet high. It was of a man with a heavily curled beard. He was wearing a crown. Kaelin's lungs were straining, and he kicked out for the surface.

Chara came up alongside him, and they trod water. "Who is it? Connavar? Bane?" asked Kaelin.

"The Dweller says it is far older than Rigante history," she told him. "Farther on there are drowned houses of white stone and many more statues. I found a small square of gold there once. It had engravings on it. The Dweller told me it was a coin in ancient times, used by a race now vanished from the world." She looked at him closely. "Your lips are turning blue with cold. You need to get out of the water."

Together they swam for the shore. Kaelin was shivering as

he waded to the bank. Chara ran past him and sat down, draping her woolen shirt over her shoulders.

"Be so good as to dress," he said, not looking at her.

"I'd like to dry off first."

Kaelin struggled into his trews and donned the buckskin shirt.

"I'll wager that feels uncomfortable," she said. "All that water dripping on your skin."

"Aye, it is," he agreed, buckling his belt.

"Why does my nakedness bother you?"

"It is not seemly."

She laughed. "That is a Varlish concept, Kaelin Ring. How many more of their ways have you drawn into your heart?"

"What do you mean?" he asked, finally turning toward her.

"The Keltoi have never been ashamed of their bodies. But the Varlish teach of the evil of nakedness."

He sat down and looked away toward the lake. Then he sighed. "I think you are right," he said. "We live among them, and we absorb their ways without even knowing it. We think we are holding to our culture, but it is an illusion. Clan children are now born and no one gives them soul-names. We buy our clothes from Varlish stores, we learn in Varlish schools, and we no longer speak the language of our ancestors. They are stealing our souls, and we do not notice." He fell silent for a while. Then he glanced at her and smiled. He looked suddenly young, she thought, almost vulnerable. "I am sorry I spoke like a Varlish. You are very beautiful. The most beautiful girl I have ever seen."

"Have you seen many naked women?"

"I haven't seen any—well, until now."

She laughed. "Then it is not much of a compliment, Kaelin Ring."

"I guess not, Chara Jace."

She lifted the woolen shirt over her head and slipped into it. Then she shivered. "That's better," she said. "Tell me, why did my name seem to upset you?"

At first she thought he had ignored the question, for he

looked away once more. When he spoke, his voice was heavy with sadness. "I knew someone with that name," he said at last. "A sweet girl. She wanted to walk with me to the Beltine Feast."

"She was smitten by you?"

"I think that she was. Because of it she was raped and murdered by two Varlish."

The words hung in the air between them. Chara did not know what to say. Rape was a rare crime in the highlands, but to murder a woman? As the silence grew, she knew she had to say something to break it. "I am so sorry, Kaelin. Did you love her?"

"Sadly, I did not, though I regarded her highly. She was attacked because of me. Had she fallen for one of her own kind, she would now be walking the hills and enjoying the sunshine."

"Did they hang the men who did it?" asked Chara.

"No. Someone hunted them down and killed them."

"Someone?"

He looked uncomfortable. "It was never discovered who did it." He looked at her and smiled, but she could see the smile was forced. "I am sorry that I lost my temper with your father and that I was gawping at you."

It was a clumsy attempt to change the subject, but she accepted it without comment. "Well, I forgive you. Perhaps my father will, too."

"And what of Bael?"

Now it was Chara who looked away. "He is a proud man, Kaelin. I think that he will challenge you."

"Do you care for him?"

"Of course I care for him. He is my brother." Pulling on her leggings and shoes, Chara rose. "We should be there by dusk," she said.

Call Jace was troubled. A strong man, he liked to believe he was in control of his life and the security of his clan. Mostly that was true, but occasionally, as now, he was forced into the realization that sometimes a situation would develop its own momentum. Attempts to change its course were fraught with peril.

Bael was right. Kaelin Ring had stared at Chara with undisguised longing. That had caused momentary irritation. As a result he had insulted the boy. Who could have foreseen the outcome? That Bael was alive was little short of a miracle. The problem now was partly one of perception. Call bore no grudge against Kaelin Ring, but that was beside the point. The Black Rigante prospered because of the tribute paid by all landowners and farmers. That tribute was not in the main paid out of love or respect. Fear was the foundation. The hard-won reputation of the clansmen was that they made merciless and deadly enemies. Now this incident would be the talk of Black Mountain and the surrounding settlements. The clan chieftain had been struck, and his son shot, by a southern boy. Without retribution the clan's reputation would suffer, and others might think of denying tribute.

The easy answer was to let Bael kill the boy. Yet easy answers, he knew, were often wrong.

He left the big house and wandered out into the foothills on the long walk to Shrine Hollow. He hoped the Dweller would be home, but she had not been seen for some months, and he doubted he would be able to call on her wisdom.

Shrine Hollow was a place of mystery and quiet beauty within the forest. In the late afternoon shafts of sunlight speared through gaps in the trees, bathing the forest floor in gold. A man could sit there, close his eyes, and almost hear the whisper of the Seidh flowing back through the centuries. Call always went there when he was troubled. He sat for a while listening to the birdsong, then climbed to the western lip of the hollow and stood looking out over the glittering waters of Sorrow Bird Lake. In the distance, due west, the mountains dipped and rose sharply, forming a V-shaped goblet into which the sun sank. At sunset the iron-gray waters would become bright bronze and crimson, as if the dying sun had melted and was flowing under the mountains. Call Jace had never lost the sense of wonder inspired by Sorrow Bird Lake and Shrine Hollow.

Shading his eyes against the harsh sunlight, he stared out at the large island at the center of the lake. Huge trees grew there: oak and ash and a few silver birch. There was a small bay on the eastern shore. The Dweller's boat was not there. Call was disappointed. She often had glimpses of the future, and he needed such a glimpse now.

He had sent Chara and Wullis Swainham to scout for Kaelin Ring. Once they had seen him make camp, Chara had ordered Wullis to return and report. There was no need to do that. Other scouts would have brought news some hours before their arrival. That meant that Chara was seeking time alone with Kaelin Ring.

Had she taken a fancy to the young man? Call hoped not. There were enough complications already.

Call walked back down to Shrine Hollow, took a silver flask from the pocket of his coat, and took a deep drink. The Uisge was cask-mellowed and twenty years old. It flowed into his throat like silken fire. Holding out his arm, he tipped a measure to the earth. "For the children of the Seidh," he said.

He heard movement from the east and turned toward the sound. Bael appeared. He had removed the bandage from his head, and the ten stitches could be seen on the scabs covering the wound. "I thought you would be here, Father," he said. "No sign of the Dweller?"

"No." Call tossed him the flask. Bael took a deep swallow. "Man, that's good."

"The water of life. What brings you here?"

"I wanted to tell you that I'd abide by any decision you make. If you desire me to offer no challenge, I'll accept it."

"You are a Rigante, Bael. You have reached majority. The clan chief cannot order you to accept an insult."

"I know. I wasn't thinking of you as the clan chief but as my father. I will do whatever you require."

"Thank you, lad. I wish that I had not insulted the boy. His reaction was courageous. Three armed highlanders, and he did not hesitate to attack. I respect that. However, the circle must be closed. Challenge him, Bael. Swords, not pistols."

"Swords, Father? He is a southerner. Swords are forbidden to them. He will have no skill."

"You said you would abide by my decision, Bael."

"And I will."

"Then let's be getting back to the house. They'll be here within the hour."

Chara Jace had enjoyed the walk with Kaelin Ring. He was not like most young clan men she knew. While in her company he did not feel the need to fill the silences with empty chatter. Nor did he seek to impress her with tales of his exploits.

She guessed, though without any real evidence, that Kaelin Ring had avenged the death of the girl back in Old Hills. Something in his expression when he spoke of the "someone" who had killed the murderers had convinced her. Added to which she had seen the sudden violence with which he had reacted to Bael's assault. Kaelin Ring was not a man to cross.

That in itself produced a disturbing thought. What if Bael challenged him and he killed Bael? The prospect made her feel cold inside. Yet what if Bael killed him? Even the thought was frightening, and Chara was not a woman given to fear.

The sun was setting as they climbed toward the stockade wall blocking the pass.

Chara paused. Kaelin walked on for several paces, then glanced back.

"Why are you waiting?" he asked.

"I think perhaps this is not such a good plan," she said. She sat down on a rock.

He strolled back to her. "What is the problem?" he asked.

"I do not want Bael to kill you. And I do not want you to kill Bael," she added hurriedly.

He looked back at the stockaded wall. "There are guards there, and they have seen me. I cannot walk away now. Perhaps there will be no fight. I shall apologize to your father."

"And to Bael?"

"Aye, if that is what you want. He struck me, but on the other hand, he could have shot or stabbed me. He was defending his chieftain."

She smiled and rose, taking his hand. "Good," she said. His hand was warm, and she squeezed his fingers, enjoying the touch of his flesh. He made no effort to pull away.

"You say there are no soul-names in the south? We could ask the Dweller to give you one," she said.

"I have one. I am Ravenheart."

"I am Flame on the Water."

They stood in silence, then Kaelin raised her hand to his lips. "It has been good walking with you, Flame on the Water," he said. "Now let us go and meet your father."

Kaelin felt a welling sense of disappointment as they passed through the stockade gates. Two sentries came down and began laughing and joking with Chara. They were speaking Keltoi, and Kaelin felt excluded. Worse, he felt as if he had lost something precious. The journey with Chara had been fulfilling in a way he had never experienced before. Her company was a delight to him. Now that company was being shared.

Chara took one of the guards by the arm, a tall man, wolf-lean and hard-featured. She led him to Kaelin. "This is Rayster, my dearest friend," she said.

Kaelin struggled to be polite. "Good to meet you," he managed to say.

"And you, Kaelin Ring." Kaelin looked into the man's bright blue eyes and saw the glint of amusement there. Rayster held out his hand, and Kaelin shook it. The grip was firm. "You've the look of the Rigante about you," he said. "Rare for southerners, I find."

"Then you do not know my uncle Jaim Grymauch."

Rayster chuckled. "Oh, I know Grymauch," he said. "He's a bull-stealing drunkard, and I love him dearly. But then, he's no southerner. He was born not three miles from here. I have not seen him in many months. I heard, though, how he thrashed the Varlish fighter. Man, but I would love to have seen that. There's no better knuckle and skull fighter than Grymauch."

Kaelin found himself relaxing in the man's company, though he wished Chara would let go of Rayster's arm. The other guard was a smaller man, wiry and round-shouldered. He had a thin, straggly red beard that barely disguised his receding chin. Chara introduced him as Wullis Swainham. Kaelin thrust out his hand. Wullis took it, the handshake soft and swift, then swung away to climb back to the stockade wall.

Both guards were wearing pale blue and green cloaks checkered with red vertical and horizontal lines, and Rayster also sported a kilt crafted from the same cloth. "I thought Rigante colors were outlawed," said Kaelin.

"Aye, they are, but this is not Eldacre, man. This is Black Rigante country. Beetlebacks do not trouble us much now. However, we remain vigilant. There's always talk of some force or other on its way to wipe us out. They are not foolish, though, these Varlish. Take a look around you. This pass is one of only three routes into our stronghold. It is guarded—as are the others—and great would be the loss of men among the attackers. The pass narrows and climbs, and we have traps all the way along it. Aye, and two cannon, both equipped for canister shot."

"What is that?" queried Kaelin.

"The Varlish developed it. Hundreds of tiny lead balls fired with a single charge. One blast could wipe out scores of attackers. My guess is they'll leave us alone for a little while yet." He swung to Chara, leaning down to kiss her cheek. Kaelin quelled his anger and looked away. "Time for you to take our guest up to the great house," said Rayster. "I'll see you at the feast."

Chara led Kaelin farther up the trail. As Rayster had said, the pass narrowed, the walls on either side sheer. It was a hard climb in places. At the top was a second set of gates, and behind them two large cannons with fluted barrels. The sentries there merely waved from the wall as the two travelers walked on.

From there the pass opened out, and Kaelin saw a beautiful valley spreading out below them. There were small lakes and a wide ribbon of a river. A water mill had been constructed on its banks, the settlement close by. The houses were well built of stone and timber, and on the flanks of the foothills below the mountains herds of cattle grazed. Kaelin drank in the scene.

"This is my home," said Chara.

"It is nearly as lovely as you," he heard himself say. "And not a Varlish in sight."

"This is only part of our lands. Across the mountains all the way to the coast there are settlements." She moved in closer and touched his arm. "See there," she said, pointing. "That is my father's house." He glanced down and saw a large, circular structure built of gray stone. It had crenellated ramparts and looked more like a fort than a house.

"It was once a keep," said Chara. "Built by the Varlish three hundred years ago. It even has dungeons, but my father uses them to store Uisge casks."

"Is Rayster your intended?" he asked her suddenly.

"Why do you ask?"

"Is he or not?" he snapped.

"He is not," she retorted sharply. "Though it is none of your concern."

Kaelin struggled for calm. "You are right. I am sorry. I don't know what is the matter with me. Must be the mountain air," he added lamely.

"I am betrothed to no one. I only reached my majority last week."

"And I yesterday," he said.

"Yesterday? I thought you were older."

"Yesterday I *was* older," he told her. "Today I feel like a child." Taking her hand, he made as if to raise it to his lips. Instead he dipped his head and kissed her mouth.

"I did not say you could do that," she said without anger.

"May I do it again?" he asked.

"You may not. This time I shall do it. Close your eyes." He did so and felt her arms encircle his neck. His head was drawn down, and he felt her lips upon his. When she drew back, he was almost dizzy.

"That was the single greatest moment of my life," he said.

"Then you have led a dull life, Kaelin Ring," she told him with a bright smile. "Now let us go down and meet my father." She took his hand, but he did not move.

"Must we go now? Can we not sit here awhile?"

"No, we must go. It is still a long walk, and you have a great deal of apologizing to do before supper."

◊ 11 ◊

CALL JACE WAS not a naturally pessimistic man. He had learned early that luck mostly favored the brave and the willing. He did not assume that events would always go the way he desired, but he trusted in his instincts, his intelligence, and his courage to win the day.

He had been clan chieftain of the northern Rigante for eighteen years and in that time had eased the Varlish from his borders. He had managed that feat by using a mixture of political skill and cunning allied with a daring that had at times been breathtaking. The lands of the Rigante were rugged, full of deep forests, high mountains, and treacherous passes. Any foe intent on destroying his people would have to risk losing thousands of men in a sustained war of attrition without major battles, thus depriving any enemy general of glory. Such a war, Call knew, would be immensely costly and politically ruinous. Only the king, far in the south, could call upon an army of the size needed to win a final victory.

The Moidart could not.

Call had understood this from the first. Yet when he had replaced the dying Laphrain, the Black Rigante had been in disarray. Beetlebacks patrolled their lands, Varlish businesses had been set up in the valley, and no clansman was allowed a sword or a pistol. Laphrain had been a good man, but he could not see the dangers.

Call Jace had. For the first two years he did nothing overtly to encourage the Varlish to believe he was an enemy. In secret, however, he formed five raiding parties and sent them out to harass and rob merchant caravans to the east of Black Mountain. None of the men wore clothes that could identify them as members of his clan. They were for all intents and purposes merely outlaws. On Call's instruction they also raided Varlish farms, stealing livestock and burning buildings. The Beetlebacks ceased to patrol Rigante lands, their time taken up trying to hunt down the raiding parties. Occasionally they succeeded, though not one clansman allowed himself to be taken alive.

In the meantime, without constant Beetleback patrols, Call began installing defenses in the high passes: stockaded walls of thick timber and solid gates of oak. With monies gained from the raids he also brought in a store of muskets and pistols.

Within four years he had bought out the Varlish businesses within the Rigante mountains and had set up several forges, ostensibly producing iron implements for farms, plows, scythes, nails, and such. But they also crafted swords and knives. Young men of the Rigante were then trained in blade skills.

Only then did Call Jace apply the first overt pressure to the ruling Varlish. The new colonel in charge of the Beetleback forces was a man named Gates. He had been sent in by an angry Moidart with orders to eliminate the outlaws. Soon after his arrival Call Jace stepped up the raids. Gates' position was becoming untenable, and he was days away from being relieved of his duties and summoned home in disgrace. Call Jace then invited him to visit the valley, along with twenty of his men. When they arrived, Call greeted them wearing a beautifully wrought half saber with a bronze fist guard.

"Welcome to you, my friend," Call said warmly, stepping forward and pumping the man's hand. "It is good to see you. Come inside and relax. I have food being prepared and a fine Uisge ready for you."

The colonel, a weary, disillusioned veteran, stared at the

sword and then into the pale eyes of the Rigante chieftain.
"The law states—"

"You are the law here, Colonel Gates," Call said swiftly,
linking his arm with the colonel's and leading him into the
great house. "We will discuss it over a drink."

Call took Gates through the central hall, where the feast
fire was blazing, past the long room with its massive rectangular table surrounded by twenty chairs, and then into the private inner study. Here there were comfortable chairs set
before a small fire. Call filled a silver goblet with Uisge and
handed it to the officer.

"You cannot wear a sword, Master Jace," said Gates. "It is a
hanging offense for a clansman."

"As I understand it, that law was passed against clansmen
who rose against the crown twenty years ago. The Black Rigante never fought against the crown. Hell, man, the king has
never even been this far north. The real concern here should
be these outlaws who are terrorizing peaceful communities.
They must be a real worry for you. I know how difficult it is to
hunt such men in this terrain, but in the south I expect they
blame you for not putting an end to the misery."

"Aye, they do. They have no idea of the problems I face.
Even so, Master Jace, the sword—"

"Do not concern yourself over such a small matter. Since
you have been a good friend to the Rigante, I have decided to
help you in the matter of the outlaws. I am sending out some
of my own men to scout for them and protect the citizens. You
cannot be expected to provide protection and hunt down
criminals with a mere two hundred men. The task is impossible. My warriors will patrol the farms and the roads leading
into Black Mountain while your Beetlebacks hunt down the
scum responsible for the atrocities."

"Your men will patrol the communities?"

"Aye. We will catch these miscreants together. Then you
will receive the thanks of the Moidart. Your reputation will be
restored. No more endless days and nights riding the mountains in the snow and the rain. Perhaps you will get a promo-

tion and return to the south. We will be sorry to lose you, but at least we will know we have a friend there."

Colonel Gates drained his Uisge. Call refilled the goblet. "Aye, it would be good to catch some of these swine."

"We'll do it," Call said soothingly.

The new policy worked well, the raids lessening dramatically. Three weeks later the colonel was back, this time even more agitated. Once more Call took him to the study, though this time the officer refused Uisge.

"By the Sacrifice, Call, your men are *armed*. Rigante warriors have been seen carrying swords and knives."

"How else could they protect communities from the outlaws?" asked Call. "Ask yourself this: How many raids have there been around Black Mountain since your plan came into operation? None. Are the merchants and farmers content with you? Yes, they are. Have the outlaws been driven back into the wild lands? Yes, they have. Everything you have done has been a huge success."

"But we have caught no one, Call."

"Your men killed five of them only last week at Col Rasson."

"Killed, yes. None were taken alive. We thought we had one of them cornered up on Jallis Crag, but he leapt to his death rather than be taken."

"It is only a matter of time before you catch one, Colonel. Either that or the outlaws will move on, seeking easier prey. Either way you have succeeded."

"I don't know, Call. One of the farmers has complained that your men have demanded tribute for the protection offered. He has, quite rightly, refused to pay. Did you know your men were doing this?"

"It is a costly business patrolling the farms. The men who do it cannot work on their own lands. But all payments are voluntary and offered freely. If the man does not want to pay, then he doesn't have to."

"Even so, this whole business is beginning to worry me."

"Put your mind at rest, my friend. Soon you will be summoned back to Eldacre in triumph. Think of it. Your reputation restored, your fame acknowledged." Gates had seemed mollified.

Then Call's raiders had intercepted a courier carrying messages to the Moidart. Gates had written that he was convinced Call Jace himself was behind the raids and that more men were needed to "pacify the Rigante."

Two weeks later a large band of "outlaws" ambushed the colonel and thirty of his men, killing them all. Call Jace sent an urgent message to the Moidart, explaining that violence and intimidation were getting out of hand in the area and requesting more troops to protect the citizens. His own men, he said, had hunted down the outlaws, killing fifteen of them and driving the others south. In a separate incident the farmer who had refused tribute was found with his throat cut.

The Moidart did send more troops, this time under a fierce and ruthless colonel named Rollin Baynock. Colonel Baynock summoned Call to his headquarters. The wily Rigante leader arrived without weapons.

Baynock was a stocky man, round-faced and small-eyed. His mouth was thin-lipped, and his receding chin was hidden by a bushy black beard. He was sitting at his desk when Call was ushered into his office at the barracks in Black Mountain. He did not offer the Rigante leader a chair.

"I have read the reports of my predecessor," he said. "This arrangement of yours ceases now. All swords held by the Rigante will be surrendered within the week. Your men will no longer patrol. You understand me?"

"Of course, sir. I was merely trying to help."

"We need no help from highlanders."

Two days later Rollin Baynock and twelve riders failed to return from a routine patrol near the Col Rasson pass east of Black Mountain. A second patrol found their bodies in a gully. Rollin Baynock's tongue had been torn from his mouth.

Within weeks the Beetleback force had doubled to four hundred men, but raids and murders continued.

Call Jace wrote to the Moidart, politely questioning the tactics employed by the new colonel and pointing out that at least a thousand men were needed to adequately safeguard the area. The Moidart responded by inviting Call Jace to visit him in Eldacre. Call reluctantly refused on the grounds that he had recently injured his leg and was confined to his bed.

The new colonel died in a brief fight at Rattock Creek when a volley of musket fire tore into his troops as they crossed the narrow bridge.

Once again Call wrote to the Moidart, requesting more troops while assuring him that he and his Black Rigante could far more effectively patrol the area than could forces from the south that did not have intimate knowledge of the terrain. He also offered to have his men escort the wagons carrying tax revenue on their twice-yearly journeys back to Eldacre. "It surely will not be long," he wrote, "before these outlaw vermin realize that the wagons contain far more riches than the farms and businesses they are attacking."

His warning proved curiously prophetic, since from that moment every tax convoy was attacked and robbed, the men guarding them killed.

Two more colonels came and went within the year. One died from a heart seizure in his office, and the other was recalled in disgrace when the second of the tax convoys was taken. Then came Colonel Lockley, an elderly man with a fine record. He rode to Call's house with only two Beetle-backs and accepted the hospitality of the Rigante leader.

"Fine Uisge," he said, sipping from the same silver goblet used by the murdered Colonel Gates.

"Aged in the cask," Call told him.

Lockley had deep-set quiet eyes that masked a fierce intelligence. The conversation that followed was coded. Call knew that Lockley was almost certainly aware of his involvement in the raids. "The Moidart has graciously allowed me to see your correspondence over the years," he said. "You have proved remarkably astute in predicting the outrages of the outlaws."

"Sadly, that is true," agreed Call. "It hurts me that my advice has not been heeded."

Lockley gave a thin smile. "The north has become a major drain on the resources of Eldacre. It seems to me there are two choices. Either we bring up an army with cannon and utterly destroy the enemy or we find a way to resolve the situation without such . . . expense. I would prefer the latter."

"As would we all," said Call. "My view has always been that having my men patrol the area would take away the need for large forces being deployed and also allow greater effectiveness for the troops under your command. They could then be used where most valuable, scouring the wild lands for brigands and thieves."

Lockley eased himself back into the deep leather chair, pushing out his booted feet toward the fire. "Which would, of course, involve armed Rigante."

"Of course. How else would they fight outlaws?"

"Indeed so," said Lockley. "This idea was employed by one of my predecessors and worked to great advantage. Attacks were few, the tax revenues got through, and the community was content."

"He was a man of great foresight and courage," said Call. "It was a sad loss when he died."

"It is my belief that this plan of yours will work wonderfully," said Lockley. "I would imagine that merely by hearing word of it the outlaws will melt away into the mountains, never to be seen again. I would further imagine that there will never be another attack on the tax convoys."

"That is certainly to be hoped," agreed Call, "though such an immediate response would be surprising."

"Of course. I am sure it will take some time for word to reach all the outlaws. But I am sure it will happen soon enough now that we are in agreement."

"Will you stay for supper, Colonel Lockley?"

"No, thank you. My wife is coming up to Black Mountain to join me, and I would like to be there to greet her. Perhaps another time?"

"You will always be welcome."

"The Moidart has asked me to reiterate his invitation for you to travel to Eldacre. He is most interested in discussing your thoughts on the administration of the area."

"That is most kind of him," said Call. "It would be an honor to meet the lord. Sadly, my health has not been good in recent months, and I fear such a journey could prove hazardous. However, I shall write to him with my thanks."

Colonel Lockley proved almost as good a prophet as Call Jace himself. Outlaw raids ceased within the month, and less than a year later the complement of soldiers had once more been reduced to two hundred.

Lockley had survived his post for another seven years before succumbing to a disease that stripped his body of flesh and left him dying in agony. Call Jace had attended the funeral. Lockley had been a career soldier, leaving little in the way of a legacy for his wife and two sons. Call Jace made them a gift of one hundred pounds in gold in memory of "a fine and honest soldier."

There had been two replacements since that time, and neither had tried to alter the agreement.

Call Jace's instincts and strategy had proved right, and the Rigante had prospered.

But now, as he watched his son fighting for his life, Call Jace knew fear. His instincts had been wrong this time. He had thought Bael would defeat the boy easily, since the southern Rigante had no experience in sword fighting. Call also knew that Bael would not try to kill him. He would seek to wound and scar him. In that way honor would be satisfied.

Not for a moment had Call considered the prospect of Bael being slain. His son was a fine swordsman. Yet the southerner fought like a veteran, his moves fast, his attacks ferocious. Both fighters had taken cuts, Bael to the upper arms and the boy to the left wrist and forearm. Kaelin also had been cut on his right cheek, and blood had drenched his shirt.

The swordsmen were fighting within a circle of watching Rigante warriors. More than two hundred had assembled for

the duel, and it had begun with great cheers for Bael. The
fight had lasted more than ten minutes so far, and the crowd
had become silent, engrossed by the skills on display.

Call glanced around for a sign of Chara. She was nowhere
in sight. He looked back toward the great house and saw her
at an upper window. Call felt his stomach tighten.

A few days earlier he had been a revered—aye, and
feared—chieftain with a doting son and a loving daughter.
Now his son faced death, his daughter had told him she hated
him, and the boy from the south was on the verge of dam-
aging fatally the Rigante reputation.

A cry of pain sounded, jerking Call from his thoughts.
Bael had taken a stab wound to the left shoulder and had
leapt back. Then he counterattacked. Kaelin Ring stumbled,
blocked a slashing blow, and sent a riposte that Bael barely
avoided.

Tiring now, the two fighters circled, looking for an
opening.

Call would have given ten years of his life to be able to turn
back time, to accept the apology offered to him the night before, during the feast, to have embraced the young Rigante
and made him a part of his own clan. The apology had been
gracefully offered, and Call had noted the approval on the
faces of the men who heard it. What he had not noticed was
the light of love in his daughter's eyes as she gazed upon the
young man. When Kaelin had concluded, he had turned to
Bael. "My apologies also to you," he had said. "I am relieved
that you have suffered no lasting hurt, and it is my hope that
as brothers of the Rigante, we can become friends. For it is
the Varlish who should be our enemies, and it shames me that
my recklessness endangered you."

Bael had stood and bowed to Kaelin Ring. "As you say, we
are both Rigante. The matter between us must be settled in
the Rigante manner. I see you have no sword. Tomorrow I
will see that several are presented to you. You may then
choose a weapon that suits you, and we will meet in the warrior's circle."

Kaelin had stood silently for a moment. Call saw him glance at Chara. Then he returned his attention to Bael.

"I do not wish to fight you," he said.

"You have no choice," Bael told him.

"Then so be it," responded the southerner. He swung to face Call Jace. "I had hoped to ask for your daughter's hand this night. I fear it is now inappropriate. I doubt she will want to wed the man who kills her brother."

With that he had left the table and walked from the long room.

The silence that followed was intense. Bael looked shocked and was staring at his father. Call turned to Chara.

"What in the seven hells was he talking about?" he demanded.

"I will hate you forever for this day," she said. Then she, too, ran from the room.

The fight was entering its last stages now. One mistake would see a man fatally wounded or killed outright.

Call could hardly bear to watch.

At nineteen, Bael had been a fighting man of the Rigante for four years. In that time he had led one of his father's outlaw bands and taken part in seven skirmishes with Beetlebacks. He had fought sword to sword eleven times and knew that he was as skillful as any man with the blade.

But this southerner was like no one else he had ever faced. His speed and aggression were inhuman. Only lack of experience had so far prevented him from finishing the fight. Bael parried and moved, saw his counterattacks brushed aside. Twice Bael had come close, once cutting the youngster's left arm. A lightning thrust, partly parried, had opened a long cut on his cheek. Against that Bael was bleeding from several cuts and gashes to both arms, and a fierce slashing blow had split his tunic shirt, slashing the skin of his shoulder.

Bael's sword arm was tiring now, as indeed was that of his opponent.

They circled warily.

Bael leapt forward. Their swords sang together, the sound
of clashing blades ringing out. Bael hacked and thrust.
Kaelin parried and countered. Then Kaelin launched an attack. Bael blocked, spun on his heel, and hit Kaelin in the face
with the back of his left fist. The youngster stumbled, righted
himself, and swiftly brought up his sword to parry what
would have been a death thrust to the neck. His riposte was
sudden. Bael threw himself to his right. Kaelin's sword sliced
the skin above his left hip, bouncing off the bone.

Now they circled again.

Bael was oblivious to the silent circle of watching warriors. He locked gazes with the young Rigante, seeing no fear
in the other's dark eyes. The left side of Kaelin's face was
blood-drenched from the cut to his cheek, his oiled doeskin
shirt heavily stained with crimson.

Despite his initial outburst about spearing the young man's
heart, Bael had always intended merely to wound his opponent and then spare him. He had been impressed by Kaelin's
acceptance of the invitation and doubly impressed by the gra-
cious apology he had offered at the feast.

He had believed it would be easy to defeat an untrained
southerner. A swift lesson in swordplay, a few cuts for good
measure, and the matter would be resolved.

Not so now.

This man, he knew, would fight on with any but the most
mortal of wounds.

Their swords clashed again as Kaelin moved in. He left no
opening for a counterattack, and Bael battled furiously, always on his back foot, to prevent Kaelin's sword from
breaching his defenses.

His arm was beginning to burn with fatigue, the sword
seeming to have magically gained twice its weight. It was no
different for the southerner, he noted, as they pulled away and
circled once more.

"Finish him, Bael!" came a cry from the crowd. He recognized the voice of Wullis Swainham.

It created a discordant moment, and Bael could feel the unease in the warriors forming the circle.

Ignoring the cry, Bael tried to gather his strength for another assault. With luck he might be able to roll his blade and make a cut on Kaelin's bicep, forcing him to drop the weapon. But Bael hesitated. Such a cut would surely cripple him for life!

You can no longer afford to think of such strategies, he warned himself.

One mistake and he will kill you.

Sweat dripped into his eyes. He wiped it away with his sleeve, smearing blood on his face.

In that moment Kaelin attacked. Bael's sword came up, but he was off balance and barely deflected the sudden lunge. Kaelin's sword thrust past his defenses, hammering into his bronze belt buckle. It did not penetrate, but the force of the blow sent Bael staggering back. Kaelin stumbled. Bael struck him in the head with the fist guard of his sword. The southerner fell heavily. Bael tried to follow in, but Kaelin rolled to his knees, then surged up to meet him.

Once more their swords crashed together.

Kaelin's blade broke, shearing off just above the hilt.

A gasp went up from the crowd.

Defenseless now, Kaelin stood his ground. Bael glanced down at the shattered blade on the churned ground. Then he looked into Kaelin's eyes. Even now there was no fear. Bael smiled. Kaelin was waiting for Bael to attack and would try to bury the jagged remains of his broken blade in Bael's belly.

"Your apology is accepted," he told the southerner. "Or would you prefer another blade?"

Before Kaelin Ring could answer the gathered warriors began to applaud and cheer. Call Jace moved into the circle. "You both fought well," he said, relief evident in his voice. "Like true Rigante warriors. Let this be an end to it."

Bael continued to watch the southerner. He had not relaxed, and Bael realized with sick horror that he was considering requesting another sword.

Then Chara pushed her way through the gathering, moving alongside Kaelin. "Let me see to your wounds," she said, gently prizing the ruined sword from his hands. He glanced at her, his expression softening, but then he looked back at Bael. The Black Rigante warrior could see him struggling with his emotions. Chara took his arm. "Come," she said, "we need to clean away that blood and seal the cuts."

Call Jace stood close, his tension rising. Then the young man let out a sigh and relaxed. Without a word to Call or Bael he allowed himself to be led back to the great house.

Bael plunged his sword into the ground, relieved to be free of its weight. Warriors gathered around him. "Man, that was some fight," said one. Others clapped him on the back. A great weariness descended on the young man.

Call Jace came alongside. "You fought well, my son," he said. "I am proud of you. Now let us stanch those wounds."

"In a moment, Father. I need to sit." Together father and son moved away from the crowd and sat on the wall of the well. "How could he have been so skilled?" asked Bael.

"Grymauch," answered Call Jace. "I should have thought of it. He trained him."

Bael let out a soft curse. "Trained him too damned well."

"I made a mistake, Son," Call said, sadly. "It almost cost you your life."

"Aye, but it didn't. You were not wrong. Had we allowed him merely to apologize, word would have leaked out and others would have begun to question the tribute. As you have always said, fear is our most potent weapon. It has ended well, Father. He will go back scarred. People will hear of his fight. The Rigante will lose nothing by it."

"Aye, it has ended well, but it might have been otherwise. Had you killed him, Grymauch would have come. He would have wanted to challenge me."

"And you would have had to kill him," said Bael. "I know that would have saddened you."

Call laughed suddenly. "Kill Grymauch? I am a good swordsman and, though I say it myself, a bonny fighter. However, in any battle anywhere, against anyone, I'd bet my fortune on Grymauch being the last man standing. No, Bael, had you killed the boy, I would have had Grymauch cut down from ambush on his way here. But you are right. It would have saddened me. Now let me fetch my needle and close those cuts."

Kaelin sat silently by the window. Chara was standing beside him, gently wiping away the blood from the deep cut on his cheek. Taking a curved needle, she threaded it with thin black twine and leaned in close. He felt the first prick of the needle but did not wince. Closing his eyes, he saw again the fight: the bright, shimmering steel of the blades, the deadly dance within the circle of warriors. Move by move he replayed them all. Three times Bael had engineered openings for killing blows and had not taken any of them. In the passion of the fight Kaelin had believed Bael to be too slow to see the openings. Now he was not sure.

The long cut to his face required ten stitches, but at the end the blood had stopped flowing.

"It will not look so bad," said Chara. "You will still be handsome."

He opened his eyes. Her face was but inches from his own. It seemed to him then to be the most beautiful face he had ever seen. Her eyes were leaf green and flecked with gold. She was examining her handiwork. He leaned in to her, kissing her cheek. Chara pulled back. "This is not the time," she said, her words stern. But she smiled as she said them. "Let us see to your arm."

He sat and watched as she expertly drew the skin together, drawing in the stitches and tying them neatly before snipping them with a tiny pair of scissors. When she had finished, he slowly clenched his fist. The wound felt tight as the muscles of his forearm rippled under the stitches. "How do you feel?" she asked, dabbing away the last of the blood from his arm.

"Tired."

She sat quietly for a moment. "I want to thank you for not killing Bael," she said at last, not meeting his eyes.

Kaelin was lost for words. She thought he had held back, which was not true. He had tried with all his might to slay his opponent. The truth burned in him, and he longed to tell her. Kaelin wanted no deceit to corrode his relationship with this Black Rigante woman.

And yet deep down he knew that this was a critical moment. The truth itself could damage what was as yet a delicate friendship.

"I am glad he is still alive," he said.

"Bael was not to blame for the duel," she told him angrily. "It was my father. He put the Rigante reputation above the life of his own son. He thought that if you were not punished, the people of Black Mountain and other lands nearby would cease their tribute."

"Aye, there is sense in that," he said.

"Sense? You take his side?"

"I'm not taking anyone's side," he said swiftly, seeing her anger. "To understand an action does not mean that I necessarily agree with it. I don't know much about the politics of these northern lands, but I know your father has maintained a Rigante culture despite living in a land ruled by the Varlish. That cannot have been easy. You should see how it is in the south. We have few rights. We cannot own a sword or a pistol or a horse above fourteen and a half hands. We have no right to vote for the councils and on feast days are penned in and not allowed to walk through Varlish areas. Beetlebacks rape our women, and the courts acquit them, often ordering birchings for any woman who complains. You don't suffer that here, Chara. I would guess that is because your father has worked hard to maintain what you call the Rigante reputation."

"You could have been killed for that reputation," she pointed out.

"Aye, but I wasn't. Are you angry with me?"

"Yes."

"You'll not want to kiss me again, then?"

"No." She grinned at him, then became suddenly serious. "Do you think I have too many freckles?"

"I think you are the most beautiful girl I have ever seen."

"That doesn't answer my question. Would I be more beautiful with fewer freckles?"

"No," he said instantly. "Without the freckles I'd have no interest in you whatever."

"Are you making fun of me?"

"Yes."

"Well, don't. I don't like it."

"I shall remember that."

Chara moved to the hearth. The fire was mostly dead, though there were a few glowing embers among the ashes. Squatting down, she added some kindling and blew gently on the coals. A tiny flame flickered, then another. She added more wood, then sat down before the fire. Kaelin joined her.

"You should have asked me before you spoke so in front of my father," she said. "What made you think I would want to walk the tree with you?"

"Because you love me," he said.

"You do not know that to be true. Perhaps I kiss all the handsome boys I meet."

"Do you?" he asked, suddenly uncertain.

"No, but you did not know that. Anyway, it was discourteous of you."

"For that I apologize," he said. "Will you marry me?"

"I need time to think on it," she said. "You have not even said why I should."

Reflected firelight shone on her red hair. He found himself staring at the curve of her neck and remembering her naked by the lake. There were many aspects of life that still confused Kaelin Ring, but here and now there was only certainty. This was the woman he was meant to be with. This was the partner of his heart. Emotion welled within him, but no words could be found to express it. He knew she was waiting for him to speak, but he could find nothing to say. The uneasy silence grew.

Finally Chara rose. "I will find you something to wear while I clean the blood from your shirt," she said.

"Thank you."

After she had left the room, he cursed himself for a fool. When she came back, he would tell her that he loved her and would make every effort to make her happy.

But she did not come back. Instead an older woman appeared, carrying a dark green tunic shirt. Kaelin thanked her and donned it. Strapping his belt around his waist, he walked out into the sunlight.

The warriors had gone, but there were several women standing by the well. None of them was Chara.

The sky was clouding, and rain could be seen falling on the mountains. The wind was cool and growing stronger. A storm was coming. Kaelin approached the women by the well. "Have you seen Chara?" he asked. They had not.

Kaelin wandered back to the great house and climbed the stairs to the room he had been allocated the night before. He did not know what to do now. It would be impolite to wander the house of Call Jace seeking out his daughter. Yet was it not also impolite to leave a guest alone, not even offering him breakfast?

He found himself becoming angry and tried to quell it. His sword arm was still aching from the unaccustomed use, and his face was sore and pinched from the stitches. He lay down on the narrow bed. Thunder rolled across the sky, and rain began to pelt down against the window.

Kaelin slept for a little while, and when he woke, it was dusk and he was hungry. Rolling from the bed, he left the room and walked downstairs to the round hall where the previous night's feast had been held. It was empty, with no fires burning.

Moving through to the kitchen, he found three men sitting and talking to several women. Two toddlers were playing on the floor alongside an old gray warhound that was watching the children with a wary eye.

No cookfires had been lit. Kaelin felt he could not ask for Chara, so instead he inquired after Call Jace.

"The chief has gone to the West Hills," a man told him. "He'll be back in a day or two."

Kaelin could no longer resist the urge to locate Chara. "And his daughter?" he asked.

"She and Bael have gone with him." The news struck Kaelin like a blow. It had been annoying to have been left for most of the day, but to find out she had just wandered off for a few days without a word of good-bye left him sick with anger. His mood darkened. If she thought that little of him, he would leave, and be damned to her and all the Black Rigante. He became aware that the man was speaking to him. "That was a good fight today, southerner. Old Grymauch trained you well."

Kaelin struggled to remain calm. "You know my uncle Jaim?"

The man chuckled. "Everyone knows your uncle Jaim, lad. He was raised here. He's one of us. Is it true he thrashed the Varlish champion, Chain Shada?"

"No, not Chain. He beat a man named Gorain. It was a grand battle."

"With Grymauch it would be," said the man. "You want some food?"

"Aye, for the road."

"You're leaving? In a storm?"

"My business here is done. No purpose would be served by staying."

The man shook his head. "They breed 'em strange in the south," he said. Pushing himself to his feet, he wandered back to a deep pantry and began to gather food.

"I'll need to borrow a cloak and a food sack," said Kaelin. "I'll see them returned at the next tribute."

"Watch out for bears," the man said with a grin. "In this weather those pistols will be useless."

"I'll remember that."

"You want me to leave a message for the chief?"

"All that needed to be said was said," Kaelin told him.

His hood held firmly in place by a borrowed scarf, Kaelin Ring made his slow way down the pass. The stockaded gates were closed, but the guards came out from under roughly made tents to open them for him.

"Steer clear of the bears," said the last with a grin. Kaelin did not respond. Shoulders hunched against the driving rain, he walked on. Chara had obviously spread the story of his stupidity throughout the clan. Yet another reason to be glad he was rid of her, he told himself.

The pass was steep, and twice he slipped and fell, once sliding on the scree for several yards. The rain beating against his face had softened the scab over the cut, and the wound tingled and stung. He tried to hold the hood over the stitches, but the wind whipped it back.

Within the hour he was wet through and desperately cold. Even in summer the mountain nights could turn savage. He shivered as he walked. Lightning seared across the sky, immediately followed by a roll of thunder so powerful that Kaelin felt the ground tremble beneath his feet.

Anger gave him strength, and he pushed on. Happily there was only one road, and Kaelin held to it. Had there been many branches to the trail, he would certainly have been lost by now.

This was a stupid act, he told himself. Since Chara and her father were going to be gone for some days, he might just as well have remained in the great house until the storm passed or the dawn came.

Best to be away, though, he argued. Best to put the bastards behind me. A pox on Call Jace and his murderous family!

Despite such dark thoughts he could not stop himself from picturing Chara's face by the firelight or erase the joyful memory of his walk with her, feeling her presence beside him.

Emerging to the flank of the mountain, he felt the full force of the storm wind in his face. It was grueling work trying to force his way through it. Although he had slept for several hours, he was still weary from the fight, and he had lost blood. He struggled on.

Lightning flashed, and he saw that the trail entered the woods up ahead. There, with the fierce winds lessened by the trees, he could make faster time.

But Kaelin was stumbling and weary by the time he reached the haven of the trees, and he sat down on a jutting root. He had been walking for almost two hours and was close to exhaustion.

His anger-fueled strength fading, he knew he needed a place to make camp. It was pitch dark there, and he waited for another lightning flash, hoping to see a rocky outcrop or an overhang beneath which he could rest awhile out of the rain.

For some while he sat there, trying to accustom his eyes to the darkness. The root was uncomfortable, and he adjusted his position. As he did so, he saw a brief flickering light in the distance. Then it was gone. He stared into the darkness. There it was again. It flickered momentarily and faded. Rising, he began to walk in what he believed was the direction of the light. He blundered blindly into bushes, having to feel his way around them. Just when he thought he was lost, the light came again. He realized it was a campfire and that the wind was occasionally flaring the flames, causing brief, bright reflections against a rock.

The ground was rising now, the trees thinning. Up ahead was a group of huge boulders against a cliff wall. Firelight could be seen glowing red on the gray rock. He approached and called out. "Hello, the camp!"

"Come on in," came a voice, the sound distorted by the storm.

Kaelin, his hand on the hilt of his hunting knife, walked to the fire, which had been set under a jutting shelf of granite.

Beside it he saw Jaim Grymauch. He grinned up at Kaelin. "By heaven, boy, what are you doing out on a night like this?"

"Felt like a stroll," said Kaelin, joy surging through him.

Moving to the fire, he sat down and removed his cloak. "I did not expect to see you here."

"I brought another of Maev's wagons to the farm. They told me of your trouble with Call. Thought I'd come and see if you needed a friend. I see I was a little late. Who cut you?"

"Bael. We fought a sword duel."

"You kill him?"

"No, my sword shattered. Then he spared me."

"He's a good boy, Bael," said Jaim. "Swift to anger, swift to forgive. I'm surprised Call would send you home on a night like this, though."

"He didn't send me home. I decided to leave."

Jaim glanced at him but said nothing. Reaching into a food sack, he produced some dried meat and a hunk of bread, which he passed to Kaelin. They sat in silence for a while, Kaelin enjoying the warmth of the fire. There was little wind there and no rain. Having eaten, Kaelin stretched out on the rock. "It is good to see you, Grymauch," he said.

"And you, boy."

"I am sorry for what I said to you back at the bridge. You are not a fool. You are a great man and my friend."

"Whisht, boy! Stop talking and get some rest." Grymauch gathered up his cloak and folded it, making a pillow, which he placed under Kaelin's head. "Dream good dreams. We'll talk in the morning."

When Kaelin woke, the sun was up and the storm had passed. Grymauch was sitting close by, chewing on a stale oatcake. Kaelin sat up and winced as the stitches on his face pulled tight. He lightly touched the wound. There was blood on his fingers as he pulled them back. Without speaking to Grymauch, he wandered from the camp and emptied his bladder. The sun was warm, making the freezing cold of the previous night's storm seem unreal.

He stared back toward the Rigante mountains. He had covered no more than four miles in the night. Had he not found Grymauch, he might have died in the woods. Berating himself for such foolishness, he returned to the camp. Grymauch was still sitting on a rock, looking off into the distance.

"Good morning, Uncle," said Kaelin.

"Aye, it is a good one," agreed Grymauch. "Tell me, did you part friends with Call?"

"I don't know. He wasn't there when I left. He'd gone to the West Hills."

"His mother lives there. The man dotes on her. So what happened?"

Kaelin told him of the fight at the farm, the invitation, and the duel. Grymauch listened quietly. When Kaelin had finished, he asked: "And what are you leaving out?"

"What do you mean?"

"Finbarr told me the trouble at the farm was caused by you ogling Call's daughter, yet not once have you mentioned her. Was she not at the great house?"

"Aye, she was there."

"Was it she who stitched your wounds?"

"Yes."

"I see."

"What do you see?" asked Kaelin, reddening.

"Not as much as I used to," said Grymauch, falling silent. Pulling off the black head scarf, he rubbed at the ruined socket.

"I thought she loved me," Kaelin said suddenly. "I told her father I wanted to marry her." The dam burst then, and the story poured out. He told Grymauch of the bear and the walk with Chara, the kiss on the mountaintop, the swim in the lake. He spoke of his anguish and hurt when she walked away from him and then left for West Hills without a word of good-bye. "I feel like a fool," he concluded.

"Aye, well, it's fitting, then, that you should have behaved like one."

"You think it was foolish to leave?"

Grymauch laughed. "You need no answer to that, Kaelin. Wounded and tired, you walk off into a ferocious storm with no real knowledge of the countryside. I'd say that was foolish.

You should have told her that you loved her, that she was the most precious creature in all the world, and that you could not imagine life without her."

"I wish I had."

"It's not too late. We're only a few miles from the gates."

Kaelin shook his head. "No. I am going back to the farm. If she wants me, she can find me there."

"What if she doesn't come, boy?"

"Then she doesn't love me, Grymauch."

Grymauch replaced his head scarf. "Perhaps that's what she'll think when she finds you left without, as you say, a word of good-bye. If you want to win the girl, you'll need to swallow your pride and say what needs to be said."

Kaelin thought about it, then shook his head and smiled. "Why is it, Grymauch, that you have never swallowed *your* pride and told Aunt Maev you love her?"

"I'm not good enough for her," Jaim said sadly. "Maev is a woman of fire and iron. I'm just a whoring drunkard—and an ugly one to boot. No, 'tis enough for me to be close to her and help her where I can."

"She's not too good for you, Grymauch. Maybe you should just ask her to wed you."

"Now it's you giving advice, is it? Maybe one day I will, boy. When the time is right." Replacing his headband, he gave a great sigh. "I have to say I'd be the proudest man who ever lived if she *were* to walk the tree with me. I love her so much, I feel that my heart will burst from it."

"That is how I feel about Chara. I feel we are meant to be together."

"My, but it is a good feeling, isn't it?" said Jaim. "Now, which direction should we head?"

"Back to the farm," said Kaelin. "I made the decision to leave, and I'll not look weak by creeping back to the great house."

"Well, I've said my piece, so I'll just walk with you."

Jaim climbed down from the rock and gathered his cloak.

From behind a rock he lifted his massive broadsword and hung it between his shoulders. He saw Kaelin looking at him.

"What are you thinking?" he asked.

"I'm thinking that you'll never ask Maev to marry you. It makes me sad."

"It shouldn't. There is nothing in the world so great as love, Kaelin. I feel privileged just to have felt it. My wife was a good woman, and though I didn't love her as I love Maev, we were content. Two bairns and a little farm. When she died and the Beetlebacks drowned my boys, I was filled with hate. The rebellion was in full flow, and I cut and killed my way from Eldacre to Three Bridges and beyond. I butchered Beetlebacks wherever I found them. After the rebellion was lost, I crossed the sea and fought in several wars. But the hate never left me, Kaelin. It burned like fire on the soul. When I came back, Maev healed me. Not just my eye but my heart. Love does that, boy. So you should understand that my life was made infinitely richer just by *knowing* Maev. I get more pleasure from seeing her smile than I have ever had from rutting with Parsha Willets or anyone else. She is the love of my life and the life of my soul. I don't need to be wed to her. I don't even need that love returned. It is enough that I am close to her and can protect her."

Kaelin saw the sorrow in the big man's face and knew Jaim was not telling the whole truth. He *did* need that love returned. Who wouldn't? thought Kaelin. The silence now was uncomfortable, and the youngster knew he needed to find something to say to restore their normal friendly banter. He stepped forward and lifted his borrowed cloak from the rock where Jaim had laid it to dry. "So," he said at last, "how is Parsha Willets?"

Jaim laughed. "Fat and willing and wonderful company. I've never regretted a single daen I've paid her."

"Judging by the amount you've given her, she must be one of the richest women in the highlands by now," said Kaelin.

"Och, it's not *that* much." Jaim thought about it. He

grinned broadly. "Maybe it is. Maybe I should marry Parsha Willets and live a life of luxury."

The mood restored, they set off toward the east.

Kaelin glanced back once, hoping to see Chara coming to find him.

But the land was empty.

◇ 12 ◇

JAIM STAYED AT the farm for less than a month. Kaelin knew he was anxious to return to Maev and made no attempt to delay him, though he dearly wanted to. The big man's presence at the farm changed the atmosphere. He laughed and joked with Finbarr and his brothers, which in turn drew Kaelin closer to the group. By the time he left, Kaelin felt more at ease with the northerners and they were more friendly toward him.

At least part of the change was due to the duel with Bael. Word of it had spread, and Kaelin's standing among the folk of Black Mountain had risen as a result. But it was mainly the easygoing presence of Jaim Grymauch that made the difference. He worked as hard as any man, repairing fences, digging ditches, clearing blocked water inlets. At night he would produce a jug or two and regale the laborers with songs or his own bawdy poems. They also witnessed at first hand Jaim's remarkable bull-charming talents. An old bull with a huge sweep of horn had become trapped on a mud bank by the river. The more he struggled, the deeper he sank. When Kaelin, Finbarr, and Senlic tried to reach him, laying long planks across the bank, the bull dipped his head and lunged at them. Jaim sat close by, drinking from a flagon of Uisge and laughing at their efforts.

Then he placed the empty flagon on the ground, looped a coil of rope over his shoulder, and walked out to stand some ten feet from the panicked animal. When he spoke, his voice was low and easy:

"Once I was lighter than sunshine on water.
I danced through the heather,
As ever I sought her.
I knew not the seasons, nor even the reasons,
Nor what I would do,
If ever I caught her.

"For life is a shadow, a cloud on the meadow,
and love is a whisper, a kiss 'neath a rainbow,
and ever we travel, and seek to unravel,
the spirit that urges us all just to follow."

The bull dipped its head and shivered. Jaim placed a loop
over its horns, then directed Kaelin and the others to continue
placing long planks around the beast. When they had done so,
Jaim spoke to the animal.

"Come, my friend," he said. "This is no place for you. Your
ladies are waiting. Let's have a little effort now." So saying, he
leaned back into the rope. The bull's shoulders heaved. He
managed to get his front legs on the nearest of the planks.
Kaelin, Finbarr, and Senlic moved in behind him, pushing
hard. With an angry bellow the bull powered himself clear.
Kaelin fell face first into the mud, and Senlic hauled him up.
The old man was laughing fit to burst, and then Finbarr began
to chuckle. The sound was so infectious that Kaelin found
himself laughing with them.

Jaim was lifting the rope clear of the bull's horns. "Are you
lads finished with your playing now?" he called. Kaelin
scooped a handful of mud and hurled it at him.

Incidents like that meant Jaim's departure was greeted
with general dismay.

"A man like you is wasted in the south," said old Senlic
Carpenter as Jaim climbed to the wagon.

"I have to be there," said Jaim. "They need to be reminded
of what a *real* Rigante looks like."

He glanced down at Kaelin. "You remember what I told
you," he said.

Kaelin nodded glumly. "Give my love to Aunt Maev, and next time you come bring Banny with you. He'd like the trip, and I miss him."

"I'll do that."

As the wagon rumbled away toward the south, Kaelin stood with Senlic and Finbarr, staring after it. "What the hell is in the south that holds him?" asked Senlic.

"He's in love," Kaelin said before he could stop himself.

"Ah," muttered Finbarr Ustal. "That explains it. Why doesn't he walk the tree with her and bring her north?"

"Maybe he will," said Kaelin.

"No, he won't," observed Senlic. "She doesn't love him."

"That's a shame," put in Finbarr. "Obviously a stupid woman." With that he strolled away.

Senlic remained. He glanced at Kaelin. "There's only one woman I've heard Grymauch talk about. And that's your Aunt Maev. I've met her, and she has a mind as sharp as a dagger. Handsome woman, too, by heaven."

Kaelin was uncomfortable with the conversation. "I should not have spoken of it," he said. "I ask you to put it from your mind when next he visits. So will you need my help marking the cattle?" he asked, clumsily changing the subject.

"No. The lads and I can tackle that. My bones tell me it's going to be a hard winter, and I reckon we should halve the herds. We'll lose many when the ice comes. Beef prices are high now. Good time to make the decision."

"I agree," said Kaelin. "Mark out half and bring me the count. Will you take charge of herding them south?"

"Not this time. I'm getting old. Finbarr can hire the men and lead them. It's time he learned a little responsibility."

"Good enough," said Kaelin.

Back at the house he made himself a second breakfast, frying several thin steaks. As he ate, he thought of the advice Jaim had given him that morning: "Don't leave it too long, boy. You don't want her marrying someone else."

Kaelin had heard nothing from Chara Jace in the last

month, and it hurt him deeply. Did she think so lightly of him? Had he been wrong to think she loved him?

"Go to her," Jaim had advised.

But pride prevented such a move. It was she who had first walked away without a word of farewell. It was she who should make the first move toward reconciliation.

What if she doesn't?

The thought was chilling. Every night as he went to his bed he thought of her. Every morning as he woke it was her face that leapt to his mind. Throughout the working days he would find himself remembering their conversations, picturing the sun on her hair, the brightness of her smile.

Perhaps she will come when the tribute is due in three days, he thought.

Holding to that hope, he ate the last of the steaks, cleaned both plate and pan, and walked out to the old barn. The supply wagon was waiting, the four horses harnessed. Finbarr's youngest brother, Killon, was waiting there.

"You want company for the trip?" asked the young man.

"That would be good," said Kaelin, knowing that Killon was wooing a Black Mountain girl, the daughter of a widow who ran a small laundry in the center of town.

With Killon beside him, Kaelin eased off the foot brake and slapped the reins to the backs of the horses. They pushed into the traces, and the empty wagon rolled forward on the long road to Black Mountain settlement.

"Be careful if you plan to tackle Grassman," Killon warned as they got onto the open road. "You don't want to be shooting any Varlish." He grinned as he said it.

"I didn't bring my pistols," said Kaelin.

"It'll do no good to report him to the Beetlebacks. A crook the man may be, but he has friends in high places. Captain Ranaud, for one. He's a cold, hard man."

"I'll just speak to the man," said Kaelin. "I'm sure he'll see the error of his ways."

The problem had begun several weeks earlier, when Kaelin

had checked out the sacks on the supply wagon and found that the supplies did not tally with the checklist. It was Finbarr who had brought them in. "It is always the same," Finbarr told him. "The trader, Grassman, is a thief. His weights are crooked, and he does not allow anyone to stand by and count the sacks as they are loaded. He will say that no highlander can enter his yard. We're all thieves, apparently. When the wagon is brought out, it is always one or two sacks short. But what can we do? The last highlander to complain to the Beetlebacks found that Grassman refused to sell him supplies. There is no other dealer in salt, white sugar, and dried fruit in Black Mountain. One man tried to set up a business, but he was thrashed by friends of Grassman and quit the town."

"I'll go in for the next supplies," said Kaelin.

It was a pleasant ride into town. The sky was clear, but the breeze carried promise of autumn, cool and fresh. The track they followed made for easy travel, though in winter it would be hazardous, Kaelin knew, for it dipped sharply as they came to the valley in which the town was situated. In winter supplies would be brought by pack ponies, adding greatly to the price of sugar, salt, and other essentials.

Black Mountain was not a large settlement. Fewer than a thousand people lived there, the stone houses clustered around the river and the three mills. From the high trail the first building to be seen was the fort and barracks housing the two hundred Beetlebacks. It was constructed in a great square, with a parade ground and an inner keep. The keep was stone built, a large round tower with no windows for the first twenty feet. There were slits known as murder holes through which musketeers could shoot at any attacking force. The outer walls of the fort were of timber. They were not high—no more than twelve feet—but a deep trench had been dug around the perimeter, and entry to the barracks was across a drawbridge. It was an old fort, built to withstand the attacks of sword-wielding clansmen. A modern army equipped with cannon would blast away the walls in minutes.

Killon was whistling one of Jaim's songs as they eased the wagon down the final slope, crossing the first of the river bridges.

"Will she be expecting you?" asked Kaelin.

"No, I'll surprise her." Killon was a slender young man, slightly round-shouldered, and though he was only in his early twenties, his hair was thinning at the crown. He had an honest, open face and a quick nervous smile. "We're going to walk the tree at the winter feast."

Kaelin found himself thinking of Chara and envying Killon Ustal's happiness.

At the town's outskirts Killon leapt down and with a wave set off at a lope down one of the narrow cobbled streets. Kaelin rode on to the warehouse. Stepping down from the empty wagon, he handed one of Grassman's loaders his order sheet and allowed the man to drive the wagon through the gates. He waited until the man returned, the wagon full, then checked the contents.

Then he climbed the wooden steps to the ramshackle office occupied by Arus Grassman.

The sturdily built Varlish trader took his money, counting it slowly before placing each coin, one at a time, in a large box on his desk. He made no attempt at conversation. Once he had finished counting, he scrawled a signature at the bottom of a checklist and handed it to Kaelin.

The young Rigante scanned the document. "It says here fifteen sacks of salt," he said.

"That's right."

"Only fourteen were loaded."

"You are mistaken."

"Then let us count them," said Kaelin.

"Fifteen were counted out of the storehouse. If one has been lost, that's not my problem. Perhaps one of the workers stole one."

"If that is what happened, then it was one of *your* workers, and that makes the loss your responsibility. That is the law."

"Don't preach Varlish law to me!" roared the man, rising from his chair, his face reddening. "I'll not take that from a kilt."

"Fetch another sack of salt," said Kaelin.

"Or what?" Grassman was a big man in his late thirties with massive shoulders and a spreading gut.

Kaelin looked around at the office. "In the south," he said, keeping his voice even, "all the warehouses are built of stone. This one is timber. I hope your fortune is not entirely held in such a building."

"What are you talking about?"

"A fire in such a place would be hard to extinguish. A man could be left penniless."

The trader blinked. "Are you threatening me?"

"A kilt threaten a Varlish? How foolish would that be? I am merely pointing out the dangers of having a wooden warehouse. A lantern falling from its bracket, a lightning strike, a disgruntled customer. So many perils."

"You *are* threatening me. By the Sacrifice, I'll have you thrown in jail."

"And all my men? My, but that will make for an interesting trial," said Kaelin. "Perhaps you will then round up all the kilts of Black Mountain who know me. And while we sit in the barracks jail, eating the Moidart's food, you can stand in the ashes of your life, among the blackened timbers." He stepped in close to the astonished man and smiled. "Now fetch me my salt or refund the price, you gutless sack of horseshit!"

For a moment it seemed the man might strike him, but then he just sagged into his chair, reached into the money box, and counted out five daens. "Take it and be damned to you," he said. "And from now on you can trade elsewhere."

"No, I don't think so," said Kaelin. "I'll come here. At least until another trader arrives."

Kaelin left the warehouse and climbed to the wagon. Flicking the reins, he moved out onto the main street and down to the barracks. Jaim had advised him to pay his respects to the colonel. "I have no respect for Beetlebacks," objected Kaelin.

"Then have respect for intelligence," snapped Jaim. "You don't have to kiss the man's boots, but it makes sense to keep him on friendly terms. You might need a friend among the Beetlebacks one day."

"When did you ever pay respects to a Beetleback?" argued Kaelin.

"I'm not running Maev's enterprise. I'm not the highlander who shot a pistol in front of a crowd of onlookers. You are right, though, Ravenheart. Offering such advice does stick in my craw. Yet it is still good advice."

Kaelin had to admit that it made sense, though it was still needling him as he drove the wagon across the lowered drawbridge. Two Beetlebacks bearing muskets stepped out to block his way.

"What is your business?" asked the first.

"I have come to see the colonel," he told them, "to . . . pay my respects."

"Do you have an appointment?"

"An appointment? No. Where do I go to make one?"

"Leave the wagon here and walk to the keep. See the clerk at the duty desk."

Kaelin drew the wagon to the left and applied the foot brake. Then he climbed down. "You can leave that hunting knife here as well," said the guard. Kaelin drew it and tossed it to the driver's seat.

He strolled to the keep and in through a massive door studded with iron.

A clerk was sitting at a desk, scribbling on parchment with a long quill pen. The man glanced up. "Yes?"

"I wish to make an appointment to see the colonel."

"And you are?"

"Kaelin Ring of Ironlatch farm."

"Ah, the duelist!" came another voice. Kaelin looked round to see a broad-shouldered young officer coming down the circular stairs. "Come up, Master Ring. I am sure the colonel will be delighted to meet you."

Kaelin stiffened momentarily. There was something about the dark-haired soldier that caused his stomach to tighten. The man was smiling, but his eyes were cold and hard.

Kaelin followed him. The stairs wound up to the first level, which was an open food hall in which a score of soldiers were sitting at bench tables, eating their midday meal. The second level was partitioned off by several doors. One of them was open, and Kaelin saw a row of pallet beds. The third level opened out onto a seating area set in a semicircle below a series of tall windows.

"Wait here and take a seat," said the officer, pausing before a door and tapping on the wood panel. Kaelin did not hear anyone call out, but the officer entered, closing the door behind him. Kaelin wandered to the first of the windows and stared down onto the parade ground. Moments later the officer returned.

"I am Captain Ranaud," he said, offering his hand. Kaelin shook it. "Colonel Linax does not have a great deal of time to spare, but he wants to meet you."

Kaelin entered the room. It was some thirty feet long, the floor covered from wall to wall with a thick carpet of sky blue decorated with swirls of pale gold. Kaelin had never seen the like. The furniture was highly polished and beautifully crafted in rich, dark glowing wood, the chair seats padded with green leather. The colonel was sitting behind a long curved desk that was also leather-topped. It was the most beautiful furniture Kaelin had ever seen. Colonel Linax had a thin, pale face and sunken eyes. His skin was dry and unhealthy.

"Welcome, Master Ring," he said, his voice faint. "Do take a seat." Kaelin sat down. "We have heard of your . . . trouble . . . with Call Jace and his son. I can see from the wound on your face that it was quite a duel. You are from the south, I believe."

"Yes, sir. Old Hills, just outside Eldacre."

"I know it well. The highlanders in that area are more, shall we say, loyal to the Moidart. They are educated. Have you been educated, Master Ring?"

"I have, sir."

"Then you know what I mean. Let me speak plainly: The Black Rigante are not educated. They make themselves rich from extortion and robbery. You have been their latest victim, and to be honest, I am surprised to see you alive. I understand your sword shattered and they spared you."

"That is so, sir. I was lucky, for I have never held a blade before."

"Of course not. There is no need for our highland people to have swords in the south. But you fought bravely, which does you credit. Are you still paying tribute to Call Jace?"

Kaelin's mind worked swiftly, and he sensed there was no point in lying. "Yes, sir. It seems . . . prudent."

"Indeed so, Master Ring. So why have you come to me?"

"To pay my respects, sir."

"Not, then, to issue a complaint against Call Jace?"

"I did consider it," said Kaelin, thinking fast. "But the fight was fair, and no one was killed. I did not know what crime I could accuse him of."

"Very wise, Master Ring. Now is not the time to deal with Call Jace, though the time is coming, I can assure you." The colonel suddenly began to cough. His face darkened, his body spasming. He grabbed a handkerchief from his desk, which he held to his face. When the paroxysm passed, he fell back in his chair. Kaelin saw blood on the handkerchief.

Captain Ranaud tapped Kaelin on the shoulder, and the young man rose from his seat and bowed to the colonel. "Thank you for offering me the courtesy of your respect," whispered the colonel. Kaelin walked to the door, following Captain Ranaud out to the top of the stairs.

"The colonel, as you can see, is not a well man," said Ranaud. "I am pleased that you came, Master Ring. Perhaps we can talk more." Ranaud led him to another room. It was

far smaller than the colonel's office, and the floor was not car-
peted. The furniture, too, was of a simple design, crafted
from highland pine. Once again Kaelin sat down. Ranaud
perched on the edge of the desk. He was a big man, his black
hair closely cropped to his skull, his brown eyes deep-set and
mournful. He had an easy smile, but there was a tightness to
the man that had Kaelin on edge. Though there was no evidence to support it, Kaelin believed him to be ruthless and
very dangerous.

"Describe to me the route you took into the Rigante heart-
land," said Captain Ranaud.

"There was a high pass with stockaded gates. After that we
came to a valley."

"The gates were guarded?"

"Yes."

"By how many men?"

"It was difficult to see, for it was raining heavily. Only one
man came down to open the gates. I would think there were
more that I could not see."

"Did you see any weapons hidden?"

"Weapons?"

"Cannon?"

"No, sir. Do they have cannon?"

"What weapons did the guards carry?"

"The man who opened the first gate had a sword and a
pistol in his belt. The next gate was opened by a cloaked
clansman, and I did not see his weapons."

"Did you observe many men carrying muskets in the town
itself?"

"No, sir."

"You stayed overnight in the great house?"

"I did."

"Were there weapons there?"

Kaelin recalled the dining hall. All around the walls there
were pikes, longbows, axes, swords, and shields. There were
also racks of muskets.

"Call Jace has many weapons on his walls: knives, swords, and suchlike. Many of them are very old."

"What makes you say that?"

"There were long pikes and what I think were called glaves. My teacher, Mr. Shaddler, told me they were weapons carried hundreds of years ago, when men wore armor."

"How many people were at the feast?"

"Perhaps a hundred."

"All men of fighting age?"

"Yes," said Kaelin.

"How many people live in the main settlement, would you think?"

"I wouldn't know, sir. Several hundred. A thousand. I didn't get much of a chance to see the settlement. I arrived at night in the rain. I fought Bael in the morning and then left in the storm that evening."

"It would be most helpful, Master Ring, if you could visit their lands again and this time take greater note of your surroundings. It is important that we gather intelligence on their community and its strengths."

"I don't know that I would be welcome, sir, but if I am asked, I will certainly take note."

"Good. Your loyalty will not go unrewarded, Master Ring. We look after our friends. I am glad you came here. I was planning to visit Ironlatch and meet you. So tell me, what caused the trouble between you and Bael?"

Kaelin guessed the man knew, but even so this was perilous ground. "He and his father came to the farm. I did not like Call Jace's manner, and I struck him. Bael hit me with his pistol, and we struggled. I managed to pull a pistol from his belt, and I shot him with it."

"Not your own pistol, then?"

"Highlanders do not own pistols," said Kaelin, "though I think that law is not held to as severely in the north as it is in the south."

"Indeed so, Master Ring. Let me show you out."

Together they walked down the stairs, past the clerk, and out into the sunshine. As they emerged, Kaelin saw Arus Grassman striding toward the keep. The man looked shocked to see Kaelin standing with Ranaud. He stood confused and uncertain.

"Arus, my friend," said Ranaud, "what brings you to the barracks?"

"I was . . . just passing," said Grassman.

"Have you met Master Ring?"

"Er . . . yes, we met this morning."

"Make sure you give him your best prices," said Ranaud. Swinging to Kaelin, he extended his hand once more. "I shall make a point of visiting Ironlatch soon."

"You will be most welcome, Captain."

Ranaud returned to the keep, and Kaelin stood for a moment, eyes locked to the Varlish trader. "See you in a month," he said, then strolled back to the wagon.

Captain Ranaud ascended the stairs and entered the office of the colonel. The older man had been imbibing the narcotic mixture again, and his lips had a blue tinge. Why don't you just die? wondered Ranaud. Your body is wracked with disease, your lungs like wet paper. Why do you hang on? Masking his contempt for the dying man, he fetched him a goblet of water.

"Do you think he will prove helpful?" asked Colonel Linax.

"One way or the other, sir."

"I don't follow you."

"He will either give us valuable information or I shall arrest him for discharging a pistol. It is a long time since we hanged a highlander publicly. It will send a message to Jace and his cutthroats."

"Jace is not to be underestimated, Ranaud. You are new here. His power is formidable."

It has been allowed to become formidable by weaklings

like you, thought Ranaud. "I bow to your superior understanding, sir. However, we did have troublesome clansmen in the isles, and we dealt with them."

"I know, I know," said Linax. "Two hundred hanged, villages burned. The fishing fleet was sunk, I understand, and there is now widespread starvation. There are those who think that a small price to pay for stability. I am not one of them. The isles now produce no tax revenue whatever."

"The isles themselves were never important, but the message of the isles and the two hundred and twelve hanged has reached the mainland. It will keep the clans in their place. We should have wiped them out a century ago and peopled the highlands with Varlish."

"We must agree to differ, Captain. Has your prisoner offered any useful information?"

"Call Jace has two cannon and around five hundred muskets."

"I am surprised you got him to talk. These Black Rigante are hardy fellows."

"He resisted all pressure until we sawed off his foot. I swear these clansmen have little feeling. They do not experience pain as we do."

"How will you use this information? With two hundred men we cannot storm Call Jace's stronghold."

"No, not yet. But I think the Moidart will begin to make plans when he learns of the cannon. Then we can burn out these rebels once and for all."

Linax began coughing again, but the spasm passed swiftly. "I knew a man once," he said, "whose house was infested with cockroaches. They drove him crazy. In the end he torched his home. It burned very brightly. And he was highly successful. As he stood among the blackened timbers the following day, he did not see a single cockroach."

"The meaning is lost on me, sir, I am afraid."

"It is one thing to light a fire, Captain, quite another to control it. And I think you may be wrong about the Moidart. Have you heard from the capital lately?"

"Not in the last month, sir."

"There is more talk of unrest. The king's popularity is not what it was, and he is still at loggerheads with the Tribune Chamber. Civil war is coming, Ranaud. Not this year, perhaps, or maybe next. But it is coming. The Moidart will have to choose sides. He will not want to commit troops so far north when he has enemies of his own far closer."

"A campaign here would be over in days," said Ranaud. "We'd hang Jace and fifty or so of his senior men, indenture half the clan to work in the mines, and build a garrison at the center of Rigante territory."

"Do not let your success on the isles go to your head, Captain. Yes, they were troublesome, but they were badly led and badly provisioned and carried no real weaponry. Call Jace has probably two thousand fighting men, and he is a real leader. He is smart—cunning, if you like—and unafraid. I do not think it would be over in days."

That's because you are old and dying, Ranaud thought savagely. *You have invested these qualities in Jace so that your own failures become more understandable.* There was little point in telling this weak and indecisive man that he had already set in motion a plan to eliminate Call Jace. The Rigante leader had built his tiny empire on bands of murderous raiders operating to the east of Black Mountain. Well, two could play that game. Ranaud had gathered intelligence about Jace for the last few months. The Rigante was known to frequent the house of a young widow woman half a day's walk from the sanctuary of his own lands. Ranaud had sent eight men into the mountains, hard, ruthless men. They would wait until Jace showed himself, then kill him. Without their leader the Black Rigante would be infinitely easier to handle.

Tense now and angry, he bowed to the colonel.

I will spend the afternoon with the prisoner, he decided. *It will be pleasant to listen to his screams as we cut away his other foot.*

* * *

The visit to the barracks had disturbed Kaelin Ring. There was something chilling about Captain Ranaud that left an edge of fear in the young Rigante. The man had known about his fight with Bael and the fact that he had used a pistol. There was no doubt about that in Kaelin's mind. So why had Kaelin not been arrested? The answer was obvious and was contained in the old proverb: The enemy of my enemy must therefore be my friend. Ranaud believed Kaelin Ring had cause to hate Call Jace and his family. As long as he continued to believe that, Kaelin would be safe. The moment the Beetleback realized his mistake, Kaelin would be arrested and hanged.

Jaim's advice had been sound. But all that had been gained was a reprieve. Kaelin Ring would never supply Ranaud with information to be used against Call Jace and the Rigante. In fact, the reverse was true. Kaelin was anxious to pass on to Jace the fact that Ranaud was gathering information about his stronghold.

He was tempted to wait until the next tribute was due and then explain what had happened to whichever of the Rigante came for the cattle. Then he thought again of Ranaud and his knowledge of the trouble with Bael. Someone had described the scene. Now, it could have been that word of it had just spread, a casual word here and there, the information pieced together by Ranaud. But even back in Old Hills there were known to be informers who would sell information to the Beetlebacks for coin. Here it would be no different. What if Senlic Carpenter or Finbarr Ustal was in the pay of Ranaud? What if some of Jace's own men were informers? If Kaelin told the wrong person, his own life would be forfeit.

No, he decided on the third day after the meeting with Ranaud, I will confide only in Jace.

Chara's face appeared in his mind, and he acknowledged that this would be a fine way to settle the impasse that kept them both from seeing each other.

The following day he spent in the company of Senlic Carpenter and Finbarr Ustal. Five hundred sixty steers had been grouped in the south pastures, ready for the drive to southern markets. Finbarr had hired twenty drovers for the trip.

Kaelin listened as Senlic offered advice to the younger man about routes, watering places, and areas to avoid. He was also given a list of the names of prominent farmers along the route who would need to be paid for grazing rights. Finbarr was obviously looking forward to the trip and pleased that this new responsibility had been offered to him.

Later that evening Kaelin confided to Senlic that he intended to travel to the lands of the Black Rigante the following morning.

"Not wise to go uninvited, lad," said Senlic. "What do you want there?"

"I want to see Chara," Kaelin told him.

"Aye, she's a fine-looking lass. I heard you asked for her hand. But if she's turned you down once, she's likely to do so again."

"She didn't turn me down. She said she needed time to think on it. A month is enough."

"You can't rush women into that kind of decision," the old man said with a smile. "Took three years before my woman agreed to walk the tree with me."

"I didn't know you were wed."

"Twenty-six years, Kaelin. Fine years, mostly. One morning I woke up and she was lying quietly beside me. I leaned in to kiss her cheek, and I realized she'd gone. Just like that. Slipped away in the night. Twenty-six years and no chance to say good-bye. Ah, but that was hard. Mighty hard."

Kaelin felt suddenly awkward. In that moment Senlic seemed old and fragile, his eyes sorrowful. The silence was uncomfortable. Kaelin broke it. "You have children?" he asked, anxious to steer the conversation away from death and regret.

"Seven. Six boys and a girl. Actually, there were ten, but three did not survive past infancy. But let's not talk about it, Kaelin. It makes me maudlin."

"I am sorry, Senlic. I did not wish to pry."

Senlic sighed, then forced a smile. "My father always told me that life was nothing but memories. He was right. As each moment passes, it becomes history. He thought it was important to hold to the moment, savoring it. He often talked of good times past and hoped that the future would supply more golden moments. The truth is, though, that memories are only golden when shared—when you can say to a loved one, 'Do you remember that walk by the orchard grove when first we held hands?' She will smile and say, 'Of course I do, you old fool.' That is the joy of memories. When Katra died, she took half my life with her, and now the memory of the orchard is at best bittersweet. Ah, I am getting old and I talk too much."

Senlic heaved himself from the chair and stretched his back. "I'll have a pack ready for you tomorrow when you leave. Try to keep it safe from bears this time." Then he patted Kaelin's shoulder and left the house.

Holding his broken left arm to his chest, Call Jace slid down the gully on his back. His leg hit a tree root, which twisted him, and he began to roll. The fractured forearm struck a rock. Jace cried out. At the bottom of the gully he lay still, gritting his teeth against the agony. Then he sat up. Blood had soaked his black shirtsleeve. Carefully he undid the button of his cuff and folded back the sleeve. The ball had hit his forearm, shattering the bone. There was no exit wound. He tried to flex his fingers, but they were stiff and swollen.

In the distance he heard the dogs barking. Jace swore and struggled to his feet. His pistol was gone, discharged into the face of one of his attackers, then knocked from his hand in the short fight that had followed. His sword, too, was lost, trapped between the ribs of another man. He hoped the bastard would die hard.

Jace moved along the gully and into the stream, splashing through the clear water and emerging on the other side. He took five steps and then stopped. With great care he extended his right foot backward, placing it into the last footprint he had made, then did the same with the left. He did that until he was standing once more in the stream. Then, with water swirling around his ankles, he pushed on, following the line of the stream as it angled northwest.

Without pursuers this route would have him back in Rigante country in around five hours. Trouble was, the hunters knew this also. If Jace headed for home, as they must be expecting, they would cut him off. With him having one useless arm and no sword, they would kill him without undue effort.

Jace kept to the stream for a quarter of a mile, then emerged on the same side he had entered, clambering up over a gently sloping rocky outcrop and then onto a deer trail that cut back toward the southeast. The fingers of his injured arm were throbbing now, the skin tight and stretched. He had been lucky.

He had seen the musketeer at the last moment and had instinctively thrown up his arm as the man fired. The shot would otherwise have struck him in the head. The musketeer had dropped his weapon and pulled a pistol from his belt. He had been marginally too slow. Jace had drawn his own flintlock and discharged it, the ball taking the assassin in the bridge of the nose, smashing his skull.

Other men had rushed from the trees. Jace had had time to draw his saber and plunge it into the body of the first. The man had screamed and, twisting as he fell, dragged the sword from Jace's hand. As the others had closed in, the Rigante leader had spun on his heel and fled into the forest.

Call Jace glanced up at the sky. Close to two hours had passed since he had been shot. Twice musket balls had screamed by him, one ricocheting from a tree trunk and spattering his face with splinters. Now they had brought dogs into the hunt.

Jace scrambled up a steep bank and paused at the top, crouching low and listening. The dogs were not barking now.

Think, man! What to do, where to go?

No longer a young man, Jace was already tired from the

chase, though there was some strength left. How many were hunting him?

He thought back to the moment he had emerged from the trees at the back of Magra's house. One man he had shot; another he had stabbed. Four had come running from the front of the house. Was it only four giving chase? If so, who was holding the dogs? Were there others in the house guarding Magra?

Only one musketeer had been at the rear of the building, the rest in hiding at the front. Had he emerged from the trail at any other point, it would have been more than his arm they would have hit.

Jace *had* approached the house from the front but had held back scanning the building. Magra had known he was coming, and they had worked out a simple code. If it was safe to come in, Magra would leave a water jug on the porch. There had been no jug.

He should have eased himself back into the trees then and returned home. But he had been concerned about Magra and so had worked his way around to the rear. It had been a mistake. Even so, you are alive, he told himself.

Once again he heard the dogs barking, this time from below and to the north. They were in the gully.

Keeping low, Jace began to climb, topping the rise and angling his route back toward the one place they would not think of searching.

It took almost an hour.

Now, once again, he was hidden in the trees by Magra's small house. The two dead men lay where they had fallen. Jace scanned the area, circling it just in case anyone had been left behind. At last he left the sanctuary of the trees and ran to the man he had stabbed. His saber was still embedded in the corpse, and Jace dragged it clear. Then he recovered his fallen pistol, thrusting it into his belt.

There was no movement from the house, and with a heavy heart Call Jace moved across the clearing and up onto the porch. He had spent many happy hours in that secluded place, and the memory of Magra's laughter filled his mind.

Her naked body was in the bedroom, though not on the bed. It lay against the far wall. It seemed to Jace that she must have cowered there, for her legs were drawn up tight against her body. Blood from her slashed throat had flowed across her breasts and then pooled on the wooden boards beneath her.

"I'm sorry, lass," said Call Jace. "Had I loved you less, no one would have come here. Had I loved you more, I'd have taken you to my home."

Turning on his heel, he strode out and returned to the trees.

Call Jace was no longer tired. He had his hunting knife, his saber, his pistol, and enemies to kill.

Aye, and a broken arm and a body past its prime! Get a hold of yourself, man, he thought. This is no time to be thinking like an old-style Rigante berserker. Magra must be avenged, that is true. But you can't do it in this condition. First you must escape the killers. His heart yearned to go hunting them, but his head remained cool. Magra was dead. Nothing could change that. Yet in order to avenge her Call needed to see the killers, to know them. He had caught only the barest glimpse in that first attack.

How could he get close without the dogs scenting him?

Turning again, he moved swiftly back into the house and through to the narrow kitchen. At the back of a small cupboard he found a pottery spice jar. Pulling clear the cork lid, he carefully sniffed the contents. As a young man Jace had discovered the joys of spiced food. Peppercorns were expensive, but he had acquired a store of them. Some he had given to Magra for when she cooked for him. From another cupboard he took a small pepper mill and ground the spice to a fine powder. Time was short, and Jace listened for the sound of the dogs.

Returning to the doorway, he sprinkled half of the black powder across the opening. Leaving the house through the rear window, he ran across to the tree line, pausing to sprinkle more powder into two of the bootprints he had made.

Once into the trees, he reloaded his pistol. It was not easy with one hand, but sitting down, he gripped the butt between his knees and tipped a measure of gunpowder from his horn, followed by a ball and then a wad to hold it in place. Filling the flash pan was even more difficult, but he managed it. Satisfied the weapon was primed, he drew back the hammer and waited.

Time passed slowly, and it was almost an hour before he heard the sounds of men moving through the trees far to his right. The first of the killers came into sight. Two sleek, powerful hunting hounds were straining at the leash, almost dragging the man forward. Call Jace narrowed his eyes. He had never seen the man before, but he would know him again. Four other men came into sight, all carrying long-barreled muskets. They, too, were unknown to Jace. A sixth man followed at the rear. His face was familiar, but Jace could not place him.

The dog handler released the leash, and the hounds bounded toward the house, barking furiously. The first of them reached the doorway, sniffed the pepper, and immediately began to shake its head and snort. But the second did not follow its example. It ran into the house, then leapt through the rear window and came like an arrow toward Jace's hiding place. It did not pause to sniff the bootprints.

Jace eased himself back into the trees. The hound cleared the first bush with a prodigious leap. The Rigante leader laid down his pistol and drew his hunting knife. As the dog leapt at him, Jace rolled to his left, slamming the blade deep into the dog's side. Its jaws raked his shoulder, tearing the skin. Dragging the knife clear, Jace plunged it three times into the beast's neck. The dog slumped to the ground.

Sheathing his knife, Jace took up the pistol and peered over the bush. Some of the men had gone into the house. Two others—one the dog handler—were moving toward the trees. The handler was calling out a name. Beside him the dying dog whimpered at the sound.

"Shella, where are you, boy?"

As the two men came close, Jace reared up. His pistol boomed, the shot taking the musketeer full in the face and hurling him from his feet. Dropping the pistol, Jace drew his saber and leapt forward. The unarmed dog handler stood rooted in shock even as Jace's blade opened his throat.

Spinning on his heel, Jace threw himself back toward the bushes just as the thunder of a musket blast sounded from the rear window. While holding the sword hilt Jace could not gather his pistol. He swore and let go of the sword. Rolling over, he grabbed the pistol, pushing it into his belt. Then he grabbed his sword, pushed himself to his feet, and began to run once more. A musket ball tore through the shoulder of his leather shirt, scoring the skin but not penetrating.

Four dead. The odds were better now but still formidable. Three men with muskets and the young fair-haired man with the familiar face. Jace doubted the surviving dog would soon recover its sense of smell.

But he was wrong.

◇ **13** ◇

PERSIS ROEBUCK HAD never desired to be a killer. It had always been his dream to attend the apothecary college in Baracum and then, perhaps, if fortune favored him, go on to become a surgeon. His father had encouraged him always to be ambitious but never haughty or arrogant.

Persis had studied hard and had even written to the apothecary Ramus in Old Hills, asking questions about herbs and their uses. Ramus had been kind enough to reply and had sent several books, complete with hand-painted illustrations, to aid the young man in his quest.

Five years earlier Persis had been a happy and contented young man living with his widowed father on their farm just east of the Black Mountain settlement. The farm was not a rich one, for the earth was thin and grazing for the cattle was sparse. His father owned only sixty head, but he had acquired a fine bull whose talents as a stud brought in extra income. It was this income that allowed Persis to acquire more books in order to prepare for the entrance examination to the college.

His father had been a fine man, upstanding and righteous. He had no hatred for the highlanders and taught Persis never to look down on another man for the sake of his blood or his religion. "The Source loves all men," his father would say.

When the Black Rigante bastard Call Jace had come to the farm, his father had greeted him cordially, offering refreshments. Persis had sat quietly in the corner. He had not fully—at thirteen—understood the nature of their conversation. It was something to do with tribute payments. His father had told Jace he saw no reason to pay for a service he did not need and had pointed out that his farm was too poor to suffer attacks from raiders. Jace had seemed to accept that but had urged his father to reconsider his position. "These are dangerous times," he said.

When Jace had gone, Persis had asked his father about the conversation. But the old man had merely smiled and shrugged it off.

The following day their stud bull had been found with its throat cut.

Father had wept at the sight, for he could not afford to replace such a fine animal. Then he had visited the barracks to tell the colonel about the incident and how it had followed his refusal to pay Jace.

Two weeks later his father's body had been discovered. His throat had been cut.

A good and a kind man had been murdered on the orders of the Rigante leader. Even at thirteen Persis knew this. All thoughts of apothecary training fled from his mind, though even if they had not, the farm could no longer support such dreams. His uncle Mathys took over the farm, and Persis worked like a slave to help keep it going. They managed to survive for four years, but in the end the enterprise failed. Mathys sold the property and lands to the farmer whose lands adjoined theirs. The price was not high, and Mathys stayed on to manage the farm for the new owner, while Persis took work in Black Mountain as a storeman-loader for Arus Grassman.

Through Grassman he had come to know the new captain of the Beetlebacks, Captain Ranaud. He had told him about the murder of his father. Ranaud had been most sympathetic. "It is a disgrace that men like Jace should be allowed to exist," he said. "But that is the way of the world, I am afraid. The problem was created by weak officers years ago and has only been exacerbated since."

Then, the previous month, Ranaud had come to see him in

his meager lodgings behind the warehouse. He had spoken of a plan to bring Jace to justice. "Not," he said, "the justice of the courts, sadly, but justice nevertheless." He told Persis of Jace's lust for a lewd woman who lived in the high hills close to Rigante country. "A few good men could end this bandit's evil forever," he said.

Persis Roebuck would have paid with his soul for the opportunity to avenge his father. He begged Ranaud to allow him to be part of the hunt. Killing Jace would mean that no other boy would have to go through the torment he had suffered. Ranaud agreed.

Now Persis Roebuck sat on the porch of the whore's home, wiping the nostrils of the hunting dog with a damp cloth. Four men were dead. Four remained. The deaths had not dampened the young man's fervor. If Jace killed all the other men, Persis would still go after him. Evil had to be countered wherever it was found. His father had taught him that.

Killers had to be punished.

Persis glanced across at the body of Keets. Jace had pierced his body with his saber, and the man had died in agony. He and Brace should never have killed the woman, thought Persis. That, too, was evil. "She's a whore, and she has seen us," Keets had said. Barley the dog handler and Persis had argued with him, and Keets had seemed to agree. Then he and Brace had gone back into the house. When they had emerged, there had been blood on Keets' hands.

"Oh, no," said Barley, the dog handler. "What in hell's name have you done?"

"I'm the leader here," said Keets, "and I have done what was necessary. But don't worry, your hands are spotless."

Brace chuckled. "I can see why Jace came here," he said. "She drained us dry to save her life. Damn, but her pleading made it all the sweeter."

"You raped her?" said the astonished Persis.

"Hardly call it rape," said Brace, a hulking, powerfully built loader from Grassman's warehouse. "She offered it to save her life."

Keets was now dead, as indeed were Barley, Jube, and Mather. The vile Brace was still alive and sitting not ten feet away, honing his saber with a whetstone.

"What shall we do?" asked Lane Pikard, a lanky young man who worked with Persis in Grassman's warehouse. Persis did not like him. Lane had an unreasoning hatred of highlanders. As far as Persis could tell, no highlander had ever harmed him, yet Lane talked constantly of the need to "exterminate the vermin." Persis guessed he had absorbed much of his hatred from Enson Giese, the aging wolf hunter. The man bragged of his grisly exploits against clansmen, how he had once castrated a highlander for an assault on a "good Varlish girl." Persis became aware that Lane was looking at him, still waiting for an answer to his question.

"We go after him," said Persis. "We find him, and we kill him. He is wounded and losing blood, and he has been chased all day. He is an old man, Lane, and will be weary by now. I think the hound is ready. We will track him. We will catch him."

"He's killed four already," put in Enson Giese. "Chances are, if we do go after him, he'll take another, maybe two."

Persis glanced up at the wolf hunter. He was the oldest man there, at fifty, and a former Beetleback dishonorably discharged for drunkenness. Despite his cruel nature, he was no coward. He was also a fine shot with a musket. "You have no choice, Enson," said Persis. "Why do you think Jace waited here at the house?"

"I don't know."

"He wanted to *see* us. Now he has. If he lives, we die—or we flee south. I'm not anxious to leave. Are you?"

"Guess not. Let's find him, then. It will be good to listen to him squeal."

"I hate him, but I don't think he's the squealing kind," said Persis.

Enson chuckled. "They all squeal, boy, when you have a knife to their balls. They beg, they plead, they promise. Even the great Call Jace. You'll see."

"I just want him dead," said Persis. "A just punishment for his evil."

"Oh, he'll die," promised Enson. "But he'll die hard."

Jace had made more than two miles over the rough country when he heard the dog barking. He cursed and struggled on. His left arm hung uselessly at his side, his fingers swollen and painful. Blood was also flowing from the bite to his left shoulder.

They were still after him. And they were gaining.

Jace pushed on, scrambling up a steep rise. Just as he reached the top, he slipped, falling hard onto his wounded arm. With a cry of pain he rolled to his back and slid down the slope. His scabbard caught on a tree root, the hilt of his saber gouging into his hip. At the bottom he lay still, breathing heavily. His strength was almost gone, and he was still some six miles from the sanctuary of Rigante lands.

Struggling to his feet, he attempted the climb again. His legs were weary, and without the use of his left arm he found the going difficult. At last he reached the top and sat down, trying to gather what remained of his strength. Too much easy living, he thought. If I get out of this, by heaven, I'll build my stamina back.

Rising, he took several deep breaths and then walked wearily along the track. From there he could see the Black Mountain road and beyond it the Rigante mountains. So close.

A shot sounded, the ball screaming by mere inches from his head. Jace hurled himself flat, then swiveled on his belly to peer down the slope. The young fair-haired man with the familiar face had released the dog's leash, and the hound was bounding up the rise. Three men had fanned out behind the handler. One of them, a gray-haired man, was reloading his musket. Jace estimated the distance. Around two hundred paces.

Damn, but that was a good shot, he thought.

Squirming back, he drew his pistol. The hound scrambled over the rise and bounded down the track toward him. Jace came up on one knee, cocked the pistol, and waited. He fired just as the dog reached him, the ball tearing into the beast's mouth and out through the back of its head. The hound's front legs collapsed under him, the body somersaulting into Jace, knocking him sideways. Pushing aside the dead hound, Jace glanced down the slope. The men were climbing it now.

With no time to reload, Jace thrust the pistol into his belt and began to run along the track.

Cutting left into the trees, he powered up another short slope and crouched down behind a thick bush to charge his pistol. His hand was trembling from exertion, and he spilled powder into his lap. Anger flowed through him. Is this how it will end? he wondered. Killed by a pack of mangy Varlish?

With the pistol loaded he waited once more. If he could shoot one musketeer and then charge into the others, he might be able to kill them all. Even as he thought it, he knew such an outcome was more than unlikely. In order to kill one with a pistol he needed to be close. That would leave two other men with long-barreled muskets and the dog handler with his own pistol. They would all have time to fire before Jace reached them. It was more than he could hope for that they would all miss.

Even so, it was his only chance. With his strength all but gone, Jace was bereft of options. If he continued to run, they would come upon him anyway somewhere down the trail, and he would be too exhausted to put up a fight. Like a stag pursued by wolves.

No, best to make his stand now.

A great calm settled on him. Laying the pistol down, he drew his saber, plunging it into the ground beside him. Then he took up the pistol and cocked it.

Dark clouds had begun to gather over the mountains. Jace glanced up. Rain might help. Only the best-crafted flash bowls would keep out water, and their muskets would be useless.

But then, so would his pistol, which was cheap and hastily made.

One against four with a saber? Could he win?

Jace smiled. He could if he were Grymauch.

The pain from his broken arm was lessening. The limb was almost numb now.

He saw movement, and two men emerged from behind the trees, muskets ready. Jace crouched lower behind the bush. The gray-haired killer was not in sight. A third man moved into the open. Where have I seen him before? Jace wondered.

Slowly and warily the three men began to climb the slope. They were fifty paces away now.

Jace took a deep, calming breath.

Where the hell was the fourth man?

Jace glanced to the right. The trees were thicker there, but there was no sign of movement. The man could not have gotten to the left of him, for he would have had to cross the trail below. This was a worry, for Jace already knew that the man was a good shot. Crouched as he was behind a screen of bushes, Jace was all but invisible, but if the man was hiding in the trees to his right, he would have a perfect target the moment Jace rose to fight. Once more the Rigante leader scanned the trees. There was nothing to be seen.

The advancing men were closer now. The first was a burly black-haired musketeer with a round face and small eyes; the second was taller and lean. His eyes were wide, his head moving swiftly from side to side as he searched for his prey. He looks frightened, thought Jace. He will fire too swiftly.

With the trio no more than twelve paces from his hiding place Jace reared up. Extending the pistol, he shot the black-haired man in the chest. As he did so, he felt a blow to his back. It was like being struck by a hammer. He staggered, dropped his pistol, and swept up his saber. Dizziness almost swamped him, but he charged from the bushes directly at the tall, lean killer. The man swung his musket and fired. The shot missed. Jace ran on, plunging the saber through his belly. The blade sliced through the killer, emerging from his back. As the man fell, Jace tried to drag the sword clear. Putting his boot on the dying man's chest, he wrenched hard. The saber hilt came away in his hand.

"The next shot goes through your head," came a voice from behind.

Ahead of him the young fair-haired man had drawn his pistol and was pointing it at Jace's chest.

The Rigante leader turned slowly. The gray-haired muske-teer had emerged from the trees and was some twenty paces behind him.

"You shoot well," said Jace. His legs almost buckled, but he steadied himself.

"Hunted wolves for most of my life," the man said equably. He advanced, but only to within ten paces. "Put your hands behind your back, Rigante."

"I wish I could," Jace told him, "but the left is shattered."

"Let us just execute him for his crimes and be gone," said the fair-haired man.

"Tie his hands," said the other. "Do it!"

"I'll not see any man tortured."

Before the gray-haired hunter could reply there came a moan from the man with Jace's saber blade through his belly. "I can't feel my legs, Uncle Enson," he said. "I can't feel them."

"He snapped your spine, boy," said Enson. "Lie still, Lane. It'll be over soon."

Lane groaned, then cried out as fresh agony ripped through him. Enson pulled a pistol from his belt and sent a shot hammering into Lane's skull.

Jace sat down, a great weariness settling over him. He glanced up at the young man. "Where have I seen you be-fore?" he asked. "It's been bothering me some."

"Bothering you, you bastard? Bothering you? I am Persis Roebuck. You came to my father's farm demanding tribute. When he wouldn't pay, you killed our only bull, then you killed my father."

"Then you have cause to hate me," admitted Jace. Transferring his gaze to Enson, he said: "And what about you? Which of your family did I kill, apart from the cow turd who broke my sword?"

Enson chuckled. "No one. I'm here for the money only. No wolves left, you see. A man has to eat. I should have put that last shot through your spine and not your shoulder. Had I done so, poor Lane would still be with us. But I wanted to see just how tough the great Call Jace would prove to be."

"Did you kill my Magra?" asked Jace.

"No, that was Keets and Brace. Both are dead, so you have your vengeance. And now, since the lily liver here will not tie your hands, I'll just have to shatter your right arm. Then we can get to know one another better."

"I know you well enough already," said Jace.

Enson raised his musket. A shot sounded, though not from Enson's musket. The wolf hunter staggered to his left and stood still for a moment. Jace saw blood pumping from his temple. He dropped his musket and pitched forward.

Kaelin Ring stepped into sight. "Put down your pistol," he ordered the fair-haired man.

"He has to die!" yelled Persis. Jace rolled to his side as the young man fired, the shot screeching past his head. Kaelin shot in the same moment, the lead ball punching through the man's chest and piercing his heart. Persis was dead before his body struck the earth.

Jace looked up at the young Rigante. "If you've come courting," he said, "you have my blessing."

Kaelin scanned the undergrowth. "Are there more of them?"

"No. These were the last."

"Can you walk?"

"Not at the moment, boy. But give me an hour's rest and I'll race you home."

The journey back to Rigante lands was long and arduous. Despite the confidence of his words, Call Jace was too weak to walk unsupported and even with Kaelin's help could make no more than a few hundred paces without needing to rest.

After two hours they had made no more than a mile, and Kaelin, too, was growing weary. Call Jace was a big man, and he stumbled often.

At last Kaelin decided he had to leave the Rigante leader and seek help. Finding a campsite close to a stream, Kaelin built a fire, gathered dead wood, and made Call Jace as comfortable as possible, covering him with his own cloak and leaving him with the loaded Emburleys. Then he set off at a run, cutting down the trail and onto the main road.

Within the hour, sweating and near exhaustion, he ran up to the first of the stockaded gates. The sun was setting, and Kaelin saw two muskets trained on him as he approached.

"What do you want, southerner?" came a voice.

"Call Jace is wounded. I need men to help carry him back," he replied.

One of the muskets was withdrawn. The gates opened, and the tall, bearded figure of the highlander Rayster appeared. "Where is he?" he asked.

"About five miles back down the road and up into the trees. He was attacked by a group of Varlish. He has been shot in the shoulder, and his arm is broken. He has lost a lot of blood."

"Wait here," said Rayster. Once more the wooden gates swung shut. Then Kaelin heard a horn being sounded. It seemed to echo through the pass, but then he realized it was a series of horns. He sat on a rock, gathering his strength.

After a while he heard the gates creak. Rayster emerged with a half dozen men. One of them was leading a pot-bellied pony.

"Show us where he is," Rayster ordered coldly.

Kaelin's anger flared. He stood and looked the clansman in the eye. "I don't like your tone, turd breath, so be careful when next you speak."

Rayster's eyes narrowed, but he forced a smile, then bowed deeply. "Be so kind as to lead us to our lord," he said. "Is that more suitable?"

The sarcasm did nothing for Kaelin's temper, but he controlled it. "If it wasn't for the fact that Call Jace needs help, I'd show you just how suitable. Perhaps we can discuss it later."

The walk was long, and no one spoke. It was dark when they came across the campfire and the sleeping Rigante leader. In the fading firelight his face seemed very pale, and they had difficulty rousing him.

Once awake, he ordered four of the men to find the bodies of the slain and bury them. "Leave no sign of the graves," he said. Two of the clansmen helped him to his feet and onto the back of the pony. Jace gripped its mane with his good hand, then sagged forward. Rayster and another clansman walked on either side of the pony, supporting Jace. The others loped off into the woods to obey the orders of their lord.

Kaelin, having retrieved his pistols, walked behind the pony. He was annoyed with himself. Yet again he had reacted with anger to a perceived slight, opening himself up to consequences far greater than the original lack of courtesy warranted. Should Rayster so choose, there would be another duel, and this time someone would die. What is wrong with you? he wondered. Why can you not learn to swallow your pride?

Because pride is all I have, he told himself. If I have to die for it, then so be it.

Two and a quarter hours later Jace was helped to his bed. Two of the women of the household helped undress him, having to cut away his shirt. The flattened lead ball was cut from his broken arm, and the limb was splinted. Then the women dealt with the wound in his back before cleaning and stitching the shallow bite from the hound. The shot from Enson Giese had cannoned off his shoulder blade, cracking his left collarbone. It was lodged just below the skin at the front of his left shoulder. One of the women sliced the skin and removed it.

Dowstairs Kaelin sat on a bench while Rayster paced back and forth. Neither spoke for a while. Then the tall clansman paused in his pacing. "You misunderstood me," he said at last. "I was concerned for my chief and intended no disrespect."

Kaelin nodded. "My temper will be the death of me," he said with a rueful smile.

Rayster held out his hand. "My thanks to you for aiding Call. How did you happen upon him?"

Kaelin shook the hand. "I was traveling here, and I heard shots from the woods. I thought it might be a Rigante hunting party, and since I was coming here uninvited, I decided to join them and explain that I needed to see Call Jace. When I climbed the trail, I saw Call attack three men. He killed one with his pistol and stabbed another. Then his sword broke."

"And you killed the other two."

"Yes."

"Those Emburleys are very fine. I have never fired one, but I have heard they are wondrously accurate."

One of the women came down the stairs. Her hands were bloody. Kaelin and Rayster both stood. The woman was middle-aged, with iron-gray hair and stern features. "He is sleeping now," she said. "But I would feel more at ease if the Dweller could see him. The shots drove cloth from his shirt into the wounds. I have seen such injuries go bad before now."

"I will send someone to Sorrow Bird," said Rayster. "Perhaps she is home now."

The woman walked away toward the kitchen area. "Where is Chara?" asked Kaelin.

"In the West Hills. She has been there for a month tending her grandmother. The old woman had a fall and can no longer walk or talk. Her body is paralyzed down one side. She is dying, I think. Bael is there also. Sad for them, for they love her dearly."

"She is Call's mother?" inquired Kaelin.

"No. She is the mother to Call's second wife, Layna. She died ten years ago in childbirth. She and the babe both. The Dweller was not here then, either."

"Who is this Dweller?"

Rayster shrugged. "She is a Wicca woman and very mysterious. She has a hut near Sorrow Bird Lake, but some men
think she dwells mostly in the shadow world where the Seidh
still live. I don't know the truth of it. She is a great healer,
though, and her spirit visions are strong."

"We have someone in the south like that," said Kaelin.
"She is called the Wyrd of the Wishing Tree woods."

"Aye, Grymauch has spoken of her. Tomorrow I will travel
to Sorrow Bird and see if she is there. Would you care to walk
with me?"

"Yes, I would. Is it close to the West Hills?"

Rayster chuckled. "She was very angry when she heard
you had left. She may not have forgiven you."

"I now have her father's blessing," said Kaelin. "You think
it might sway her?"

Rayster shook his head. "I have known Chara since she
was a wee bairn. She has a temper like yours, Ravenheart.
But she is quick to forgive. You may, however, need to curb
your tongue, for I don't doubt she will lay into you with
mighty ferocity at first."

Kaelin sighed. "I'll bear that in mind."

Although Chara Jace hoped that the Dweller would be at the
lake, it was not the only reason she had traveled to Sorrow
Bird. A month of tending her sick grandmother had exhausted her spirit, and the sense of freedom she felt as she
walked the high country was beyond joy.

Rayga had been a vibrant woman, fiercely intelligent, swift
to anger, yet with a sense of humor that was often self-
mocking. One moment she would rail at someone, the next
collapse into a fit of giggles and laughter that was totally infectious. Chara had always enjoyed her company. The older
woman had been a font of wisdom and someone Chara had
always relied on. Seeing her paralyzed, incapable of speech,
and mewing like a babe brought a pain into Chara's soul she
could never have imagined. It led not only to feelings of
sorrow but to anger that fate could deal so harshly with such a

good woman. And there was guilt, too, for sometimes Chara would find herself thinking that it would have been better if the stroke had killed the old woman. Then Chara would have been able to remember her as she had been.

Here, in the high hills overlooking Sorrow Bird Lake, the wind was fresh and cool, the air sweet as honeyed wine. Birds were singing, and the sunlight shone on the blue waters of the lake. Chara sighed. From this high vantage point she could not see whether the Dweller's small boat was moored on the island, and she found herself reluctant to journey farther. She was hoping that the Dweller could cast a spell and restore Rayga to health. Deep down she sensed that this hope would be dashed. Rayga was over eighty years old.

Chara sat on the hillside, remembering the day almost ten years earlier when Rayga had first brought her to the lake. "Why is it called Sorrow Bird?" the child had asked.

"It is a long-ago tale," said Rayga, "of a time when the Seidh walked among humans. There was a tribe living in these mountains that turned against the ways of the gods. The tribe was led by a woman. She was tall and haughty and filled with ambition. She sought to dominate the other tribes by war, assassination, and duplicity. One day an old shaman called upon the Morrigu—a powerful goddess—for aid. The Morrigu brought a plague upon the woman's tribe. It killed everyone. Every man, woman, babe. All dead. Save for the queen herself. She walked among the dead, her ambitions in ashes. The Morrigu came to her there. 'And now you must kill me,' said the queen, 'for my people are gone and my heart is broken.' 'No,' said the Morrigu. 'You will live on.' And she changed the queen into an owl. For many years the queen-owl dwelt on the island. At night her moaning could be heard for many miles. That is why it is called Sorrow Bird Lake."

"That is very sad," Chara said.

"All actions have consequences, child," Rayga told her.

"Is the queen-owl still there?"

"Perhaps. Or perhaps the Morrigu forgave her. I do not know."

The two images of her grandmother merged in her mind, one bright and vibrant with twinkling eyes and the sweetest of smiles and the other slack-jawed, spittle running down the twisted lips. Chara felt tears spill from her eyes, and she sat on the hillside weeping.

It is so unfair, she thought as the tears subsided. Why must life be so cruel? Had Rayga died when the stroke hit, then all her loved ones would have remembered her as she was, bright and full of life and wisdom. Now all memories would be stained by the mewling, self-soiling creature she had become.

Chara wiped away the last of her tears, then stared down at her hands and arms, at the supple young skin. Rayga's hands were dry and covered with liver spots. Once they, too, had been young and flawless. Chara shivered as the thought came to her that one day her own granddaughter might be sitting at the bedside while Chara was drooling and near death.

Pushing such images from her mind, Chara gazed out over Sorrow Bird Lake: the bright, shining water and the distant sunlit mountains.

She saw movement down near the lakeside: two men emerging from the trees and walking down to the waterline. In that instant her heart soared, for one of them was Kaelin Ring. Scrambling to her feet, she began to walk down the slope, then stopped. Anger flared. He had left the Rigante lands in a storm, not waiting to say good-bye or to offer her comfort for the tragedy that had befallen her grandmother. Chara sat down again as the clash of emotions raged on. Every day for the last month she had thought of him, re-calling their walk together and the kiss as they stood on the high pass overlooking the valley. Every night before she slept his face appeared in her mind. She wanted to run down the slope and throw her arms around him. She wanted to run down the slope and slap his face.

I will go down, she thought. And I will be cool and distant. I will not let him know the hurt he did to me.

Having a plan helped settle her mind, and she rose again

and strolled down toward the lake. As she came closer, she saw that the Dweller's small boat *was* moored in the tiny bay on the island. Rayster and Kaelin were standing at the water's edge talking. Kaelin heard her approach and turned. She was pleased to see the joy on his face as he saw her.

Ignoring him, she moved to Rayster, linking her arm through his. "What brings you to the Dweller?" she asked.

He disengaged her arm but held to her hand. "Your father was wounded—not badly," he added swiftly. "He was attacked in the woods when he went to visit . . . a friend."

"I know about Magra," Chara said brightly, enjoying Rayster's embarrassment. "What happened?" She cast a sideways glance at Kaelin and saw that his initial joy had vanished and his face had darkened with anger. Good, she thought.

"Magra is dead. Murdered," said Rayster. It took a moment for the words to sink in.

"They killed a woman?"

"Aye. Your father has a broken arm and a musket ball in his shoulder. He slew several of the killers. He would have been killed himself had Kaelin not rescued him."

The words did not fully sink in. Chara was still horrified over the murder of Magra. "Why would they kill her?" asked Chara. "What harm has she ever caused?"

"Who can understand the hearts of evil men?" answered Rayster. "How is your grandmother faring?"

"She is dying—slowly," Chara told him, aware that Kaelin Ring had walked away. For one dreadful moment Chara thought he would continue walking all the way back to the great house, but he paused close to a cluster of boulders and sat down. Rayster saw the concern in her eyes.

"He has come to apologize to you," he said softly. "If you care for him, you had better consider some conciliatory move. He has great pride, and if he walks away now, I doubt he will come back."

"I have pride, too," she snapped. "I won't crawl to any man."

"Then have the courtesy to thank him for saving your father's life," he responded. Only then did she recall his earlier words. Kaelin Ring had rescued Call Jace.

Glancing to her left, she saw that Kaelin had stood and was once more moving away. "Kaelin," she called out. He stopped and half turned. Chara approached him. "I want to thank you for what you have done."

"And now you have," he said, his voice angry. "So goodbye to you."

"Is it good-bye that you want?" she countered. "For if it is, you can have it."

"What right have you to be angry with me?" he asked her. "I told you how I felt, and you walked away from me. You left me in your father's house without a word."

"My grandmother was taken ill."

"And that prevented you from leaving a message for me? I asked you to marry me. You left the room. That was it. You treated *me* with disrespect, and now *you* are angry?"

"She is coming!" Rayster called out.

Chara and Kaelin glanced toward the water. A white-haired woman in a tattered robe was slowly paddling the boat toward the shoreline.

Kaelin moved past Chara and ran down to the water's edge, wading out to haul the small craft up onto the bank. Reaching out, he lifted the Dweller clear of the boat. "It is good to see you again, Wyrd," he said. "You gladden my heart."

"In this land, I am the Dweller on the Lake," she said, "but it is good to see you, too, my dear. And you, Chara," she added as the red-haired girl approached them.

"What of me?" asked Rayster. "Will no one ever be pleased to see me?"

The Dweller smiled. "Always, clansman. Come, let us sit in Shrine Hollow. It is a peaceful place, and it radiates harmony. I do not need angry thoughts around me."

The white-haired woman led them up the short slope and into the trees. Chara followed her, Rayster and Kaelin bringing up the rear. The Dweller seated herself on a flat rock.

"Call Jace does not need me," she said. "His wounds will heal, though his left arm will ever be weak and his shoulder will pain him when the cold weather comes." She glanced at Chara. "Rayga died this morning as you were walking the mountains. She slipped away peacefully, and she was not in pain. I was with her as she began her journey, and she sent you her love."

Tears spilled to Chara's cheeks. "Her life was good," said the Dweller. "She added to the magic of the land. By all means grieve at her passing but know that only her body is dead. Her spirit has moved on and will find great joy."

The Dweller looked up at Kaelin. "What would you ask of me, clansman?"

"How is Grymauch? Has he declared his love for Aunt Maev?"

"No. He will. I have seen it."

"And will she wed him?"

"He will take her in his arms, and she will love him," said the Wyrd. "Now let us talk of you, Ravenheart, and of you, Flame on the Water. What is it you desire? Is it to rail at each other, scratch and claw?"

"No," said Kaelin. Chara shook her head but said nothing.

"Take each other by the hand," ordered the Dweller. Chara and Kaelin glanced at one another, then Kaelin reached out. Chara put her hand in his. "Life carries many perils and much sadness," said the Dweller. "Against this we have only love to feed us on the journey. Do you love each other?"

For a moment there was silence, then Chara saw Kaelin relax and felt his hand squeeze hers. He was about to speak when the Dweller interupted. "Do not tell me, Ravenheart. Tell her."

Kaelin turned toward Chara. "I love you," he said.

"And I you," she replied.

"Then you should walk the tree," said the Dweller. "But will you accept the advice I am ready to offer you, hard though it be?"

"I will accept," said Chara. "You are the wisest of us all."

"And you, Ravenheart?"

"I will."

"Then walk the tree, but not now. Wait for two years."

"Two years?" said Kaelin. "That is an eternity!"

"Only to the young," answered the Dweller. "I know that you burn for each other. The burning is a fine feeling, full of life and lust. But you will need more to carry you through the decades. You will need to be friends as well as lovers. You will need to trust one another, to understand one another. If after two years you still burn, then that flame will last to the end of your lives. This is my advice. And now I must return to the island. I have much to do."

Kaelin and Rayster eased the boat back into the water, and the three of them watched as the Dweller returned to the tiny bay, mooring her boat and walking into the trees without a backward glance.

Rayster watched Kaelin take Chara's hand and kiss it. The rangy highlander chuckled. "I'll see you both back at the house," he said. "I'm beginning to feel like the third pigeon on the branch."

With that he strolled away. Kaelin looked into Chara's eyes. "Can you wait two whole years?" he asked.

"I don't want to," she said. "I want to throw off my clothes and make love here on the earth."

"As do I," he said, reaching for her.

Chara stepped back swiftly. "The Dweller is never wrong, Kaelin. I want our flame to last all our lives. I want to live with you and grow old with you. I want to love you till the stars die. If waiting two years will bring us this joy, then we should wait."

"It is going to be a long, long two years," he said.

◇ 14 ◇

ALTERITH SHADDLER SAT on the rickety bed in his small room, watching the snow forming ridges on the leaded window. It was cold, and his meager store of fuel was exhausted. A thick blanket was wrapped around his skinny shoulders. There had been low moments in Alterith's life but none as bleak as this. He gazed around the room: four bookshelves groaning under the weight of historical tomes, a chipped and ancient chest containing his spare clothes and the certificates and prizes he had won as a student. On top of the chest lay his white horsehair wig, threadbare now, the canvas lining showing through at the temples. The west wall was bare. The dripping water upon it gleamed in the pale light, as did the black mold staining the wall above the floorboards. His was the highest room in the old boardinghouse and was directly below the cracked roof. His best frock coat had been ruined a year earlier when he had inadvertently left it on a chair against this wall. The summer rain had seeped in, carrying tar and muck from the roof felt, and when autumn came and he needed the coat, he found it stained with a gray fungus that had eaten away at the fibers.

Alterith had always hated this room, yet now that he was about to lose it, he found himself filled with despair.

The last year had been one of his best as a teacher. The conversation with Mulgrave regarding the great king Connavar had caused him to reexamine the histories. He had found many records that contradicted the official view. In the spring he had saved enough daens to subscribe to the *Journal of*

Varlish Studies, published in Varingas, and had sent away for the back issues regarding the wars between Vars and Keltoi. Some of those issues had proved fascinating, especially a section on the battles of King Bane that detailed the nature of Rigante society in the years after the death of Connavar. Alterith had discovered a new respect for the ancient people and their way of life. He had tried to impart this new respect in his teaching of the clan children. It had been most succesful and rewarding, for truancy fell and his classroom was always packed. His students endeavored to complete their homework assignments, and there was little dissension during lessons.

The summer had been golden. At the end of the term his clan pupils had even given him a present: a small box of vanilla-flavored hard candy purchased from the apothecary Ramus. Alterith had been touched by the gesture, though the first of the sweets had made his teeth ache and he had shared the rest with the class.

With his pupils more attentive, he had decided to teach more than history, reading, and writing and had included lessons on arithmetic and mathematics. To his surprise he found that some of his students were quick to grasp the concepts and that one in particular was exceptionally gifted. Arleban Achbain soon learned to work out complicated sums in his head.

It was still hard to believe that such a gift could prove to have such heartbreaking consequences.

Banny had worked hard, often staying behind after class to talk to Alterith about figures and their magic. Alterith's bleak mood lifted as he recalled Banny questioning him about the figure nine. "It is a pure figure and never diluted," said Banny one day.

"In what way, Banny?"

"No matter how many other figures are used to multiply it, the base figure always returns to nine," the boy told him.

"Explain."

"Well, sir, five times nine is forty-five. Four plus five

equals nine. Sixteen nines equals 144. One plus four plus four equals nine. All multiplication of nine returns to nine. Isn't it wonderful?"

Alterith smiled at the memory. So impressed had he been with Banny that he had entered him for the school examination in arithmetic. The application had been denied. Worse than this, Alterith had been ordered to cease teaching beyond his brief. All lessons, apart from reading and writing, were canceled forthwith. The problem did not end there, however. At the end of the winter term the headmaster, the elderly Doctor Meldane, had attended one of Alterith's lessons, sitting quietly at the back.

The lesson had been a triumph, a class full of attentive pupils, with one of them reading an essay aloud to the others at the close. It told the tale of Bendegit Bran, one of Bane's greatest generals. Alterith had been full of pride.

Two days later Doctor Meldane had summoned Alterith to his plush office on the first floor of the school proper. He did not offer Alterith a seat. "I am puzzled," he said, "as to why a competent teacher such as yourself should take it upon himself to alter known history. Perhaps you would explain."

"I have altered nothing, sir," Alterith told him. "All of my teachings are based on known records of ancient events, based on the findings and research of the *Journal of Varlish Studies*."

"Do not bandy words with me, sir," snapped Doctor Meldane. "I listened to a nonsense essay with an underlying premise that the Keltoi were a great people, noble and just. You did not dispute this . . . this fabrication."

"What was there to dispute, sir? Everything the boy said was true. King Bane did lead an army to defeat Stone at the height of its power. He did institute laws which were just. The people were happy under his rule. Where is the error?"

"Bane was the son of Connovar, a Varlish king. Therefore, Bane himself was Varlish, at least in part. The Keltoi of themselves have never achieved anything of note. If they were noble and intelligent, where was their empire? Where are their scientists and philosophers? The Keltoi are an inferior race, Shaddler. *This* is what is known."

"Perhaps, sir," said Alterith, "it was their intelligence and nobility which prevented them from creating an empire. Perhaps they decided that butchering other races and stealing their lands was barbarous and inhuman."

"This conversation is concluded," said Doctor Meldane. "The experiment of teaching highland youngsters has proved a failure. The class will not resume after the winter break, and your services are hereby terminated."

"Terminated? You are dismissing me?"

Meldane reddened. "You were offered this position, Master Shaddler, because you were known to be sound. In short, a man who understood the glory that is the Varlish destiny. I overlooked your humble origins and your lack of social graces. But you, sir, are a traitor to your race. I'll not have your like polluting my school. Be so kind as to remove yourself from my sight."

That had been three weeks ago. Alterith's small store of daens had been used up now, and he had no coin for the rent, which was due the next day. He had tried to find employment as a clerk, but word had gone out that he was "suspect" and a "kilt lover." No Varlish businessman would even give him the benefit of an interview.

The winter was proving a harsh one, and many of the roads south were blocked by snowdrifts. With no income, no savings, and no work Alterith faced a bleak future. If he sold his books, he might have enough money to buy passage to Baracum, but he knew no one there.

Life had been good this year despite the departure in the spring of Gaise Macon to the capital and the loss of income that had entailed. Now he was to pay for his happiness.

Discarding his blanket, he put on his shoes, locked his door, and descended the three flights of stairs to the dining room. The other ten guests were already at the table. They ignored Alterith as he took his place. He ate in silence, listening to the conversation. More talk of civil war in the south. The legendary cavalry general Luden Macks had been arrested for treason but had been acquitted by the people's court. He had been rearrested on the orders of the king and tried by the privy council. He was due to hang within the month. There was also talk of unrest in the north. The Black Rigante had apparently murdered Colonel Linax, and the Moidart was mustering troops to move against them in the spring.

Alterith finished his meal, mopping up the last of the gravy with a piece of bread.

The landlady, a sour-faced widow named Edla Orcombe, approached Alterith as he left the table. She had always been polite, though never friendly. During the last few difficult weeks that politeness had worn thin. "I have had inquiries regarding rooms, Mr. Shaddler," she said. "Will you be keeping your room past this present month?"

"We will speak tomorrow, madam," he said, aware that the other guests were listening.

"Indeed," she told him. "Oh, by the way, a young kilt came by this afternoon to see you. Called at the front door, if you please. He left a note. It is upon the table by the door."

Alterith thanked her and walked out into the corridor. The note was where Edla Orcombe had said. It was wax-sealed, though the seal had been broken, the note obviously having been opened and read. Alterith swallowed his annoyance. Opening it, he saw that it was signed in black ink by someone called Maev Ring. He had heard the name. The clanswoman had a small business making clothes. She was also, he seemed to recall, the mother of the troublesome Kaelin Ring. The note was short and to the point. It invited Alterith Shaddler to call upon Maev Ring the following day two hours before noon. Cursory directions were provided.

Under normal circumstances Alterith would have sent back a note politely refusing the invitation. He was not comfortable in the presence of women. On this occasion, however, it gave him an opportunity to leave his lodgings for a day, avoiding the questioning of Edla Orcombe and the embarrassment of admitting that his funds were gone.

He slept badly, the wind rattling the window and ice forming on the inside of the glass. The morning sky was dull and overcast, the temperature well below freezing. Alterith rose and dressed. He shivered as he did so, his hands blue with cold. He descended the stairs to the dining room. Breakfast was being served, and a fire was blazing in the hearth. Alterith poured himself a cup of hot tisane and sat by the fire.

It would take him almost an hour to walk to Maev Ring's home. His teeth would be chattering by the time he reached it.

Edla Orcombe moved into the dining room, heading past the tables, her small eyes fixed on Alterith. His heart sank. "Good morning to you, Mr. Shaddler."

"And to you, Mrs. Orcombe."

"Will you be requiring dinner this evening?"

"I will, Mrs. Orcombe."

"We need to discuss certain matters, then, for I run no charity here."

Normally Alterith Shaddler found himself nervous in the company of women and experienced great difficulty focusing his thoughts. But something snapped in him now. "Indeed not, madam," he said. "In fact, you are as renowned for your lack of charity as you are for the squalor of your property."

Her jaw dropped. "How dare you?"

Alterith stood. "I would continue this conversation, madam, save for the fact that it is both boring and annoying. Please have my bags packed. I shall be quitting this pestilential place upon my return."

Sweeping past her, he returned to his room, wrapped a heavy scarf around his neck, put on his frayed topcoat, and left the house.

It was bitterly cold outside, and he slipped and slithered on the icy street.

He had been walking for around twenty minutes when a pony and an open-topped trap came into sight. It was being driven by Banny Achbain. He waved at Alterith and drew on the reins. "I have been sent for you, sir," he said. "There are blankets by the seat."

Gratefully Alterith opened the side door and climbed in. He was too cold to make conversation and wrapped one blanket around his shoulders and another over his thin thighs. When he had thawed out a little, he called out to Banny. "Do you know why Mrs. Ring wishes to see me?"

"No, sir."

"What is she like?"

"Frightening," replied the boy.

Time was running out for Maev Ring. Already there were whispers in Eldacre about the highland woman and her burgeoning wealth. She heard them through her workers and from warnings offered by two of her oldest partners, Gillam Pearce and Parsis Feld. It would not be long before the Moidart's cruel eyes turned toward her. Perhaps a month, perhaps a year. It would be so much simpler to be poor, she thought. Yet everything she touched turned to profit, and with no opportunity to spend her wealth on extravagant homes or jewels, she continued to invest in businesses both large and small.

The previous night she had had a dream. She was riding upon the back of a huge and terrifying bear. At any moment it could throw her off and devour her. So she fed it honey cakes to keep it friendly. The honey cakes made it grow. And soon it was big as a house, its claws like sabers. She could not get off, for the fall would kill her, and she was running out of honey cakes.

Shula Achbain was preparing breakfast for Jaim. She could hear them chatting amiably in the kitchen. Shula was normally shy and stuttering in company, but Grymauch had won her over, and she teased him, making him laugh. Maev liked to hear Jaim laugh. It was a sound full of life. He had just returned from a trip to the north, and the news he had brought back was worrying. The colonel of the Beetlebacks had been killed, supposedly during a meeting with the Rigante leader, Call Jace. Jaim had told her that Jace knew nothing about the killing. The new colonel was a former captain named Ranaud. He was known to be a kilt hater.

Kaelin, however, was doing well at Ironlatch. He was in love with a girl named Chara, and if all went well, they planned to marry on Kaelin's seventeenth birthday the next year.

Time is flying by, thought Maev, moving to a mirror on the tall cabinet. There was more gray in her red hair now and a deepening of the tiny lines around her eyes. "You are getting old," she said aloud.

"Aye, but still the most beautiful woman in the highlands," said Jaim Grymauch.

"You shouldn't sneak up on people," she snapped. "A big man like you has no business moving so silently. What do you want?"

He grinned at her. "Nice to see you blush, Maev," he said.

"You are an irritating man, Grymauch, and I don't know why I keep you around."

"Old White Wig is here. He looks like an icicle."

"Then go and make him welcome. Offer him breakfast."

"They say he's broke and ruined," said Grymauch.

"I have heard that. Now, go and greet him."

Jaim chuckled and shook his head, but he obeyed her, as he always did. Maev sat down in a wide chair, gathering her thoughts. Then she listened as the former schoolteacher entered the kitchen.

"This is Shula," he heard Jaim say. "Best cook in the highlands and a beauty to boot. What will you have? Steak and eggs, hot oats, fresh bread and cheese?"

"Just a little water, if you please."

"By the Sacrifice, man, there's not an ounce of flesh on you. You need to eat. It'll drive the cold out faster. Shula, fry a little bacon and eggs for our guest and cut some of that bread."

"I don't want to be a burden," said Alterith. "Perhaps you could let Mrs. Ring know that I am here."

"She knows, sir teacher, and she's told us to feed you. So sit yourself down."

"Do I know you, sir?"

"I am Jaim Grymauch."

"Ah. I do believe I have heard the name."

"Most people have. I am renowned for my many good works. Some tell me that when I die, I shall be named among the saints."

"Yes, indeed," Maev heard Alterith reply. She smiled. She could hear the nervousness in the Varlish teacher's voice.

"How do you like your eggs, sir?" she heard Shula ask.

"With the yolk firm, madam, thank you," replied Alterith.

"My nephew Kaelin asked to be remembered to you," said Jaim.

"Did he? I doubt he recalls me fondly. I had occasion to discipline him many times. The last time, however, still causes me grief."

"Why so, sir teacher?"

"He argued about the nationality of King Connavar, and I caned him for it. I have since discovered he was quite right to argue, for he was correct. Connavar was undoubtedly a full Rigante."

"It takes a man to admit when he is wrong," said Jaim, and Maev heard a grudging respect in his voice. "I shall tell Kaelin what you said when next I see him. Ah, Banny boy, come in and fill your belly."

Maev heard a chair leg scrape on the floor. "So, boy, how many is twenty-five times twenty-seven?"

"Six hundred and seventy-five," Banny said instantly.

"You made that up," Jaim said with a laugh. "That was too quick."

"Because it was too easy, Grymauch," answered Banny.

"No one can do a sum that quickly. Isn't that right, schoolteacher?"

"Banny is correct," said Alterith. "He has a wonderful mind for numbers."

Maev heard plates being laid on the table, and conversation ceased as they ate. She guessed that Jaim was also tucking into a second breakfast. Rising from her chair, she added coals to the fire. The conversation had taught her more about Alterith Shaddler, and she liked what she had heard. The man was more open-minded than she had expected and obviously had affection for Banny. Added to that she sensed that Grymauch also liked him, and despite the big man's many faults he was a good judge of character.

With the breakfast concluded Jaim returned to the room. "Are you ready to see your guest yet?" he asked.

"Yes, show him in."

Alterith Shaddler was ushered in, and Jaim left quietly, pulling shut the door behind him. The teacher wore no wig. His hair was cut short and was thinning at the temples. He was stick-thin, his clothes almost threadbare.

"Thank you for coming at such short notice," said Maev Ring. Alterith bowed and said nothing. "I have a proposition for you. Please take a seat." Alterith settled himself on the edge of a nearby chair. He was monstrously ill at ease. "I want to open a school for clan youngsters," said Maev Ring.

"A school, madam?"

"Aye. I have a building I believe would be suitable, and I have ordered fifty desks and chairs. Now I need a teacher to run it."

"A clan school? I fear that the authorities will not allow it."

"They cannot prevent it. The king issued the proclamation five years ago that highland youngsters were to receive schooling. Doctor Meldane can do nothing to prevent such a school."

"I was not thinking merely of Doctor Meldane. The civil authorities will present objections."

"The Moidart is a loyal follower of the king, and all lessons will begin with the prayer for his health. I understand that was the policy in your classroom."

"Indeed so, madam. Yet I fear there will be many difficulties."

"I will tackle each as it arises."

"What of textbooks and writing implements?" he asked.

"The man who runs the school will have a budget to purchase such items as are necessary."

"What will be taught?"

"Initially? Reading and writing, arithmetic, and history. After that we shall see how the project fares." An uneasy silence developed.

Alterith Shaddler stared at the floor. Maev watched him closely, sensing his disquiet. Alterith Shaddler, she surmised, was conservative by nature. There was nothing rebellious in the man. From everything Kaelin had told her of him, he was proud of his Varlish heritage. The thought of being considered a kilt lover would probably appall him. Maev felt a touch of anger but kept her face expressionless. Perhaps it had been a mistake to invite this skinny Varlish to her home. Then Alterith spoke: "Firstly, madam, I must raise the matter of salary. My funds are . . . my funds are gone. I am living in lodgings and have no money for rent. From today I also have nowhere to live."

"I have furnished two rooms above the classroom, Master Shaddler. There is a bedroom and a study. I shall pay you five chaillings a month, and you will have a budget of three pounds a year to purchase books and any items you deem fit. How much rent do you owe?"

"One chailling, three daens."

"I shall give you the first month's salary in advance. You may take with you today five chaillings to settle your debts."

He took a deep breath, then looked into her eyes. "I appreciate this offer, madam. I have to say, however, that I will brook no interference in the way I teach my classes or the methods I use. I will teach both clan and Varlish history. If that is acceptable, then I will willingly—even gladly—take on this role. If not, then I must decline."

Maev nodded and gave a small smile. "I appreciate a man

who stands by his principles in the face of disaster. You will run the school the way you see fit. I shall not interfere. If it is successful, we will talk of hiring another teacher to help you in your duties. There will also be a housekeeper to clean your rooms and a cook to prepare meals."

"Then I accept, madam, with grateful thanks."

"Good. Banny will take you back to your lodgings. You may collect your belongings, and he will then drive you to your new home. Please prepare a list of items you will need, and we will meet next week to discuss them."

Alterith rose but did not leave.

"Was there something else, Master Shaddler?" Maev asked him.

"Why have you asked me to undertake this role, madam? My dealings with your nephew were hardly conducive to such trust."

"There are many reasons, Master Shaddler, but the only one which counts is that I believe you will excel in the role." Stepping forward, she handed him a small pouch. "Here is your first month's salary. And now you will find Banny waiting to take you to your lodgings."

The apothecary Ramus disliked traveling to the poorer quarters of Eldacre. In the heat of summer the narrow streets stank of refuse piled up against the walls, and there were beggars, hard-eyed men and women who would cut a man's throat for a copper daen. In winter there was less stench, though half-starved dogs roamed the streets, occasionally attacking travelers. The decaying houses were set close, with people living in cramped quarters, huddling together against the cold. The poor of Eldacre were miserable indeed: thieves, cutthroats, beggars, and whores. Received wisdom was that these people were lazy and shiftless and therefore predisposed to crime. Ramus often wondered about the veracity of such claims. Was it surprising that the starving stole bread or that a man weighed down by failure would become bitter at the success of others?

Every week there were hangings in Eldacre as thieves were dragged to the scaffold. Yet there was no shortage of crime thereafter. Would laziness alone cause a man to risk the rope?

Ramus heeled the pony on through the icy streets. Snow was swirling again, and the night was bitter cold. Two soldiers of the night watch, heavily wrapped in black cloaks, appeared from Potter's Street. They stood for a moment watching the old man on the fat pony, then moved on. Ramus rode halfway down Potter's Street and turned left into Shoe Lane. The streets were unlit, but candles and lanterns shone in windows, casting a glow over the snow-covered cobbles.

The pony plodded on. Ramus found the gate leading to Bramble Field. There, on what was once common land, some twenty or so roughly built huts had been erected. Originally they had been for transient workers who arrived in the summer seeking casual employment. Now run-down, they were used to house the sick and the dying who had no homes of their own and no money for rent.

Ramus saw a watchman sitting before a glowing brazier. He rode his pony to the man. "Good evening to you," said the apothecary.

"Are you lost, man?" asked the watchman.

"No. I am seeking the house of Maldrak."

"Don't know the name."

"A retainer of the Moidart's. I am told he was moved here some days ago."

"Oh, aye. Stinks of piss and blood. I know him. Fourth hut on the right."

Ramus thanked the man and rode on. Tethering the pony behind the hut and out of the wind, Ramus entered the ramshackle building. There was but a single room with a narrow bed and two rickety chairs. There was an old brazier, but it held no coals, and there were no candles. In the faint light of the moon shining through the doorway Ramus could see old Maldrak lying on the bed. He appeared to be asleep.

Ramus trudged back to the watchman. "I need a lantern and some coal and kindling," he said.

"It'll be wasted on him, man. He's dying. He's been pissing blood ever since he came here." The watchman made no move to rise from his stool.

"Tell me where I might find what I need," said Ramus.

"It'll cost you. Coal don't come cheap."

"My understanding is that the poor souls here are guaranteed food, coal, and candles until they die," said Ramus, his voice calm. "But I shall pay you two daens for fetching what I need."

"Three daens might persuade me to leave my fire," said the watchman.

"Then three daens it shall be," said Ramus. "But I'll require a full lantern, if you please."

Within the hour Ramus had the brazier glowing in Maldrak's hut and, by the light of a lantern, examined the old man. His skin was hot and dry to the touch, and there was a large lump just above his groin. The thin sheet below him was stained with blood and urine. Maldrak drifted in and out of consciousness.

"I'll be right as rain in a few days," he said, opening his eyes and seeing Ramus. "Just need a bit of rest is all."

"You are losing blood, my friend."

"No, not blood," insisted Maldrak. "I been eating beetroot. Just beetroot, see?"

Ramus sat quietly. The fear in the man's voice made him pause. The apothecary had brought with him several bottles of fever-reducing potions and one that would help dull the pain. Only the last one would be of any use to the old man. Ramus looked around the squalid room. Maldrak had served the Moidart's family for more than fifty years, and this was his reward: left to die in a cold and barren hut. "Can I get you something to eat or drink, Apothecary?" asked Maldrak.

"No, thank you," answered Ramus, aware that there was nothing there, not a water jug, not even a stale loaf.

"Good of you to visit. My wife is out tonight. Otherwise she'd cook you a meal."

His wife had been dead for twenty years.

"How's the little pony?"

"She is well."

"Nice little creature. I'll give you some apples to take away with you."

"How are you feeling, Maldrak. Is there much pain?"

"Just a bit. Pulled muscle, I think. It'll heal, right enough." The old man dozed for a while. When he awoke, he talked again for a while, then paused. "Are you the priest?" he asked.

"No, I am Ramus."

" 'Course you are. Stupid of me. Don't ever get old, Ramus." He looked around. "Why am I here? Don't see none of my stuff. I wish the priest was here. Need to talk to him. Put things right. Because it wasn't my fault, and I could do nothing. It was all over by the time I got there, you see. Bothersome, though."

"What is bothersome to you, my friend?"

"Best not to say. Best not. How is the old pony?"

"She is well. Rest a little. Gather your strength."

"There's apples in the orchard. I'll fill you a sack. They'll only go bad otherwise."

Ramus felt a weight of sorrow on his soul. He had heard only the day before that Maldrak had been moved to Bramble Field. A young retainer had called at the apothecary to collect the balms needed by the Moidart. Ramus had asked about Maldrak. "He's gone, sir. He'd started acting odd, you know. And he stank something terrible. Bramble Field is the best place for him. He'll get food and medicine and stuff."

There was no food there. This was a place for the discarded, somewhere to die out of sight and out of mind. It was rare for Ramus to feel anger, and even now it was tinged with sadness and disappointment. "Are you the priest?" asked Maldrak. "I need a priest."

"Yes, I am the priest," Ramus said sadly.

"I have sins, you know. I haven't been a good man. But I

want to see my wife again, you know. I don't want the gates shut on me."

"They won't be shut," promised Ramus.

"I couldn't have done nothing. When he killed her, I was downstairs. I wasn't supposed to be, you see. He'd told us all to take the night off and go into town. But I didn't. It was raining, and I had on my old boots, and they leaked. I came back to change them. That's when I heard her scream."

"Who screamed?"

"His wife, Rayena. Lovely girl. It was only a few days after the birth. She was still recovering. I thought she was just— you know—in pain. I was by the stairs, and I saw him on the upper landing. He come out of the bedroom, and there was blood on him. He didn't see me. Then I saw he had something stuck into his belly, low down. He dragged it out and flung it away. It was a pair of scissors. She'd obviously stabbed him as he strangled her. I ducked down. Didn't want him to see me. For years I've been wondering whether I could have saved her if I'd run upstairs when I first heard the scream. And then later I thought I should have gone to the captain and told him what I'd seen. But I didn't. Is that a sin?"

"Why did you not report the crime?"

"I was frightened. Would you like something to drink, sir? A little wine or something?"

"No, I am fine. Who was the killer?"

"The Moidart. Most of the servants knew Rayena had been seeing the highland boy, Lanovar Ring. The Moidart found out. Don't know who told him. He hunted Lanovar down and killed him. Then he waited until his wife had the child, and he killed her, too. When I got out of the house, I just ran down to town. Didn't care that my feet were wet. I sat in the tavern and said nothing to nobody. He was bleeding bad when I left, so I thought he'd probably be dead when I got back. But he wasn't. Then word went around that assassins had come and killed the wife and stabbed the lord. I didn't say nothing then, either. Then, when little Gaise was a few weeks old and his eyes changed color, I thought the lord would kill him, too."

Ramus was puzzled. All babies were born with blue eyes, the natural color appearing later. But why should Gaise Macon's peculiar green and gold eyes have put him in danger? The portrait of the Moidart's grandmother showed that she had such eyes.

"Did you know Lanovar Ring?" he asked Maldrak.

"Met him once or twice. Fine-looking man."

"And his eyes were also green and gold?"

"Oh, yes, sir. Just like Gaise. But the Moidart didn't kill the boy. Gave him no love, though."

What a quandary, thought Ramus. To be so full of hatred that he would kill his wife and then not to know whether he was raising the son of his enemy. Did Gaise inherit his looks from his great-grandmother or from the highlander who had cuckolded the Moidart? The Moidart could never know.

"Then came the night of the fire," said Maldrak. "It was only a few months later. It was awful. The Moidart came out, but we could hear the screams of people trapped inside."

"The Moidart was burned badly," said Ramus. "He still suffers."

"No, he came out unscathed," said Maldrak. "He shouted to someone: 'Where is my son?' Nobody answered. The Moidart gave a terrible cry then and ran back into the inferno. I've never seen the like. We all thought he was dead. Then he appeared at an upper window. His cloak and shirt were on fire, and he was carrying little Gaise wrapped in a blanket. And that had started to smolder. The Moidart kicked out the window and jumped. When he hit the ground, he rolled to protect the babe. We all ran to him and beat out the flames. The baby had a little burn on his face, but he was all right. The Moidart was burned bad and had a broken ankle. After that I knew he would never kill Gaise. Not after risking everything to save him."

The old man drifted off to sleep. When he awoke some minutes later, he blinked and seemed confused. "What happened to the priest, Apothecary? Did he go?"

"Yes."

"Did he damn me?"

"No, my friend. He blessed you." Maldrak winced and groaned. "Hurting a lot now," he said. Ramus opened a bottle of potion and helped the old man drink. "Man, that's bitter," said Maldrak.

"It will ease the pain."

"Am I dying, Ramus?"

"Yes."

"Oh, dear. I don't want to."

"Drink some more. Finish the bottle."

Maldrak did as he was bidden. Then he sank back. After a while he said: "That's a little better. I think I'll sleep now. I'll be right as rain when I've rested. Thanks for all you've done for me. He blessed me, you say?"

"Aye, he did."

"Don't want the gates shut when I get there."

"Rest, Maldrak. Sleep."

The old man closed his eyes. Ramus waited quietly by the bedside. The potion was a powerful one, and soon Maldrak was sleeping deeply. Ramus had seen such cancers before. Death from them was always agonizing. Maldrak would suffer no such agony. A few drops of the potion would take away the pain. A little more and sleep could be induced. But to drink the whole bottle would slow and then stop the heart.

Ramus took hold of Maldrak's wrist, feeling for the pulse. It fluttered weakly for a while, then faded away.

"I hope your wife is waiting for you," he said.

Then he blew out the lantern and left the hut.

Since the attack on him eight months earlier Call Jace had been a changed man. His left arm ached continuously, and his shoulder pained him when the weather was cold or wet. His men noticed the change in his mood. Rarely did Call Jace take part in the joking and camaraderie of the Rigante, keeping to the great house or wandering by himself at Sorrow

Bird Lake. His son Bael carried out most of his duties, though Call himself always led the twice-monthly clan meetings with his captains.

The winter had been especially harsh, and that meant there was little trouble with Ranaud and his Beetlebacks, but no one doubted that the spring would see trouble. Throughout Black Mountain the word had gone out that Call Jace had been responsible, either personally or by order, for the murder of Colonel Linax. The ailing officer was said to have traveled to a meeting with Jace to discuss various aspects of the unwritten treaty between Rigante and Varlish. He had ridden out one early autumn morning in the company of Captain Ranaud. That night Ranaud had returned, telling a tale of treachery. They had arrived at the meeting place only to find a group of highlanders waiting in ambush. Colonel Linax had, according to Ranaud, been shot in the head. Ranaud himself had escaped by drawing his saber and charging the ambushers. Only the intervention of the Source had saved him.

The news split the community. Highlanders did not believe Jace would kill a man he had invited to a meeting. The Varlish felt vindicated in their mistrust and hatred of all clansmen.

Jace himself was furious. At first he had believed a renegade group of highlanders might have been responsible and had sent out scouts to track them. Except there were no tracks. The ground where Linax had been murdered was badly churned by the soldiers who had ridden out to recover the body. But higher in the hills, where the killers probably would have fled, there was no sign of a large party of travelers.

"They'd have to have been ghosts," Rayster told him upon his return. "The whole area is unmarked. Not a single boot print. No evidence of a recent campfire, no discarded bones from a meal."

"They must be somewhere!" snapped Jace. "An armed group cannot simply kill a Beetleback and then vanish."

"No, indeed," agreed Rayster.

"Then how do you explain the killing?"

Rayster shrugged. "We can eliminate the claim that a group of raiders killed the colonel. There were no raiders. Unlikely as it sounds, the only person who could have killed him is Ranaud himself."

"That is ridiculous."

"We know there was no meeting planned with you. Our people in Black Mountain say that Ranaud himself arranged it. He is known as a clan hater. Linax was not. The colonel's death has left Ranaud in command and given him freedom to act against you."

Call cursed. "Damn, but it galls me to think people believe me to be so stupid as to arrange a meeting and then kill a Beetleback. It is insane. If I wanted Linax dead, I'd have planned it with at least a little subtlety."

As the vicious winter finally gave way to the brighter, warmer days of spring, fresh news reached Call. A regiment of the king's army and an artillery battalion were said to be preparing for a march to the Black Mountains. Five thousand men and fifty cannon would be heading north in less than a month.

Ranaud had also reinstated the law concerning highlanders carrying weapons. Any clansman found with sword, pistol, or musket would be summarily hanged.

Worse was to follow. A young clansman was arrested for wearing a Black Rigante cloak. Put on trial for treason, he had been beheaded in the town square. Call Jace sent out two hunting parties in the hope of assassinating Colonel Ranaud. Unfortunately, the man was wily and rarely rode without fifty men at his back. One of the parties was ambushed. They managed to escape, but not without losing three men and killing five Beetlebacks.

For several months Call Jace had journeyed at least once a week to Sorrow Bird Lake, seeking the wisdom of the Dweller. Throughout the winter she was missing, but then, in the first week of spring, he saw her small boat moored in the bay. He sat in Shrine Hollow until she came to him. His arm was aching badly, and his mood was sour. "Where do you go, woman?" he asked her. "Why do you spend so little time with your people?"

"I spend almost all my time with my people, Call Jace. What do you require of me?"

Her voice, as ever, was cool, her manner distant. "You do not like me, Dweller. I know this, but I have never asked why. Now I am asking."

The white-haired woman remained silent at first, staring at him intently. When she finally spoke, there was sadness in her voice. "It is not about dislike, Call Jace. The Varlish are a cold race, and they—and others like them—are draining the magic from the land. What they do not realize is that in the end the magic is all we have. Without it the world will die. Why do I seem cold to you? You may have the blood of a Rigante, but you have the soul of a Varlish. Nothing you do adds magic to the earth. You scheme, you plot, you murder. Every day a little more of the magic dies."

"I always appreciate straight talking," he said sourly. "I live with regrets for some of my deeds. I will answer for them to the Source one day. I don't doubt that. I will, though, leave the Rigante stronger than I found them. Or do you wish to deny me that also?"

"I do not deny you your achievements, Call Jace. I admire you for some of them. You did not ask me about my admiration."

"Ah, well, your likes and dislikes are not important now. Tell me why this Ranaud would kill his own colonel."

"He lusts after glory, highlander. He wants to be famous. He thinks there are no battles left to fight—save one. If he defeats the Rigante, he will be honored. His name will be enshrined in the history of the Varlish. He is, like all vain men, a fool. If he were to wait but a little while, he could have all the battles he dreams of. A civil war is coming among the Varlish. It will drench the land in blood."

"I care nothing for wars among the Varlish," said Call. "My only desire is to save my own people."

"That does you credit, Call Jace."

"How do I fight him?"

"You do not need me to guide you in the planning of a war," she told him. "What is to come is hateful to me. You must hold out until the winter. After that the Moidart will need all his troops, for the clans in the south will rediscover their pride and their manhood."

Call gave a derisive laugh. "Nothing could make those puppies wolves again. You think I am like the Varlish? All in the south are tainted with Varlish thinking."

"Yes, they are. The flame in their hearts has gone out. But they are like dried grass, Call Jace. One spark will ignite them, one glorious spark, one moment of true Rigante greatness. It will break my heart to see it and at the same time gladden my soul, for the magic will flow out and be carried upon the winds. It will flow over the land and feed the parched souls of every highlander. Even you."

"What are you speaking of?"

"You will know when the moment comes. You will hear of it. You will even weep, Call Jace."

"I have not shed tears since I was a wee lad and my father died."

"I know. Too much of your Rigante heritage is locked away, buried deep. But remember my words when the day comes. Now go and prepare for your war, Call Jace. Choose your captains wisely."

As the snows melted, Call instructed Bael and Rayster to double the training of clan warriors.

"Can we win this war?" Bael asked him.

"One day at a time, boy. We will need to hide supplies farther back in the mountains in case they breach the gates and take the valley. Food, salt, powder, and shot. We must also build secondary lines of defense. The West Hills is where to start. Build gates across the pass and move two cannon back there."

"If they push us back into the West Hills, there'll be nowhere else to run, Father," said Bael. "We'll have our backs to the sea."

"I know. Call a meeting for tomorrow. It is time to appoint group leaders and plan our campaign."

◇ 15 ◇

THE EXECUTION OF Killon Ustal stunned the highland
community of Black Mountain. The youngster had been
wooing a town girl and had gone to see her one morning. The
law regarding the wearing of Rigante colors had not been en-
forced for more than a decade, and Killon had been wearing
an old cloak to ward off the winter cold. News of his arrest
reached Ironlatch only two days later. His brothers, Finbarr
and Jabe, had gone into town prepared to pay whatever fine
the magistrates demanded. They came back with his decapi-
tated body.

Finbarr and Jabe had quit the farm the following morning
and had headed west to join Call Jace.

Shorthanded now, Kaelin, Senlic Carpenter, and Bally
Koin worked the high pastures, driving cattle back down into
the valley. Of the six hundred head at the beginning of winter
more than sixty had died in fierce blizzards and snowdrifts
or been torn apart by starving wolves. It was hard, grueling
work, and Kaelin wished he had time to travel to Black
Mountain to hire other herders.

He had changed in the last year. Laboring on the farm had
widened his shoulders and strengthened his arms, and he had
grown taller by almost two inches.

Kaelin had seen Colonel Ranaud only once since that first
meeting. The soldier had ridden to the farm five months earlier at the onset of winter. He had arrived in the company of
thirty soldiers. Kaelin had welcomed him with false warmth,

inviting him into the house. Ranaud had seemed tense and on edge. "Have you been back to Rigante lands?" he asked.

Kaelin had discussed with Call Jace what to say to the officer. "I have, sir."

"Did you note their armaments?"

"They have seven cannon, and every clansman has access to a musket." Ranaud relaxed and sat down by the fire, extending his hands toward the flames.

"Seven, you say. Good. Where are they placed?"

"They are set in the two passes leading into the valley: three in the first, four in the second."

"Excellent, Master Ring."

"Let me fetch you some wine, Colonel," said Kaelin, walking through to the kitchen. Call Jace had been right. Ranaud had shown no surprise at the news. He already knew the number of cannon and their positions.

Kaelin handed the colonel a goblet of mulled wine. Ranaud sipped it. "I understand congratulations are in order. You are to be wed."

"Yes, sir. Sadly, though, I must wait another year."

"Really? Why is that?"

"The advice of a Rigante wise woman," Kaelin told him. "Each day now passes like a month. I feel I will have a white beard before I walk the tree."

Ranaud laughed. "Abstinence makes the heart grow fonder, as my mother used to say. Who is the lucky girl?"

"Chara Jace."

"The chieftain's daughter. My, my, but you have set your sights high, Master Ring. I understand she is quite pretty."

"Indeed she is. May I also offer my congratulations to you, Colonel. The promotion is richly deserved."

"Linax was a good man in his way, but he did not know how to deal with rebels. Do you still hate Call Jace?"

"My feelings for him have not changed at all," said Kaelin.

"Good. Then let us talk about their defenses."

The colonel stayed for just under an hour. Kaelin answered

all his questions with honesty, and Ranaud was in a better mood when he left. For some while after his departure Kaelin sat alone. Ranaud obviously had other sources of information. Call Jace had lost several scouts and believed them to have been taken to the keep and put under torture, their bodies disposed of in secret. It was a good theory. Yet there was another. What if there was a traitor among the Rigante? Call had scoffed at this. "There's not a man—or woman— here who would betray me," he said.

After the murder of Killon Ustal the Rigante withdrew to their heartlands. That meant that Kaelin had not seen Chara for weeks. Working fifteen-hour days, he had no time to journey west, and Call Jace allowed no highlanders to venture out into the valleys. Beetleback patrols had tripled, and Kaelin constantly saw soldiers riding the hills in groups of fifty or more.

The town of Black Mountain seethed with Beetlebacks, and many of the surrounding fields were covered by tents and picket lines.

One morning in late spring Colonel Ranaud rode up to Ironlatch farm, leading a hundred soldiers and a score of wagons. Kaelin walked out to meet him. The colonel stepped down, then waved the wagons forward.

"What is happening, sir?" asked Kaelin.

"This is the most westerly farm, Master Ring. It commands fine views of the valley. If Call Jace leads out his Rigante, they will first be seen from here. I am commandeering the farm buildings. My men will build perimeter defenses and a watchtower. We will disrupt the work of the farm as little as possible, and any beef that needs to be slaughtered to feed the soldiers will be paid for."

"You think Call Jace will lead his men against you?"

"Indeed I do, Master Ring."

"Why would he do something so foolish?"

Ranaud smiled and shrugged. "Why indeed?" he said.

The soldiers worked for several days, digging a long trench

across the new western wall and dragging up five cannon to face the western approaches. Two watchtowers were erected, one towering above the milking sheds and the other on a small hill to the north of the house. Kaelin watched the enterprise with growing concern. Ranaud was right. Ironlatch was a strategic location. Any attacking force would have to cross some three hundred yards of open ground with no cover.

The hundred soldiers pitched their tents fifty paces to the east of the farm. Kaelin offered the four officers rooms in the house, which they gratefully accepted, for the nights were still cold and sleet showers were still common.

Senlic Carpenter avoided the soldiers as much as possible, and Bally Koin took to sleeping in one of the hill huts above the pasture. It was from that hut early one morning that he saw a column of soldiers coming from the west and taking the road into Black Mountain. He told Senlic what he had seen, and the old man approached Kaelin.

"They had two prisoners," he said. "Bally's eyes are not what they were, and he didn't recognize the men. He did, however, recognize the clan colors they wore."

"Must be two of Call's scouts," said Kaelin. "I pity them."

The following day Kaelin saw a tall man with a staff herding a small group of cattle toward the farm. He was dressed in leather leggings and a weathered brown leather jerkin. Several soldiers stood watching, and one of the officers, Lieutenant Langhorne, came out of the house and stood alongside Kaelin. "One of your men?" he asked.

"No," said Kaelin. He strolled out to meet the man. "Good morning to you."

"And to you, sir," said Rayster. "I found these cattle in the thickets to the north. They were carrying your mark, and I thought it might be worth a meal if I brought them back to you."

"Aye, it is worth a meal at least. Are you looking for work?"

"They said in Black Mountain that you were shorthanded. I'd be obliged for a month's labor."

Lieutenant Langhorne came alongside. He was a tall man with a finely trimmed beard and a heavy southern accent. "Where have you come from, fellow?" he asked.

"North, sir. I am a Pannone from Styrline. Great shortage of both food and work there, sir. Thought I'd try my luck in the warmer south."

The officer stepped in. "You think this is warmer?"

"Aye, it is, sir. Up north you have to piss fast. It freezes the moment you release it, and if a man is not careful, he'll have a three-foot icicle hanging from his rod."

Langhorne laughed aloud and wandered away.

Rayster moved in close to Kaelin. "Soldiers captured Chara late yesterday."

Kaelin stood rooted to the spot. "Chara? How?"

"For some reason she left the valley. I don't know why. She was with Wullis Swainham. One of our scouts saw them entering the woods. He followed. Soldiers were hidden nearby, and both Wullis and Chara were taken. Call is beside himself. He is talking of gathering the clan and sacking Black Mountain." Rayster paused. "Are you all right, man? You are pale as a ghost."

Kaelin fought for control as a cold panic swept through him.

He could not stop himself from seeing Chara in a dungeon in the keep, facing the hot irons, the thumbscrews, and the other instruments of torture he had heard about as a boy. He took a deep breath and tried to think. "Call must not come out," he said at last. "It is what they want. It is what they have planned for."

"He'll not let them harm Chara, Kaelin. I know the man."

"I need time to think," said Kaelin. "Go and see Senlic and have the meal you asked for. We will speak later."

Rayster nodded and moved away.

Kaelin gazed out over the distant mountains.

If Call Jace was to lead out the Rigante, they would be massacred. And even if by some miracle they reached Black

Mountain, they could never take the keep. Musketeers manning the murder holes would cut them down.

The panic in his soul threatened to swamp him.

The day he had killed Bindoe and Luss Campion had been a watershed in the life of the young Rigante. It had changed him forever. The Varlish had murdered Chara Ward, and he had been unable to save her. Now another Chara was threatened by the same vileness that characterized, for Kaelin, the Varlish race.

He had *liked* Chara Ward, but he *loved* Chara Jace. She was, he knew, the partner of his soul, the one woman he would love for all of his life.

Conflicting emotions raged within him. He wanted to take his pistols and ride into Black Mountain, blasting the life from Ranaud. He wanted to join Call Jace and be part of a Rigante army that would tear down the keep stone by stone, killing every Beetleback in the territory. Neither action would save Chara.

Five thousand Beetlebacks were now camped around Black Mountain, waiting for the opportunity to wipe out the Rigante.

Kaelin walked out into the pasture, past the cattle Rayster had driven in. Anger and the need for revenge had driven him to kill Bindoe and Campion. Anger and loss of control had caused him to punch Call Jace and shoot Bael. Now was not the time for uncontrolled fury.

Chara Jace would have been taken, with Wullis Swainham, to the keep and there imprisoned. Kaelin pictured the building and its approaches. Sentries patrolled the walls, and other soldiers manned the small guardhouse set within the gate arch. Then there was the open parade ground and the keep itself. Kaelin recalled the large mess hall on the first floor. There was also a set of steps behind the clerk's desk, leading downward. He guessed they led to the dungeons below the building. How many guards would be stationed there? Two? Ten? How could he know?

Anger flared again, but he quelled it savagely.

Despair touched him. An army would be hard pressed to take the keep. What could one Rigante clansman in his seventeenth year hope to achieve?

Kaelin thought of Grymauch, but there was little satisfaction to be gained. Grymauch would probably just take his giant broadsword and walk boldly into the compound in an attempt to fight his way to the dungeons. No, Grymauch would be no help. Aunt Maev would offer better advice. She had an almost uncanny ability to strip away nonessentials, paring down a problem until the answer shone like a jewel. What would she say now?

Kaelin considered the problem. She would say that taking the keep was not the issue here. The objective was to release Chara Jace. How, then, could one man defeat five thousand Beetlebacks? Kaelin could almost hear her answer: "There will not be five thousand Beetlebacks guarding Chara Jace. There will be sentries on the wall and sentries in the guardhouse. Once inside, there will be a guard or guards outside the dungeons."

If the gatehouse sentries could be neutralized swiftly and silently, the guards on the walls would prove no part of the equation. They would carry on their patrolling oblivious to what went on below. Yet they would see intruders moving toward the keep.

That could be overcome.

Kaelin continued to plan, thinking through each potential problem.

Then he sought out Rayster and walked with him out onto the open land behind the milking sheds.

"Man, that's insane," said Rayster as Kaelin outlined his plan. "I can think of a score of things that could go wrong."

"Then I'll try it alone."

"I didn't say I wouldn't go with you," snapped Rayster. "But we'll need a mountain of luck."

"We'll make our own. Get Senlic to harness the wagon. We'll leave within the hour."

Kaelin walked back to the house. Two of the officers were

seated at the dining table, having consumed most of a jug of fine wine from a barrel Kaelin had supplied. "You are a fine host, Master Ring," said Lieutenant Langhorne. The other man raised his goblet to Kaelin and smiled drunkenly.

"I am pleased to be able to honor those who serve us so bravely," said Kaelin. "I am going into Black Mountain this afternoon. Is there anything I can bring back for you?"

"A woman with big breasts," said the drunken officer.

Lieutenant Langhorne shook his head. "We have all we need, Master Ring."

Kaelin moved past them and up the stairs. Once in his room, he loaded the Emburleys and tucked them into his belt. Putting a small powder horn, a dozen balls, and a pack of wadding into the deep pocket of a black overcoat, he donned the garment. From a drawer in the chest beneath the window he took a pouch of coins, adding to it a small store of ten golden coins hidden in the paneling of the wall behind his bed. Lastly he gathered up two wooden-handled knives with four-inch blades, which he slipped into the inside pocket of his greatcoat.

Kaelin glanced around the room. It was unlikely he would return here.

He smiled grimly.

It was unlikely he would return *anywhere*.

Buttoning his coat, he moved downstairs. The second officer was asleep, his head resting on the table. Lieutenant Langhorne was stoking the fire. He looked up as Kaelin reappeared.

"This week's password is Valhael, Master Ring," he said. "Should you be stopped, mention my name and the password. It should ease your passage."

"Thank you, Lieutenant. I was thinking of paying my respects to Colonel Ranaud. Are you sure there is nothing I can fetch for you from the barracks?"

"No, though it is kind of you to offer. I thought you already had your supplies."

"The roof has leaked and ruined our salt," Kaelin said swiftly.

Once outside, he saw Senlic standing with Rayster beside the wagon. Kaelin offered the old man his hand.

"Take care, boy," said Senlic.

"You, too," he replied, climbing to the driving seat. "Look after the farm." Rayster stepped aboard and sat beside him. Just as Kaelin took the reins, Senlic dipped his hand in his pocket and produced a small charm, which he passed up to Kaelin. It was the head of a bear in a circle of silver. Kaelin looked into Senlic's eyes. "What is this for?"

" 'Tis a good-luck piece. My father told me it was once blessed by the Veiled Lady. Don't know if it's true. Wanted you to have it."

Kaelin closed his hand around the charm. "Thank you, my friend. A man never knows when he'll need good luck."

Senlic nodded, then turned away and walked back to the barn.

"Did you tell him?" asked Kaelin.

Rayster shook his head. "No, but he's canny, is Senlic. His mother had the second sight. Maybe he inherited it."

Kaelin flicked the reins, and the wagon lurched forward on the long road to Black Mountain.

The Dancing Bear tavern was one of the oldest buildings in Black Mountain. It had begun life as a barracks and supply depot for Varlish soldiers building the new keep some four hundred years earlier. Then it had been a warehouse and finally a tavern.

It was a large building, originally two-storied, but a fire had gutted it a century before, leaving the outer walls standing but burning away the upper floor. Now it had a high vaulted roof above a collection of bench tables and leather-topped stools and chairs. The tavern keeper, a wily ex-soldier named Grabthorne, had constructed a partition wall of wicker, separating the drinking area from the dining tables. His cooks supplied no fancy fare and spices were in short supply, but the Dancing

Bear was renowned for its beefsteak pies, venison, and mutton. Grabthorne's wife would also produce fine pastries, apple bakes, and custard delicacies.

Kaelin Ring and Rayster were seated at a table by the window overlooking the gatehouse arch of the keep. Occasionally both sentries would come into sight, usually to greet soldiers crossing the drawbridge after a night of revelry. On the battlements above another four sentries patrolled.

"What are we waiting for?" asked Rayster.

"The last changing of the guard," said Kaelin.

Rayster glanced out of the window. The keep reared up against the night sky, majestic and powerful.

"You are not eating your pie," said Kaelin.

"My appetite is not what it was," admitted Rayster.

The tavern keeper, Grabthorne, sidled over to them, wiping his hands on a gravy-stained apron. "Is everything to your liking?" he asked. He was a small man in his fifties with sharp blue eyes.

"The pie is superb," said Kaelin. "My compliments to Mrs. Grabthorne."

"I have seen you, young man," said Grabthorne. "You are from Ironlatch farm?"

"I am, sir."

"Colonel Ranaud speaks highly of you. Good man, Ranaud."

"The best," agreed Kaelin.

"He'll put these rebels in their place, and we can get back to living in peace and making money, eh?"

"It is certainly to be hoped, Mr. Grabthorne."

"We'll be closing down the kitchens soon," said the tavern keeper. "If you'll be wanting apple pie, you'd best place your order now."

"Thank you. Two portions, if you please."

Grabthorne wandered away. Many of the diners were now leaving. In the tavern itself a group of soldiers was singing raucously. "Are you sure you want to go ahead with this plan?" asked Rayster, leaning across the table.

"I can think of no other."

Rayster sighed. "I had always hoped to die in my bed, my grandchildren weeping around me."

"Maybe you will."

Rayster glanced back at the forbidding keep. "Doesn't seem likely at present."

Grabthorne returned with two plates bearing thickly cut portions of apple pie dusted with sugar. Rayster had finished only half of his meal and pushed away his plate.

"Not to your liking?" asked Grabthorne.

"It was good," said Rayster, "but I needed to leave room for the apple pie. My friend tells me it is magnificent."

"Aye, the wife is a fine pastry cook and no mistake."

Kaelin paid for the meal, adding two daens "for the cook."

"Good of you," said Grabthorne.

Kaelin tucked into the apple pie.

"I don't know how you can eat at a time like this," said Rayster. "My stomach is shrunk so tight, I doubt I could swallow an apple pip. Are you not at least a little frightened?"

"I'm not usually frightened when I eat," Kaelin said with a smile. "There is not much danger at the moment. Ask me again when we reach the gatehouse."

"I will probably have other matters on my mind around then," said Rayster.

The two clansmen were the last to leave the tavern, and Kaelin led Rayster into the shadows of an alleyway overlooking the gates. The guards had still not been changed. The two men waited silently. Just after midnight two more guards appeared, had a brief conversation with the men they were replacing, then entered the gatehouse.

"Now?" whispered Rayster.

"Wait awhile. Let them settle down and become bored."

"By heaven, you are a cool one, Kaelin Ring."

Kaelin did not reply. He did not feel cool. His heart was beginning to beat faster now, and tension was tightening his belly. Taking his money pouch from his pocket, he tipped out the coins into his hand. Pocketing most of them, he put several chaillings and daens back into the pouch.

Another hour slowly passed. Small groups of soldiers continued to return to the keep. Kaelin noted that the guards did not bother with passwords. It was easy to be complacent when five thousand fighting men were stationed in and around Black Mountain.

"Now," said Kaelin, and strolled across the open ground. Rayster followed him.

Kaelin crossed the drawbridge and reached the wrought-iron gates, which were now closed. "Hello the gatehouse," he called softly.

A soldier appeared. "What do you want?"

"Mr. Grabthorne sent us. One of the soldiers left his money pouch at the Dancing Bear. I am to return it."

"Hand it through, then."

"Mr. Grabthorne asked me to fetch a signed receipt and see the money counted."

"You don't trust me?"

"Of course I trust you," said Kaelin. "You are a soldier of the king. 'Tis Mr. Grabthorne who doesn't trust *me*. He counted it out before I left."

Kaelin reached into the pocket of his dark coat, producing a bottle of Uisge, which he uncorked and sipped. "Ah," he said, wiping his mouth on his sleeve. "Twenty-year-old single malt. Nothing like it."

"Damn, but that's too expensive for the likes of common soldiers," said the man.

"I'll share it with you while you count the money," offered Kaelin.

The soldier slid back the gate bar and ushered them inside. Kaelin walked into the small gatehouse. A second soldier was sitting at a table there, a deck of playing cards spread out before him. The first guard explained to the man about the money pouch. Kaelin passed the Uisge bottle to him, then tipped out the contents of the pouch to the table. Both guards sat down, their eyes on the silver and copper coins glinting in the candlelight.

"Must be near five chaillings here," said the second guard. "I'd like to know how a soldier came by five chaillings."

The first guard pulled the money toward him and began separating the coins. Kaelin glanced at Rayster and nodded. Then he dipped his hand into his pocket, curling his fist around the hilt of a knife. Rayster moved closer to the table, looking as if he were reaching for the Uisge bottle.

Kaelin's blade came clear of the pocket. With one swift movement he rammed it into the throat of the first guard. Rayster plunged his knife into the neck of the second. Kaelin's opponent struggled to rise, blood pumping from his severed jugular. He fell across the table. Kaelin caught him, lowering the body to the floor. The second soldier was grappling with Rayster. They kicked over a chair. Kaelin moved in, stabbing the man twice more in the back. The soldier made a gurgling noise, then fell into Rayster's arms.

"Strip them of their armor," said Kaelin, kneeling beside the first corpse and swiftly unbuckling the straps of the black breastplate.

Within moments the two clansmen had donned the breastplates and black leggings and shirts of the dead Beetlebacks. Rayster struggled into the larger of the boots. They were still too tight. He stomped his feet. "This is uncomfortable," he said.

Kaelin heard a rapping at the gates. Rayster jerked. "Stay here and pull those bodies behind the table," said Kaelin. Lifting a round black helm from a hook by the door, Kaelin donned it, then stepped outside. Three soldiers and an officer were standing there.

"Password?" asked Kaelin.

"Just open the bastard gate," said a drunken soldier, his voice slurring. "Do I look like a sheep-shagging clansman?"

"My orders are to ask for a password," said Kaelin.

"And quite right, too," said the officer. "The password is Valhael."

Kaelin pulled back the bar, allowing the men inside. "I don't know you," said the officer, peering at Kaelin in the moonlight.

"I'm with Lieutenant Langhorne and the Fifth, sir," Kaelin said smoothly.

"I didn't know the Fifth were operating within the barracks."

"I was only told this morning, sir."

"Very good. Stand easy."

"Thank you, sir," answered Kaelin, copying the salute he had seen among the soldiers at Ironlatch.

The officer walked away. The drunken soldier remained behind, leaning against the gatehouse arch. "You made me look bad, you prick," he said. "I shan't forget it." He pushed himself away from the wall, half fell, then righted himself. Staggering off across the parade ground, he called back: "I'll remember you!"

Kaelin returned to the gatehouse. "You man the gates," he told Rayster. "If anyone asks, you are from the Fifth and your officer is Lieutenant Langhorne. Ask for the password, which is Valhael. You understand?"

"Aye, I heard you talking to the soldiers."

Kaelin strapped on a saber and slid his knife into his belt. "See you in a while," he said.

"May the Source make that true," replied Rayster.

Kaelin Ring strolled across the parade ground toward the keep. The main doors were open, and he stepped inside. The clerk's desk was empty now, but he could hear the sounds of men in the mess hall above. Moving behind the clerk's desk, he climbed slowly down the circular stair beyond. It was unlit, and he placed each boot with care. The lower steps glinted with reflected light, and he paused momentarily.

If there were two guards, he might be able to kill them before they either raised an alarm or made enough noise to alert other soldiers. More than two? What if there were four or five? Kaelin's mouth was dry. However many were waiting there, he would walk in and take them on. It would be better to be dead than to know he had failed Chara. He leaned forward to peer along the dungeon corridor.

One guard was asleep, his head resting on a table and his unbuckled breastplate on the floor beside him. Kaelin could see no one else.

Taking a deep, calming breath, he moved silently down the last of the stairs and eased his way toward the table. The man was snoring gently. Kaelin stepped behind him, drawing his knife. The blade was razor sharp, and it slid through the flesh of the man's throat without at first waking him. Then the pain cut through his dreams, and he jerked upright, opening his eyes. Blood pumped from the wound, drenching his shirt, and he slumped forward once more.

There were twenty dungeon cells. Half of them were open. Lifting the lantern from its wall bracket, he ran to the first locked door, sliding back the metal grille and shining the lantern inside. A white-haired man was asleep on the floor. One by one Kaelin checked all the dungeons. Three times he had to open the doors, for the occupants were not in sight of the grille. In the last he saw a sight that would haunt him for years. A man was lying unconscious on a pallet bed. He had no hands or feet, the stumps having been covered with black pitch. His eyes had been put out. He made a low moaning noise as the dungeon door swung open. The sound was barely human. Kaelin heaved the door shut.

The horror of what he had seen did not register at first. What did was that this was the last locked dungeon and neither Chara nor Wullis Swainham was there.

He had failed.

Kaelin struggled for calm. His plan had worked perfectly to this point, and he had penetrated the keep without being caught. Yet it was all pointless now. He tried to think clearly. If she was not in the dungeon of the keep, where would she be? Were there other cells?

He had no way of knowing, and the thought of failure was bitter.

Then he heard sounds upon the stairs. Kaelin swore softly

and ran to the dead guard, grabbing him by the arms and hauling him from his chair. Swiftly he dragged the body into one of the empty cells. Moving back into the corridor, he saw that blood had drenched the table and the floor beneath. The dead guard's cloak was hanging on a hook. Wrenching it clear, he draped it over the table.

Two guards came into sight, half carrying a prisoner. The soldiers were not wearing breastplates or swords, though both had sheathed daggers at their waists.

The prisoner was Chara. Her face was swollen, the lower lip split and bleeding. Her clothes were torn, the leggings half open at the waist, exposing her belly and right hip. Anger flowed through Kaelin, but he fought for calm.

"Where is Bay?" asked one of the guards.

"He had a bad throat," said Kaelin. "I'm standing in for him."

"Your lucky night," said the second. "You get a nice piece of a highland arse. Course, it comes used, if you know what I mean." The man laughed.

Kaelin saw Chara's swollen eyes open, and she looked up at him. "It is your lucky night, too," he told the guards, moving in closer. "But not all luck is good." As he stepped in, he put his hand behind his back, drawing the knife from his belt. Chara began to struggle. Both men looked away from Kaelin. The knife plunged into the chest of the first, passing between the ribs and skewering the heart. Chara rammed her head into the face of the second man. He staggered back. Releasing the knife, Kaelin drew his saber. The man let go of Chara and turned to run. Kaelin caught him, bearing him to the ground. The soldier's face struck the stone floor, smashing his teeth. He cried out. Kaelin dropped his saber and knelt on the man's back, his hands tight around the guard's throat. The soldier struggled for a few moments, then went limp. Kaelin did not move and continued squeezing the throat until he was sure the guard was dead. Then he pushed himself to his feet.

Chara was sitting on the floor, her back to the wall.

"We must get out of here," he said. "Can you walk?" He reached for her.

"Don't touch me," she snapped. She closed her eyes and drew in several deep breaths. "I can walk."

Kaelin lifted the guard's breastplate from the floor. "Get into this. I will buckle it."

"I can do that myself," she replied, her voice cold and distant.

Kaelin lifted the blood-drenched cloak from the table. "Tie this on. It will not pass close muster, but the guards on the battlements may be fooled."

Chara did so, and Kaelin led her up the circular stairs, pausing in the doorway at the top and listening. There were still sounds from the mess hall above, but they were muted now.

"Let's go," he said, moving out through the keep doors and onto the parade ground.

The walk to the gatehouse seemed interminable. He tried not to look at the sentries on the wall. Then he saw one of them wave. Kaelin waved back.

Rayster was waiting. He saw the injuries to Chara's face, and his mouth tightened. "They'll pay for this," he promised.

"Some of them already have," said Kaelin. Moving inside the gatehouse, he tore off the breastplate and put on his black greatcoat. Then he retrieved his pistols, pushed them into his belt, and stepped back out into the night. "Now let's be gone," he said.

Easing open the gate, the three highlanders crossed the drawbridge and moved toward open ground. Kaelin's mouth was dry. At any second he expected to hear a sentry call out for them to stop. He imagined long muskets trained on them, lead shot ripping into flesh. Into his mind's eye leapt the image of the mutilated man in the cells. Kaelin shivered and walked on.

No challenge came from the barracks, and the three highlanders disappeared into the alleyways behind the Dancing Bear.

* * *

Rayster and Chara ditched their breastplates in the alley, then Kaelin ordered Rayster to return to the wagon and head off toward the west. "Chara and I will go directly south," he said.

"Why south?" asked Chara.

"We will not have long before they find the bodies. They will expect you to run for home. That is where the search will begin. We will go south and then turn west into the forest. It will be slower travel, but we'll have more chance of moving undetected."

Rayster and Kaelin had bought supplies earlier that afternoon, and Kaelin took a small sack of provisions from the wagon. Rayster gripped his shoulder. "Good luck to you, Kaelin," he said. Then he climbed aboard the wagon and flicked the reins.

Kaelin and Chara set off through the night-deserted streets, keeping to the darkest places until they reached the edge of the town. The southern road was empty as they left Black Mountain. "It would be good if we could run for a while," said Kaelin. "How is your strength?"

"Not good, but I can make a mile or two," she told him.

Together they began to lope along the road. Ahead, just over a mile away to the right, Kaelin could see the dark outline of the forest. Fear was heavy upon him, for out in the open like this they could be run down by a horse patrol within minutes. He sent up a silent prayer to the Source and increased his pace. Only then did he realize how exhausted Chara was. She struggled to keep up, then stumbled. They had made less than half a mile. Kaelin dropped back. "Let's walk awhile," he said, glancing back toward the town, expecting at any moment to see horsemen thundering into sight.

How long would they have? It was unlikely that the whole night would pass before a soldier noticed that no one was guarding the gates.

They pushed on, running and walking. Chara did not complain, but Kaelin could see she was almost at the end of her strength.

At last they reached the rising slope leading to the trees.

Chara struggled on, then suddenly sat down, her breathing ragged. Kaelin knelt beside her. "Let me help you," he said, taking her arm. She snatched it back.

"I told you not to touch me."

"Aye, you did. I understand why. And you should understand that it is stupid. I have strength, and you do not. If we do not put distance between us and Black Mountain, you will be back in that dungeon cell by daybreak."

"They'll not take me alive again," she said.

"Take my arm, Chara. Then it won't be me touching you but you touching me. Use my strength."

She hesitated for a moment, then hooked her arm in his. Smoothly he drew her to her feet, and they continued up the slope and into the trees.

There he allowed her to rest. There was no point pushing into the forest at night. The moonlight was thin and obstructed by clouds. Here at the edge of the trees there was still some light, but if they moved deeper into the forest, they would be stumbling in pitch darkness. Best now to wait for the dawn and watch the road. Kaelin's fear was that the enemy would bring tracking dogs to the scene.

Chara lay down on the soft earth, covering herself with the blood-drenched cloak.

In the faint moonlight he gazed upon her bruised and swollen face. These wounds were as nothing to those which burned like fire on her soul, he knew. Two years earlier a highland woman had killed herself after a rape by Beetlebacks. The young Kaelin had not understood her despair. He had voiced his confusion to the Wyrd one afternoon in the woods just beyond Maev's house.

"Why would she do it?"

"I don't think any man can understand, Ravenheart," she told him. "It was not just the act of rape, which is evil enough. It was all the vileness that accompanied it: the fear, the self-loathing, the realization, maybe, that her life was not hers. Rape is the opposite of everything that lovemaking should be. Instead of being life-affirming it degrades the very value of life. Parsha Willetts was raped many years ago. It still scars her."

"Parsha? But she is a—"

"I know what she is," snapped the Wyrd. "She sells her body for money. A man might therefore think that a rape would be a small matter for someone in her profession. It is never a small matter, Kaelin. Rape has little to do with lust. It is about domination and humiliation, the stripping away of dignity, the scarring of the soul. It is about pain. Parsha still has nightmares about it."

"Does Jaim know?"

"No, and I will trust you not to speak of it to him. Jaim is a good man, the finest of the Rigante. His heart is huge, and he carries within him great magic."

"Jaim is not a sorcerer," said Kaelin.

"No, he is not. The magic I speak of is elemental. He does not know it is there. Grymauch lifts the soul, Kaelin. Have you not noticed how in his presence your spirit soars? He radiates all that is fine in the Rigante. He touches hearts. Were he to know of Parsha's suffering, he would set out to kill the men responsible. That would stain him. Parsha knows this also."

"They *should* be killed," said Kaelin.

"Maybe they should, Ravenheart. Maybe they will be."

Kaelin sat now at the edge of the trees, watching the road.

His heart was burdened, and he felt a great sadness overwhelm him. Before this night he had killed only two men. Both had deserved it, for they had murdered Chara Ward. Yet what had the guards at the gatehouse done? They were merely soldiers doing their duty. Perhaps they were married and had children of their own. Perhaps they were good men.

The sleeping guard might have been dreaming of his wife or son. At least with the last two they were planning to rape Chara and, as such, deserved their fate.

Curiously there was no sense of achievement or exultation. He had walked into a fortress and rescued the girl he loved, and all he felt was a sense of melancholy. Kaelin looked down

again at the sleeping Chara. Would her wounds ever heal?
She shivered in her sleep. Removing the greatcoat, he laid it
over her.

Sitting with his back to a tree, he dozed a little and
dreamed of the man in the dungeon cell whose hands and feet
had been cut away.

The sound of hoofbeats on the road awakened him. Kaelin
crept to the tree line and saw four riders moving at speed.
They were Beetlebacks. He waited until they had passed out
of sight along the southern road. Were they searching for
him? It seemed unlikely, for they were moving too fast to see
tracks.

Even so their appearance brought back his fear of capture.

He saw that Chara was awake. She was lying quietly, staring at him.

"You feel rested?" he asked her.

"Yes."

"Would you like some food?"

She sat up and nodded. Opening the canvas sack, Kaelin
produced two oatcake biscuits sweetened with honey. He
passed one to Chara. They ate in silence. There came a
rustling in the undergrowth behind them. Kaelin wrenched a
pistol from his belt and cocked it.

"It is just a fox," said Chara.

"Yes," he said, uncocking the Emburley and returning it to
his belt. Chara ate two more biscuits, then lay back down.
Within moments she was asleep again.

Kaelin waited until the dawn, then woke her. He did not
touch her but called her name softly. "Time to be moving on,"
he said.

She was stronger for her rest, and they made good progress
for several hours. They moved warily, stopping often to listen
for sounds of horsemen. By midmorning they had reached
high ground, where the trees were thinner. It was unlikely that
any Beetlebacks would be that high, but Kaelin remained
cautious.

Colonel Ranaud would stop at nothing to recapture Chara

Jace, and there were thousands of men at his disposal. He knew also that Chara would try to make it home, and this would give him an advantage. No matter how circuitous the route, Chara and Kaelin would have to emerge by the pass.

When they stopped to eat by a stream, Kaelin asked Chara if there were any other routes into Rigante territory.

"No. The mountains cut away for a hundred miles, then curve toward the sea."

Throughout their rest Chara volunteered no other conversation. She would reply if spoken to, but apart from that she merely sat, her eyes fixed on some distant point. Kaelin knew instinctively that this was not the time to talk of her ordeal, but he tried to find some other means of drawing her out.

"Why did you leave Rigante lands?" he asked at last.

She looked at him, and he saw the anger in her eyes. "Wullis Swainham told me you were sick. He said you had a fever and were likely to die."

"Why would he say that?" asked Kaelin, surprised.

She looked away for a moment. "He sold himself to the Beetlebacks," she said.

"He gave you up for *money*?"

"No. For revenge. I do not want to talk about it." Chara turned toward him. "Let me have one of your pistols and a knife."

"You do not intend to harm yourself?"

"Harm myself? What are you talking about?"

"I knew of a woman once who, after she was . . . attacked . . . killed herself."

Chara laughed then, but it was not a merry sound. "I will not harm myself, Kaelin. If there is justice at all in the world, I will one day meet Wullis Swainham again. And I will kill him."

Kaelin drew one of the Emburleys and passed it to her. "It pulls a little to the left," he said. Then he gave her one of his knives.

"I need to wash," she said. "I stink of Beetlebacks."

"The stream will be cold," he warned her.

"I expect so." She made no move to undress, and Kaelin found the silence uncomfortable.

"Are you not going to bathe now?" he asked.

"Would you turn your back?" she said.

The words stunned him. "Turn? Why? I have seen you naked before. You told me I was Varlish-tainted because I was embarrassed by your body."

"Well, now I am Varlish-tainted," she said softly. "And no man will ever see me naked again."

Kaelin said nothing for a moment. "I will scout a little and be back in a while," he said sadly.

Then he strode away toward the west.

Ranaud's fury raged for most of the morning. The bodies of the guards in the gatehouse had not been discovered until just before dawn, when the relief sentries arrived. Ranaud himself had been jerked from sleep by someone pounding on his door. It was the young officer in charge of the night watch.

"What the hell is it, man? Are we under attack?"

"No, sir. Two gatehouse guards were killed in the night."

"What?"

"They were stabbed and stripped of their armor, sir."

Ranaud's sleep-befuddled brain tried to make sense of the attack. What was the point of such an enterprise? Moving to his bedside table, he poured a goblet of watered Uisge and drained half of it. The spirit flowed like fire in his throat. "No one else was attacked?" he asked.

"No, sir."

"It makes no sense." Ranaud climbed into his leggings and pulled on his boots. Why would the attackers want the guards' armor? The answer was obvious. To pass unobserved within the barracks and the keep. Were they here to assassinate him? Ranaud strapped on his sword belt. No. Had it been a murder attempt, they would have found him long before the dawn. What, then, was the purpose? Suddenly he swore. "Has anyone been to the dungeons, Lieutenant?"

"The dungeons, sir?" replied the startled man.

"You idiot!" stormed Ranaud, pushing past the man and heading for the stairs. The startled officer followed him. Soldiers were milling outside the mess hall. Ranaud ordered three of them to follow him and ran downstairs.

The lantern in the dungeon corridor had guttered and died. All was dark and silent. Ranaud ordered a soldier to fetch another lantern and waited on the stairs. When the man returned, he eased past his colonel, holding aloft the light. It shone on the two corpses and the blood that had flowed across the floor.

"Check the cells," ordered Ranaud, knowing that Chara Jace would not be there.

Filled with cold fury, he swung on the young officer. "You were in charge of the night watch?"

"Yes sir."

"Tell me, Lieutenant, do you have friends in high places?"

"No, sir."

"Are you noble-born or rich?"

"No, sir."

"Then you are doomed, you pitiful wretch! You'll hang later. Take this man and lock him in a cell," he told the soldiers. Pushing past the doomed officer, he strode upstairs. Outside the mess hall he ordered the men there to wake every soldier in the barracks and gather reports from everyone who had come into the fortress during the night hours.

Back in his room he washed and shaved, then walked into his office to wait.

Within a short time a second officer appeared at his office. He knew the man, a career soldier from Eldacre, a solid if unimaginative officer named Bardoe Jaekel. The lieutenant saluted.

"I believe I saw the killers, sir," he said.

"One of your brother officers will hang today for dereliction of duty, Jaekel. This story of yours might see you swing alongside him."

"Yes, sir, I understand that," answered the man.

"Go on, then."

"Just after midnight I returned to the barracks in the company of several men from my squad. We were met at the gates by a young sentry who demanded the password. This was entirely correct. When I gave it, he opened the gates. I questioned him, for I had not seen him before. He told me he was with the Fifth, under Lieutenant Langhorne. I had no reason to suspect him. He had followed the orders you yourself laid down. I did seek out Prelling to question him about the use of southern units, but I could not find him and decided to wait until morning. It was a bad mistake."

"Prelling?"

"The man you are to hang, sir."

"Yes. Describe the guard you saw."

"He was young, sir, not yet twenty, I would say. Tall. He had a scar on his face."

Ranaud swore loudly. "Kaelin Ring," he said.

"Sir?"

"He runs Ironlatch farm. He is betrothed to Chara Jace. Lieutenant Langhorne and sections of the Fifth are stationed there. Send out riders to the west. Give them a description of Ring and the girl."

"Yes, sir."

"And send Wullis Swainham to me."

Bardoe Jaekel saluted and left the office. Minutes later Wullis Swainham tapped at the open door. Ranaud gestured the former clansman inside but did not offer him a seat. He looked into the man's small eyes. "You have heard?"

"She is gone," said Swainham. Ranaud could smell the fear upon the stocky red-bearded Rigante.

"Aye, she is gone. If she gets to Call Jace, he will hear of your infamy. One wonders how far you will have to go to escape Rigante vengeance, Wullis. I understand rape is considered a heinous crime among the clans, though for the life of me I cannot understand why."

"You promised to protect me," said Swainham, a whine appearing in his voice.

"First you must protect yourself. Ring and the girl are on

foot. They will not head west. Too much open country. They will have gone south and then cut northwest through the forest. You are a tracker, are you not?"

"Yes," Swainham answered miserably.

"Then track them. Find them. Kill Ring and bring me the girl."

"I'll need some men."

"No, no. You clansmen are hardy and used to rough travel. You will catch them the sooner if you are alone. Do this, Swainham, and I will give you ten pounds more so that you can travel south and find a new life."

"You said I would become clan chief of the Rigante once Call was dead. You said I would be an important man in your new administration."

Ranaud shook his head. "That was when your . . . valuable work for me was a secret. It is likely that before this day is out word of your deeds will be spreading throughout Black Mountain. Even when we have crushed Jace, there will be those left alive who will stop at nothing to see you dead. Sadly, Swainham, a traitor is never popular even among those with the most to gain from such treachery. I will furnish you with pistols and a good mountain horse. Find their trail. Find *them.*"

Swainham stood for a moment, then backed away toward the door.

"Oh, and Swainham," Ranaud said with a cold smile. "If it should cross your mind just to ride south, I shall have you declared a horse thief and an outlaw. Then my soldiers and the soldiers of the Moidart in the south will hunt you down."

Like all truly weak men Wullis Swainham saw life through a distorting mirror. Wiser men whose ideas and philosophies soared over his head like geese departing for winter were all talk and no action, lacking common sense. Brave men who risked their lives for the clan were foolish and needlessly reckless. Wullis saw his cowardice as intelligent caution and his failure to advance himself in the ranks of the Rigante as evidence of the jealousy of his peers, most especially Call Jace.

Oh, yes, Jace above all.

He had not betrayed Call Jace. Call Jace had betrayed him.

The thoughts of Wullis Swainham, as he rode his horse along the southern road, were full of bitterness.

His keen eyes had soon spotted where the fleeing Kaelin Ring and Chara Jace had left the road, and he cantered his mount after them. The dawn sun was clear of the eastern mountains now, and Wullis urged his horse up the long slope toward the trees.

Dismounting, he led the horse into the forest, tethering the reins against a jutting branch. Scanning the ground, he soon found the spot where the two had rested. Wullis turned his eyes toward the west. How long had they rested there? The undergrowth ahead was thick and dense. It was likely, therefore, that Kaelin Ring had decided to wait for dawn. If that was the case, then the southerner and Chara were only a little way ahead. Certainly no more than a mile.

The horse would be useless in this terrain. Wullis left it tethered and began to follow the tracks.

As he moved, he found himself thinking of Call Jace and the anguish he would suffer when he learned of the fate of his daughter. These were pleasing thoughts, though it would be more satisfying if the man could know exactly *why* he had earned such suffering.

Almost two years earlier Wullis had gone to Jace. Wearing his best cloak and leggings and carrying an offering of an embossed hunting knife, he had asked for the hand of Chara Jace. The girl was almost of marriageable age, and Wullis believed she had some feelings for him. Not that she had said anything, but he could see it in her eyes when she looked at him.

Jace had listened politely as Wullis delivered his carefully worked out speech. Then he had begun to laugh. The sound had torn through Wullis Swainham, and he stood blinking and confused before his chieftain.

"Ah, Wullis," said Call Jace as his laughter finally subsided, "that was a rich jest. Who put you up to it? Was it Bael? Rayster?"

"Jest, lord? I don't understand?"

All humor faded from Call Jace's eyes. "Not a jest? Are you insane, then, Wullis? What could possibly have led you to believe that I would allow my only daughter to wed a timid man? No, no. Put this nonsense from your mind. By heaven, Wullis, a man should at least understand his limitations. You are a fine tracker, but you have the heart of a corn mouse. Now let us say no more about this matter."

The heart of a corn mouse. The insult had burrowed into his soul like a maggot. And as the months passed, the hurt he felt had swelled and grown from hurt to bitterness and bitterness to hatred.

Well, the corn mouse had been among the men who had deflowered his precious Chara. The corn mouse had seen three of Call's best scouts taken by the Beetlebacks. Now the corn mouse would kill Kaelin Ring and bring Chara back to the fortress. And he would be there when the great Call Jace was dragged to the executioner's block. Call Jace would live to rue the day he had spoken so scathingly.

Wullis moved swiftly through the undergrowth, following the tracks. The southerner was not taking any pains to disguise their passage. He also noted that Chara's smaller prints showed occasional scuff marks as her feet dragged. She was exhausted. As well she might be, he thought.

She'll be more exhausted yet by the time I've caught her, he decided.

Wullis thought of Kaelin Ring. His hatred of the southerner was intense. He had watched with awe the fight with Bael, but then he had seen Chara run to him, taking his arm and staring up at him with undisguised adoration. The sight had sickened him to the depths of his being.

It would be good indeed to stand over his body, to make Chara stare into his dead eyes.

Wullis came to a rise before a sharp dip. He paused, kneeling behind some bushes. Down below a group of hunters was gathered around a fire. Wullis saw that the tracks of Kaelin and Chara moved away toward the south. They were seeking to avoid the men below. Wullis had no such fear. With luck, if he took the straight path, he would be ahead of them.

Moving down the slope, he passed the campfire, waving to the men seated there. They waved back and then ignored him.

Wullis clambered up the opposite slope and began to move with great care, pausing often to listen and scan the surrounding trees. He had no wish to be surprised by Kaelin Ring or to get into a sword fight with him. What he wanted was to find a good place for an ambush.

Then he spotted them. They were sitting beside a wide but shallow stream. Wullis ducked down and began to crawl through the undergrowth. Painstakingly, moving inch by inch, he came closer.

Now he was within fifteen paces of them. Drawing his borrowed pistols, he eased back the hammers. All he needed to do was to rear up and blast the life from Kaelin Ring. Just then Kaelin rose to his feet and walked away toward the west. Wullis swore.

Chara swung her head to watch Kaelin leave, then climbed out of her clothes and waded into the stream. There was blood on her face, and her body was badly bruised. Even so, she was still beautiful, the sun glinting on her red-gold hair. She sat down in the stream and washed, then lay flat on her back, allowing the water to slide over her.

Wullis lay very still. Where in the seven hells had Kaelin gone? His hands were slippery with sweat. Carefully putting down the pistols, he rubbed his palms on his leggings.

Chara rose from the water and returned to her clothes. She sat down, and Wullis saw that she was weeping. He could not hear her above the rushing of the stream, but he could see her shoulders heaving as she bent double, her face in her hands.

Blame your father for this, he thought. Blame Call Jace for what you have been through.

At last the weeping ended, and Chara donned her torn shirt and leggings. Then she sat, hugging her knees and staring out over the mountains.

Wullis waited patiently, his pistols ready.

Kaelin Ring emerged from the trees and strolled down to the water's edge. He squatted down. Wullis cursed softly, for Chara was now in the line of fire. Moving carefully to his knees, Wullis lifted the pistols.

Kaelin Ring stood and moved away to Chara's left. Wullis surged to his feet. Kaelin saw him. He should have been rooted in shock. Instead he dropped to his knee just as Wullis fired his first shot, the ball sailing over Kaelin's head. Steadying himself, Wullis readjusted his aim. Kaelin Ring had drawn his pistol. Panic touched Wullis then, and he shot too fast. Kaelin's pistol boomed. The ball smashed into Wullis' chest, searing into his lungs. He staggered.

All he knew in that moment was that he had to run, to get away. He heard his name called. His gaze flicked to Chara Jace. She was wading through the stream toward him. In her hand was a silver pistol. Wullis felt his strength ebbing away. She was closer now.

"Not my fault," he said, backing into a tree.

The pistol came up. Liquid fire tore through his groin, and he screamed in pain and fell writhing to the ground. Chara dropped the Emburley and lifted her knife. Kaelin Ring ran alongside her, grabbing her arm. "Leave him," Wullis heard him say.

"He has to suffer more," shouted Chara.

"Believe me, he will. But if you do this, you will always regret it. I know. It will stain you forever."

"I am already stained."

"There is a difference. The horrors you suffered were perpetrated by evil men. Do this and the horror will be on your soul and yours alone."

Wullis heard this through a sea of pain. He thought it could get no worse, but the fire flared higher into his belly and his body spasmed. He twisted on the ground, drawing his knees up toward his belly. The skin split, and his entrails bulged against his shirt.

Opening his eyes, he saw Chara and Kaelin wading back across the stream.

And all he could do to stem the pain was to scream . . .

And scream.

The death of Parsis Feld, the owner of the Eldacre forge, caused quite a stir in the town: a married man with three sons and a doting wife. His heart gave out while he was being "entertained" in the town's most illustrious brothel.

Yet even that news was dwarfed by the revelations that followed. The Varlish community reacted with astonishment when it was learned that forty percent of Parsis Feld's business empire was in fact owned by a highland woman.

The sons of Parsis Feld were outraged. None of them wished to continue their father's business but were seeking to sell it and retire to graceful homes far away in the south. Now the amount they could expect was almost halved.

The eldest son, Jorain Feld, took his complaint to the Moidart, and so it was that on a bright autumn morning Galliott the Borderer, with ten soldiers, rode to Maev's home.

Galliott was uneasy. As captain of the watch he had many informants and had known for some time about Maev Ring's astonishing successes. They did not concern him, for Maev Ring conducted herself with a commendable lack of ostentation. He did wonder at times what on earth she did with the money she earned, but apart from that he turned a blind eye to her business dealings. Now, despite Maev's attempts to remain inconspicuous, her name was being spoken all over town.

Galliott reined in his mount in the yard behind the house and dismounted. Maev herself walked out to greet him.

"What can I do for you, Captain?" she asked.

"Is Jaim here?" he replied.

"No. He has gone north on an errand for me."

Galliott was relieved. The last person he wanted around at this bitter moment was Jaim Grymauch. "I am sorry, Maev, but I am here to escort you to Eldacre Castle. The Moidart wishes to question you."

"Shall I harness my buggy, Captain, or are you to drag me there in chains?" There was anger in her green eyes.

"Harness your buggy, madam, by all means. I shall drive it for you."

"I am quite capable of driving it myself, Captain."

"Very well."

Crowds gathered in Old Hills to watch Maev Ring as she passed. They noted the way she sat, head high and proud, as she steered the pony. There was no fear showing. In Eldacre itself more crowds lined the streets, many just anxious to catch a glimpse of the "rich clanswoman."

Maev rode her buggy through the great gates of the castle and followed Galliott to the steps leading into the castle proper. Galliott dismounted, passed the reins of his horse to a servant, then helped Maev from the buggy.

He walked with her through the great doors, then led her up a flight of stairs to the first level. There he bade her sit on a velvet-covered couch in a red-carpeted corridor. Galliott sat beside her. "Answer all questions truthfully, Maev," he said. "Do not make him angry. You have broken no law. Hold to that."

"I have waited for this moment for some years," she said with a sigh. "I am prepared for it."

"Wait here. I will see if the lord is ready to see you."

Galliott strolled away. He returned some twenty minutes later, leading Maev along the corridor and up a further flight of stairs. Tapping on a door, he opened it. Maev found herself in a circular room with white-plastered brickwork. The floor was fitted with a thick gray carpet. At the center the fawn in brambles motif had been skillfully embroidered.

The Moidart was sitting at a desk beneath a tall window. Maev had never been this close to the lord. His white hair was drawn back in a tight ponytail, his hawklike features were tanned, and his dark eyes radiated power. He was dressed in black, though his tunic was edged in silver and white lace cuffs showed at the wrist.

Galliott walked Maev to the desk. There were no other seats in the room, and she stood silently waiting.

"You know why you are here?" asked the Moidart.

"Parsis Feld died, and his children are greedy," said Maev.

"Very succinct," the Moidart said softly. "Since you are a highlander and as ill bred as the rest of your mangy clan, I shall ignore your lack of respect. But only this once, Ring. The next time you speak, you will call me 'lord' or I shall have you flogged for discourtesy. Is this clear to you?"

"It is, lord," she replied.

"Good. Now tell me how you became . . . embroiled with Parsis Feld."

"He had pinned his company's fortune on supplying your soldiers with weapons, lord, and had no other outlets. Also, his pistols were cheaply made with poor materials. He was close to bankruptcy. I went to him with a proposition, which he accepted. From that moment we were partners."

"Tell me of the proposition."

"A student of the gunsmith Emburley was seeking employment. I hired him, lord, and I organized shipments of high-quality iron to Feld's armory."

"And how, pray, did you find the money to hire a gunsmith?"

"From the profits I made from Gillam Pearce."

The Moidart leaned back in his chair. "You have an interest in Pearce's business?"

"I do, lord."

"Let me guess. You went to Gillam Pearce and suggested he make a pair of fine boots for me, which were then delivered as a present?"

"Yes, lord."

"How many other business interests do you have, Ring?"

"A little over twenty, lord."

"Twenty-seven," he said. "The profits must be very high now."

"Yes, lord."

The Moidart fell silent. Then he gave a bleak smile. "You are an interesting woman, Maev Ring." He glanced up at Galliott. "Fetch her a chair," he ordered.

Galliott did so, and Maev sat down. "Let me run over the facts again," said the Moidart. "You acquired minority interests in twenty-seven failing businesses, and now each one turns a profit?"

"Yes, lord."

The Moidart lifted a heavy sheet of paper and scanned it. "Parsis Feld paid three hundred and twenty pounds in tax this year. Five years ago he supplied eleven pounds, eight chaillings. That is a handsome turnaround. My congratulations to you."

"Thank you, lord," said Maev, surprised by this turn of events.

"The law specifically states that no clansman—or woman, for that matter—can own a Varlish business. You, however, do not own the businesses. Jorain Feld understands this. He has, therefore, laid another charge against you. No clansman can own a pistol."

"I own no pistol, lord."

"Jorain claims that since the forge currently has one hundred and forty pistols stored and forty percent of the business is yours, you currently own forty pistols."

Maev felt cold inside.

"However," continued the Moidart, "I find this to be a specious argument. As you said so aptly upon your arrival, Parsis Feld has greedy children. That will be all, Madam Ring."

Maev sat stunned for a moment. "You mean I can go . . . lord?"

"Of course you may go. You are guilty of no crime."

Maev struggled to rise. Her legs felt weak. Galliott, seeing her distress, took her arm. "Thank you, lord," she said. "I am most grateful."

"Thank you for the boots," said the Moidart.

Galliott led her out of the room and back down the stairs. "This is good news, Maev," he said. "The best. Congratulations."

"I still cannot quite believe it. I am free?"

"You are free," said Galliott.

The freedom lasted two days.

Unable to convince the Moidart that Maev Ring had broken Varlish law, Jorain Feld took his case to the bishop of Eldacre and invoked church law. He also made a payment of five hundred pounds to the cathedral.

Maev Ring was arrested again and this time was taken before the bishop.

She was charged with witchcraft and taken in chains to the cells below the cathedral.

◊ 16 ◊

THAT NIGHT KAELIN and Chara made a cold camp in a shallow cave. They could not risk a fire, and even though the night air was chilly, Chara sat apart from Kaelin, huddled against the rear wall, her cloak drawn tightly around her.

The screams of Wullis Swainham had followed them, occasionally dying off, only to come again just when they thought his agony was over. Kaelin sat at the mouth of the cave, staring out over the moonlit forest. He wished Grymauch were close and half hoped—as had happened once before—that he would see a small campfire and the giant clansman would be sitting there waiting for him. The Wyrd was right. Jaim was a magical man. No matter how difficult the situation, the presence of Grymauch always brought hope. Kaelin had a feeling that the one-eyed clansman might even be able to break through the wall around Chara Jace.

He glanced back at her. She was gazing at the rock face, but he knew her mind was far away.

"Are you hungry?" he asked. She shook her head. "Perhaps you should eat, anyway. It will give you strength."

"All right," she said.

Kaelin moved back into the cave and searched through the canvas sack, coming up with some strips of salted beef. Chara ate in silence. Kaelin felt there was a chasm between them and did not know how to cross it.

"Why did you stop me from taking my vengeance?" she asked suddenly.

"He was dying, anyway," he replied. "And in great pain."

"I hope that his pain lasts for an eternity," she said.

"Why did he betray you? Do you know?"

She shook her head and lapsed once more into silence.

"You said it was for revenge," he prompted.

Chara sighed. "He wanted to marry me. My father laughed at him. I knew nothing of this. He told me as he . . ." Her face reddened. "He told me that everything I was suffering was the fault of my father. I should not have let you stop me. I should have cut his eyes out."

"It would not have brought you peace," he said.

"Peace? You think I will ever have peace? How would you know? You are a man, just like those stinking men back in the keep." The force of her anger shocked him, yet it did not spark his own. Instead it saddened him.

"I am not like those men," he said at last. "I would never harm a woman. No true Rigante ever would. Get some rest."

Returning to the mouth of the cave, he sat in despair. Wullis Swainham was dead, yet his evil lived on. Kaelin was powerless to change that. The night grew colder. He saw that Chara was sleeping, and once more he covered her with his greatcoat. It began to rain, and he drew back from the mouth of the cave. Chara suddenly screamed and sat bolt upright, scrabbling for a pistol.

"It is all right!" shouted Kaelin. "You are safe. I am with you."

"They are coming for me again," she cried.

"I will not let them harm you."

She blinked, and her breathing slowed. "You will not let them take me?"

"I promise."

"You will kill me?"

"I will not let them take you."

"I need more than that, Kaelin. Promise you will shoot me."

"It will not come to that. But if it does, then yes, I will kill you. You have my promise."

By late afternoon of the following day they had reached the western flanks of the mountains. Kaelin climbed a high tree to look out over the valley and the road to the pass. Hundreds of soldiers were garrisoned there. Kaelin could see men pitching rows of tents. A line of twenty cannon had also been drawn up. Horses were being picketed to the east.

Climbing back to the ground, he told Chara what he had seen.

"Can we slip by them?" she asked.

"No."

"What do we do? We cannot just sit in the forest until we starve to death."

"I need time to think," he replied. Moving away from her, he approached the towering cliff face and stared up. They were already high, and the cliffs soared for at least another six hundred feet. Wispy clouds prevented him from seeing the very top. He walked along the base of the rock face. It was not the soft sandstone of the southern hills. There were many cracks and juts that would make fine handholds and footholds. This would not be the problem, though, he knew. Grymauch had taught him to climb, and he had learned that the greatest danger to a climber came not from the rock face but from within. A handhold that was merely ten feet above the ground felt solid and large. The same handhold a hundred feet up seemed tiny. The higher one climbed, the more dangerous it felt. Fatigue would seep into the muscles; the wind would tug at the climber's clothing. Fear sometimes led to a dizzy feeling where it seemed the mountain was swaying back and forth, seeking to dislodge the arrogant human clinging to it.

In perfect conditions Kaelin knew he could make this climb, then angle along the highest ridge, coming down into Rigante territory beyond the pass. These were not perfect conditions. It had been raining in the night, and the granite was greasy and slick. Added to which Chara was in no fit state to tackle such a task.

Yet what were the alternatives?

They could cut away to the south and hope to survive. He had coin, and if they reached distant settlements, he could purchase food and supplies. Always supposing they could stay clear of Beetleback patrols. And what would happen here if Chara did not return home? Call Jace might lead his Rigante out against the cannon. They would then be massacred.

At last Kaelin returned to Chara. "We need to scale the cliffs and move along the ridge of the mountain," he said.

Chara looked aghast. "No one can climb the cliffs, Kaelin. They are hundreds of feet high, and there is no knowing what lies at the peaks."

"If we stay here, they will find us eventually or we will die of hunger and cold. There is no going back, and there is no going forward. All that is left is up. I have climbed cliffs. It is not so difficult as long as you keep your head and keep a firm grip on your imagination. Do not look down. Concentrate only on handholds and footholds."

Chara stared up at the towering cliff face. "It is madness," she said. "We will fall and be dashed to pieces."

"As I said, you need to keep a firm grip on your imagination."

"I can't do it," she said, backing away from the face.

"I'm sorry," he said. "I do not want to do this, either." He told her of his fears concerning a Rigante attack on the cannon and how Rayster had warned him that Call Jace would risk everything to save her. "I can think of no other way to bring you home," he admitted.

She sat in silence for a few moments. "Have you ever climbed a cliff as high as this?" she asked him.

"No."

"We don't know what is up there. There might be no route through to the valley. Then we'd have to climb down again."

"Yes," he agreed.

"I do not like heights. They make me dizzy."

"You do not look at the height; you look at the rock face. And you climb one move at a time, from ledge to ledge." He explained all that Jaim had told him about exposure and the need to climb slowly and smoothly, conserving energy. She listened intently.

Kaelin saw her turn back to look at the rock face. "We will be climbing into clouds," she said.

"Yes. It will be cold and hazardous."

"Will you go first?"

Kaelin knew that he should. Experienced climbers always took the lead, working out the route. If he climbed second, he risked Chara falling and dragging him down with her. Better that, he thought, than having to see her fall alone. "No," he told her. "You will go first. I will climb just below you. That way I can help you with footholds."

Chara's expression showed that she was still far from convinced. "Where do we start?" she said.

Kaelin rose from the rock and walked along the cliff face, gauging the best route. Finally he stopped. Removing his stolen saber, he dropped it to the ground. "Take off your cloak and roll it into a bundle," he said. "Otherwise it will flap in the wind. I will tie it across your back."

"What about that greatcoat?" she asked. "Is it not too heavy to climb in?"

"I will need it when we reach the peaks. It will be cold up there. The coat is loose. If it proves too cumbersome, I will ditch it later."

Chara rolled the black cloak, then looped it over her shoulder and under her left arm. Then she fastened it with a brooch pin. Kaelin drew the pistols from the front of his belt and placed them at the rear. "Ready?" he asked her.

"Aye, I am." Her eyes were less swollen now, the bruises on her face fading.

Kaelin held her gaze. "I know you have been hurt, Chara . . ." She swung away from him, her eyes blazing with anger. "Wait, let me finish!" She paused. "What I want to say is this: You were taken in order to force your father to come out of his stronghold and be massacred by the Beetlebacks. That was Ranaud's plan. That plan fails only when you walk into the great house. If you die here, Call Jace will likely respond with blind rage. He will come out and fight. And he will lose. The Rigante will lose. I want you to think of this as we climb. I want it in your mind as your muscles ache and you fear you cannot go on. Anger is good, Chara. Hold to it. Let it give you strength."

"Are you finished?" she said. "Just tell me where to begin."

He approached the face and pointed up to a deep crack some fifty feet above them. "We need to reach that chimney in the rock. Once inside, we will find the climbing more easy. Move slowly. Rest often. Try to use the muscles in your legs more than those in your arms. The arms will tire first."

Chara stepped up to the face and began to climb. Kaelin waited until she was more than six feet above him, then climbed after her. The handholds and footholds were good, and they moved steadily up the face. Just below the chimney was a narrow ledge. Chara climbed onto it. She glanced down. Kaelin saw her face lose its color. Vertigo swept over her, and she closed her eyes, her body swaying. Swiftly he hauled himself up alongside her, propelling her into the wider ledge within the chimney. "Look at me!" he snapped. "Open your eyes and look at me!"

Her eyes flared open. "Do not look down. Concentrate only on the climb."

"I am all right now," she said.

Releasing her, he stared up the three-foot-wide fissure in the rock. It snaked up for at least another forty feet, then it narrowed. The rocks were slick with the previous night's rain, but handholds were plentiful. "Wait here and watch where I climb," he said. He began on the jagged left side of the chimney, then stepped across to the right, climbing ever higher. When he reached the narrow section, he paused to scan it. Then he descended to where Chara waited. "It is easy to the point where the fissure closes. After that you will need to use your fist to help you climb. I'll show you how." Lifting his hands, he held the palms together as if in prayer. Then he drew them an inch apart. "Slide your hand between mine. Once inside, try to make a fist." She did so, and he felt her knuckles pressing against his palms. "That is good. It is called a hand jam, and that is what you must do with the narrow fissure while you search for a foothold. Once your foot is secure, release the fist and press your hand a little higher into the fissure. You understand?"

"I am not a dolt. Of course I understand."

"Then climb."

She scaled the chimney with ease, but where it narrowed, she stopped. Kaelin moved closer to her. "I cannot find a foothold," she said.

"Move your right foot up another two feet," he told her. As she did so, he guided her foot to a small jut in the face.

"I'll slide off it," she told him. "It is too small."

Steadying himself, he pressed his hand under her foot. "Push now," he said. Chara levered herself up—then slipped. She cried out as her hand wrenched clear of the fissure. Kaelin grabbed her as she slid into him. Her foot hit his left leg, dislodging it from the face. He clamped his right hand tight to the rock on which he hung. Chara reached out and grabbed a tiny overhang, relieving Kaelin of some of the weight. Then she levered herself clear. Kaelin regained his foothold. He glanced across at her. There was blood on the back of her left hand where the skin had been gashed. Ignoring the wound, Chara moved back to the fissure and, pushing her hand into it, drew herself up. Kaelin followed close behind.

They were now almost a hundred feet above the forest. The wind was blowing strong, and there was rain in the air. Kaelin prayed that it would hold off.

As the fissure finally closed, they came to a ledge of rock some five feet deep. Chara sank down, her back to the face. Kaelin drew himself alongside her. "Any tremble in your arms yet?" he asked.

"Not yet."

"Let me know when there is. Jaim says that is when the muscles are about to give out. We'll need to rest then."

Kaelin eased his way along the ledge. It ran for almost sixty feet. The rock face was smooth almost all the way. Kaelin, who had been climbing rocks with Jaim since he was a child, knew he could find holds. Chara could not. Stepping back as far toward the edge as he could, Kaelin scanned the cliff. There was another ledge some thirty feet higher but no obvious route to it. Returning to where Chara was resting, he stepped over her outstretched legs and examined the rock above the chimney. Centuries of rain had washed over the stone, smoothing it. But there were holds that Chara might manage. The problem was that an overhang obscured his view of the upper face. What if they were to climb past that, only to find no way forward? Would they be able to descend again?

Passing Chara again, he walked the ledge, seeking a better way. He did not find one.

"Time to go," he told her.

It took more than half an hour to reach the overhang. For most of that time Chara clung to the face, unable to reach the only handhold available. Kaelin tried to help her, but his own footholds were so small that he could not risk trying to push her. Eventually Chara took a chance and hurled herself up, her left hand scrabbling at the rock. Kaelin's heart was in his mouth. Had she fallen, there would have been no way to stop her. They would both have been swept from the face. But she did not fall.

They reached the overhang, traversed along a ledge, then faced an easier climb to a wide shelf of rock. Wispy mist floated by them, and the air was cold and damp.

"You are walking in the clouds now," Kaelin told her. "How does it feel?"

For the first time since the rescue Chara smiled. "It feels good. How high are we now?"

"Four hundred feet. Perhaps a little more. We need to push on. The light will be fading soon."

For another hour they climbed steadily. In places they were able to walk and scramble up slopes created from fallen rock. At last they reached the crest of the mountain, a huge cleft between two peaks. To the west they could see the gentle slopes of the Rigante valley. Chara turned back and stared down the way they had come. The light was fading, and now the drop seemed even more dizzying. Suddenly giddy, she sat down. "I cannot believe I climbed that," she said.

"But you did, Chara," said Kaelin. "You conquered your fear and conquered the mountain. And you are free."

Wearily she pushed herself to her feet. "I am free thanks to you, Ravenheart," she said. "I am sorry I have treated you so badly."

"You have nothing to apologize for. I mean that with all my heart. Now, let us get to the great house. We did not come all this way to die of cold on a mountainside."

The wind was shrieking around them as they began their descent. There were no sheer faces there, only a series of downward slopes. Chara lifted her bundled cloak clear of her shoulders, shook it loose, and wrapped it around herself.

They trudged on through the dusk and into the night, coming at last to within sight of the main Rigante settlement. Chara was close to exhaustion. They were seen by scouts from the high pass to their right. Two men came running down to intercept them. One was Rayster.

"By the Sacrifice, where the hell did you come from?"

"From the clouds," said Chara.

The preliminary hearing into the case of the church versus Maev Ring was held in the Holy Court, a marble building set in the grounds directly behind the cathedral. It was a beautiful copy of the ancient temple in Stone where Persis Albitane was said to have delivered his first sermon. For more than a hundred years the Holy Court had been the main church in Eldacre, until the construction of the colossal cathedral.

Some two hundred feet long and supported by fifty-six columns, the building was mainly used now as a museum and a repository for books and scrolls depicting the spread of the faith through these northern lands in the last eight hundred years. The prime exhibit was a golden urn said to contain the ashes of Persis himself. Once a year the urn was carried into the cathedral for the Service of Healing, and pilgrims would travel hundreds of miles for the opportunity to touch it and beg Saint Persis to intercede on their behalf, healing their bodies or the illnesses of their loved ones.

There were no pews now in the main hall of the Holy Court, but there were two hundred seats in the high galleries, one hundred on each side. At the western end of the hall, set upon a raised dais beneath an arched stained-glass window, stood the judgment table.

The bishop of Eldacre sat at the velvet-covered table, two abbots and three senior priests filling the other chairs. On this day the galleries were empty, for the trial proper could not be set until the judging panel had decided the merits of the case. Despite this, the trial date had in fact been organized for the following day.

Maev Ring stood before the table, her hands behind her, her wrists manacled together. Two priests, swinging bowls of holy incense on slender chains, were stationed alongside her. According to church ritual, no evil demon or spirit could be released while the incense burned.

Maev glanced up at the tall stained-glass window. It showed the saint Persis Albitane kneeling before a veiled woman. Golden light was flowing from her fingers and forming a halo around the head of the saint.

"Let the hearing begin," said the bishop. "I have many duties today, and my lunch is waiting."

A black-garbed cleric moved into sight. He was a short man, potbellied and wearing an ornate white wig. He bowed to the panel. "Lords and Brothers," he said, "I represent the church in this matter and have affidavits and depositions to present."

"The court recognizes Arlin Bedver," said the bishop. "Let it be so recorded." The priest at the farthest end of the table took up a quill and began to write. The bishop leaned forward and stared at Maev Ring. "The trial is set for—," he began.

"I appear for the accused," came a voice that echoed from the back of the building. The bishop appeared startled. His eyes narrowed.

Alterith Shaddler moved past the equally surprised Maev Ring and bowed low before the panel.

"You were not summoned here, schoolmaster," snapped the bishop.

Alterith opened a leather satchel and produced a sheaf of papers and an elderly leather-bound volume of Holy Law. "According to the laws of church and state—and I have here the relevant documents and texts—any Varlish of good standing, with a degree in theology, can represent himself as an advocate. I also have here copies of my degree from the Academy for the Instruction of the Righteous."

"You wish to be recorded as a speaker for witches?" asked one of the abbots, a thin, elderly man with a reedy, high-pitched voice.

"As I recall, sir, Saint Persis Albitane began his career by appearing for other saints accused by the church of the day. He, too, was derided for speaking up on their behalf."

The abbott reddened. "Are you suggesting, sir, that this holy and august panel can be compared to barbarians? Have a care, Master Shaddler."

"What I am saying, Lord Abbot, is that it is the right of every defendant to have an advocate. Maev Ring is an honest highland woman, accused by men who have much to gain from her downfall. I have my credentials with me. Do you deny me the right to represent her? I urge you to think carefully on this matter, for I also have here a letter which I shall dispatch to the church authorities in Varingas, making it clear that should I be denied, this hearing should be voided as an illegal action. A second letter will be sent to the king's privy council charging church leaders in Eldacre with breaking the law of the king himself."

"You are threatening us?" said the bishop.

"Indeed I am, my lord. I will also petition the Moidart to arrest those who break the king's law. Since the Moidart himself has found Maev Ring innocent of earlier charges, I feel sure he will listen most attentively to my plea."

"This is insufferable!" shouted the bishop. "I shall have you flogged for your impertinence."

"May I speak, my lords!" said Arlin Bedver, stepping forward to the table. He leaned in close to the bishop and spoke too softly for Maev to hear what was said. The silence grew. Then the bishop waved Bedver back.

"Alterith Shaddler will be recorded as advocate for the witch," said the bishop. "The trial is set for—"

"If it please the court," interrupted Alterith Shaddler. "I will need at least three days to gather affidavits and depositions to support the defense. Such a right is enshrined in—" He drew more papers from his satchel. "—clause seventeen, paragraph nine, of the Church Constitution regarding heresy, sedition, and acts of desecration."

The bishop flicked a glance to Arlin Bedver, and Maev saw him nod in agreement.

"The trial is set for three days' time," said the bishop. "Do you have any other demands, Mr. Shaddler?"

"I would ask, my lord, that Maev Ring be released from custody until the trial."

"Denied!" The bishop heaved his huge bulk from his seat. "This hearing is over," he said. Then he stalked from the dais. Two guards, bearing ornamental lances, took Maev Ring away. "I will come to you presently," Alterith Shaddler called after her. Then he replaced the papers in his satchel and approached Arlin Bedver.

"I would appreciate sight of your affidavits," he said.

"Of course, Master Shaddler. They make for grim reading."

"How so?"

"Fifteen of Maev Ring's . . . partners . . . have stated under oath that she cast spells upon them in order to swindle them out of their businesses. The widow of Parsis Feld maintains he was a changed man after Ring came to him. Before that he was a churchgoer and a man steeped in goodness. After they became partners, he began consorting with prostitutes and took to strong drink. The case is enormously strong against her. My advice to you is to urge Maev Ring to plead guilty and show genuine remorse. The church will then strip her of her ill-gotten gains, sentence her to a public flogging, and then release her. Should she make a vain effort to plead innocence, the church will ask for the full penalty under the law. She will be flogged and then hanged or burned."

Alterith looked into the man's dark eyes. "I wonder, Mr. Bedver, if you realize that this is a travesty or you genuinely believe this is a case of witchcraft."

"What I believe—or do not believe—is incidental, Mr. Shaddler. The church has brought the case, and I am the appointed advocate for the church. Now, the depositions and affidavits are here. Please feel free to read them. I shall wait until you have finished."

Alterith carried the documents to the table so recently vacated by the panel and began to read. What he found there sickened him.

An hour later he was ushered into the cell at the rear of the cathedral. It had been built not as a dungeon but as a bedchamber for priests. There was a bed and a small table with two wooden chairs, and a lantern was hanging on a wrought-iron bracket on the far wall. A small window looked out onto gardens.

"Not so terrible a place," he said as he entered.

"No," agreed Maev Ring.

Alterith thought she looked tired. "Are they feeding you well?" he asked.

"Aye, they bring me food. Why are you doing this, schoolteacher?"

"I believe you to be innocent, madam."

She shrugged. "What does that matter? Innocent or guilty, they will burn me."

"They have fifteen witnesses who say you bewitched them," said Alterith. "I have copied out their names. My understanding is that you have more than twenty partnerships."

"Twenty-seven."

"Then at least twelve of your partners refused to condemn you. I shall seek them out and ask them to speak on your behalf at the trial."

"They won't," said Maev Ring. "The Varlish will close ranks. They will think of all the money they can make, of the debts they will not need to repay. I wish you had not made them wait another three days."

"We need that time, madam."

"I do not need that time. The result is a foregone conclusion. Better to let it reach that conclusion with speed."

"I don't understand."

"I don't want Jaim here. Can you understand that? When Parsis died, I knew there would be trouble, so I sent Jaim to the north. He will be back within two weeks. It must be concluded before then."

"You do not want him to have to watch you die. I understand that."

She laughed then. "You don't understand, schoolteacher. My death is written already. I don't want to see *him* die. We are not talking about an ordinary man here. Jaim Grymauch would walk into the fires of hell to rescue me. He must not be here."

"I think we are getting ahead of ourselves," said Alterith. "The most important matter to focus on is your innocence and the proving of that innocence. Now, give me the names of all your business partners. We have three days, and I intend to use that time wisely. I do not share your cynicism, Maev Ring. There will be good men prepared to stand up for the truth."

Call Jace gazed around the room at his thirty war chiefs and listened as one by one they reported the progress of the fighting men under their command. Kaelin, sitting across the table from the clan leader, watched him intently. Call had spent an hour with Chara and when he had returned had questioned Kaelin about her state of mind. Kaelin had little to offer. He told the Rigante leader that she had been withdrawn and hostile for most of the journey. Call's hands had trembled with suppressed fury, and he had spoken of "taking his vengeance" and killing every Varlish in Black Mountain.

Even now, with the meeting into its second hour, Call's face was still ashen, his eyes angry.

Rayster gave a report on the enemy's strength at both passes. Two thousand men were camped before each one. Both forces had twenty cannon. "If we come out of the mountains," said Rayster, "they will cut us to pieces before we get within sword range."

"What about a night attack?" asked Call.

"Losses would still be enormous. They have fires burning behind each cannon. It would take mere moments for them to haul away the canvas covers on the weapons and set flame to the touch holes."

"They will have to pull back once winter sets in," offered another warrior.

"No," said Call. "They will not wait for winter. Reinforcements are on their way. Five thousand men of the king's regiment. Then they will launch a twin assault, blasting away our gates and then swarming into the valley. The Dweller tells me that another three thousand Beetlebacks are on the southern road, heading north. They are the king's troops and are coming from as far south as Baracum."

"The king's troops?" put in Rayster. "Why would the king seek to destroy us?"

"The murder of Colonel Linax is being attributed to me," said Call. "Linax had friends at court. The question is: How do we counter this threat? If we attack, we lose. If we defend, we also lose—albeit more slowly."

There was silence around the table. Kaelin pushed himself to his feet. "I know that I am not of this clan, though I am Rigante," he said. "Might I speak?"

"You have earned that right, boy," said Call. "By heaven, you have."

"Then I say we should attack one of their forces, but not through a pass. I came here over the mountains. I could lead a force back the same way during the night. We would emerge from the forest on their unprotected left flank at dawn. All the cannon are pointed at the pass. If the cannoneers were routed or killed, there would be nothing to stop our main force from coming out of the valley. Then we would have them between hammer and anvil. We would also—if successful—capture twenty cannon, plus powder and shot and whatever weapons and stores they have." Kaelin sat down.

"The cliffs above the forest are sheer," said Bael. "I applaud your skill in bringing Chara over them. Many of us here have climbed rock faces. It is far easier to go up than down. And at night? We would lose men, Kaelin."

"I agree," said Rayster. "Even the thought of such a climb makes my stomach churn. I'll risk dying facing an enemy with a sword in my hand, but to topple from a cliff face in the darkness—I don't think so."

"There are a series of ledges," said Kaelin. "With enough ropes we can lessen the danger. But you are both right. Men will likely fall and be dashed to the rocks. If the plan works, however, we will destroy one Beetleback army. That will demoralize the Varlish and perhaps make the winter safe for us."

"How many men would you need in this force?" asked Call Jace.

"At least three hundred," said Kaelin.

Call Jace glanced down the table to where a powerfully built middle-aged man had been sitting quietly for the entire meeting. "What think you, Arik?" he asked.

Arik Ironlatch gave a bleak smile and rubbed at his graying beard. "My men are fine climbers, Call Jace. I don't doubt I'd get volunteers for such an enterprise."

"You think it will work?"

"It will or it won't," Arik answered with a shrug.

"Are you for it, though?" persisted Call, an edge of irritation in his voice.

"Always preferred *doing* to *jawing*," answered Arik. "I say let's have at it."

"Then you'll lead the raid?" said Call.

"I could," said Arik, "but it's the southerner's plan, and I'll follow any man with the guts and the ice to walk into an enemy castle and spirit away a prisoner. Leaders need a little ice in their veins. They need to think coolly at all times. Me, I get carried away in the heat of battle. Let Kaelin Ring lead."

Call looked suddenly uncomfortable. "We are talking of the future of our clan," he said. "If we win, we gain time. If we lose, we are finished. I mean no disrespect to Kaelin Ring— for he has proved himself an exceptional warrior—but he is untried in battle and leadership."

"I disagree, Call," said Rayster. "I followed Kaelin's lead when we entered the fortress. If we are to try this hazardous plan, then I agree with Arik. Kaelin Ring is the man for it."

Kaelin saw Call glance down at the splint on his left arm and guessed that the Rigante chieftain was wishing he were strong enough to lead the attack himself. "Let us put it to the vote," said Call. "Those in favor of our friend Kaelin leading this attack raise their hands." Of the thirty men present, seventeen voted in favor, including Bael and Rayster.

"Then it is decided," said Call. He swung to Kaelin. "How soon?"

"Tomorrow night," answered Kaelin.

"Very well. This meeting is now over. Arik, will you join Kaelin and myself for a dram before you leave."

"I never say no to Uisge," said Arik.

For Alterith Shaddler the next twenty-four hours were filled with disappointment. Of the twelve businessmen left on the list, seven had left Eldacre unexpectedly, traveling south to Baracum. Four refused point blank to speak up for Maev Ring, and Gillam Pearce was "not available" to speak to the schoolteacher. His wife maintained that Gillam was ill with a fever.

Close to despair, Alterith sat in a small eating house, sharing a meal with Banny. The youngster had grown in the last year. Though still slim, he had strong shoulders, the legacy—though Alterith did not know it—of days spent with Jaim Grymauch, learning to fistfight and to wield a wooden sword. He was more confident now, especially after the fight in the summer with Kammel Bard. He had downed the Varlish youth three times, the last with a left hook that had spun Kammel from his feet and pitched him to the cobbles unconscious.

"There is still time, sir," Banny told the dispirited Alterith. "We have two more days."

"There is no one left to call, Banny. I am filled with despair—not just for the admirable lady but for the soul of the Varlish. I know the clans believe us to be cruel and spiteful, but there is in our race courage and nobility of spirit. To see so many of my people ready to lie for wealth, to see a good woman die in order that a few more coins can line their pockets—it is a disgrace, Banny."

"Those we saw today were not willing to lie for gain, sir. Could you not see that they were just too frightened to speak the truth?"

Alterith nodded. "I saw. They have been visited by the knights, who have filled their heads with tales of burning and retribution."

"I saw two of them today," said Banny. "They looked very fine with their white cloaks and their silver armor."

"They are—were—a fine order," Alterith told him. "I don't know what to make of them anymore. They are pledged to uphold the purity of the tree and to combat evil wherever they find it. Yet in the last few years I have heard tales of torture and murder. The knights, by the nature of their order, do not pledge allegiance to the king. And with the trouble in the south between the king and the covenanters, they are a law unto themselves now."

"What can we do?" asked Banny.

"I will return to Gillam Pearce. By all accounts he is an honest man. I cannot bring myself to believe he will allow Maev to face execution."

They finished their meal in silence. Alterith gave Banny

money to pay for the meal and left the eating house. It was dark as he stepped into the narrow street.

Three men emerged from the shadows. Alterith stood very still. All three wore white cloaks and silver helms.

"A word with you, schoolteacher," said the first.

"What can I do for you, sir?" asked Alterith.

"Step away from evil," he answered, "for a man is judged by the company he keeps, and the company of witches can lead only to the burning. The witch Ring will be punished. As will all those who seek to aid her in her dark ways."

"We must be talking of another Maev Ring," said Alterith. "The woman I know is a good woman with no pretensions to dark powers."

"I see that I am not making myself clear, Mr. Shaddler." He stepped in close. Something struck Alterith on the side of the head. He fell back against the wall, dizziness swamping him. A mailed fist hammered into his belly. Alterith fell to his knees, vomiting his meal to the cobbles. "If you approach Gillam Pearce, you will die. I promise this," said the man. "I tolerate no evil and crush it wherever I find it."

Alterith struggled to his feet. "If you . . . tolerate no evil," he said, "how is it that you can look in a mirror?"

The mailed fist struck him in the face, and he pitched once more to the ground, blood seeping from a cut under his right eye.

The three knights of the Sacrifice walked away. Alterith vomited once more. Banny found him there.

"What happened, sir?"

"Help me up." Banny lifted the skinny schoolteacher to his feet. "Fetch the pony and trap. I need to see Gillam Pearce tonight."

"Yes, sir."

Twenty minutes later Alterith, still shaken from his beating, pounded on the door of Gillam Pearce's house. His wife opened it. "I told you," she said, "my husband . . ." Her voice trailed away as she saw the blood on Alterith's cut and swollen face. "You are hurt," she said lamely. Alterith looked into her eyes. She was past middle age, her face lined and heavyset. But all traces of irritation had passed when she saw his wounds, and that showed Alterith that she had a kind heart.

"I was set upon, madam, by men who do not wish to see Maev Ring defended. I was told that if I came here, I would be killed."

"Then you should understand why my husband cannot help you."

"What I understand is that a great injustice is being perpetrated and a good woman—a woman like yourself—faces execution. I cannot let that pass. I will not be frightened into allowing such an evil."

"Bring him in, Ilda," came a voice from inside the house. " 'Tis too cold to talk on the doorstep."

Alterith stepped into the small living room. A fire was glowing in the hearth, and a small man was sitting before it. "Shall we compare wounds?" he asked, rising from his chair. Alterith saw that his left eye was black and swollen and there was a deep cut on the bridge of his nose.

"Bruises will heal," said Alterith. "They want to kill Maev Ring."

"I know, and that saddens me," said Gillam Pearce. "She is a fine, shrewd businesswoman. But what can I do, Master Shaddler? Fifteen upstanding citizens claim she bewitched them. If I say they are all liars, I will be ruined. No one will buy from me. Worse, when she is found guilty, I will be accused of being her accomplice, and then I will face the rope or the burning. So what is it you will ask of me? To stand up before the church and tell them the truth, though it destroys me?"

"Yes," said Alterith, "that is what I ask."

"And what would the purpose be, pray? We will not save Maev Ring."

"All trials are recorded, Master Pearce. Recorded for posterity, with the evidence sent on to the church authorities in Varingas. That is why the knights are so anxious that you do not speak. Not because you will make a difference to the verdict, which has already been bought and paid for by Jorain Feld, but because their infamy will be seen in your testimony. This trial is a sham, a mockery of all we should believe in. Someone needs to say that on the record. If Maev Ring must go to her death over this, then she should know she had loyal friends, men of honor and courage, men unafraid to speak the truth and shame the vile."

Gillam Pearce began to laugh.

"Have I said something to amuse you, sir?" Alterith asked stiffly.

"Of course you have, my friend. Look at us: a skinny schoolteacher and a small cobbler. What a terrifying army we make against the might of the church and the knights of the Sacrifice. We shall have them quaking in their boots."

"Then you will speak for Maev?"

Gillam moved to a small desk by the far wall. From a drawer he took a sheaf of papers. "This is my affidavit, sworn out three days ago and witnessed. Take it and keep it safe. It will still be admissible in evidence even if they do carry out their threat to kill me."

Alterith pushed the papers into the pocket of his coat. "I am in your debt, sir," he said.

"Not at all, Master Shaddler. I thank you for reminding me what honor means. I shall—if the Source is willing—be at the Holy Court."

◇ **17** ◇

KAELIN RING SAT on the ground, waiting for a break in the clouds. The weather had not favored the 322 men, and the night was pitch dark, with storm clouds rolling across the sky.

Arik Ironlatch moved alongside him. "What is your plan?" he asked.

Kaelin could scarcely make out the man's grizzled features. "We go down in squads of twenty," said Kaelin. "The ledges will not accommodate more. That is, of course, if the clouds break and give us the moon."

"They will or they won't," said Arik. "No point worrying about it."

Kaelin did not reply. His stomach was tight with worry, and there was little he could do about it. When they had first reached the peaks, there had been a little light and Kaelin had walked to the lip and gazed down. The rock face he had climbed late the previous day seemed doubly daunting now, dark and sheer, the trees far below. His confidence, so high when he had spoken at the meeting, was draining away by the moment. The wind was gusting, and there was the smell of rain in the air.

Climbing was perilous in good conditions, but to attempt a night descent was fraught with problems. In climbing up a man could see the holds just above him, but descending meant feeling one's way. The face was exposed. Billowing winds could dislodge a climber, or rain could make the holds slippery and treacherous.

Kaelin's mouth was dry. He pictured the climb, breaking it down in his mind. The ropes would help. There were a number of trees near the lip, and the men could lower themselves to the first of the ledges. He tried to recall if there were jutting rocks that would support ropes farther down. Then he realized that Arik was speaking again.

"So, how is my farm prospering?" he asked.

"Your farm?"

"The farm I sold to Maev Ring."

"It is making a good profit, sir," answered Kaelin.

"We don't 'sir' each other in the highlands," Arik told him. Then he chuckled. "That farm made no money for me. I danced for joy when I tricked your aunt into buying it for half again what it was worth. Now it is valued at six times what she paid for it. A shrewd woman is Maev Ring."

"Aye, she is." Just talking about the mundane realities of life away from war and peril relaxed Kaelin. He felt the tension and the fear easing out of him.

Arik leaned in. "Now tell me again what we are to do when we reach the ground."

"We wait for the dawn, and then you take a hundred men and charge the cannoneers. I will lead the rest against the main force," Kaelin told him, surprised that his voice sounded calm and confident.

"Then Call brings his men out of the pass?"

"Let's hope so," said Kaelin.

The clouds parted. Kaelin glanced up. Moonlight shone down upon the peaks, but the clouds were still thick and the light would not last long. Pushing himself to his feet, Kaelin gathered a rope and walked to the edge of the cliff. Gazing down, he could see the first ledge some forty feet below. Moving back from the edge, he tied the rope to the trunk of an old tree. Tossing the coil out over the cliff, he watched it snake down. While the moon was still bright he hooked another rope over his shoulder and lowered himself to the ledge. It was around four feet deep and thirty feet long. Kaelin scanned the area, seeking a jutting rock to which he could

belay the second rope. There was nothing. The moon vanished again, and Kaelin sat down quietly in the darkness
to wait.

His thoughts turned to Chara and her ordeal. He had not
seen her since she had walked into the great house and, despite his memories of his conversation with the Wyrd, had no
depth of understanding of her suffering. He hoped with all his
heart that as the days passed, she would rediscover her joy of
life. Then he recalled the words of Call Jace after he had
spoken with her.

"I thank you, Kaelin, for bringing my daughter home. You
are a good man and a brave one. I will always be in your debt.
I also want you to know that I will understand if you withdraw your offer of marriage."

Kaelin had sat silently, trying to make sense of the words.
Call misunderstood his silence. "I am sure Chara will understand, too," he said.

"I love her, Call. Nothing has changed for me. When she
recovers, we will wed as we planned. If that is what she
wants."

Call Jace placed his hand on Kaelin's shoulder. "Spoken
like a Rigante. We will see."

"I'd like to speak to her."

"She doesn't want to see anyone. Give her time, boy."

The wind gusted again, shrieking across the rocks. The
clouds broke, and within minutes the moon shone bright once
more. Kaelin looked at the heavens. Stars were glinting, the
sky beginning to clear.

The next ledge was sixty feet down and slightly to the
right. Kaelin swung the second rope from his shoulder and
tied it to the first with a reef knot. Dropping the coil, he
watched it fall. It dangled some five feet to the left of the
ledge below. Needing more ropes, he scaled the face, pulled
himself back over the lip of the peak, and strode back to
where Arik was sitting beside Rayster. It had surprised Kaelin
that the tall clansman had joined them, for he had made it
clear at the meeting that he had no wish to meet his doom on a

cliff face in the dark. "A man should always face his fears," was all Rayster had said.

Kaelin dropped down alongside the men. "I'll take another rope down. Watch for my signal and then let the men follow in groups of no more than twenty. The climb must be done as silently as possible. If we are discovered on the face, we'll be wiped out."

"We're not noisy climbers," said Arik. "We won't be singing battle songs."

"I know," said Kaelin. "What I am trying to say is that any man who falls must not cry out."

"They all know that, Kaelin," Arik said softly.

"Let the first of your climbers bring down more ropes. We'll need at least ten more." Kaelin turned to run his eyes over the waiting warriors. "Some of them still have scabbards at the hip," he said. "Get them all to loop them over their shoulders."

"I'll do that, General," Arik said with a wink.

Kaelin relaxed and smiled. "I must be the youngest general in Rigante history," he said.

"Bendegit Bran was about your age," said Arik. "And Bane was only a little older when he became a gladiator. We Rigante grow fast to manhood."

The sky was clear of clouds now, and Kaelin took a deep breath. "It is time," he said. Taking another rope, he returned to the edge and swung himself over. Once on the ledge, he signaled for the first of the climbers to follow him.

Rayster came down, bringing another rope. He reached the ledge and looked over at the forest hundreds of feet below. "I do not like this at all," he muttered.

"Warn the men that on the next drop they will need to swing across to the ledge. The rope is a little shy."

"Oh, what a nice thought," said Rayster.

Kaelin glanced up. "Best move aside," he warned. The second of the climbers was on his way down.

Once the first twenty had safely reached them, Kaelin lowered himself until he was alongside the second ledge. Gently swinging on the rope until he was above it, he dropped to the shelf of rock. Signaling Rayster and the others to wait, he examined the area. Here there was a chimneylike fissure, and within it a small column of stone some three feet high. Belaying another rope around it, he tied it securely and watched as the coil unraveled on its fall to the next shelf of rock. From here he could not see how far down the rope hung. It seemed, though, that it was shy of the ledge. Kaelin waved to catch Rayster's attention and gestured him down.

The clansman came down smoothly, then swung on the rope as Kaelin had done. Only he did not let go as his feet swung over the ledge. Kaelin saw that he was very pale, his knuckles white as they gripped the rope. Panic was on him, and he could not let go. He swung back and forth over the dizzying drop.

"Rayster, listen to me. You will not fall. I will catch you. You hear me?"

"Damned hands won't obey me," said Rayster. He was sweating and staring down into the darkness.

"Look at me!" Rayster's eyes met his. "Keep looking at me." Kaelin held out his hand. "Now swing, and when I tell you, release the rope. I will catch you. Trust me, Rayster."

"I'm not sure that I can do it."

"I am sure," Kaelin said softly. "You are a brave man, and you *are* facing your fears. Now we are going to climb down this cliff, and we are going to smite the enemy. We are going to fight for the Rigante and avenge Chara. So start to swing."

Rayster pushed his feet against the rock face. The rope groaned as he swung back and forth.

"Now!" said Kaelin.

Rayster let go and cannoned into Kaelin, almost knocking him from his feet. Rayster stumbled and fell. Kaelin reached out, grabbing his shirt and hauling him back from the edge. The clansman's face was ghostly white.

"Breathe deeply and slowly," said Kaelin.

"I am all right. I'll not panic again."

"Wait here," said Kaelin, taking the coiled rope from

Rayster's shoulder. Then he lowered himself onto the face, moving down hand over hand.

The first rope ended some eight feet short of the shelf. Kaelin found a foothold and steadied himself against the face. The wind was blowing strong over the exposed rock. Kaelin played out a little of Rayster's rope, then looped the remainder back over his shoulder. Adjusting his feet more securely, he half turned his body and slowly tied the two ropes together. Once the reef knot was tight, he dropped the coil to the ledge and climbed down.

As the night wore on, Kaelin slowly moved down the rock face, tying ropes to jutting rocks so that the clansmen could follow. At last he reached the chimney fissure above the final ledge. Rayster swung down to join him and stared gloomily down into the pitch darkness of the chimney. "It looks worse than it is," said Kaelin. "There are handholds and footholds aplenty. Then there is one last ledge. After that it is the soft earth of the forest—and the cannon and muskets of the Beetlebacks."

"I shall never climb again," said Rayster. "I feel I have used up just about all the luck I have."

Above them the majority of the 320 warriors were on the face.

Five hours had passed since the climb had begun, and Kaelin estimated that at least that much time again would be used up. Carefully he climbed down the chimney, not using the rope. Rayster followed him.

A sound came to them, a wet thud followed instantly by a loud crack. Then another. Something dark swept past the opening of the chimney. Kaelin could not see what it was. Perhaps someone had dropped a rope or dislodged a rock.

Emerging from the chimney to the ledge, Kaelin saw a dark stain on the lip of the rock. Then he looked over the edge. Two bodies were lying on the rocks, limbs splayed grotesquely.

Kaelin fastened the last rope around a large rock. Rayster emerged. "Time to feel solid ground again," said Kaelin.

Rayster gave a tight smile. "Not before time. It will be pleasant to be the first to the forest."

"You will not be the first," Kaelin said softly. "Two men fell."

Rayster swore. "I'll see you below," he said. Swinging his legs out over the edge, he disappeared from sight.

Kaelin did not follow him. Instead he scaled the chimney again, climbing swiftly. When he emerged once more into the moonlight, he saw that a rope had given way on the ledge above. Clansmen were huddled there, with others clinging to the rope above, unable to descend. Kaelin untied the rope Rayster had used to descend the chimney, drew it up, and coiled it swiftly. Looping it over his shoulder, he climbed to the ledge. His limbs were tired as he reached the lip, but the ledge was packed with men and there was no room for him to clamber over.

He could see the jagged end of the sheared rope. It had rubbed against a sharp edge on the lip and given way. Clinging to the rock face, Kaelin thought the problem through. The new rope would also grind against the lip, and with a mass of men filling the ledge he could not seek out any other means of securing the rope. A man stumbled above him, and for a moment it seemed he would fall. A comrade grabbed him. Kaelin eased himself up until his arms were over the ledge. Then he carefully tied the end of the new rope to the severed section of the first and dropped the coil down the face. He glanced up at the nearest man. He was short and slim, and his face showed his fear. "Pick up the rope and pass it to the man beside you," said Kaelin. "Carefully now!" There was no room to bend, and the man slowly went into a squat, retrieving the rope. Slowly and smoothly he rose, passing the rope to a bigger man beside him. "Loop it over your right shoulder and down around both hips. Hold it firmly." The big man did so, and the rope slid along the lip to a more rounded section of stone. "You need to hold it there as the men climb down. Do not allow it to slip left or right. You understand?"

"Aye," said the big man.

"When you start getting tired, pass on the duty to another." Kaelin glanced at the clansman closest to the rope and the edge. "You climb down now," he said. "When you reach the ledge below, you will see a fissure. Move into it. There will be no rope, but it is an easy climb. Start now!"

The warrior took hold of the rope and swung himself over the edge, descending swiftly. Then another man followed him, and another. Soon the ledge began to clear, allowing the climbers above to descend. Kaelin returned to the chimney, climbed swiftly down it, then lowered himself to the forest, where Rayster and several others were waiting.

The bodies of the two clansmen had been covered by cloaks.

"Were they friends of yours?" asked Kaelin.

"All Rigante are my friends," said Rayster. "One of them was my cousin. A good man. Four sons, two daughters. The other I could not recognize. He must have struck the ground headfirst. There are bits of skull and brain everywhere."

Three hours later 140 clansmen were gathered close to the foot of the cliff. Many were sleeping, wrapped in their cloaks; others sat watching their comrades slowly descending the great cliff.

Arik Ironlatch joined Kaelin. The old man looked weary. He patted Kaelin on the shoulder, then walked away and swung his sword and scabbard from between his shoulders. Lying down on the ground, he rested his head on his arm and fell asleep.

All the men were tired, and Kaelin wondered how much strength they would have come the dawn.

Banarin Ranaud's dreams were never happy ones. For as long as he could remember he had dreamed about being trapped underground, the walls around him writhing and swelling and thick with slime. Unable to stand on the shifting ground, he would crawl on hands and knees, repeating over and over again: "I will be good, Mama. I will be good. I promise."

Upon waking, he would at first be relieved, but then there would always follow a fierce and terrible anger.

It had never mattered how good he was as a child, how much effort he made to please her. Invariably she would drag him to the cellar, shouting and screaming at him. Then she would lock him in the old, discarded closet and leave him in the dark, listening to the sound of rats scampering across the dusty floor outside.

But this dream was different.

The writhing walls contracted, the slime covering him. Pressure on his body propelled it through the narrowing confines of his prison until he tumbled against something hard and unyielding. He heard a door close, a lock being fastened. "I will be good, Mama!" he yelled.

There was no light at first, but then he saw a faint glow begin close to his face. He tried to back away from it, but the closet was small. The glow became a twisted face. There was a bloody gaping hole where the right eye should have been.

"Such a bad, bad boy," said Colonel Linax. As he spoke, several bloated maggots fell from his blue lips.

Banarin Ranaud screamed—and sat bolt upright.

His breathing was fast and ragged, and he stared panic-stricken at the canvas walls of his small tent. Rolling from his blankets, he scrambled out into the predawn light. The ground was wet beneath his feet, soaking the thick socks he wore. Gazing around, he saw the sentries patrolling near the picket lines, the cannoneers sleeping by small fires set behind every cannon. Already some of the men were emerging from their tents, and there were breakfast fires burning.

Colonel Ranaud ducked back into his tent and removed the wet socks. He sat on his blankets, still shaken by the dream. Truth was, he regretted the murder of Colonel Linax. The man had been kind to him, and kindness was something Ranaud had little experience of. At first he had been content to wait for Linax to die of the lung disease that was rotting his body from within. Yet the man had clung to life for month after weary month. And all the while—as Ranaud saw it—the

Black Rigante were growing stronger and more confident. Sooner or later there had to be a reckoning. Wullis Swainham's reports claimed that Call Jace had ordered the construction of a new forge capable of producing bigger cannons. Ranaud had begged Linax to write to the Moidart for more men in order to lead an assault on Jace's stronghold. Linax had refused. "We would need thousands of soldiers, Banarin. Even if we breach their gates, they will fall back to the mountains within. There will be no major battles but a long war of attrition. The cost of maintaining an army in the north would empty the Moidart's treasury within two months. Only the king could supply a standing army in this area, and he has troubles of his own in the south. And even had he not, Call Jace has done nothing yet that would convince the king he needs to be exterminated."

Banarin Ranaud had spent a great deal of time considering just what action of Jace's might alert the Moidart—and the king—to his infamy.

That was when the plan had occurred to him. If Call Jace were to murder Colonel Linax while under a flag of truce, it would send a clear message to the south that he was an enemy of the state. The king would be forced to act. Linax had many friends in Varingas.

Ranaud planned the murder with meticulous care. He told Linax that Wullis Swainham had come to him with a request from Call Jace for a meeting. Jace, it seemed, was under pressure from his fiery clan chiefs to start a war. He was seeking ways to avert such a calamity and needed to discuss them with Colonel Linax. It was vital, however, that he and Linax should meet in secret.

Linax had agreed and had ordered Ranaud to conduct negotiations as to where and when the meeting should take place.

They had ridden from the barracks at dusk five days later, heading west before cutting into the forest. Linax had been exhausted as they had dismounted in a small clearing. He had coughed blood into his handkerchief, then had slumped down beside a stream. Ranaud had drawn his pistol and cocked it, walking swiftly to where the colonel sat. As Linax had looked up, Ranaud had leveled the pistol and fired, the ball slamming through Linax's eye and exploding out through the back of his skull.

Leaving Linax's horse behind, Ranaud had ridden at speed back to the barracks, where he had relayed the news of Call Jace's treachery. Then he had sent a dispatch to the Moidart.

Now, with four thousand men under his command and a full regiment of the king's musketeers on their way, he was about to achieve the fame and glory that would once and for all put to rest his mother's prediction. "You are a useless creature, Banarin, stupid and weak. You will amount to nothing in this life. You understand? Nothing! You are a worm. And worms live in the dark."

Ranaud pulled on his boots and buckled on his black breastplate. Today he would ride the twelve miles to the other encampment to ensure that discipline was being maintained. He was sure that Call Jace would attack. The escape of his daughter was a setback, but when Jace learned of her ordeal, he would be filled with rage. He would *need* revenge. Passion was the one great virtue of the highland race but also its greatest weakness. Jace would have to seek battle. The only question that remained was which pass he would choose to sally forth from.

Ranaud had two thousand men at each pass. Both groups were equipped with twenty cannons loaded with canister shot. When Jace did attack, at least half his men would be wiped out in the first volley.

The colonel emerged from his tent and stared up at the entrance to Jace's stronghold. Six hundred yards of open ground stretched from his cannons to the mouth of the pass. In the time it would take charging men to cover the distance his cannoneers could load and fire twice. It would be a massacre, and Ranaud's fame would be established.

Banarin Ranaud, the Hammer of the North. He liked the sound of it.

A trumpet sounded, the notes shrill in the cold morning air. The dawn was breaking, and he saw men streaming out from their tents. Ranaud moved swiftly across the camp, heading toward the cannons. He did not run, for such haste would look unseemly in the commanding officer.

The artillerymen were dragging the oiled canvas covers from the huge, flaring barrels of their cannons, while other men stoked up the fires behind each weapon. Ranaud reached them and saw the reason for the trumpet call.

Hundreds of armed men were gathering in the pass. They were out of range at the moment.

"Ready the formation!" ordered Ranaud. Officers relayed his orders. Cavalrymen ran for their mounts, saddling them swiftly. Musketeers gathered in line behind the cannons. Ranaud returned to his tent, loading his two pistols.

Today he would see glory.

Strapping on his saber, he pushed his pistols into his belt.

By the time he returned to the front line his six hundred cavalry lancers had ridden out to the right flank, ready to sweep down on the charging clansmen. Seven hundred musketeers marched toward the left flank and the forest. They, too, would send a hail of shot into the highlanders.

Three hundred musketeers remained stationed behind the cannons just in case any highlanders should reach the line.

The soldiers moved smoothly into position, the musketeers on the left flank forming two lines, one kneeling and one standing. The commanding officer gave the order to load. The musketeers opened the black pouches at their hips and removed the egg-shaped powder flasks.

A thunderous volley came from the trees. Scores of musketeers went down. Ranaud stood rooted in shock. Black smoke from the volley was billowing in the trees. The stunned survivors of the musketeers were huddling together around the bodies of their comrades.

Then the highlanders charged from the forest, rushing into the demoralized musketeers. Sabers and knives ripped into the soldiers, who panicked and began to stream back toward the apparent safety of the center. The highlanders raced after them, hacking and slashing.

Ranaud swung to see the musketeers behind him desperately trying to bring their weapons to bear, but their line of fire was blocked by their own fleeing soldiers. Chaos descended on the battlefield. The panicking soldiers ran into their own lines, obstructing their comrades, while the highlanders swarmed after them, shrieking battle cries. Ranaud saw a white-haired and grizzled warrior slashing his saber through the throat of a cannoneer. At that moment Ranaud also saw something infinitely more terrifying. The main body of the highland army had emerged from the pass and was running silently toward them.

"Fire the cannons!" yelled Ranaud.

But it was impossible. The routed musketeers, in their desperation to get away from the ferocious assault from the forest, had spilled out through the gaps in the line of cannon and were directly in the line of fire.

A highlander ran at Ranaud. Dragging a pistol clear, he discharged it into the face of the attacker, who was smashed from his feet. Some of his own musketeers began to shoot. Several highlanders went down. Others scrambled across the bodies, hurling themselves at the soldiers. Despite being vastly outnumbered, the highlanders had all the advantages now. Musketeers were invaluable only as long as the enemy could be kept at bay by volley fire. At close quarters, without knives or swords, they were virtually defenseless.

Ranaud ran toward the right flank, signaling furiously for his cavalry to intercept the charging highlanders. Then he swung back just in time to see two more highlanders bearing down on him. He shot the first, who staggered and fell. Throwing away his pistol, Ranaud wrenched his saber from its scabbard, blocking a fierce overhand cut and sending a slashing riposte across the attacker's face. The man stumbled. Ranaud plunged his blade through his chest.

Then he saw Kaelin Ring. Their eyes met. Ring ran at him. At that moment a musketeer fired. The ball sent a spray of blood from Ring's hip. The highlander was spun in a half circle. Ranaud charged in. Ring recovered his balance and parried the thrust. Ranaud rolled his wrist, his blade slipping over Ring's saber and lancing toward the highlander's throat. Ring swayed back and slashed his own blade in a ferocious cut that cannoned off Ranaud's breastplate and up across his right cheek, slicing the skin. Ranaud fell back. Ring followed him. Ranaud was an expert swordsman, but the ferocity and speed of Ring's assault were astonishing. Ranaud desperately parried and blocked. A cannon fired, then another.

We can still win, thought Ranaud.

Ring attacked again. Ranaud parried and launched a counter, his saber spearing toward Ring's heart. Ring swayed to his right, Ranaud's blade slipping by him. Pain exploded in Ranaud's chest as Ring's saber slid between his ribs. Ranaud grunted and fell back. His legs were weak and gave way. As he hit the ground, another cannon fired. Through a gap in the ranks of fighting men he saw that it was not his cannoneers who were discharging the cannons. The highlanders had swung several artillery pieces and had sent a murderous volley of canister into the charging cavalry. Scores of men and horses littered the ground.

Ranaud tried to rise, but he had no strength. His face was resting against the hard earth, and he could smell the mustiness of the soil.

"You are a worm, Banarin," he heard his mother say, "and worms live in the dark."

The surviving cavalrymen fled toward the north. The musketeers tried to follow, but they were pursued by clansmen whose blades were hungry for blood. What had begun as a battle and then had become an instant rout was now a massacre.

Call Jace strode across the corpse-littered area, Arik Ironlatch beside him. The older man's clothes and hair were blood-spattered, but his face was calm. They came across the body of Colonel Ranaud. Call flipped him to his back. "I'd like to have killed him myself," he said.

Rising to his feet, Call stared out toward the north. Clansmen had reached the far hill and were still pursuing the remnants of the musketeers. The Rigante chief swung around. Arik Ironlatch was kneeling beside Kaelin Ring. Fear touched Call then, and he ran to where the body lay.

"Is he dead?" he asked.

"Close to it," said Arik. "He has two wounds: one above the hip and one high in the back."

Call swore. "Plug them as best you can. We'll have him carried back to the valley."

Arik nodded. "Best you summon the men back, Call," he said. "Them cavalry might turn again and catch our boys in the open."

Call walked away. Bael was standing with Rayster by one of the captured cannons. "Sound the recall," said Call. A long, black horn was hanging from Bael's shoulder. He swung it to the front and lifted it to his lips. A single eerie and melancholy note echoed through the hills. Bael repeated it three times.

When the last note faded away, Bael looked at his father and grinned. "We won," he said.

"Aye, now let us count the cost," replied Call. "Arrange stretcher parties to carry our wounded back and number the dead."

Both young men moved away. Call gazed around the battlefield. Hundreds of musketeers lay where they had fallen, but the Rigante chief saw few Rigante corpses. Even so his mood was dark. This victory would merely delay the inevitable. With five thousand of the king's soldiers on their way and another two thousand men at the second pass, there was little hope of sustained success. Ranaud had seen to that with the murder of Linax. A few thousand Rigante could never stand against the full might of the Varlish.

Several men came by, leading captured horses. The men were laughing and joking with one another. Call moved past them. The tents of the Varlish were still standing, and Call could smell soup. He strolled to one of the cookfires. A cauldron of broth was bubbling there.

An hour earlier the men, now dead, had been looking forward to breakfast.

Now it was the crows and the foxes who would feast. Aye, and later the worms, Call thought darkly. To the rear of the camp was a picket line and a group of wagons. Some twenty ponies were tethered there.

Call's broken arm was paining him as he turned back toward the cannons. As he picked his way through the bodies, he heard someone moan. Glancing down, he saw a young musketeer, barely more than a boy, who had been stabbed in the belly, his entrails beside him on the ground. Call drew his dirk and cut the boy's jugular. "Should have stayed home a while longer with your mam," he said. With a sigh Call heaved himself to his feet.

Rayster and Bael returned. "We lost just seventeen men," said Bael. "Another thirty-three wounded, only six badly. It was a great victory, Father."

"Aye, it was," said Call, forcing a smile. He had no wish to dent their pride or let them know how hollow this victory would feel in a month's time. He looked at Rayster. "Gather some men and collect the Varlish stores and weapons. Get them back to the valley. I doubt the enemy will march against us today. But they might, so do it swiftly. Bael, you organize the movement of the cannons. Use the captured horses to haul half of them back into the pass. The other ten should be taken to bolster our northern defenses."

"Prisoners, Father," said Bael, pointing back to the hills. Clansmen were herding around twenty musketeers down to the low ground.

"Have them brought to me," said Call.

Rayster ran across to the men guarding the musketeers. Moments later the prisoners shuffled forward to stand before Call Jace. Their eyes were fearful. Some were trembling, and one man's breeches were stained with urine.

"I bear you no hatred," said Call, "and not one of you will be harmed. So relax now. Many of your comrades are wounded. Some will die. Others can still be saved. I will leave you two wagons and some supplies. Tend the wounded, then get them away from here."

With that he turned away from the astonished prisoners and strode to where Arik Ironlatch was supervising the stretcher men. They lifted the unconscious Kaelin and began to carry him away.

"You think he will live?" asked Call.

"He will or he won't," said Arik.

"I don't know why I bother to ask you anything," muttered Call.

"You are in a sour mood," observed Arik. "Do you know why?"

"Of course I know why."

"Aye, so do I, Call Jace. You are getting ahead of yourself, man. Tomorrow's evils are not our concern now. There is nothing we can do about them. So enjoy the day. It was hard won."

"Seventeen clansmen are dead, Arik. Seventeen men with families and loved ones."

"I know that, Call. Saeka was one of them. He fell from the cliff in the night. I did not know until the dawn."

Call gave out a deep sigh and laid his hand upon Arik's shoulder. "Your son was a fine man. I liked him greatly. I mourn with you, Arik."

"Fathers should not outlive sons, Call. It is against the order of nature. My heart is broken, but I will still enjoy this day. You hear me? On this day Rigante courage overcame the might of the Varlish. We did not yield. We did not beg for mercy. So I am proud today, Call. Proud of my son and proud of my people. I like to think that somewhere, far along the Swan's Path, Connavar is proud, too, and Bane, and Calofair, and all the heroes of the Rigante." There were tears in the old man's eyes, and his voice broke.

Call felt his tension and brooding fears drain away.

"Tonight we'll get drunk together," he said. "I have a cask of forty-year-old Uisge. We'll toast the fallen and salute the day."

Arik brushed the tears from his eyes. "Aye," he said, "we'll do that."

The first morning of the trial of Maev Ring was filled with legal arguments concerning the presentation of evidence, the legality of the affidavit of Gillam Pearce, and the presence of two clerics hired by Alterith Shaddler to document the statements of witnesses.

The Holy Court's galleries were packed, and twenty armed guards stood by the entrances and exits. The bishop, in ceremonial robes of purple and white, sat at the center of the judgment table, flanked by three senior abbots and two court-appointed clerics.

The first news of the day was that the body of the boot-maker Gillam Pearce had been discovered in a side street that morning. He had been disemboweled and beheaded.

Alterith Shaddler had learned this only when presenting Gillam's affidavit to the court.

"The affidavit is signed and witnessed," said Alterith, "and according to the law can still be recorded. I also have statements from the witnesses testifying that the affidavit is exactly as Gillam wrote it. It cannot be denied." He glanced across at the four knights of the Sacrifice who were standing alongside the judgment table. Turning to face them, he continued: "The fact that vile and evil men, seeking to pervert the cause of truth and justice, have murdered him should not prevent his statement being heard."

The bishop lifted a gavel and hammered it three times on a wooden block. "You will address the judgment panel, Master Shaddler."

"Which judgment panel would that be, my lord?" replied Alterith. "The panel of the Holy Court or the panel of murderers who stand alongside it?"

"How dare you?" thundered the leader of the knights, stepping forward, his hand on the hilt of his sword.

"Here is my head," shouted Alterith Shaddler, touching his brow, "and here is my belly. I doubt you have the courage to strike either while witnesses are present, you vile cur! You are a disgrace to the armor you wear. You are abhorrent to me—and to every Varlish who entertains notions of honor."

"Be silent!" raged the bishop. "One more outburst, Master Shaddler, and I shall have you removed from the court."

Alterith, white-faced and trembling, took several deep breaths. Then he bowed to the bishop. "The affidavit of Gillam Pearce is hereby offered in evidence according to the law."

The bishop gestured to Arlin Bedver. The potbellied cleric rose and bowed. "Do you have any objection to the affidavit being presented?" asked the bishop.

"No, my lord. The law is the law. However, the observation I would make is that since there will be no opportunity to question Master Pearce, there is no way to tell whether the affidavit was made while under the bewitchment of the accused."

"True," said the bishop. "Let it be recorded, then."

Alterith stepped forward and placed the scroll on the judgment table. The bishop glared at him balefully.

"Tell me, Master Shaddler," he said, "why there are two clerics scribbling at your table."

"They are documenting all that is said, my lord."

"We already have clerics attending to that task. Are you suggesting they are not to be trusted?"

"Not at all, my lord. It would be churlish in the extreme to suggest that this panel was so corrupt that it would doctor the evidence to see an innocent woman convicted. It would be unseemly of me to even hint at such a grotesque perversion of justice."

"Then why do you have clerics at your table?" asked the bishop, ignoring the heavy sarcasm in Alterith's comments.

Alterith Shaddler returned to his table and lifted a heavy

tome. Finding the marker, he opened the pages. "According to clause twenty-six, Chapter Seven, of the Articles of Holy Law, an advocate may hire up to three clerics to record the evidence. This is, apparently, to offset any honest mistake made by court-appointed scribes. It is my intention to send all documents to Varingas so that the events of these proceedings achieve a far wider audience."

Maev Ring stood quietly during the discussions, her wrists chained, her lungs burning with the smoke from the incense pots carried by the priests alongside her.

"May it please the court," said Arlin Bedver, "I wish at this time to present a petition from Sir Gayan Kay of the Holy Order of the Sacrifice."

"Do so," said the bishop.

Alterith surged to his feet. "I object, my lord," he said.

"How can you object when you haven't heard the nature of the petition?" asked the bishop.

"These knights have no knowledge of Maev Ring and are strangers to Eldacre. What, then, can they bring to this trial?"

"Let us hear the petition and find out," replied the bishop.

"Thank you, my lord," said Arlin Bedver. "Sir Gayan offers to use his considerable expertise and experience to test Maev Ring. He has in the past elicited confessions from witches, bringing a speedy conclusion to such affairs, thus saving the courts both time and expense."

Alterith's laughter pealed out. "Are you now suggesting that these . . . monsters . . . be allowed to torture Madam Ring into a confession? Have you no shame, Master Bedver?"

"That comment will not be recorded!" stormed the bishop.

"All comments are recorded, my lord," said Alterith. "I would have thought that the mountain of lies already gathered to support this trial would be enough for Mr. Bedver. Such, it seems, is not the case."

His face crimson, the bishop rose to his feet. "I find your comments discourteous to this court," he said. "And I sentence you to twenty lashes, this sentence to be carried out when the trial is over. Any more outbursts and I will add to that sentence. Do you understand that, Mr. Shaddler?"

"I do, my lord." Alterith sat down and began to leaf through the Book of Holy Law. Arlin Bedver continued with his petition, bringing forward Sir Gayan Kay to explain the nature of the tests he would use to get the truth from Maev Ring. Alterith made no move to interrupt but continued to study the tome before him.

Sir Gayan Kay, in full ornamental armor of silver plate, his broadsword by his side, told the court that witches were always demon-possessed and that the only way to reach the truth was to drive the demon—albeit temporarily—from the body. That was done by the application of pain. Demons, being cowardly by nature, could not tolerate such pain, which left the human host able to answer questions with honesty.

Alterith tried to shut his ears to the nonsense as he scanned page after page of the Book of Holy Law. Finally he found the section he needed. It came under the heading "Trials by Ordeal." He read it swiftly.

Sir Gayan concluded his statement and stepped back. The bishop conferred with the two abbots. Then he spoke. "We will allow Sir Gayan to conduct his examination this afternoon," he said.

Alterith rose. "May it please the court, I refer once more to Holy Law. Questioning under ordeal can take place only with the consent of the civilian authorities. Therefore, no questioning under physical duress can take place without the permission of the Moidart. Any such questioning undertaken without permission would be in breach of the law, with the results voided."

"With the court's permission," said Arlin Bedver, "I could petition the Moidart for approval."

Alterith watched the bishop intently. The Moidart had already found Maev Ring innocent of all charges. The bishop knew that. An application to the Moidart would almost certainly be refused.

"That will not be necessary, Master Bedver," he said at

last. "We will delay no longer. Are your witnesses ready to give evidence?"

"They are, my lord."

"Then let us move on."

By the evening recess Alterith's early jubilation at his successes had been severely dented. Five witnesses had so far given evidence against Maev Ring, their testimony—at least to Alterith Shaddler—appearing ludicrous in the extreme. One man had spoken of dreaming of a white goat that spoke to him following the afternoon when Maev Ring had become his partner. After that, he said, he had felt compelled to abstain from church and was filled with the desire to frequent brothels.

What surprised Alterith, who felt like laughing out loud, was that no one in the galleries seemed to find the evidence amusing. The audience sat in grim silence, listening intently to the evidence.

"How many dreams did you have of this white goat?" asked Alterith.

"Several," replied the witness, a thin man named Nade Holder, a carpet maker from the northern quarter.

"And at what point did you begin to believe that the goat dream was a direct result of your partnership with Maev Ring?"

"I don't understand."

"Shall I speak more slowly?"

"I was bewitched by her," said Holder. "She cast a spell to steal my business."

"Would it surprise you, Mr. Holder, were I to tell you that I have statements claiming you have been visiting whorehouses for years?"

The man blinked and licked his lips. "But not as often as I have done since the spell was cast," he said.

"So it was not a spell that first sent you to prostitutes?"

"It was the devil tempting me," said Holder. He pointed at Maev Ring. "She is a servant of the Devil."

"When did this become apparent to you? Two years ago

when first she supplied you with capital to expand your business? A year ago when you began making handsome profits? When exactly?"

Holder looked uncomfortable. "I suppose it was when Parsis Feld died. Yes, around that time."

"After you had spoken to Jorain Feld?"

"About the same time, yes."

"I see. So it was not when you dreamed of goats, or when you were rutting with whores, or when you were counting the large profits you had made from Maev Ring's business acumen. How very revealing, Master Holder. How much do you expect to profit by this prosecution? Will it be worth ten pounds to you? A hundred? How much?"

"I never gave it a moment's thought," said Holder. "I am only here to do my civic duty."

Alterith laughed scornfully. "You are scum, Holder. Of the worst kind. You are an ingrate and a liar, a whorer and a villain."

"Here, he can't talk to me like that!" said the outraged Holder.

"Indeed he cannot," said the bishop. "You will apologize for that outburst, Mr. Shaddler."

"I would sooner dine on dog's vomit," Shaddler told him.

"Another twenty lashes will be your reward, you impudent rascal!"

"Thank you, my lord. I have no more questions for this witness. He may now crawl back under the rock whence he came."

"And another twenty!" shouted the bishop.

The following morning Arlin Bedver called Jorain Feld to the stand. Feld was a sallow-faced individual in his late twenties. Tall and stooping, he stood in the witness box, his long thin hands clasped together as if in prayer. His voice was deep and sepulchral. Under Bedver's questioning he told how his father, Parsis, had become a changed man in the years after he had been partnered with Maev Ring. He had taken to strong drink and to visiting houses of low repute. His language had coarsened, and he had begun to gamble heavily. Once, while drunk, he had told Jorain that he had "sold his soul for the sake of his business."

In cross-examination Alterith asked him at what point he had begun to believe that witchcraft was responsible for his father's condition.

"As soon as we discovered he had given half of his business to an ill-bred highlander," he answered.

"I see. Why was it, then, that when you petitioned the Moidart, you said nothing about witchcraft? You asked the Moidart to rule on the legality of the business dealings. You suggested that Maev Ring might be guilty of owning pistols. But not sorcery, Master Feld. Why was that?"

"I don't have to answer to you," Feld told him.

"You do, Master Feld. That is the beauty of the Varlish legal system. While you stand in that box, you will answer to me, and to Mr. Bedver, and to the bishop and his panel. Later you will answer to a higher authority. One day, Master Feld, you will stand before the Source of All, and you will answer him, too."

"My conscience is clear. The woman bewitched my father. She will pay for it."

"Do you support the church, Master Feld?"

"I do."

"Have you made donations to it?"

"Yes."

"When was the most recent, and for how much?"

"I do not see what that has to do with anything," answered Feld, transferring his gaze to the bishop.

"Nor do I," said the bishop. "Where is this leading, Master Shaddler?"

"It is my understanding that Master Feld made a donation of five hundred pounds on the day that Maev Ring was arrested, my lord. I find the timing interesting and wished to see that it was placed on record."

The bishop sat very quietly, and a silence fell over the courtroom. "Are you suggesting," the bishop said at last, "that Maev Ring's arrest was bought for five hundred pounds? Are you accusing me of corruption?"

"What I am doing, my lord, is ensuring that *all* relevant information is being recorded. I have no doubts as to the initial outcome of this abominable action. I also have great faith in the Varlish system, which despite what many in this area believe to be iniquitous and cruel, is based on principles of justice and truth. Truth has a habit of making itself known no matter how well it is hidden within an army of falsehood and deceit. The truth will come out, my lord."

"You sanctimonious wretch!" shouted the bishop. "I've had my fill of you." He signaled to the guards at the rear of the building. "Take this man out and administer twenty lashes to his back. By heaven, I want to see blood on him when he returns!"

Alterith was removed from the Holy Court and taken to the rear of the building. He was allowed to remove his coat and shirt, then his hands were tied to a stake. A guard appeared alongside, holding a small strip of leather. "Put this between your teeth, sir," he whispered. "It will stop you from biting your tongue." Alterith bit down on the leather. The guard put his mouth close to Alterith's ear. "I am sorry for this, sir. I'll go as easy as I can. You're a good man."

Alterith tried to count the strokes, but searing pain made him lose all sense of reason. Somewhere during the lashing the leather fell from his mouth, and he began to scream with each stroke. At the end he was hanging by his thin wrists and sobbing like a child.

The guards helped him to his feet. One sponged his back. "Steady yourself now, sir," the guard said gently. "We'll not let the air get to the wounds. I've sent for some wine and honey. We'll dab that on."

Alterith felt humiliated by his screams and tears. "I am not a brave man," he said. "I'm not good with pain."

"Don't you worry about it, sir. There's all kinds of bravery.

I haven't the balls to stand in front of the bishop and speak like you have. Don't talk yourself down."

The second guard returned and bathed Alterith's back. The mixture of wine and honey stung at first, but then the pain eased. The first guard helped him put on his shirt and coat.

The sounds of hammering filtered through from beyond the cathedral.

"What is that noise?" asked Alterith.

"They're building the scaffold and pyre to burn Maev Ring," said the guard. "We're told it will be the day after to-morrow at noon."

Alterith's head dropped, and he felt close to tears once more. "We'd best be getting back, sir," said the guard.

"I am so ashamed," said Alterith.

"No need to be, sir. Most men cry out when the lash strikes."

"You misunderstand me. I am ashamed of being Varlish."

Despite the pain from his raw back, Alterith cross-examined each of the prosecution witnesses during the long afternoon and early evening, asking each of them the current state of his businesses and the condition it enjoyed before the arrival of Maev Ring. When faced with prevarication, he produced figures showing the level of tax paid before and after Maev Ring's involvement.

It was dark, the night wind cold, as he walked back to the lodgings he had taken during the trial. As he had told the doomed Gillam Pearce, there was little chance that his advocacy would sway the judgment panel. Its decision had been made before the first words had been spoken at the trial itself. Even so he had retained the faintest of hopes that decency would prevail. He knew now that this was not so.

There was, he saw now, an institutional evil at work, the might of which could not be overcome. The fat bishop was a corrupt lecher, the abbots at his side career clerics borne upon whichever wind would carry them to comfort and riches. The dread knights of the Sacrifice were killers who hid behind a shield of apparent sanctity. Yet by far the most depressing aspect for Alterith was the evidence offered by the many witnesses. These were ordinary men fueled only by greed. Where, he wondered, in all of this could he find any indications of Varlish nobility of spirit?

The face of Gillam Pearce appeared in his mind. Yes, he thought. One good man.

He trudged on through the dingy alleyways. His back was a sea of fire, and it was lucky, he thought, that he had no intention of sleeping this night. There was too much to do. He had only one witness on the morrow, but after that he would give his summation. It was mostly written out already in his mind, but he felt it needed more power. He could not sway the panel, but his words, when they reached the authorities in Varingas, must be coherent and compelling.

It was while thinking this that he crossed the last road before the lodging house.

As he did so, two figures emerged from the shadows. One grabbed his arm, and the other cracked a fist into his face. Half-stunned, Alterith Shaddler was hauled from the road and into an alley. The side door of his lodging house was within sight, but there was no light shining above it.

In the moonlight he looked upon the faces of two of the knights of the Sacrifice. The men were not wearing armor now but were dressed in black clothes, more suited, he found himself thinking, to the dark deed they planned.

Alterith was thrown against a wall. Strangely, this dulled the pain from the lashing. Both men had drawn knives.

"You were warned about the evil of your ways," said the first. "You did not heed the warning. Your fate was in your own hands, and you chose death. Now you will pay for the corruption of your soul."

"How can you use those words?" asked Alterith, amazed that his voice did not quaver. "Can you really believe that the Source favors murder in alleyways? That he smiles down upon those who kill innocent bootmakers and teachers?"

The man smiled. "The demons may have blessed you with a silver tongue, schoolteacher, but it will avail you nothing. If you speak words of repentance, however, then you will not burn in lakes of hellfire but will be welcomed in paradise."

"If paradise is filled with the likes of you, then give me hellfire," said Alterith Shaddler.

The second man sheathed his dagger and pulled an oddly shaped implement from his belt. It looked to Alterith like a pair of tongs except that the ends were curved and sharp. "What is that?" he asked, fear in his voice.

"I promised Sir Gayan I'd bring him your foul tongue," the man told him. "I would have drawn it out once you were dead, but you need punishing for your insults."

Alterith felt his legs giving way. The first knight stepped in, grabbing him by the throat and hauling him upright.

"My, my," came a deep voice, "but you are an unpleasant pair."

The knight with the tongs spun around. Alterith saw a huge figure standing in the alleyway. He was cloaked and hooded but appeared to be carrying no weapon. "Begone, rascal," said the knight. "This is no business of yours."

"Aye, I am a rascal, no doubt of it," the man said amiably. "By heaven, I'm renowned for it."

The knight slipped the tongs back into his belt and drew his dagger. "This is your last chance, fool," he said. "Leave now or the wrath of the righteous will end your miserable life."

"Isn't that the schoolteacher?" responded the man. "Never liked him. Spent too much of his time thrashing my nephew. Just goes to show how wrong it is to make swift judgments. For here he is defending a highland woman and being lashed for it. Now, my little mice, my good humor is fading. It is cold, and I am hungry. So be on your way while your faces are still pretty."

The knight suddenly lunged. The big man's right hand blocked the dagger, his left thundering into the knight's face. Stepping forward, he grabbed the knight, spinning him.

Then, with one hand gripping the back of the knight's belt and the other holding him at the nape of the neck, he rammed the man's face into the alley wall. Shards of broken teeth scattered to the pebbles. Alterith stood transfixed. The knight holding his throat released him and leapt at the newcomer. Once again the dagger was brushed aside, and the knight was hauled into a sickening head butt that smashed his nose. That was followed by a punch to the solar plexus that doubled the knight over. He, too, was then spun and hurled headfirst into the wall, where he sank to the ground alongside his comrade.

Alterith slid down the wall. The pain in his back flared again, and he felt sick.

The big man approached him and, pushing back his hood, squatted down. Alterith recognized him as the man who had been at the farm when he had first visited Maev Ring. "What an exciting life you lead, schoolteacher," Jaim Grymauch said, with a grin.

"I . . . I thank you, sir," said Alterith. "Those men planned to murder me as they murdered Gillam Pearce."

"Aye, I heard. I wish I'd been here sooner. Come, let us get you inside. I don't doubt you'll be wanting your dinner."

"I couldn't eat," said Alterith.

"I could," said the man. "I've been walking for fifteen hours, and I'm weak as a newborn calf." He hauled Alterith to his feet. "So invite me to dine with you, man, for I've no coin."

"Your company would be most welcome, sir. I am indebted to you."

"I'll not talk of debt with a man who risks his life to save my Maev."

"She has spoken to me of you, Master Grymauch."

"I expect it was nothing good. A hard woman is Maev."

"Oh, it was good, sir. But she was concerned that you would . . . how shall I phrase it?"

"Do something foolish?" offered Jaim.

"Indeed so, sir."

"Let us talk while we eat," said Jaim Grymauch.

* * *

Kaelin Ring sat by the edge of a black river. The sky was gloomy, and though there was light enough to see the barren landscape, there was no sign of moon or stars. The trees by the river's edge were all dead, not a leaf to be seen.

On the far side of the river Kaelin watched as a slender boat was launched into the water. A hooded ferryman stood at the stern, a long pole in his hands.

Kaelin Ring felt burdened by weariness, and he sat slumped against a gray rock, waiting as the ferryman slowly poled the boat across the calm iron surface. He felt a weight in his hand and opened his fingers. A thick, round black coin appeared there, then faded away before reappearing again. Each time he tried to close his hand around the coin, it disappeared.

The boat reached the river's edge, and the ferryman stood waiting. Kaelin Ring pushed himself to his feet and approached the man. The ferryman held out his hand.

"Do not give him the coin," said the Wyrd.

Kaelin turned slowly. "Why are you here?"

"To bring you home, Ravenheart. This is not your time. Nor is this the place you should cross."

"I am very tired, Wyrd."

"I know. Come, let us talk awhile."

Kaelin glanced back at the ferryman.

"He will wait," the Wyrd said swiftly.

She walked back up the slope and stopped once on level ground. Here she sat and waited. Kaelin hardly had the strength to follow, but he stumbled on before slumping down alongside her.

"Chara is waiting for you," she said.

"Chara is lost to me, Wyrd. I thought I had saved her, but I was too late. They destroyed her spirit."

"No, they did not. Chara Jace is Rigante. She may be young, Ravenheart, but she has an old soul. It is strong, and it will recover. Even now she sits at the bedside of the man she loves, nursing his wounds, praying that his fever will break and that he will not die."

"The man she loves?"

"I am speaking of you, Kaelin. This is not the world you know. Your body lies in the great house. It is wracked by fever."

"Where, then, is this place?"

"The Black River. A place of lost souls, Kaelin. The brokenhearted come here, the lost, the despairing, and the defeated. It is not for you. We must journey back to the land of the living."

"I have no strength, Wyrd."

"You have more strength than you know. In you runs the blood of Connavar. You are Rigante, Ravenheart."

"Leave me be, Wyrd. I am tired, and the ferryman is waiting."

"Maev Ring is imprisoned," said the Wyrd. "They plan to burn her as a witch."

"Aunt Maev? A witch? That is nonsense."

"Aye, it is. Jaim is there now. Soon they will bring her to the stake, and fifty guards will be there to see her burn."

"Jaim will not stand by, Wyrd."

"No, he will not. His heart is as big as Caer Druagh and filled with the magic of the land. In every sense he *is* the Rigante: big and braw and magnificent. You love him, do you not?"

"Of course I do. He means the world to me."

"And to me, Ravenheart, for in Jaim we see all that is wondrous in the Rigante spirit."

"I must get to him. I must help him."

"You cannot. Your body is weak."

"There must be something I can do, Wyrd. Tell me. Anything!"

"You can open your heart, Kaelin, and you can hold Jaim within it. You can live your life as he would have you live it, unfettered by hatred, free to love. Not an easy path."

"Are you saying that Jaim is going to die?"

"All that lives and breathes will someday die, Ravenheart. When Jaim's time comes, the magic will flow out from him like a flood and touch every heart. That is his *geasa*. And believe me, when that day comes, he will not travel to this river of despair. Not Jaim Grymauch. There will be no ferryman."

"How do I get home?" asked Kaelin.

"Do you want to?"

"I do, Wyrd."

"Then let it be so."

Kaelin closed his eyes.

Pain seared through his side, and he groaned and opened his eyes. Above him was a roughly plastered ceiling and two beams of dark oak. He felt a hand in his. Rolling his head upon the pillow, he saw Chara Jace sitting by the bedside. There were tears on her face. She squeezed his fingers.

"It's good to see you, boy," said Call Jace, leaning over the bed. "You had us scared for a while."

"Where . . . is the Wyrd?" asked Kaelin.

"The Dweller has gone back to Sorrow Bird Lake," said Chara. "But she was here through the night."

"I'll leave you two to talk," said Call. "You rest, Kaelin. Let those wounds heal."

Kaelin heard the door close and looked into Chara's green eyes. "I love you," he said.

"I know."

"That's what I wanted to say that day by the fire. I wish I had."

"Don't talk now. Lie quiet, Ravenheart."

"Ranaud is dead."

"I know that, too. You led us to a great victory. You are a hero among the Rigante. Men speak of you with awe." She smiled at him and squeezed his hand. Seeing her smile filled him with a joy so great that his eyes misted, and he felt tears spilling to his cheeks. His throat tightened, and he could say nothing, but he clung to her hand as if his life depended on it.

"I love you, too," she told him. Then she leaned down and kissed his cheek.

* * *

Galliott the Borderer had endured a troubled night. This
was unusual for the Beetleback captain. Normally he slept
soundly and dreamlessly, waking refreshed. Yet last night he
had twisted and turned in his bed, unable to close his mind to
the events of the day.

The result of the trial was not in doubt. Maev Ring would
burn. Galliott tried to tell himself that this did not matter. The
death of one highland woman would not shake the founda-
tions of Varlish rule. He had rolled his pillow, thumped it to
make it more comfortable, then lay on his back and then on
his side. Finally, aware that his tossing and turning were disturbing Morain, he rose from his bed and walked downstairs
to where the evening fire was burning low behind its screen of
iron mesh.

Galliott's house was small, the outer walls covered in ivy
and the roof thatched. It was an old building with beamed
ceilings and a brick-built fireplace with recesses for logs. A
brass bucket sat on the hearth, half-full of coal. Galliott did
not light a lantern but sat in his favorite armchair. He added
three log chunks to the dying blaze and poured himself a
small glass of Uisge.

Many highlanders had been executed in the last ten years
on the orders of the Moidart. Some of them had been innocent. Yet it was more than innocence that worried him. He
sensed it deep beneath his practiced pragmatism.

The Uisge was warming, and he felt his muscles slowly
relax.

Earlier that morning he had been surprised to see the
schoolteacher Alterith Shaddler walking to the Holy Court
flanked by a dozen highlanders. It was like an honor guard.
Then one of Galliott's informants came to him, telling him
of the return of Jaim Grymauch. "Widow Barley says he
downed two of the Sacrifice knights last night as they were
setting upon the teacher." Galliott paid the man three daens
for the information.

Within the hour Sir Gayan Kay came to his office, demanding that officers seek out and find the villain who had savagely assaulted two of his men the night before. Galliott sat quietly while the knight spoke. Gayan Kay was a tall man, broad-shouldered and lean of hip. Like all the knights of the Sacrifice he was highly trained in all matters martial, an expert in the use of sword, ax, mace, and dagger. Most knights, Galliott knew, were also highly proficient with musket and pistol. They made deadly enemies, and not merely as a result of their dueling skills. Enemies of the order always died, some by assassination, most by burning, and Galliott had no wish to be added to the death list. So he listened politely, determined not to offend the knight. When Gayan Kay had concluded his report, Galliott asked: "They were attacked by one man, you say? Do you have a description?"

"He was powerfully built, maybe six and a half feet tall. He was obviously demon-possessed, for no mortal man could so easily defeat two of my knights. He had but one eye. The other was covered by a black piece of cloth."

"Well, Sir Gayan, such a man should stand out in a crowd. I will inform my soldiers to watch out for him."

"You have no idea as to his identity?"

"Indeed I have, sir. Leave the matter with me."

"Will you share this information?"

"It would do you little good, Sir Gayan. The man is a highlander and a rogue. He has many hiding places, but I will not need to search them."

"And why is that, pray?"

"Because he is a close friend of Maev Ring. He will come to the execution, and he will try to save her. That is his nature."

"Someone else she has bewitched."

As Galliott sat by the fire, he recalled his reply. Where the anger had come from he had no idea even now, but he could still recall its cold power. He had looked up at the arrogant knight and been unable to keep the contempt from his voice. "There is no one else present, Sir Gayan, so let us drop this ludicrous pretense. Maev Ring is no more a witch than I am.

She is a victim of the greed of small men and the corruption of the mighty. Her death will be a stain on the Varlish. The man who will try to save her is not bewitched—save by love and notions of honor. He is a great man. By the Source, I wish I had one-tenth of his courage."

Sir Gayan Kay stood and stared malevolently at Galliott. "How many men will you have under your command at the execution?"

"Fifty. I will do my utmost to see he is arrested *before* he commits any indiscretion."

"If he is there on the day, I shall kill him," said the knight.

Galliott suddenly laughed. "Kill Jaim Grymauch? Not on your best day. He is not a tiny bootmaker or a skinny school-teacher. He's a man, by heaven!"

"I see that this area has many heretics," Sir Gayan said coldly. "When this is over, I shall make it my business to root them all out. There is no place in all of Varlain for those who offer defense to our enemies. You will come under the question on that day, Captain Galliott."

"Try to tackle Jaim Grymauch and you won't live to see it," Galliott told him.

Sir Gayan Kay gave a thin smile. "Watch carefully when the witch burns, Galliott. Listen to her screams. Before the year is out they will be yours."

The threat had frightened Galliott. It still caused a small knot in his stomach as he sat before his fire. Yet curiously he did not regret speaking out. He had watched the events of the trial that day and had felt a growing sense of unease. It had begun when Alterith Shaddler's clerics had failed to arrive and there was no one at the defense table taking notes. Alterith had asked for a recess while he sought reasons for their absence. That had been refused.

The first person to be called had been Onray Shelan, the talented gunsmith who had designed many of Parsis Feld's new range of pistols and muskets. Shelan was a man in his mid-thirties, a full Varlish of impeccable breeding. When his name had been called by Alterith Shaddler, there had been some consternation in the judgment panel. The prosecutor, Arlin Bedver, had leapt to his feet, voicing an instant objection. "Master Shelan's name is not on the roll of material witnesses," he pointed out.

"Indeed not," replied Alterith Shaddler, "for he can offer no evidence to contradict allegations of witchcraft. I am calling Master Shelan to speak of his work for Parsis Feld."

"And how, pray, does this further your cause, Master Shaddler?" asked the bishop.

"Perhaps it will not, my lord. I felt it would be helpful if the court understood the nature of Parsis Feld's business prior to and following Maev Ring's involvement. Master Shelan is, if you like, a character witness." Shaddler had returned to the volume of Holy Law, opening it to a marked page. "If you please, I refer the court to Chapter Eleven—"

"Yes, yes, yes," snapped the bishop. "I don't doubt you have some scrap of ancient law to justify this waste of time. You may proceed. But be brief."

Galliott, sitting high in the gallery, watched as Shaddler moved around the table to approach Onray Shelan. His movements were awkward, and there was sweat on the schoolteacher's face. He had removed his black coat, and the gray shirt he wore beneath it was streaked with blood from the lashing he had suffered the day before.

Shelan's evidence was compelling. He had been approached several years earlier by Maev Ring, who had paid for his journey north. He had then examined the weapons produced by the Feld forge, pronouncing them of mediocre design and poor craftsmanship. Maev Ring had offered him a four-year contract to design and produce superior pieces, which he had done. They were now highly sought after, creating large profits for the Felds and for himself.

"Do you use witchcraft in your work?" asked Alterith Shaddler.

Shelan laughed. "No, sir. Merely good design, quality metals, and wood. I also have pride in my work and will not allow a single piece to be sold unless it is to the highest standard."

"Did you have many dealings with Maev Ring?"

"I did not, sir. We communicated by letter mostly, though I have met the lady on three occasions."

"Did Parsis Feld ever speak to you concerning her?"

"I object to this," said Arlin Bedver. "Words which may or not have been spoken by the late Master Feld cannot be corroborated."

"The witness will not answer that question," said the bishop.

"How was your relationship with Parsis Feld?" asked Alterith Shaddler. "Were you friends?"

"I liked the man greatly," said Shelan. "There was no arrogance in him. He knew that he was less than brilliant as a businessman, and many's the time he blessed the day that Maev Ring rescued his forge."

"Objection!" roared Arlin Bedver.

"So noted," said the bishop. "You will refrain, sir," he told Shelan, "from making observations. You will answer questions directly and not elaborate on them."

"What are your plans now, Master Shelan?" asked Alterith Shaddler.

"I shall resign from the forge," said Shelan, "and travel south to the capital. I stayed longer than I had anticipated because of my liking for Parsis Feld and my respect for Maev Ring."

Bedver made no attempt to cross-examine the gunsmith. Galliott glanced along the gallery, looking at the faces of the spectators. They were sitting quietly but listening intently. Onray Shelan came across as a man speaking the simple truth. When his evidence was finished, he stepped from the box and offered a deep bow to Maev Ring. She nodded to him and gave a small smile.

To Galliott's surprise, Alterith Shaddler did not call Maev Ring to give evidence. Instead he launched into his summation. Galliott could not recall all that he said, but the spirit of it burned in him even now. As Shaddler spoke, Galliott became aware that he was not really addressing the judgment panel but was speaking instead to the packed galleries of Varlish onlookers. He talked of failing businesses and Maev Ring's skill in assessing problem areas and overcoming them. He listed the years of increasing profits for each of the enterprises. But it was the closing remarks that plunged home like arrows of fire.

"Imagine if you will," he said, "a foreign land, far from Varlain. A brilliant young Varlish entrepreneur travels there and finds that there are laws preventing him from using his skills to found a business. So he sets out to make his fortune by investing his genius in the businesses of others, bringing his Varlish skills to bear. As the years pass, this young Varlish becomes more and more succesful. All who know him are impressed by his acumen. But then some of the people of this land, people he has helped make rich, decide that he is too powerful. So they go to the king and ask that this Varlish be arrested. The king, an honest and good man, interviews and questions the young Varlish and finds him innocent of all charges. He has killed no one, cheated no one, and broken no law. Indeed, his success has also seen the king's treasury swell as tax revenues have increased. But his enemies are determined to bring him down, and they decide that since they cannot emulate his success, he must be in league with dark forces. So this young Varlish is brought before another court. Witnesses who would speak up for him are threatened, and those who resist the threats are foully murdered. What would we think were we to hear this story? Would we come to believe that he was truly a sorcerer? Or would we know in our hearts that a terrible injustice was being perpetrated?

"Here in this Holy Court we see a highland woman whose crime is that she is remarkably intelligent. What iniquities has she been accused of? Making people rich has never been considered a crime. No. What we have heard is greedy men talking of goat dreams and whoremongering, of mysterious bewitchments that they did not complain of until they saw an opportunity to become even wealthier. What we see is a judicial system manipulated and corrupted for the sake of money."

The bishop hammered his gavel to the table, the sound echoing up into the galleries. "Have a care, schoolteacher. You still have forty lashes to endure for your impertinence. The Book of Holy Law, which you have become so fond of, states that it is within my power to add forty more. Now are you finished?"

"Aye, my lord, I am almost done here. I do not expect those whose hearts are blacker than the pit to care about principles of truth and justice. But know this: If Maev Ring is found guilty, I will make it my life's work to see that the perpetrators of this evil are brought to book."

"And I am sure your life will be a long and happy one," the bishop said with a smile. "You have made so many friends, Master Shaddler. It is almost inconceivable that anyone would set out to harm you. Now sit down." Shaddler did so, and Galliott leaned forward as the bishop rose from his seat.

"Maev Ring, many witnesses have given evidence under oath concerning your foul activities, which are a stench in the nostrils of the holy. You have bewitched and seduced good and upright citizens and not once offered a word of remorse. Do you have anything to say before sentence is passed?"

All eyes swung to the tall, red-haired highland woman. She stood quietly for a moment, and when she spoke, her voice was firm and strong. "I wish to thank Alterith Shaddler for removing my distaste for all things Varlish. And I offer my sincere condolences to the widow of Gillam Pearce, another good man whom it was my privilege to know. As to this court I have only the utmost contempt. That is all I have to say."

Someone in the gallery began to applaud, and to Galliott's surprise others joined in. The Varlish spectators—except Jorain Feld and other prosecution witnesses—rose to their feet and clapped their hands. Galliott saw the shock on Maev Ring's face. She looked up at the massed ranks of Varlish and bowed to them.

"There will be silence!" bellowed the bishop. "I will not have this court made a mockery!"

"Too late," shouted someone in the gallery. "You've already done that yourself, you fat swine!"

"Guards! Find that man!" screamed the bishop. Two red-liveried guards ran up the inner steps to the left-hand gallery, but once they reached the crowd, everyone had resumed his seat, and they stood helplessly. The bishop was breathing heavily, and his face was streaked with sweat. He glared at Maev Ring.

"You will be taken from here to your cell. Tomorrow at noon the demons will be burned from your body, and your soul consigned to the master of hell you have served for so long. Take her away."

"Shame!" came another voice, this time from the right-hand gallery. Then the booing began. Seat cushions were hurled down at the judgment panel.

The bishop, abbots, and clerics all departed swiftly through the rear of the building, but the four knights of the Sacrifice stood their ground, staring up at the jeering crowd. As Jorain Feld rose to leave the gallery, someone pushed him. He stumbled into another man.

"Watch where you're going," said the second man. "I don't want to be polluted by touching you."

Jorain rushed for the exit, the curses of the spectators ringing in his ears. On the stairs he was pushed again. He slipped and fell, tearing his breeches. Some of the other witnesses were also being manhandled.

Galliott eased his way through the angry crowd and walked out into the dusk. Alterith Shaddler was once more met by a group of highlanders, who escorted him away. Galliott saw the giant figure of Huntsekker emerging from the other door. The man walked over to where he waited.

"A black day, Captain," he said. Huntsekker tugged at the twin spikes of his iron-gray beard. "And it will get worse."

"I fear so," agreed Galliott.

"Have you heard that Grymauch is back?"

"I have."

"He'll come, you know."

Galliott sighed. "There'll be fifty men here and twenty musketeers. I have men looking for him now. If we find him, I'll have him arrested on some pretext and keep him in the cells until this . . . this obscenity is over."

"You'll not find him, Captain. He'll wade into your fifty men. Truth to tell, I'll be tempted to join him."

"As would I, under other circumstances," admitted Galliott. "But we won't, Master Huntsekker, for we are Varlish and pledged to uphold the laws of state and church."

"Even when the church is riddled with corruption?" queried Huntsekker.

"Even then."

Huntsekker swore softly. Then he chuckled. "Did you hear about the time Grymauch stole my bull? We spent the night searching for him, and when we returned, it was back in the paddock, a sprig of heather tied to its horn."

Galliott smiled. "I remember. I always thought you would hate him for that."

"You don't hate a man like Grymauch. You thank the Source for him. I'll never forget that night or watching him beat the fighter Gorain. He is a man to match the mountains, Captain."

Alone now by his fire, Galliott poured another Uisge. Given the choice, he would have ridden far from Eldacre on the morrow, putting as much distance as possible between himself and the vileness of the execution. Yet he did not have the choice. He would have to stand in the open ground before the pyre and listen as Maev Ring burned to death.

Galliott thought of Jaim Grymauch. He would come to the execution. Of that there was no doubt. The one-eyed clansman would try to save Maev Ring.

With a deep sigh the Borderer replaced the mesh screen before his fire. Tomorrow he would have to kill Jaim Grymauch, and the prospect filled his heart with an abiding sorrow.

* * *

The morning was bright and clear, and Galliott washed, shaved, and dressed in black boots and leggings, putting on two white woolen shirts beneath his black breastplate. Strapping his saber to his hip, he swung his black cloak about his shoulders and set off for the castle.

As he walked through the streets, he saw people gathering, talking on street corners. He also saw highlanders coming into the town, scores of them. Reaching the castle gates, he stared off toward the hills. The roads were thick with people.

He had anticipated that several hundred would attend the execution, but now he revised that estimate. If the highlanders were coming, there might be as many as a thousand filling the cathedral square. His fifty men would be hard-pressed to control such a crowd.

In his office at the castle he summoned Duty Sergeant Packard. The man saluted and stood before his desk. Packard was a veteran, hard-eyed and square-jawed. He had been a close friend of Bindoe's and was known for his hatred of highlanders.

"Any sign of Grymauch?" asked Galliott.

"No, sir."

"Have you seen the crowds gathering?"

"I have, sir. A lot of highlanders coming in. None of them are armed, though. Still, there could be trouble. I've posted guards throughout the town in double shifts."

"Good thinking."

"You think she is a witch, sir?"

"No. But that is not our concern."

"Didn't think she was. It's not right, sir."

"No, it isn't right, Sergeant. Our job, however, is to marshal the crowds and see that there is no trouble. In situations such as this the wrong word or action can spark a riot. I want all the men told to maintain their tempers. If we have any hotheads in the troop, assign them duties at the castle."

"If the crowd tops a thousand, our fifty won't be able to control them, sir."

"I know. How many men do we have on castle and patrol duties?"

"One hundred and thirty, sir. We had to send five hundred north for Colonel Ranaud."

"Double the execution guard to one hundred. Equip the men with quarterstaves. They can use them to keep the crowd back."

"Yes, sir. There's a whisper that Jaim Grymauch might cause trouble."

"Believe it, Sergeant. As soon as he shows himself, I want him taken. I'd prefer it were he to be taken alive."

"That might not be possible, Captain. He's a big bastard, and if he's armed, he'll be a handful."

"I think a hundred men should be sufficient to render him harmless."

"Yes, sir," said Sergeant Packard, his voice doubtful. "Why would he come? He can't stop it. He'll just be throwing his life away."

Galliott rose from his desk and walked to the window. In the far distance he could see clouds over the snowcapped mountains. "He'll come because he has to," Galliott said sadly. He turned back toward Packard. "He'll come because that's what heroes do. They fight for what is right, no matter what the cost."

"If he's a hero, sir, doesn't that make us villains?"

"It does today, Sergeant."

Alterith Shaddler swung his skinny legs from his bed and sat up. The morning was cold with the promise of winter. He had, despite his grief and the pain from his back, dozed a little during the long night. There was a little blood on the sheets, but the wounds from the lash were healing fast. The apothecary Ramus had visited him the night before, giving him, free of charge, a cooling balm. Alterith had accepted it with thanks and had managed to smear some on his shoulders and sides. But he could not reach the cuts between his shoulder blades, and they pulled tight whenever he moved.

The schoolteacher crossed the small room and placed kindling atop the ashes in the fireplace. Several long sulfur sticks had been placed in a narrow brass cylinder by the fire, and he struck one upon the brickwork. It flared into life, and he touched it to the kindling. After a little while, his fire burning merrily, he added small coals. The north wind rattled the window. It was past dawn, and Alterith padded to the window, gazing out over the town. In the street below ten highland men were standing silently, seemingly impervious to the cold.

Alterith Shaddler had never known popularity. In all his years he had never developed the social skills necessary. When he had left the Holy Court the previous day, crowds had cheered him—and not just highlanders. Black-garbed Varlish had applauded as he passed. The persecution of a good woman was too high a price to pay for such regard. Alterith would swap it in an instant and accept a life of cold loneliness for the chance to turn back the clock and see Maev Ring free.

He had seen the clanswoman the previous night. She had given Banny enough money to see the school run for another five years without further input. "After that I am sure my nephew Kaelin will continue to support you," she said.

"I am so sorry, madam," he told her. "I fear you needed a better advocate."

"You will call me Maev, Alterith Shaddler. And I could have wished for no better man to speak up for me. I meant what I said in that court. I have spent my life hating all Varlish. I saw no good in them. You and Gillam Pearce and Master Shelan have given me peace of heart."

They had sat quietly then in the small cell. Alterith had not told her of the return of Jaim Grymauch even when she spoke of him. "When he does come back, you will make it clear to him that I do not desire vengeance. He should marry Parsha Willets and put this . . . this tawdry business behind him."

"Parsha Willets?"

"She is a friend of Jaim's," said Maev. Suddenly she

laughed. "Why am I being coy? Parsha is what we used to call an Earth Maiden. Jaim is fond of her, and she loves him utterly."

"I have no experience of such matters," he said, "save what I have read in the great romances. However, in my readings I have come to the conclusion that 'fond' is not enough. Is that how you feel toward Jaim? Are you fond of him?"

"My feelings are my own," she replied testily.

"I am sorry," he said instantly. "I did not wish to be discourteous."

Maev reached out and patted his shoulder. "I am too sharp sometimes, my friend. To be truthful, I do not really know what I feel for Jaim. I think of him constantly, and I feel empty when he is gone. If I close my eyes, I can see that big, ugly face with its childlike grin. I sometimes think that living with Jaim is like having a pet bear." He saw her smile then. "In another time we would probably have wed. A safer time, when I didn't have to worry constantly about him being taken and hanged. Now there will be no such time."

Alterith had wanted to tell her about Jaim's rescue of him, but he could not. In all their conversations her biggest fear had been of Jaim Grymauch being hurt. If she knew he was back, she would spend her last hours fretting and anxious.

"The apothecary Ramus has given me a potion," he said, dipping his hand into his pocket. "If you take it an hour before the . . . the allotted time, it will remove all pain. He says you will feel nothing."

"I want no potions," she told him. "I want nothing to dull my eyes or my heart or leaden my limbs. I will walk from here as a Rigante should, head high."

A guard had opened the door then, telling Alterith his time was at an end. Maev had risen from her chair and taken hold of his hands. "You take care, Alterith," she said. Then she leaned in and kissed his cheek. The last person to kiss him thus had been his mother, twenty years before, and tears fell from his eyes.

Then the guard took his arm and led him from the cell. As the door closed, he saw it was the same guard who had administered his lashing.

"How is the back, sir?" he asked.

"It is healing, thank you."

"The bishop has not yet ordered the remainder of the sentence to be carried out. That's good. Gives the scars time to form."

"Yes," said Alterith.

"She's not going to suffer, sir. The lads have doused the lower pyre with black oil. The smoke will—you know—make her pass out before the flames reach her."

Alterith looked into the guard's open and honest face. "She is an innocent woman," he said. "This should not be happening."

"I know that, sir. We all know that. It's a terrible thing, no mistake. You did your best, though. A man can do no more. Now you better be going. There's a dozen highlanders outside waiting to walk you to your lodgings."

Now, with the dread day upon him, Alterith had no wish to witness the outcome of the evil. He could not bear the thought of watching Maev Ring burn.

On the tiny table beside the bed were all his notes from the trial. He sat quietly, arranging them, then rolled them into little bundles tied with string. Those he pushed into an old leather shoulder satchel. What will it be worth, he wondered, when they are read in Varingas? The previous night he had gone to the house of his clerics. Both men had been visited by the knights, who had removed their records of the trial and warned them not to appear for the final day. Without those records would anyone be impeached? Would the bishop face censure? And what were the chances of his own notes reaching Varingas, or indeed of his being alive to give evidence should he be so called?

Alterith had always believed that evil should be faced and that good would ultimately triumph if men stood their ground. Yet in this place the evil had been institutional, pervading all areas. Good men had been coerced into silence or murdered, and the power of the church had been behind the killers. Throughout the centuries fine, brave people had suffered and died to establish a religion based on love and tolerance, to build a society whose laws protected the poorest. Yet within a generation vile men had corrupted the purity of the law and the spirit of the faith. It was enough to make a man doubt the existence of any higher celestial power. What kind of a god would allow such iniquities? Where in all this sea of corruption, greed, and vengeful malice was there a single indication that the cause of good had any strength?

Alterith washed his face, then dressed. Both of his shirts were now bloodstained, and his threadbare coat would not keep out the cold.

With a heavy heart he threw the satchel over his shoulder and walked downstairs.

Just after midmorning Galliott the Borderer was summoned to the offices of the Moidart. As he climbed the stairs, he saw Huntsekker coming down. The big man nodded to him as they passed but did not speak.

Galliott tapped on the Moidart's door, heard the command to enter, and walked inside.

The Moidart, dressed all in gray, was sitting at his desk. "I see the hills are emptying," he said. "Clansmen are everywhere."

"Yes, my lord."

"I want no riot, Galliott. Our forces are stretched thin."

"I have doubled the guard at the execution, lord. One hundred to control the crowd and twenty musketeers."

The Moidart rose from his chair and winced as the unhealed burns on his body drew tight. "There was a dispatch last night from Baracum," he said, pointing to an opened letter on the desk. "Read it."

Galliott leaned over the table and lifted the document. The writing was small but beautifully crafted. Holding it at arm's length, Galliott squinted to read it. When he had finished, he carefully laid it on the desk. "It cannot be," he said. "It is madness."

"Madness or not, it is true," said the Moidart. "The king has fled the capital and is raising an army against Luden Macks and the covenanters. It is civil war, Galliott. Heaven knows where it will end."

"Surely the king will crush them, my lord."

"Perhaps, though I doubt it. However, that is not our concern now. Insurrection in the highlands will not—for the foreseeable future—allow us to summon reinforcements from the king. All we have is our own troops. I have sent a rider to Colonel Ranaud, ordering him to withdraw from his attacks on the Black Rigante. Another rider has already been dispatched to order the king's regiment to return south. These are dangerous days, Galliott."

"Yes, my lord. Might it not be best if the bishop could be prevailed upon to pardon Maev Ring?"

The Moidart's face darkened. "That is a course I urged upon him last night. He is worse than an idiot. He lectured me about the majesty of the church. Fresh from the bed of his strumpet and with Jorain Feld's bribe jangling in his purse, he talks to me of Holy Law. But enough of that. Tell me of your plans for the execution."

An hour before the execution the crowds were already gathering in force. Galliott stood just in front of the scaffold surrounding the twelve-foot-high pyre. Maev Ring would be brought out through the cathedral doors, walked to the steps of the scaffold and then up to the narrow platform, and tied to the stake. The walk from the cathedral would take less than a minute. Galliott placed twenty men to the right of the cathedral doors some fifty paces from the entrance. "Hold the line there," he told them.

The stone-flagged cathedral square was in fact rectangular, 300 feet long and 210 feet wide. There were four entrance points: three from the town of Eldacre itself and one across a

bridge leading out to Five Fields. Already there were some
six hundred people congregating close to the bridge. Forty of
Galliott's men, their six-foot quarterstaves held across their
bodies, were maintaining a line some eighty feet from the
scaffold. Twenty-five more Beetlebacks were struggling to
control the highland crowds emerging from the entrance on
the left. More and more were arriving, creating pressure on
those in front, inexorably moving them forward against the
officers. There was no ill intent as far as Galliott could see,
but the press of the crowd was so great that the Beetlebacks
were forced back a step at a time. Galliott issued orders to
pull back the line, allowing more room for the newcomers.
That eased the pressure for a while.

Sergeant Packard approached him. "They just keep coming, sir," he said. "Reckon there'll be a damn sight more than
two thousand."

Hundreds more people began to arrive from the Varlish
areas. Originally Galliott had planned to keep the crowd at
least a hundred feet from the pyre. He had revised it to sixty,
and now he revised again. Once the fire was lit, the heat
would drive people back, but until then Galliott was forced to
allow the crowd to move closer. Even then his men were
struggling to hold the lines, and there was no sign of the
twenty musketeers. Their presence would certainly help maintain order.

Galliott climbed the scaffold steps, gazing out over the
crowd, seeking a sign of Jaim Grymauch.

Suddenly booing and hissing began. Galliott glanced
toward the cathedral and saw the four knights of the Sacrifice
walking out into the sunshine. They were wearing their ceremonial armor of silver plate and handsome white plumed
helms. White cloaks hung from their shoulders, the emblem
of the tree embroidered in silver upon them. By their sides
hung old-fashioned broadswords with flaring quillons. Galliott stared at them. In bygone days the knights of the Sacrifice had been heroes, men of courage and compassion whose

deeds were legendary. Now the beautiful silver armor was worn by men like Gayan Kay: malevolent, spiteful, bigoted, and merciless. Their presence had enraged the crowd, but Galliott had no power to order the knights to withdraw.

They walked to the foot of the scaffold. Galliott descended to meet them.

Gayan Kay lifted the ornate face guard of his helm. "No sign of this Grymauch?" he asked.

"Not yet, sir knight. Is your presence here necessary? It is difficult enough to control the crowd."

"Controlling crowds is your job, Captain. We are here to witness justice being done."

Galliott bit back his anger and moved away from them.

As the time for the execution drew close, more than two thousand people were crammed into the square. The booing at the knights had faded, and most people were staring at the great arched doors of the cathedral. Galliott was sweating. The musketeers were still missing, as were around ten of the men charged with patrolling the entrances.

Galliott strolled around the inner perimeter, watching the crowd and gauging its mood. He sensed that they were becoming more passive now. There was no immediate threat to his men.

Ten more soldiers eased their way through the front ranks of the crowd and made their way to where Galliott was standing. The first of them saluted. "Travelers are thinning now, sir," he said.

"Any sign of the musketeers?"

"No, sir."

Suddenly the crowd went very still, and silence fell on the great square. Galliott turned to see two priests bringing out Maev Ring. The sunlight glinted on her silver-streaked red hair, and she walked with great dignity toward the scaffold. Two red-garbed cathedral guards had positioned themselves below the pyre, lighted torches in their hands.

Galliott strode to the foot of the scaffold. Maev Ring paused before him.

"I am sorry, Maev," he said.

She did not reply and moved past him, lifting her heavy skirt and climbing the steps. The priests followed her. On the narrow platform above they tied her hands to the stake, then withdrew. Galliott glanced toward the cathedral. There was no sign of the bishop. Galliott climbed the first five steps of the scaffold and gazed out once more over the crowd.

There was movement in the center, the highland crowd parting to create a pathway. Walking slowly along it was a huge figure in a hooded black cloak. He was carrying a quarterstaff.

Galliott ran to where the ten new arrivals were still standing. "Stop that man," he told them.

Jaim Grymauch emerged from the crowd and began to walk toward the scaffold.

From high on the scaffold Maev Ring saw him coming, and her heart was close to breaking. "No, Jaim," she whispered.

The ten soldiers ran at him, forming a half circle. Jaim kept moving. Two of the Beetlebacks darted in. Jaim's quarterstaff, tipped with lead, flashed out, striking the first on the temple and catapulting him from his feet. Jaim blocked the second soldier's staff, cracking his own against the man's leg. The soldier stumbled. Jaim's staff rapped against his skull, and he fell face first to the flagstones.

The other soldiers rushed in. Some blows cracked against the giant hooded highlander, but his own staff whirled and thudded against skulls, arms, and legs. One by one the Beetlebacks fell. The crowd was cheering now. Other soldiers tried to aid their comrades, but people in the crowd grabbed their staffs or took hold of their cloaks. And not only highlanders; on the Varlish side soldiers were also held back.

Galliott drew his saber and ran in to help his men. Jaim downed the last of them and stepped across the sprawling, half-stunned men. Galliott lunged at him. Jaim parried the blow with his staff, bringing it up and over the captain's blade and rapping him hard against the temple. Galliott fell to his knees, dropping his sword.

Jaim Grymauch walked by him.

Sir Gayan Kay and the knights of the Sacrifice drew their broadswords as Jaim Grymauch bore down upon them. Gayan swung toward the cathedral guards. "Light the pyre!" he bellowed.

Neither of the men moved. Gayan ran toward them, wrenching a torch from the first guard and tossing it to the wood. Flames flickered immediately.

"That you should not have done," said Jaim Grymauch, tossing aside his quarterstaff and ripping away his hooded cloak. Reaching up, he curled his hand around the massive hilt of the glave hanging between his shoulders. With one wrench he swept the fifty-two-inch blade from its scabbard. Two of the armored knights rushed him.

The glave swept up, then slashed down, striking the metal neck guard of the first knight. The plates parted. One snapped off and flew into the air. Beneath the plates the knight was wearing chain mail. It prevented the glave from cutting into his skin but not the terrible force of the blow from smashing his neck into shards. Even as the knight's dead body was toppling toward the flagstones, Jaim's giant sword hammered into the breastplate of the second knight. The man grunted as the metal collapsed inward, snapping three of his ribs. He fell to his knees and did not see the terrible stroke that burst through his helm, splitting his skull.

The third of the knights advanced more cautiously, followed in by Sir Gayan Kay.

Grymauch, in no mood for caution, charged them both. Blocking Gayan Kay's sword, Grymauch spun and shoulder charged the other knight. The man fell heavily, then struggled to rise. Jaim's sword hammered into his helm, ripping away the visor. The force of the blow hurled the knight to the ground unconscious. Gayan Kay hefted his broadsword and launched a murderous cut toward Grymauch's head.

Grymauch ducked, then thrust his sword like a lance into Gayan Kay's belly. Chain mail once more prevented the blade from piercing flesh, but the pain of the blow was indescribable. Gayan Kay screamed and dropped his sword. Grymauch let go of the glave and stepped in, grabbing the knight by his throat. "Burn my Maev, would you?" he said. Then he dragged the terrified knight toward the burning pyre, lifted him from his feet, and hurled him headfirst into the blaze. The force of the throw scattered burning kindling around the base and plunged Gayan Kay deep into the pyre.

Gathering his sword, Grymauch ran to the scaffold steps and climbed through the swirling smoke. Maev was almost unconscious as Jaim cut her free. Sheathing his sword, he lifted her into his arms and, flames licking at his boots, ran along the narrow platform and back to the steps.

The crowds were cheering at the top of their voices now.

Maev's eyes opened, and she stared up into Grymauch's ugly face. He grinned down at her. "You think I'd let them kill my woman?" he asked.

"I'm not your woman, you lummox!" she said.

The flames had really caught now, and the heat was intense. Jaim carried Maev to the cathedral steps, then faltered, looking around.

"Well?" asked Maev, "what is your plan?"

He shrugged. "Don't know. Never expected to get this far."

"Put me down, you idiot. I can walk. We should go through the cathedral. There are stables at the rear of the Holy Court." Jaim lowered her to the ground.

Galliott had regained his senses and rose unsteadily. He saw the giant highlander holding Maev Ring, and deep down he was glad. His ten men were still on the ground, some holding their heads, others groggy from the beating. Jaim and Maev began to walk toward the cathedral doors.

Suddenly there was a commotion in the crowd, and some of his musketeers pushed through. Seeing the sprawled bodies and the highlander with the sword, they raised their weapons. Time slowed in that instant. Galliott saw Jaim Grymauch turn his back on the musketeers, hauling Maev Ring into a protective embrace and shielding her with his body. Taybard Jaekel ran from the crowd, throwing himself at the musketeers, knocking aside one of the weapons, and cannoning into several of the other men. In the same moment Galliott shouted at the top of his voice: "Don't shoot!" But it came too late. Five of the guns boomed, the sound crashing like thunder. Galliott ran at the musketeers. "No firing!" he bellowed. "Cease fire!" The men lowered the weapons. Taybard Jaekel struggled to his feet and swung to look at Jaim Grymauch.

At the top of the steps Maev Ring hugged Grymauch. His body had jerked when the muskets had fired, but he was still standing. She felt the strength of his arms around her and the warmth of his chest against her face. She wanted the moment to last forever. The smell of woodsmoke and sweat was on his clothes. *"You think I'd let them kill my woman?"* he had said. Deep down she had always known he would come for her, if only to die trying to save her. "We must go now, you foolish, wonderful man," she said. He did not answer, nor did he move. She pulled back gently and looked up into his face. "We must go, Jaim," she said again.

There was blood on his lips, and she felt the desperation in his embrace. He was clinging to her now. "Oh, no, Jaim," she cried. He sagged against her, and she could scarcely hold the weight. A huge man appeared alongside them. Huntsekker grabbed Jaim and lowered him to his knees. Blood gushed to Grymauch's beard, and he held to Maev's gaze. Maev took hold of his hand, squeezing his fingers. "Don't go, Jaim," she pleaded. "I love you. Don't leave me. Not now!"

"Never . . . will," he said, his voice breaking. He fell against Huntsekker, who threw his arm around Jaim's shoulder, holding him.

"I'll get her safe from here, big man," said Huntsekker.

"You have my pledge on it. No harm will come to her while I live."

"Go . . . now," whispered Jaim, his body convulsing.

"No," said Maev. "I'll not leave you!"

But Grymauch could not hear her. Huntsekker laid his body on the steps, then took Maev by the arm. She clung to Jaim's hand, staring at his still face. "His death will be for nothing if they take you now," said Huntsekker. "Let him go." Huntsekker gently laid his hand over hers, loosening her fingers. Then he drew her up and led her into the cathedral, pausing only to push shut the great arched doors.

Maev Ring stood silently. Brilliant sunlight was spearing through the smoke outside, and Jaim Grymauch was bathed in gold.

Then the doors swung shut, the light disappearing from view.

Galliott walked slowly up the steps and knelt beside Grymauch's body. Placing his hand on the dead man's chest, he said: "I knew you'd come." Galliott looked out over the crowd. They were standing quietly now, not a ripple of movement to be seen. His own sadness was mirrored on every face, yet there was something more.

They had witnessed something majestic, and it had touched all their hearts. No one wanted to move. In all of them was a desire to hold to this moment, let it soak into their souls. Even the musketeers made no move to arrest Taybard Jaekel. He stood alongside them, tears in his eyes.

Sergeant Packard climbed the steps and stood staring down at Grymauch. Packard had a lump on his brow, and the skin was split and bleeding. "You want us to go after the woman, sir?" he asked.

"No, Sergeant. That is a church matter. We are here only for crowd control."

Packard swung to stare at the burning pyre. "That knight didn't get out," he said. "Proper fried he was, and good riddance."

"I told him not to tackle Grymauch. Some men don't listen."

"Grymauch damn near cracked my skull, but I'm glad I was here to see this," said Packard. "Something to tell the grandchildren, eh?"

"Yes," said Galliott, wearily pushing himself to his feet.

A group of highlanders, flanked by soldiers, came walking up the stairs. "Can we take his body, Captain?" asked the first.

"Of course," said Galliott. Six men moved around the corpse, lifting it gently. One of the highlanders pulled Jaim's huge glave clear of its scabbard and offered it to Galliott. No highlander was allowed to own a sword, not even in death.

Galliott shook his head. "Bury it with him," he said, laying it on the body.

The crowd parted once more for Jaim Grymauch. Highlanders and Varlish pulled off their hats and caps as the bearers of the body passed by and bowed their heads in silent tribute.

"So, the villains won today, eh, Captain?" said Sergeant Packard, genuine regret in his voice.

Galliott shook his head. "He came to rescue the woman he loved, and he did that. He won, Sergeant. We lost. We all lost."

"Aye, and I'm glad we did," said Packard. "Tonight I'm going to raise a tankard to the big bastard and wish him well on his journey."

Sixty miles to the south, at the center of the Wishing Tree woods, the Wyrd waited. She could have used her power to see Jaim Grymauch's last moments, but she could not bear it. She sat in the shadow of the great stone at the center of the old circle and waited, her spirit in harmony with the land.

The Wyrd heard the creaking of the ancient oaks and the gentle rustle of the breeze across the grass and felt the power of the sun bathing the land. Beneath these indications of life she also held to the magic, tiny and insubstantial now but still pulsing in the soft earth.

These woods had once known the Seidh, the old gods of

fire and water. The Morrigu had walked here with the storm crow, Babdh, upon her shoulders. Riamfada had dwelled in the wood and here had made the magical sword carried by Connavar the king. It was here still, awaiting the stag.

He had come to her in a dream the night before, as she had hoped he would. Once more she had conjured the image of a campfire in the woods, and his spirit had taken form alongside it. "Welcome to my fire, Gaise Macon," she said.

"Why do I wear this cloak in my dreams?" he asked her. "It is badly patched and old."

"It is the cloak of Connavar. Each patch represents a different clan, stitched to the blue and the green of the Rigante. It was a cloak of unity. It told the world that Connavar was Keltoi and above clan rivalry."

"Why do I wear it?"

The Wyrd thought for a moment, then smiled. "Ask yourself this: Do you feel it belongs around your shoulders?"

"Aye, I do."

"Then that is why you wear it. Why have you come to me, child of the Varlish?"

"I have a commission in the king's cavalry. Tomorrow I join my regiment. A war has begun."

"I know all this. Why are you here?"

"I have never been able to push from my mind our last meeting. I miss the mountains of my home. I miss the land. In my dreams I walk the slopes of Caer Druagh. I am drawn to it. And yet . . . I feel the land does not know me. It cannot feel my presence or my love."

"It knows you, Gaise. It is part of your blood," she told him.

"I want a soul-name."

"You have always had one. You are the Storm Rider."

He sighed then and smiled. "I like that. It feels like a cool breeze on my soul." His green and gold gaze locked to her eyes. "Will we meet again, lady?"

"Oh, yes. In triumph and sorrow, Rigante."

The Wyrd shivered at the memory, then glanced up at the

sky. It was nearing noon, and at this moment Jaim Grymauch was still alive.

Regret touched the Wyrd, soft and sad and of infinite weight.

He had been on his way north and had camped in a cluster of rocks. The Wyrd's spirit had found him there. He had been humming a song and drinking from a flagon of Uisge when she had appeared at his fire. Jaim had stared blearily at the apparition, then rubbed his eye. "A powerful brew," he said, sniffing the neck of the flagon.

"It is not the Uisge," the Wyrd told him. "I have been searching for you."

"And you have found me. Would you care for a drop of the water of life?"

"In this spirit form I cannot drink, Jaim Grymauch."

"Aye, you do seem somewhat insubstantial, woman. Are you here to cast some spell upon me?"

The Wyrd smiled. "I cast few spells now, Grymauch. The magic is almost gone from the land."

"Then to what do I owe the pleasure of your company?"

"The woman you love is in danger, Jaim," she said. Grymauch lurched to his feet. "No, no, it is not immediate. Sit yourself down and listen to me." He slumped back by the fire, dropping the flagon. Then she told him of Maev's arrest. He listened in silence and then, when she had finished, moved to the stream and drank a copious amount of water. When he returned, his eye was no longer bleary.

"I shall go back and take her from the cathedral. There won't be enough guards to stop me."

"Aye, that might work," she said.

"I hear a doubt in your voice. I can do it, Wyrd."

"I know you can. But it is important that the trial take place, Jaim. That it is concluded."

"They'll burn her."

"Yes, she will be sentenced to burn. The injustice of the sentence will sway the crowd, both Varlish and Highlander. It will change hearts and minds, Jaim. And from it will come a greater understanding between the races."

"I'll not let her die, Wyrd, even if it means the Varlish and the clan hate each other for a thousand years. Maev is the love of my life. Can you understand what I'm saying?"

"I do understand, Jaim. But even as we speak the school-teacher Alterith Shaddler is preparing to defend her. He is no warrior, yet he will stand against the knights of the Sacrifice and risk his own life for Maev. We cannot go on as two peoples filled with hate, Jaim. It is draining the magic from the land, and without the magic there will be nothing. The land will die little by little. I do not ask that you leave Maev to her fate. I ask that you wait until the trial is over."

" 'Tis the same thing," he argued. "There will be scores of soldiers at the execution, pikemen and musketeers."

"And against them will be Jaim Grymauch, the greatest of the Rigante. You know me, Jaim. You know I have pledged my life for the clan. You know I would not lie to you. Trust me when I tell you that the future of the Rigante rests now in your hands."

He stared into the fire. "I don't know what to do," he said.

"Then trust your heart."

"I can save Maev and help end the hatred?" he asked.

"Yes."

"A long time ago I failed to save a friend. I have lived with that regret as a wound on my soul which has never healed. It would kill me to fail my Maev. You understand? I'd sooner be dead."

"You will reach her, Jaim. I promise you that. You will hold her. Maev will live, though you will not."

He said nothing for a while. "I am destined to die there?"

"Yes. If that is the path you choose."

"But Maev will be safe?"

"She will go north, Jaim, and dwell among the Black Rigante."

"I'd die willingly for Maev. But tell me this: If I took her from the cathedral before the trial was over, would she walk the tree with me?"

"Yes, Jaim, she would. You would have some years together. Happy years. I'll not deny it. But then the Rigante would be wiped out, the clan destroyed. Hatred and violence would swamp the highlands."

"Tell me what to do, Wyrd."

"I cannot do that, Jaim. You will know when the time comes. Go to Eldacre. Stay low and watch over the schoolteacher. He is staying at a lodging house in Peartree Lane. The knights will try to kill him. You must keep him safe."

The Wyrd's spirit had faded away, and she had opened her eyes back in the Wishing Tree woods. Her fire had burned low—almost as low as the flames of her soul. Her words had doomed Jaim Grymauch.

Now she waited. The sun drifted past noon. The air suddenly freshened, and a cool breeze blew. Closing her eyes, she felt the first rippling wave of magic flow across her. She cried out with the joy of it, forgetting for an instant what had caused it.

Here, sixty miles from the cathedral, the wave was gentle. Yet even so the magic seeped into the earth and the trees, the rocks and the water. Those closest to the center would have felt it most strongly. It was the kind of magic that changed hearts and opened minds.

Against her better judgment the Wyrd opened her spirit eyes and floated back along the wave, peeling back the curtain of time. She saw the giant Grymauch standing at the top of the cathedral steps, Maev Ring in his arms. She heard the muskets roar, she saw him stiffen as the lead shot ripped into his back.

A choking sob came from the Wyrd, and she fled back to her body. For a long while the tears flowed. When they faded away, the Wyrd was exhausted and the sun was setting. With trembling hands she lit her fire.

The magic of Jaim Grymauch was still strong in the Wishing Tree woods, and tomorrow she would begin again her life's work. The perils were still great, but the Rigante were about to be reborn. There would be battles ahead, and triumphs and tragedies.

But now there was a glimmer of hope.

Epilogue

FOUR VARLISH ATTENDED the funeral of Jaim Grymauch: Alterith Shaddler, Huntsekker, Taybard Jaekel, and Shula Achbain. More than fifteen hundred highlanders gathered to see him laid to rest in a small plot behind Maev Ring's house. Maev herself placed the first shovel of earth upon the coffin.

The following morning she harnessed a wagon and prepared to set off for the north.

Huntsekker offered to go with her, but she refused. She lifted the reins, then glanced down at the powerful Varlish. "I thank you, but you have a farm to run," she said. "People rely on you." Then she paused. "I am glad Jaim did not kill you," she added.

"He was a good man, Mistress Ring."

For a moment she did not answer, and Huntsekker saw she was fighting for control. "He was . . . ," she faltered, then took a deep breath, her eyes full of tears. "He was a rogue, you know. A drunkard who stole bulls for enjoyment. But he was always true, Master Huntsekker. Always. I think . . . I think that I shall miss him greatly." Unable to say more, she flicked the reins, and the wagon moved away.

There were fires in Eldacre that night. The Feld forge went up in flames, with all the stock destroyed in the process. Jorain Feld and his brothers were ruined. Several other businesses owned by witnesses against Maev Ring were also destroyed.

The most shocking news to surface after the death of Jaim Grymauch explained the absence of the bishop at the execution. His body was found stretched out upon the judgment table of the Holy Court. His neck had been crushed. There had been no witnesses to the murder, though a priest talked of seeing a large man, with a twin-spiked silver beard walking away from the building.

The king's regiment withdrew from the north, as did half of the Moidart's soldiers, and an uneasy truce developed between the Beetlebacks and the Black Rigante.

When news of Grymauch's death, and the manner of it, reached the north, Call Jace walked away alone to Shrine Hollow, carrying with him a jug of Uisge. He sat there drinking it as the sun set over Sorrow Bird Lake. He had grown to manhood in the company of Jaim Grymauch, and many were the jugs they had shared. He recalled the sound of the big man's laughter and remembered the many escapades of their youth.

Call bowed his head and realized that tears were dropping from his eyes. He wiped them away, cursing himself for a soft fool. Then a sob broke clear of his control, and he wept uncontrollably for a while.

Only then did he remember the words of the Dweller:

"For the clans in the south will rediscover their pride and their manhood . . . One spark will ignite them, one glorious spark, one moment of true Rigante greatness. It will break my heart to see it and at the same time gladden my soul."

"What are you speaking of?"

"You will know when the moment comes. You will hear of it. You will even weep, Call Jace."

"I have not shed tears since I was a wee lad and my father died."

"I know. Too much of your Rigante heritage is locked away, buried deep. But remember my words when the day comes."

Kaelin Ring found him there. Call knew that the young man was suffering, and the two sat in comfortable silence as the moon rose.

"I cannot believe he has gone," Kaelin said at last. "A part of me won't accept it."

"He hasn't gone," said Call. "You carry him here," he added, tapping Kaelin's chest, "in your heart, as I carry him in mine. The clan will do the same, boy. Mark my words. You don't forget a man like Grymauch. They'll be talking about him in a hundred years."

"What will they say, do you think?"

"They'll say he was a hero. They'll say he was a legend. But best of all, boy, they'll say he was Rigante!"

The epic of Ravenheart continues,
as war sweeps across the land of the Rigante in

STORMRIDER

The explosive new novel by David Gemmell
An April 2002 hardcover from Del Rey® Books

Prologue

THE NIGHT sky was lit by flames, and black smoke swirled across the valley as the town of Shelsans continued to burn. There were no screams now, no feeble cries, no begging for mercy. Two thousand heretics were dead, most slain by sword or mace, though many had been committed to the cleansing fires.

The young knight of the Sacrifice stood high on the hillside and stared down at the burning town. Reflections of the distant flames shone on his blood-soaked silver breastplate and glistening helm. The wind shifted, and Winter Kay smelled the scent of roasting flesh. Far below the wind fanned the hunger of the flames. They blazed higher, devouring the ancient timber walls of the old museum and the carved wooden gates of the Albitane church.

Winter Kay removed his helm. His lean, angular features gleamed with sweat. Plucking a linen handkerchief from his belt he examined it for bloodstains. Finding none, he wiped the cloth over his face and short-cropped dark hair. Putting on armor had been a waste of time this day.

The townsfolk had offered no armed resistance as the thousand knights had ridden into the valley. Instead, hundreds of them had walked from the town singing hymns and crying out words of welcome and brotherhood.

When they had seen the knights of the Sacrifice draw their longswords and heel their horses forward, they had fallen to their knees and called on the Source to protect them.

What idiots they were, thought Winter Kay. The Source

blessed only those with the courage to fight or the wit to run. He could not recall how many he had slain that day, only that his sword had been blunted by dusk and that his holy white cloak had been drenched in the blood of the evil.

Some had tried to repent, begging for their lives as they were dragged to the pyres. One man—a stocky priest in a blue robe—had hurled himself to the ground before Winter Kay, promising him a great treasure if he was spared.

"What treasure do you possess, worm?" asked Winter Kay, pressing his sword point against the man's back.

"The orb, sir. I can take you to the Orb of Kranos."

"How quaint," said Winter Kay. "I expect it resides alongside the sword of Connavar and the helm of Axias. Perhaps it is even wrapped in the Veiled Lady's robe."

"I speak the truth, sir. The orb is hidden in Shelsans. It has been kept there for centuries. I have seen it."

Winter Kay hauled the man to his feet by his white hair. He was short and stocky, his face round, his eyes fearful. From all around them came the screams of the dying cultists. Winter Kay dragged the man toward the town. A woman ran past him, a sword jutting from her breast. She staggered several steps, then fell to her knees. A knight followed her, wrenching the sword clear and decapitating her. Winter Kay walked on, holding his prisoner by the collar of his robe.

The man led him to a small church. In the doorway lay two dead priests. Beyond them were the bodies of a group of women and children.

The prisoner pointed to the altar. "We need to move it, sir," he said. "The entrance to the vault is below it."

Sheathing his sword, Winter Kay released the man. Together they lifted the altar table clear of the trapdoor beneath. The priest took hold of an iron ring and dragged the trapdoor open. Below it was a narrow set of steps. Winter Kay gestured the priest to climb down and then followed him.

It was gloomy inside. The priest found a tinderbox and struck a flame, lighting a torch that was set in a bracket on the gray wall. They moved down a narrow corridor that opened out into a circular room. There were already torches lit there, and an elderly man was sitting before an oval table. In his hands was a curiously carved black box some eighteen inches high. Winter Kay thought it was polished ebony. The old man saw the newcomers and gently laid the box upon the table.

"The orb is within it," said the captured priest.

"Oh, Pereus, how could you be so craven?" asked the elderly man.

"I don't want to die. Is that so terrible?" the prisoner replied.

"You will die anyway," the old priest said sadly. "This knight has no intention of letting you live. There is not an ounce of mercy in him."

"That is not true," wailed the prisoner, swinging toward Winter Kay.

"Ah, but it is," the knight told him, drawing his sword. The little priest tried to run, but Winter Kay sprang after him, delivering a ferocious blow to the back of the man's head. The skull cracked open, and the priest crumpled to the stone floor. "Is that truly the Orb of Kranos?" Winter Kay asked.

"Aye, it is. Do you have any inkling of what that means?"

"It is a relic of ancient times. A crystal ball, some say, through which we can see the future. Show it to me."

"It is not crystal, Winter Kay. It is bone."

"How is it you know my name?"

"I have the gift, Sir Knight, though at this moment I wish I did not. So kill me and be done with it."

"All in good time, priest. My arm is tired from constant work today. I'll let it rest awhile. Show me the orb."

The elderly priest stepped away from the table. "I have no wish to see it. The box is not locked."

Winter Kay strode forward. As he reached out for the lid, he realized the box was not made of wood at all but had been cast from some dark metal. "What are these symbols etched upon it?" he asked.

"Ward spells. The orb radiates evil. The box contains it."

"We shall see." Winter Kay flipped open the lid. Within the

box was an object wrapped in black velvet. Putting down his bloody sword, Winter Kay reached in and lifted it out. Carefully he folded back the cloth. The priest was right. It was no crystal ball. It was a skull, an iron circlet upon its brow. "What nonsense is this?" demanded Winter Kay. Reaching out, he touched the yellowed brow. The skull began to glow, as if a bright candle had been lit within its hollow dome. Winter Kay felt a powerful surge of warmth flow along his fingers and up his arm. It was exquisite. It continued to flow through his body, up through his chest and neck and into his head. He cried out with the pleasure of it. All weariness from the day of slaughter fell away. He felt invigorated.

"This is a wondrous piece," he said. "I feel reborn."

"Evil knows its own kind," said the old man.

Winter Kay laughed aloud. "I am not evil, fool. I am a knight of the Sacrifice. I live to destroy evil wherever I find it. I do the work of the Source. I cleanse the land of the ungodly. Now tell me what magic has been placed in this skull."

"Only what was always there. That . . . that creature was once a mighty king. A great hero destroyed him and freed the world of his evil. However, the darkness within him cannot die. It seeks to reach out and corrupt the souls of men. It will bring you nothing but sorrow and death."

"Interesting," said Winter Kay. "There is an old adage: 'The enemy of my enemy must therefore be my friend.' Since you are named by the church as the enemy, then this must be a vessel for good. I find no evil in it."

"That is because its evil has already found you."

"And now you begin to bore me, old man. I shall give you a few moments to make your peace with the blessed Source, and then I shall send you to him."

"I will go gladly, Winter Kay. Which is more than can be said for you when the one with the golden eye comes for you."

Winter Kay's sword swept up and then down in a murderous arc. Having been blunted by a day of murder, the blade did not completely decapitate the old man. Blood sprayed across the room. Several drops splashed to the table, spattering the skull. Light blazed from the bone. As Winter Kay gazed upon it, an ethereal face seemed to form for a brief moment. Then it faded.

Wrapping the skull in its hood of black velvet, Winter Kay returned it to its box and carried it from the burning ruins of Shelsans.

Thrill to the epic saga of
The Rigante
by David Gemmell

SWORD IN THE STORM

Fierce and proud, the Rigante dwell deep in the green mountain lands, worshipping the gods of Air and Water, and the spirits of the Earth. Among them lives a warrior, born of the storm that slew his father. He is Connavar, and tales of his courage spread like wildfire. The Seidh—a magical race as old as time—take note of the young warrior, and cast their malignant shadow across his life.

For soon a merciless army will cross the water, destroying forever the timeless rhythms of life among the Rigante. Swearing to protect his people, Connavar journeys straight into the heart of the enemy. Along the way, he receives a gift: a sword as powerful and deadly as the Seidh who forged it. Thus he receives a name that will strike fear into the hearts of friend and foe alike—a name proclaiming a glorious and bitter destiny. . .

Demonblade.

MIDNIGHT FALCON

Bane the Bastard is the illegitimate son of Connavar the Demonblade. Born of treachery, Bane grew up an outcast, feared by his fellow highlanders, denied by the father whose unmistakable mark he bore—the eyes of Connavar, one tawny brown, the other emerald green.

Hounded by the country of his birth, Bane found acceptance across the seas—only to have it stripped away in an instant by a cruel and deadly swordsman. Now fighting as a gladiator in the blood-soaked arenas of the Empire, Bane lives for one thing: revenge. And he pursues his goal with the same single-minded determination that won his father a crown.

But more is at stake than a young warrior's quest for vengeance. The armies of the Stone are preparing to march on the lands of the Rigante. The fate of human and Seidh alike will be decided by the clash of swords—and by the bonds of twisted love and bitterness between a father and a son.

Don't miss any books in
The Stones of Power series!

GHOST KING
LAST SWORD OF POWER
WOLF IN SHADOW
THE LAST GUARDIAN
BLOODSTONE

"The stuff of true epic fantasy."
—R. A. Salvatore,
New York Times bestselling author

Be sure to check it out. . .

The Drenia Saga
by David Gemmell

Legend

The King Beyond the Gate

Quest for Lost Heroes

Waylander

In the Realm of the Wolf

The First Chronicles of Druss the Legend

The Legend of Deathwalker

Winter Warriors

Published by Del Rey Books.
Available wherever books are sold.

Visit Del Rey Books online and learn more about your favorite authors

There are many ways to visit Del Rey online:

The Del Rey Internet Newsletter (DRIN)
A free monthly publication e-mailed to subscribers.
It features descriptions of new and upcoming books,
essays and interviews with authors and editors,
announcements and news, special promotional offers,
signing/convention calendar for our authors and
editors, and much more.

To subscribe to the DRIN: send a blank e-mail to
join-ibd-dist@list.randomhouse.com
or you can sign up on Del Rey's Web site.

The **DRIN** is also available for your PDA devices—
go to www.randomhouse.com/partners/avantgo for
more information, or visit http://www.avantgo.com
and search for the Books@Random channel.

Del Rey Digital (www.delreydigital.com)
This is the portal to all the information and
resources available from Del Rey online including:

• Del Rey Books' Web site, including sample chapters
of every new book, a complete online catalog, special
features on selected authors and books, news and
announcements, readers' reviews and more

• Del Rey Digital Writers' Workshop, a members-only,
FREE writers' workshop

Questions? E-mail us...
at delrey@randomhouse.com